One Time in Paris

ANNABELLE McCORMACK

Published by Annabelle McCormack

Edited by Marion Archer

Proofreading by Caitlin Lengerich, @chronicledbycait

Cover by Patrick Knowles

Cover Art used with permission from Shutterstock.

www.annabellemccormack.com

One Time in Paris

Wanderlust Families

The Camden Brothers

Quinn Camden (married to Elle Winnick)
Aiden Camden
Mason Camden
Logan Camden

The Winnick Siblings

Elle Winnick (married to Quinn Camden)
Lydia Winnick (married to Callum Scott)
Kyle Winnick

The Scott Siblings

Callum Scott (married to Lydia Winnick)
Isla Scott

1

———

ISLA

LAS VEGAS, NEVADA

THE WEIGHT of a male arm around Isla Scott's waist registered for half a second before her stomach did a full somersault.

Nope. Bigger problem. She was going to hurl.

Scrambling for the side of the bed, Isla tripped, her foot still tangled around the bedsheet. *Thunk.* Her hands smacked against the tiled floor, and she winced, then straightened, scanning the unfamiliar bedroom.

Oh God. Where the hell is the bathroom?

And why was this whole—absurdly enormous—suite so blindingly white? It looked like a spa threw up in here.

Do not think about vomit.

Barreling toward the first door she saw, Isla caught sight of herself in the mirror—tanned skin, light brown hair streaked with pink, wearing nothing but a pink cheetah-print thong and a matching bra that screamed *shots were involved.*

Head pounding, she opened the first door she found, hoping—praying—it was a bathroom.

It was a closet.

And she was too late.

The stomach-souring taste of last night's shots came back up with full force as she vomited.

Isla shakily wiped her mouth with the back of her hand, trying to get her bearings.

A groan from the bed. A shuffle of sheets. Isla squeezed her eyes shut for a beat before turning, stomach still churning.

He propped himself up on his elbows, disheveled dark hair falling into sharp blue eyes. Familiar. Too familiar.

Her pulse stuttered.

Oh hell no.

Not him.

Aiden Camden.

Waking up practically naked after a drunken night in Vegas was bad enough. But waking up beside someone she'd known all her life? A man who was one of her older brother's best friends?

Aiden winced, looking as rough as she felt. His blue eyes narrowed. "Isla? Oh. Bloody brilliant."

"Please, for the love of my future mental health, tell me we did not have sex." She tiptoed toward the bed, yanking a blanket from the edge to wrap around her.

"Um—" He moistened his lips, dark eyebrows furrowing as he slumped back onto the pillow. "I don't believe so."

"Pants. Are you wearing any pants?"

Aiden peeked under the covers, then shook his head. His well-muscled arms flexed as one arm crossed his bare chest, rubbing a knot out of his shoulder.

Fucking fantastic. I can't remember if I had sex with my brother's best friend.

They'd kissed. She was sure of that. The flash of his smile, the Eiffel Tower glowing behind him, the warm press of his hands against hers—

Then his mouth on hers. It had been unexpected. Rough

and desperate and—*God help her*—exhilarating. A low laugh. His fingers brushing the strap of her dress. Her breath hitching—

Blank.

Aiden Camden was infuriatingly good-looking. He knew it, and so did a string of brokenhearted women. Isla had sworn she'd never be one of them. And she wouldn't be.

So how the heck did we get here?

Goddammit.

"Um . . ." Isla glanced over her shoulder toward the closet.

"You feeling poorly?" Aiden squinted at her like she might spontaneously combust.

On the other hand, she wouldn't mind spontaneously combusting right now. *Where's a good bolt of lightning when you need it?*

She nodded. "Uh . . . yeah. Your closet has seen better days. So has my dignity."

He grimaced. "I'll take care of it."

"Then you can start by helping me find my clothes." All she wanted to do was get the hell out of there. *Right now.* Get back to her room and find out why Davy had abandoned her in the middle of the night. Where had the rest of the girls in the bachelorette party gone?

Wrapping a sheet around his waist, Aiden stumbled out of the bed. It wasn't fair, really. He was just as hungover as she was, but she looked like she'd been dragged by a bus and he looked, well, beautiful. Chiseled abs. Dark hair just slightly ruffled. Five o'clock shadow.

Damn those Camden brothers. Every single one of them was stupidly good-looking.

Even if she wasn't slightly interested in Aiden, she could admit that fact.

Okay, so maybe being here proved that some subconscious

drunken part of her *was* interested, but it didn't make the situation any better. Callum would kill her if he knew. *For that matter, Callum would kill Aiden.*

Aiden grabbed a pair of trousers from the floor as he scooted past her, then left the room, going farther into the suite. A minute later, he returned—trousers on—with her slinky silver minidress in his hand. "Found this by the door. Presumably flung there in a moment of artistic abandon."

She did her best not to react. *By the door?* Her clothes had come off that quickly?

Holy shit.

"Turn around," she demanded, taking the dress from him.

He didn't hesitate. "We need to get our story straight. Callum . . . he *cannot* know about this."

"There's nothing to figure out," she said, shimmying into her dress. "I won't tell him and neither will you. That's simple enough. You've got a girlfriend anyway, so I very much doubt either of us wants *anyone* to find out."

"Lola's not my girlfriend," Aiden said flatly. "I told you that last night."

"*Currently.*" Isla checked around for the strappy heels and clutch she was sure must be somewhere nearby. "Every other time I see you, you're back together again."

Aiden didn't respond, going over to the closet. He opened it, blinked once, then promptly shut it again. "Right. Well. That's traumatizing."

Good God, the embarrassment. How was she ever going to look Aiden in the eye again?

It wasn't like she never saw him. She'd be seeing him soon enough at Liddy and Callum's post-elopement party in London, which her brother and his new wife had finally managed to plan despite the logistical nightmare of having Isla's divorced parents agree on one place to celebrate. Isla had suggested they do the party in Costa Rica at *La Hacienda*, which would have been perfect because she wouldn't have had to travel now that she was running the boutique inn full-time.

But her parents *hadn't* agreed to Isla's suggestion, and now she had to go all the way to London for a party where the Camden brothers would all be in attendance since they lived in London *and* were Callum's closest friends.

"Um. Yes, well. This . . . was . . . something. I'll see you in London." She slung her clutch's strap around her wrist and started for the door.

"Isla, wait."

She turned in the hallway to find Aiden standing there, hands in his pockets. She bit the inside of her lip, stomach roiling with the same nausea she'd woken up with.

"For what it's worth—not that I have much memory of the blessed event, thanks to a massive amount of gin—I don't think much happened between us. I was practically non-functional. I can't even remember the last time I got this smashed, and as soon as you leave, I'm going straight back to sleep."

"Okay . . . thanks?" She furrowed her brows. Was he trying to make her feel better? Piss-poor attempt, if so. They'd ended up in bed together, and the fact that neither of them remembered *how* did nothing to alleviate that problem. "Good to see you," she managed, then continued forward.

"But—"

"Don't worry, I won't tell Callum," she said, not bothering to glance back at him. Her hand was already on the knob. Her stomach was really starting to churn.

"I just don't want to leave you thinking I have a habit of preying on unconscious women in cheetah print."

"Let's just forget you ever saw my knickers." Isla's fingers tightened around the doorknob. "But for your peace of mind, I don't believe that."

"Good."

She opened the door.

And froze.

Standing in the doorway, suitcase at her side, sunglasses perched low on her nose, was Lola. Her red lips parted with surprise. "Isla?"

A bubble of anxiety rose in Isla's stomach.

No. Not anxiety.

Then she threw up on Lola's Louis Vuitton suitcase.

If humiliation were an Olympic sport, she'd just stuck the landing.

2

AIDEN

24 HOURS EARLIER

The last thing Aiden wanted was to sit at this table with his ex. The coffee was abysmal, and the Vegas lights were a migraine waiting to happen, the pounding in his head only getting worse.

He should have known Jorge Salas would tell his daughter about their meeting in Vegas. He just hadn't expected her to show up uninvited—especially when her presence had already complicated Camden Enterprises' negotiations with Ipolymer.

Nothing had been kosher in his business relationship with Salas Group since the moment he'd made the mistake of sleeping with Lola Salas.

That had been playing with fire. His older brother Quinn had warned him, but he hadn't listened because Lola was beautiful, polished, and knew exactly how to handle herself at any function.

A power couple, people said. He'd never liked the term— too American, too optimistic. She, the daughter of a powerful international investment banker. Him, the CEO of Camden

Enterprises, a top defense contractor in the UK, with major dealings in the United States.

Everyone thought they were *perfect* for each other.

But three months into dating, Lola had started ring shopping.

Three months.

Maybe it shouldn't have rattled him. But it had. He hadn't nearly been thinking "marriage is the next step"—they'd never even talked about it. Or said *I love you.* He'd never *been* in a relationship for three months, even. *Ever.*

In every relationship he'd been in—including the one with Lola—something had always been . . . *missing.* Not that he could name it. He wasn't *that* interested in psychoanalyzing himself. He'd just known he wasn't ready to marry her and had broken it off.

She'd wisely dropped the wedding talk after that first breakup.

"Why do you keep checking your cell phone?" Lola snapped, pausing mid-cut into a pastry. "I told you, he'll be down soon enough."

Aiden frowned and cleared the notification from his watch. "We agreed to meet at the convention because it was neutral territory, Lo. Him sending you takes it a bit into less friendly waters."

"Oh, for Pete's sake. We can have a civil conversation, can't we?" Lola arched a perfectly shaped reddish-gold eyebrow, then stabbed her pastry.

Every time they sat across from each other at a meal, Aiden remembered the way she stabbed her food, and the way it made him feel. Like she was going to turn the tines of that fork on him someday if he pushed hard enough.

"The last time—"

"The last time was the last time. We agreed to that. I don't want your scraps, Aiden. And I mean it. I'm here only as a favor to my father."

Somehow, he didn't believe her.

Just like he didn't believe the messiness of their relationship hadn't affected the acquisition of Ipolymer Synthetics. Jorge had been advising the board of Ipolymer, and *somehow* everything about the deal had just gotten messier after the last breakup with Lola.

He undid the top button of his collar and leaned forward, the blast of the air-conditioning not nearly strong enough to keep the sweat from dampening his neck. "Listen, I really don't have time for this. I have back-to-back meetings scheduled during this convention. Yes, we want Ipolymer—we need them. But that doesn't mean we won't walk from the negotiations if—"

"Like I said, he's coming. You and I don't need to hash out the details now; Daddy's on his way. I just thought it would be nice for us to grab a cup of coffee and catch up." She flashed a perfectly innocent smile at him—if he could believe anything Lo did was innocent.

Hell, innocent and Lo Salas were the two furthest terms from each other in the dictionary, and he knew that from experience.

But thinking about her that way now won't help anything.

That lack of innocence had been precisely what had roped him back in—not once, not twice, but four times.

A chance meeting. A tempting smile. A reminder of how good they'd been together. And every damn time, he'd fallen for it, conveniently forgetting how ruthless she could be. Then at dinner or at the till at a market, she'd remind him—an offhanded insult, a condescending remark. And just like that, the spell would break.

Not this time, though.

This time, the ambush wouldn't work.

This time, he was here for a damn work convention, and hopefully, he'd close the acquisition with Ipolymer before returning home to London.

He was *not* here to make a massive mistake with a woman.

But he'd be nowhere closer to that acquisition if he pissed Lola off enough.

He glared down at his coffee, wishing he'd ordered the tea he really wanted. But the last time he'd ordered tea at a coffee shop in the US, the damn thing had taken a full half hour to cool to a drinkable temperature, and he'd still scalded his tongue on the first sip.

"I know that look," Lola said, her voice suddenly softer. "You don't have to be so angry. Is it wrong for me to want to know how you are?"

"I'm not angry." Aiden frowned at her. "I just don't think this is particularly productive. The last time I saw you, Ipolymer walked away from the negotiating table the next day. It's taken me a full eight weeks to get them back for discussions. I can't afford for my personal life to have an impact on the business dealings of Camden Enterprises."

Her hazel eyes darkened. "If you're implying that my father did anything illegitimate as a result of our last breakup, that's just disgusting."

Fuck. The bloody woman was putting him in a damned-if-you-do, damned-if-you-don't situation.

"Lo, I really don't want to do this again."

She changed her tactic, her eyes growing shiny. "You won't even have coffee with me? Really, Aiden? Is that how things are? Coffee for fifteen minutes while my father—whose plane landed late, I might add—gets settled into his hotel room? You're unbelievable."

Aiden pressed his lips to a line. *Mayday. Bloody mayday.*

But no one would be coming to save him because he was thirty-one years old, and if he couldn't manage a civil coffee with his ex, he had no business running a multinational defense contracting corporation. He settled on a neutral, "I don't know what to say."

She stood, crumpling her napkin onto her plate.

Dammit.

"Lola, hang on—"

"No, we're done here. I can see from your expression that this was a massive mistake." She shook her head, a scowl on her pretty face. "Honestly, Aiden, you're such a man-child. You can't even handle sitting with me civilly. It's ridiculous."

"It's not about not sitting with you. I've just got loads of meetings, and I'm not here for pleasure. Vegas isn't my dream destination. I'm here for a convention, and that's it."

"Of course you are. You wouldn't know the meaning of fun if she sat on your face." Lola grabbed her purse. "Which she has. Several times, I might add. I can't believe I lost nearly a year of my life on this back-and-forth, wishy-washy *nonsense* from you." With a glare, she turned and stalked away.

Aiden stared into the void she'd left, unsure if he should feel relieved, offended, or both.

Was that it?

Had getting rid of her been that easy?

Of course, he did have a few onlookers staring at him as though he'd just struck the woman—Lola had never known volume control. He gave them a stiff nod, then lifted his mobile to avoid any eye contact.

His mobile buzzed, and Aiden glanced down at an email.

Sender: *Jorge Salas*

Subject: *The meeting is off.*

He exhaled sharply, fingers curling tight around the table's edge, the cheap laminate pressing against his palm.

Fucking fantastic.

He pushed his chair back, wanting to storm out of the café. Instead, he gathered his paper cup, and the plate and cup Lola had left behind, and carried them over to the bin.

Ridiculous. This was how Jorge Salas did business?

But, deep down, he knew it wasn't *just* about Lola. Salas was guiding Ipolymer on the acquisition. He knew how much Camden Enterprises wanted it, and he was driving a hard bargain because they could afford to.

The board had sent him to Vegas with one order—make that acquisition happen.

And now everything was bleeding at the seams.

Fuck.

3

ISLA

"You're here!" Megan squealed as Isla rolled her suitcase through the door of the Paris Las Vegas suite.

The blast of cool, air-conditioned luxury barely eased the travel fatigue pressing behind her eyes. The suite was bright, polished, too perfect—much like the five smiling faces waiting to pounce. The replica Eiffel Tower loomed beyond the window, a gaudy reminder of exactly where she was.

Subtlety, thy name is Vegas.

Isla sucked in a deep breath and surveyed the smiling faces of "the Squad"—her five closest friends from her years at Trinity All-Girls Preparatory, the exclusive boarding school her father had shipped her off to in Connecticut during high school, when Mum had finally relented to his pestering to put her in a "place that will expand her possibilities."

"There they are," Isla said as brightly as possible, tossing her hair over her shoulder as she stopped in the foyer.

Megan—the bride-to-be and the only reason the Squad had gotten her to agree to come to Vegas in the first place—came at Isla with arms outstretched and wrapped her in a bear hug.

"I'm so happy you made it. I kept telling the girls I really, really wanted you here!"

Isla returned the hug and then looked beyond her toward the other women gathered on the couch. Somehow, if it was possible, none of them appeared to have changed. Like, at all.

They probably haven't.

A voice from an adjoining room filled her with relief. "Is she here?" Her best friend and former roommate, Davy, hurried out, jet-black hair streaming behind her.

Even in high school, Isla and Davy had bonded over being the outsiders among their blue-eyed, blond classmates. Both of their fathers were English, but unlike Isla's Costa Rican mother, Davy's mother was Indian. They'd clung to their shared love of film and acting, a friendship that had followed them well past graduation—Isla to London's theater and film scene and Davy to the BBC.

Isla grinned at Davy. "How's the jet lag?"

"Oh, I have the *worst* jet lag," Piper said from the couch. Out of their group of six, Piper was always the most likely to insert herself into a conversation, though it was always harmless. "I spent last week on the coast of Croatia, and I swear, it was exhausting coming back to Greenwich, let alone here."

Exhausting? Must have been rough alternating between cocktails and yachts.

"Oh, Bobby and I went there last year," Blair said, stretching back on the pristine white couch. Even from here, the giant diamond on her hand sparkled. *That* was a wedding Isla had missed. Blair and Bobby had done a destination wedding in Bora Bora—*say that five times fast*—where the rooms they reserved for their guests cost four grand a night. Isla could practically feel her bank account clenching at the memory of receiving that invite.

Fortunately, running *La Hacienda* full-time gave Isla a

better out to some of these invitations now. It was an upgrade, at least, from having to claim the *poor starving actress* card.

As the other girls resumed their conversation, Davy joined Megan. The three of them exchanged a smile, and for the first time all day, Isla felt a shred of genuine excitement about this trip. Davy and Megan had gotten her through most of the roughest parts of high school. "I'm really so glad you could come." Megan reached over and squeezed Isla's hand. "How's the hospitality industry treating you?"

"It's great. Insanely busy," Isla said. "Rainy season will be coming up in a couple of months, so things will slow down then, but it's been a wild winter. Lots of honeymooners and special events nonstop." She glanced back at her suitcase. "Where should I put my stuff?"

"You're rooming with me, of course." Davy took the handle of the suitcase. "Come on, I'll show you where to stash everything."

Isla followed Davy into the bedroom she'd come from, glad for the excuse to put her things away before she really faced the rest of the Squad—and their inevitable questions.

Love life?

Nonexistent.

Career?

Busy. And not her first choice, but hey—at least *La Hacienda* still belonged to her family.

Skincare routine?

Tears and sunscreen.

"Oh my God, I have never been so happy in my life to see your face," Davy breathed as they stepped into the room. "If I have to hear one more word about 'Bobby' or tennis matches or their new diets, I might actually scream."

Isla smiled and set her carry-on on the made bed in the room. It had been ten years since they'd finished high school, and she hadn't spent much time with the Squad since then. She knew they had her back—*sort of*—but she had always felt . . . different to them. "How much of this bachelorette party do we all have to spend together?"

"Too much. But I'll do my best to keep my complaints to a minimum." Davy sank onto the bed beside Isla's carry-on. "But seriously, last night. My God, Isla. We went to one of those hibachi places, and I have never been more embarrassed to be out at a restaurant with people—and that includes being with my *mom,* who returns every meal she gets. First, every single one of them had special, off-menu requests. Then Kelsey told the chef—after he'd already started cooking—that she had a shellfish allergy, even though she doesn't. She just thinks shrimp juice is 'gross.' That was fun."

She flopped onto her back.

Isla sat beside her. "Makes you wonder what we thought we had in common in high school, doesn't it?"

Davy shook her head, pursing her lips emphatically as she scowled at Isla. "No, I know exactly what *you* had in common with them. You're a trust fund baby too, even if you pretend not to be."

"If by trust fund baby, you mean I'll inherit some money from my father when he dies—assuming my stepmother doesn't spend it all first—then sure, I'm a trust fund baby." She nudged Davy. "And you're acting like your dad isn't Greenwich's top plastic surgeon and your mom their top cardiologist."

"Yeah, yeah, don't remind me." Davy covered her face with her hands. "I have to hear about what an absolute disappointment I am every time I go home. *If you'd just gone to medical school like we planned . . .*" Davy shook her head bitterly. "My mom still wants to send me to India to become a doctor."

"At least you're still chasing what you love. I bailed the second I had to pick between my dreams and my mother's."

The words sat heavy in her chest—heavier than she expected. But it felt so good to tell *someone.*

She couldn't tell Callum that, of course. Callum had shelled out the money to save the inn from financial ruin when Mum had gone bankrupt. And he'd done it, in large part, to save the only childhood home that Isla had ever really known.

He'd done it for Isla, not for Mum.

But after having walked away from acting almost twenty months earlier, if she had to make the same choice all over again . . . would she?

She'd loved acting. Few places felt as comfortable as a stage did for Isla. *Like another home, really. One I gave up.* And because the film and theater worlds in London were more closely linked than they were in Hollywood, she'd seen some success in both.

Isla had been at the cusp of *something,* too. The audition before she'd gone to Costa Rica for Elle and Quinn's wedding—when everything in her life had changed—had been one for a film where the producer had personally invited her.

And when the producer had called her to tell her he wanted her for the part? She'd felt like such a flake for turning it down.

Just that easily, she'd left behind a lifelong dream. She'd told herself she was all right with it—and maybe she was—but damn if she didn't miss the excitement of *creating.*

Davy was quiet.

Too quiet.

Isla had seen that look before. The way Davy bit her lip, eyes just a little too shiny.

"What is it?" Isla asked gently. Davy had just started a job at the Travelog Channel—a huge promotion. "Did something happen?"

With a sharp sniffle, Davy blinked back tears. "No. Not yet.

But I'm one bad pitch away from getting fired. My boss called me into his office last Friday and told me that if I didn't have an innovative idea on his desk when I return from this trip, I may as well pack my things."

Oh no.

"What? Davy! What about the cheese adventure?"

Davy sat, shoulders slumped. "Turns out they did that exact segment four years ago. Cheese capitals of Europe. Tanked harder than my high school math scores. So not only did I pitch something that's already been done but I also pitched a failure of a concept, too."

"I know of an exciting boutique inn in Costa Rica that would be happy to host you for a travel docuseries." Isla slipped her arm around her shoulder with a comforting squeeze.

"Do you know that I tried to pitch something like that to them? Antony said I had to do better than a Costa Rican inn and rolled his eyes. He *actually* rolled his eyes at me in a meeting. In front of everyone, Isla. I almost evaporated into my seat I was sweating so badly."

"You can't let him intimidate you. You're good at this. This is what you were born for—you said it yourself."

"Oh, who am I kidding? My parents sent me to school hoping I'd get an MD and an MRS., and so far, I've failed on both accounts. I'm a has-been wannabe filmmaker who can't even pitch a tantalizing idea to keep my entry-level job at the Travelog Channel. This isn't National Geographic, Isla. They give shows to *influencers* on a regular basis. Most of our shows are on YouTube—only a few make it to the cable channel or get picked up by a bigger network. The only film that got me noticed was because you starred in it, and you're so freaking beautiful that no one was paying attention to the filmmaking."

"Stop it." Isla shoved her away. "Listen, this is what we're going to do. Between scheduled selfies and whatever horrors

Kelsey has planned, we're going to brainstorm ten killer ideas. Minimum. Okay?"

"Okay," Davy answered tearfully, clearly unconvinced.

Isla stood, determined to cheer her up. "What's on the agenda for tonight?"

"Silver dresses, dinner, Chippendales show at nine thirty, then time in Ellis Island Casino." Davy sighed with about as much enthusiasm as Isla felt.

"Sounds like we need to pre-game." Isla unzipped her carry-on and pulled out a bottle of tequila she'd picked up duty-free at the airport. "To solving our problems," she declared with a confidence she didn't know she possessed.

"How much of that bottle do you think it will take before I believe it?" Davy groaned.

Isla poured two shots and raised hers with mock solemnity. "Let's find out."

4

———

AIDEN

"THIS IS BLOODY MAD." Aiden pinched the bridge of his nose, exhaling slowly to keep his temper in check.

"Sit down. Grab a drink." Felix peered up at him from the bar with a chagrinned expression.

With a clenched jaw, Aiden slid into the barstool beside Felix. He'd always hated Las Vegas. Probably unreasonably so. But something about it had always seemed so . . . irritatingly dirty. Infuriatingly sleazy.

This wasn't helping.

"Look, we've known each other for a long time, Aiden. I told you from the start that I'll always shoot straight with you. And I'm warning you now because I consider us friends."

Friends? He barely knew Felix Covington. His company was among many that Camden held contracts with, and the two men were friendly *enough*, but Aiden didn't know if he could name three personal facts about the man.

Felix sipped on his Manhattan and winced. Perhaps at the drink. Perhaps at his own lack of subtlety.

"This is business, pure and simple," Felix said. "The

company just isn't impressed by the way this whole Ipolymer deal has gone down. You keep saying it's going to happen, and —look—I'm sure you're trying your best, but you can't shit where you sleep. Frankly, that sort of behavior just hasn't impressed my board. I'm doing what I can, but partnering with another company is looking more appealing to them the longer this drags out."

Aiden let his eyes drift from the bar toward the chaotic, blinking lights. No wonder people lost all sense of time in here. The noise, the crowds, the flashiness, the fliers of mostly naked women *everywhere*—it was overstimulation dressed up in neon —even with the jet lag. If he tried to lie down and go to sleep right now, he'd struggle to shut his brain off. It was like drinking inside a pinball machine.

He ordered a gin and leaned back, thinking before he responded. Felix's news wasn't just a blow—it was earth-shattering. If Covington Biotechnics partnered with another company, the repercussions would be felt in every single division of Camden Enterprises.

How in the hell was he supposed to go to London with this news?

But the truth was that he had fucked up. He had made such a disaster of the Ipolymer acquisition, however unintentionally.

"You want my advice?" Felix asked unhelpfully.

Aiden's drink arrived, and he lifted the glass. "Is it the kind I ask for, or the kind you give anyway?"

"Just make nice with Lola until the acquisition is secured. After that, it'll be a done deal. You can break up with her— again—or divorce her, or whatever the hell it takes. But business is business. At the end of the day, sure, you shouldn't have gotten involved with her, but now that you can't unfuck that mess, you may as well enjoy yourself until you get what you want out of the deal. You could do a hell of a lot worse than Lola Salas."

Aiden's jaw flexed.

Christ. That's what passed for romantic endorsement now? What a charming approach to corporate strategy—marry, merge, move on.

He'd worried about this sort of thing when he'd considered leaving the military and taking over at Camden. He wasn't a paragon of morality, but he had standards. Ethics.

His father had built this company from the ground up. If not for the stroke, Arthur Camden would still be at the helm—gruff and demanding but honest. Aiden could respect that. What he couldn't respect was this underhanded bullshit.

No wonder Quinn had bolted off to save the world with philanthropy while Aiden was stuck saving the balance sheets.

Second-born, second-choice, and just the sort to live this interminable, soulless monotony until he became just as rotten as the colleagues around him.

After secondary school, he'd tossed his reputation to the wolves by trying to save Ciara, a family friend, from humiliation after she'd wound up pregnant by some bastard who'd abandoned her. Aiden had claimed the baby was his and ruined his family's faith in him. Ciara had miscarried, but the damage was done.

He'd already joined the British Army's Intelligence Corps and was gone.

For six years, he tried to earn back credibility by completing a secondment with MI5 and developing counterterrorism and diplomatic security skills. It was enough to impress his father when Aiden was needed for the CEO role at Camden, but not enough to shear the wool as the black sheep of the family.

And maybe someday, I'll be just as soulless as they believe. But not today.

He slung his drink back, slammed the glass on the bar top, and stood. "I'm not for sale, Felix. If your company is so worried about my so-called *bad behavior*, surely getting involved with Lola Salas for a fifth time won't impress anyone. Good night."

Without giving Felix a chance to respond, Aiden left, searching for the exit. He needed to go outside and get a breath of fresh air.

Today had been a catastrophe from start to finish. The conference hadn't started so terribly—Pinnacle was always one of the most notable events he attended. He'd spoken yesterday and been on a panel, and everything had felt surprisingly . . . positive.

But after today, all he wanted to do was cancel his meetings for tomorrow, get the first flight out, and go spend the weekend somewhere—anywhere—else.

Of course, he couldn't do that.

He had duties. Responsibilities. His family's business weighed on his shoulders.

Perhaps the mistake had been assuming he was cut out for this in the first place.

When he started working at Camden five years ago, even his father hadn't been certain he would be dependable. But Aiden had wanted to prove him wrong, show his worth. After the disaster with Ciara from his foolish teenage years, everyone had painted him as a villain anyway.

That's what you get for being soft.

Maybe he just wasn't cut out for this.

Or maybe Felix was right.

He'd made a mess of things. Maybe the easiest way out was playing the game—just long enough to win.

But was he really willing to sink to that level?

He didn't have to like doing it, but it wasn't really his fault, was it? Lola and her father were the ones who blurred the lines between business and personal where they shouldn't have.

The cool night air struck his flushed face as he walked out, heading for the Strip.

In a different life, he would have been drinking the night away with his army friends, finding comfort in alcohol and women. Back when he'd been "irresponsible." *The good old days, apparently.*

And now, look at him—*Mr. Responsible.*

And miserable.

He unbuttoned his tailored suit jacket, then pulled off the conference lanyard from his neck, blinking in the glow of the nearby Eiffel Tower, a frivolous replica that paled in the shadow of the real thing. A cardboard cutout of culture.

God, I miss Paris. Miss traveling for fun.

Felix's words rang in his head. *"You may as well enjoy yourself until you get what you want out of the deal."*

The temptation curled through his throat with sickening disgust. Was he being short-sighted here?

I need the night off from this.

Whatever problems he had would still be waiting for him in the morning—but a night of well-deserved relaxation might help him set his mind straight.

Sucking in a deep breath, he raised his chin, scanning the Strip.

Maybe I just need to shut up and let Vegas do its worst.

5

———

ISLA

"THAT GUY IS STARING at you again," Davy purred from beside Isla, her head leaning back against the booth.

Isla cracked an eyelid open and scanned the casino floor, then saw the man in question—a bearded guy wearing a cowboy hat and a hockey jersey. *Quite a combo—Nashville meets slap shot.* Looking over had been a mistake, though, as the guy saw her staring and winked.

Isla tore her gaze away, straightening in her seat.

"You should totally go for it," Piper said from Isla's other side. "He's kinda cute."

"I'm not that desperate, but thanks." Isla laughed and finished her drink. She needed to slow down, but the moment her glass emptied, another one always magically appeared. She adjusted the "bachelorette" sash around her torso with discomfort.

They were nearing eleven, and *dammit*, when she'd lived in London, this had been the time of night she frequently went *out*. But after living in Costa Rica for so long, she was ready for bed.

Mornings at *La Hacienda* started before sunrise, preparing the inn for the guests—those already there and those arriving later. Then, after a long and often brutal day that ran the gamut of helping the guests with anything they needed, playing a pseudo concierge, managing all the staff, and fixing travel emergencies—all with a smile on her face—she usually collapsed into bed early with aching limbs and depleted energy.

"Who's ready for the Eiffel Tower?" Kelsey asked, approaching the table with Blair. Each of them carried more drinks for the table. They set them down in the middle since only Isla had an empty glass. "It closes in an hour, so we need to hurry if we're going to make it."

Great.

"Wait, that's tonight?" Davy groaned. She shook her head, looking a bit ill. "I thought we were doing that during the day tomorrow."

"Yeah, but Megan thought it would be more fun at night," Blair said, flipping her long hair over her shoulder. "I mean, I'm not sure it'll be *that* impressive, considering Bobby and I went on a private tour of the real tower last summer."

Megan's smile faltered, a mist of insecurity in her eyes. And there it was—the Squad's signature move—subtle status assassination.

Isla leaned forward and gripped her friend's hand. Coming to Vegas had been Megan's idea, and Isla wasn't about to let their other snobby friends make her feel bad about it. "I think seeing it at night sounds amazing. Actually, I've always thought it would be so fun to visit all the Eiffel Tower replicas. There are like twenty towns named Paris in the US alone. Wouldn't it be wild to visit them all?"

"Oh, that would be fun," Davy said. Then her eyes widened, and she grabbed Isla's hand. "*A Tour of Paris.* Oh my God. Isla. That's perfect for a pitch!"

"What's perfect?" Piper asked, leaning over Isla to peer at Davy.

"Um—" Isla glanced at Davy. Her friend wouldn't want everyone else knowing about the job situation. "It's nothing. Why don't you all go on ahead to the Eiffel Tower, and I'll catch up? I have to run to the loo. Want to come with me, Davy?"

"What about all the drinks?" Kelsey asked, setting one of the new glasses in front of Isla.

"We could chug them all." Isla shrugged and took a sip.

"I think we should take it easy." Davy gave Isla a pointed, warning look.

"Oh, just leave them. I'm sure we'll get more. I'm with Isla —we can start toward the Eiffel while Davy and Isla go to the *loo*. I love the way you still keep some of those English terms and accents when you talk," Kelsey told Isla with exaggerated eyebrows. "It's so cute."

Crap. Isla hadn't even noticed she'd let that slip. She normally tried to use English expressions and terms around her English friends and American ones around Americans, but when she was drunk, all bets were off. And even then, it wasn't an exact science. The only reason she probably even had an English accent was because she'd lived in England until she was seven.

Isla smiled tightly. "Thanks. It's not an affectation. It's just . . . how I speak." *But sure, let's exoticize the British/Costa Rican hybrid like I'm a novelty at the zoo.* Going to boarding school in Connecticut after living in Costa Rica with Mum for years had been the hardest transition. Her English father had moved there to be with his new American wife, and her mum had managed to convince him to let her stay with her for grade school.

But once the pressure of "getting into a proper Ivy League"

became more pressing to her dad, Mum had finally relented and sent her to Connecticut. Holidays were split between England at her grandparents' and Costa Rica with her mum and her partner. Talk about culture shock.

She nudged Davy to exit.

Davy climbed out of her seat on wobbly legs. "Actually, why don't I sit here and drink as much water as possible while you go to the bathroom? I'll wait for you, and everyone else can go on ahead."

"Are you sure?" Megan asked, worry creasing her brow.

"Yeah, go on. We'll be right behind you." Isla winked at Megan, then hurried off in the direction of the bathroom.

The alcohol buzz settled into her limbs as she walked, her legs feeling oddly bouncy. She couldn't remember the last time she'd gone out like this. Back home, most of her drinking was with Sergio, her friend and the manager of the inn.

Thank God for Sergio. He was the only thing keeping her sane at the inn. He'd started as a full-time tour operator and then seamlessly transitioned to manager when the inn booked out and work had gotten busy.

She smiled to herself, feeling lighter than she had in weeks. For the first time on this trip, she felt relaxed. No drama or forced laughter. Just warmth and a buzz in her bloodstream. Maybe this trip hadn't been a total mistake after all—

A hand clamped around her elbow.

"Hey there," a male voice said in her ear. *Too close.*

Isla turned to find herself only inches away from Cowboy Hockey Man. She froze, her stomach roiling at the strong scent of beer coming from his breath.

"Uh . . ." She shifted her elbow, but his grip was firm. Uncomfortable.

Shit.

This was why she always went to the bathroom with a girlfriend.

"How's about you and I get out of here?" Cowboy Hockey Man said, edging even closer.

Isla's eyes narrowed. "How's about you take your hands off me?" She pulled her arm away forcefully, but he still didn't let go.

"Don't play shy. I saw you eye fucking me from that table."

Oh my God. So foul. "Yeah, never. I prefer real men to wankers." She yanked herself free and turned to go, but the man was still too close behind her.

A cold spike of fear slithered up her spine. *Fuck.* She should have brought pepper spray.

"There you are," a male voice came suddenly. She knew that voice. And those eyes. Ice-blue and currently trained on her unwanted shadow with surgical precision. His hand gripped hers, and she turned, the familiarity of him flooding her with relief—*Aiden Camden*.

What in the hell was he doing here?

There is a god. Not Aiden, of course, but the one who'd sent him here like a guardian angel.

"Aiden," she managed.

His eyes flicked toward the man following her. "I believe my wife asked you to leave her alone, didn't she?" He tilted his head in challenge.

Wife? Never had that word sounded so unbelievably sexy, even if it was from one of her brother's best friends.

Cowboy Hockey Man took a faltering step back, his gaze swiveling to Isla. "Oh sorry, man. I didn't know she was married."

"That really shouldn't have made a difference. She said no. Now get the fuck out of here," Aiden snapped, drawing himself to his full height. Which was over six feet.

Had he always been this tall? Or broad-shouldered? Or was that just the adrenaline talking?

"Go back to England," the guy slurred, his face red. "We don't need more of your tea-drinking bullshit."

Isla relaxed, then hugged Aiden. "Wherever the hell you came from, I've never been so happy in my life to see a Camden."

"I don't know if I should take that as a compliment," Aiden said with a chuckle, then released her. "What are *you* doing here? I'm in town for a conference."

"Bachelorette party." Isla threw her hands up. "Obviously."

"What else?" He smiled. "For a moment, I thought maybe I'd had one too many and hallucinated the scrawny girl who used to trail us, begging and whining to play tag."

She slugged him playfully with a roll of her eyes. "You're quickly wearing out your welcome."

He gave her a charming smile. "Just teasing, of course. But I really didn't expect to see you here. How's Costa Rica?"

"Not too different from when I saw you over Christmas in London." She shifted with discomfort. "But actually, I was on my way to the loo and then I have to run to catch up with my friends—we're going to the Eiffel Tower. Though I'd love to catch up—"

"Why don't I hang around? In case that fellow comes back. I can walk with you until you're safely reunited with your companions."

She gave him a grateful look, then smiled. "Thank you." She hurried into the bathroom, feeling thankful already. Aiden's sudden appearance had been not only wonderful—but she was truly glad to see him. He was safe—felt like home— someone she'd known her whole life.

She grinned at her reflection as she passed a mirror.

Vegas, you sneaky little minx.

6

———

AIDEN
NOW

"Oh, for fuck's sake." Lola gagged, stumbling back like she'd been physically struck.

Turning a deep shade of red, Isla whirled toward Aiden, eyes wide, then she looked back at Lola. "I am so sorry!" She dashed back into the room, hurrying past Aiden. A few moments later, she returned with a wet towel in hand and bent to clean Lola's bag. "I'm not feeling so well this morning."

"I can see that," Lola said tersely. She crossed her arms, eyes shooting daggers at Aiden, who rubbed the back of his neck.

This . . . looked *bad*.

Because it is. Catastrophically bad.

How in the hell had Isla wound up back here with him last night? One drink too many and suddenly he was the protagonist of a bloody farce.

His memory was a blur. Not hazy—blank. His stomach cramped in pain as though he'd swallowed broken glass.

This didn't feel like a typical hangover, if he was honest.

Isla straightened, started to hold the dirty towel out toward him, then stopped. Folding it in her hands, she gave him a faltering smile. "Talk soon," she said, then flipped the barest glance at Lola. "Good to see you again, Lola."

She was gone before Aiden could say anything else, leaving a thick, uncomfortable silence.

What the hell is Lola doing here now? To rub salt in the wound?

Lola stared at him for a few beats longer, one dark brow arched with disbelief. "Well." She crossed her arms. "I suppose I know who's been occupying your thoughts lately."

Shite. Having someone like Lola be in possession of this information was so explosively dangerous. Callum would kill him. He'd never explicitly banned Aiden or his brothers from pursuing Isla, but he hadn't needed to. Some rules didn't need to be spoken—a rule he'd never intended to break. Especially since he and Callum had grown so much closer in the past several years after Quinn had moved to Nashville.

He and Callum saw each other nearly every day because they lived a few blocks away from each other and went to the same gym. They ran together five days a week. Got together for drinks and dinner.

Fuck.

"Ah, Lola, it's not what you think." He was acutely aware of his lack of a shirt right now, and the searing look from Lola told him she was too.

"Oh, really? I'm not an idiot, Aiden. Please don't sink to that level."

"I'm serious." He fought for absolute deadly composure. "We had some business to discuss this morning, but she was out late. I think she has food poisoning."

"Business?" Lola gave a sharp laugh, cutting and cold. "Oh my God, you really do think I'm stupid, don't you? I know what the walk of shame looks like. Look, I get it. You're in deep shit.

She's Callum's little sister. I saw the way he doted on her at Christmas when she was in London. I wonder what he'll say when he learns—"

"You're jumping to conclusions," Aiden said cooly, though his gut churned with something disturbingly protective. He hated that Lola's family ran in the same circles as his did. It meant that she not only knew exactly who Isla was, but that Lola also had access to Callum.

"Like I said, she was here for a business-related thing," he added.

"Dressed in last night's clothes? While you're shirtless? Right." She set her hands on her hips. "Are you going to invite me in at least or do I have to stand here at the door covered in your girlfriend's vomit?"

Aiden ground his teeth. He hadn't even surveyed the room yet. What if there were . . . signs? Condoms? Clothing. *Christ.*

The idea that they might've done something he couldn't remember—something Isla might regret—made him feel physically ill.

"She's working on a project and needed my input," Aiden said, feeling downright pathetic. Hopefully, he didn't sound it. As long as he stuck to the story, she couldn't know what she didn't know.

Lola poked him in the ribs as she pushed past him, dragging her suitcase. "Yes, and I know the sort of *input* you love to give." She smirked grimly, hurt flashing in her features as she turned to look at him.

She couldn't stay here long. He had to get rid of her. *Carefully.*

He couldn't afford to piss her off further, though, because he needed Ipolymer. And he sure as hell didn't trust her not to do something unhinged, like call Callum out of spite. She might not have Callum's number, but he wouldn't put it past her to get it.

"What are you doing here?" he asked at last, crossing his arms. He had the odd sensation of wanting to find a shirt, but if he was going to pretend that he'd been fine hanging out here with Isla half-dressed under so-called "normal" circumstances, then he needed to play it cool. "How did you know where I was staying?"

Lola surveyed the room, her gaze sharp. Penetrating. As though laying his secrets bare.

"I asked around," she said with a disaffected shrug. "I'm going back to New York this morning. My father's given me oversight of the acquisition—the one you've been fumbling. I would have told you yesterday, but you refused to talk—"

"What?" Aiden restrained the flare of ugly anger that shot through him.

But seriously. What. The. Fuck.

Lola held his gaze. "I can do more than hang off your arm like candy, you know. I went to Harvard Business."

"I don't know what you or your father are playing at, Lo, but this is absurd. Given our background and the trouble we've had with this acquisition—"

"We're not *playing* at anything." Lola pursed her lips. "Letting you know is a courtesy. I don't have to talk to you directly, you know. Neither does my father. That was a courtesy, too. You seem to forget who we are and what we do in Salas Group, and it's high time you had a reminder. We won't be having any further meetings about the acquisition in Vegas. I'll set something up for the next round of talks once I'm back in New York. Probably next month."

Bollocks.

Another month of waiting to *attempt* to close this deal? *The board at Camden will be furious.*

Visceral pain shot through him, his stomach cramping harder. He flinched, trying not to let it show.

"Why, Lola?"

Lola gave him a hard stare. "This is just business. And, honestly, I'm glad I came this morning. This was enlightening. Told me everything I needed to know."

He wanted so badly to just toss her out.

Stick to the lie. "Isla is *only* a friend. I've known her since she was a girl."

"Well, she's clearly not a girl anymore, Aiden. She's a grown woman, and you seem to have finally noticed." She smiled patiently. "Anyway, we'll be in touch. Enjoy the rest of your trip."

Blessedly, she let herself out.

Aiden sank onto a sofa, his stomach churning.

If only there was a way to *prove* to Lola that nothing had happened. For Isla's sake.

But I don't even know if nothing happened.

The gap in his memory was seriously alarming.

So much for one carefree night. He'd woken up with no memory, a pissed-off ex, and Callum's sister in his bed.

Bloody. Fucking. Fantastic.

7

——

ISLA

THE ENTIRE SUITE was still and silent until the bloody swing bar caught Isla at the door.

Dammit.

She pulled her phone out and dialed Davy, hoping and praying her friend would have her ringer on.

"Hello?" Davy croaked sleepily.

"At the door. Let me in."

Davy didn't answer, and the line went dead. But a minute later, the soft metal click of the security lock slid into place, and the door creaked open. She scanned Isla, a mischievous grin on her face. "Have fun last night?"

"Don't start," Isla hissed, then hurried into the room. She'd already thrown up once on the way back—right into a casino trash can. The towel from Aiden's room? Ditched. Like her dignity.

She could *not* afford to let any of the girls know about this. Thank goodness they appeared to still be sleeping.

Once they were in the safety of their room, Isla shut the door. "Oh my God, I feel so sick."

Davy hadn't appeared to have been sleeping after all—her laptop was open on her bed, papers scattered beside it. "I told you to take it easy," Davy said with a shake of her head. "You need some water?"

"Water. Ibuprofen. Gatorade." Isla slipped into the adjoining bathroom and clicked the light on. Blinking at herself in the mirror, she cringed. She looked *rough*.

She tied her hair back and washed her face and neck, desperate to get rid of the smell and taste of vomit.

"Luckily for you, I think Kelsey scheduled one of those mobile nursing units to come give us all IV fluids this morning. She swears by them for hangovers." Davy leaned against the doorframe to the bathroom. "Well, that and Adderall. Didn't even know that was a method of treatment, but according to Kelsey, it's the only way to go. Not that I have access to prescription drugs for you."

What? God, she really was a foreigner now.

"Mobile IVs?" Isla raised a brow. "I think I've been living abroad for too long."

"I think you're just a foreigner to the *Squad*," Davy said, putting sarcastic emphasis on the last word.

Isla left the bathroom and changed into pajamas, then pulled out a bottle of water from the mini fridge. She sipped it, stomach feeling sickly, then sat shakily on the bed. "What the hell happened last night? How in the *world* did I end up with . . ."

Maybe Davy doesn't know.

"Aiden?" Davy smirked. "I don't know. You came back from the bathroom with him after everyone left for the Eiffel Tower."

"I remember that part." Isla groaned and curled up on the bed, tucking her knees in and covering herself with a blanket. "But what happened after that?"

Davy shrugged. "I don't know. You guys sat there talking and drinking, and then I left because I was so excited about the Paris idea." She got up, a wide smile on her face. Plopping down beside Isla, she continued. "Speaking of which, I was up all night working on that. I pitched Antony, and he called me already. He loves the idea, Isla. *Loves it.* And with you and Aiden on board, he's completely sold to move forward with a contract."

Uh . . . what?

"Pitched what idea?" Isla blinked up at her, brow furrowing.

"Don't you remember?" Davy gave her an odd look. "The Paris thing. You and Aiden and I sat talking about it for like a half hour. Then you two walked me back to the hotel so I could work on the pitch." She touched Isla's face gently. "My God, how much did you have to drink last night?"

Then they'd never met up with the rest of the bachelorette party?

Isla scanned her memory, the fuzziness of it all now even more alarming. Bits and pieces were at the fringe—like Aiden kissing her—but a complete picture?

What was the last thing she remembered?

Or even the last thing she remembered drinking?

A slick feeling broke out on the back of her neck, a *very* disturbing thought occurring. "I feel like I might have been drugged last night."

Davy's eyes widened. "Are you kidding?" Then her chin dipped. "Aiden? Isn't he like family?"

"Oh, gross. First of all, no." Isla squinted at her. "His sister-in-law's sister is my sister-in-law—"

"Say that ten times fast."

"Exactly. But no, we're not anything. Now, my *brother* is one of his best friends, but that's about it. But . . . Aiden?

Drug me?" Isla squeezed her eyes shut, trying to think straight.

Would Aiden really do something like that?

He'd been reckless as a teenager—sure. The troublemaker of the Camden brothers.

But drug me?

She'd woken up in his bed.

That had been shocking enough.

How well did she really know Aiden?

Her palms grew clammy as she tried to think harder. He'd rescued her from that creep and then—

Isla's eyes flew open.

"He walked me back to the table, and then we sat and had those drinks Kelsey and Blair brought before the Eiffel Tower thing. I gave one to Aiden since no one drank any . . ." Isla made a weak attempt to sit and peered at Davy. "Did you drink any of those?"

Davy shook her head. "But, I mean, Kelsey and Blair got them. They wouldn't put anything in our drinks, and I sat with them the whole time."

"Yeah, but they didn't drink them either, did they? They left for the Eiffel Tower right away, while I was gone."

Concern frosted Davy's expression. "You think it was those drinks?"

"That's the last thing I really remember, Davy. Sitting at the table with you, drinking those drinks. Then . . . nothing. I don't remember talking about any Paris thing with you at all. I have no idea what you're talking about."

A crestfallen look came across Davy's face, but she flicked it away. "That's not important right this second. It had to have been Aiden, Isla. No one else came near those drinks." She lowered her voice, then touched her hand gently. "Did you have sex with him?"

Isla curled her arms around her waist, a heavy feeling of violation roiling her gut. "I don't remember. And he says he doesn't either. We just sort of . . . woke up together."

How could I let this happen?

I feel so dumb.

"Do we need to go to a hospital?" Davy's voice was soft and comforting, grounding her.

"I just don't . . ." Isla shook her head. "I don't *believe* Aiden would do something like that." She rolled off the bed and unzipped her suitcase, hands trembling. Grabbing a pair of flip-flops, she slipped them on then, left the room, and headed back into the main area of the suite, glancing around at all the closed doors.

Davy was at her heels. "What are you doing?"

"Which one is Kelsey's room again? I want to know where she and Blair got those drinks."

Davy led the way, and Isla followed, shaking. They entered the darkened room, and Davy went toward the bed, where Kelsey was sleeping with a sleep mask. "Hey, Kels," Davy said, bending at her side.

Kelsey rolled over and tugged the mask off. She blinked at them in the dim light. "What's going on?" she asked in a rough voice.

Davy nodded toward Isla, who hugged her arms to her chest.

"Just a quick question about last night. Those drinks you got before you all left for the Eiffel Tower . . . where did you get them?" Isla asked as calmly as possible.

"You woke me up for that?" Kelsey scowled and sat. "Don't think I didn't notice that you guys didn't ever meet up with us. Megan was really hurt, you know."

"Isla thinks she might have been drugged, Kels. That's why we need to know where the drinks came from."

Kelsey's expression changed immediately. "Oh my God." She tucked her blond hair behind her ears. "Are you okay? What happened?"

Isla moistened her lips. "I-I'm fine. I think. Just feeling really sick at the moment."

Kelsey blinked, clearly still processing. "Um, those drinks? There was a guy. He had like a cowboy hat and a hockey jersey . . . he gave them to us."

Oh . . . fuck.

Isla sat on Kelsey's bed shakily. "Oh no."

He'd given them the drinks *before* Isla had gone to the bathroom.

Before she'd run into Aiden.

"That was the guy who was harassing you, wasn't it?" Davy bit her lip.

Isla nodded. "Yeah."

Kelsey's eyes grew even wider. "D-did he hurt you?"

"No, a friend of mine from London just so happened to show up and chased him off." And thank *God* for that. What in the hell would have happened if she hadn't run into Aiden?

Then again . . . she might not have sat at that table and had those drinks. She would have gone to the Eiffel Tower with her friends.

A part of her wanted to scream at Kelsey for taking drinks from a stranger—but what was the point? They'd all been doing it. The whole night had been a parade of free drinks from random men, and no one had thought twice about it.

And she didn't want to have to admit to Kelsey what had happened afterward either.

"Let me see if I can get that mobile nurse thing to show up faster and take care of you." Kelsey grabbed her phone off the nightstand. "But you're okay otherwise? My God, that's so scary. I'm so sorry—and here I was thinking you guys blew us off."

Thanking Kelsey, Davy helped Isla back to their room and Isla curled up on the bed again, mind spinning. She wanted to sleep, but she was also too agitated for that.

"Do you want to go to the—"

"Hospital? No." Isla squeezed her eyes shut. "If that creep did put something in the drinks, then Aiden is no more responsible about what happened than I am. Like I said, he couldn't remember what happened either."

"And you're sure you believe him?"

Sure?

Mostly. He *had* seemed pretty confused.

But why had Lola been at his door when she'd left? Just minutes earlier, he'd said they weren't together anymore. Yet Lola had been carrying a suitcase. *And she knew where he was staying.* Had Aiden lied about that? If so, what else would he lie about?

This wasn't what she wanted to deal with right now.

Not ever. If she could erase last night, wipe it clean from her brain—*the parts she remembered anyway*—she would.

"We might want to contact the casino, too. If that other guy did put something in our drinks, their security team will probably want to know about it."

Ugh.

Isla shook her head. "Maybe. I can't think about that right now. What was this Paris thing you were so excited about?"

Davy sat on her bed and shut the open laptop. "It's nothing—"

"No, don't do that. You were excited. I want to know."

"Um, considering what happened, it's really nothing in the grand scheme of things."

Isla shot her a mock glare. "It's clearly not nothing. Now

tell me. I need to think about something else. Please." She fluffed her pillow, then sat back against it.

Davy tied her hair back into a ponytail, then sighed. "You had mentioned that tour of Paris thing, and I spent the night researching the different Parises. I pitched a travel program to Antony about it—a six-episode program exploring six different Parises and ending in France, of course—and he loved the idea."

"That's amazing, Davy. See? I told you it would all work out."

"Mm-hmm," Davy said, her lips pressing together in a smile that didn't meet her eyes.

"What's that look for?"

Davy looked away, gathering the papers and stacking them on the laptop. "Don't worry about it."

"Davy Mehta. Don't you dare." Isla sipped at the bottled water she'd opened. "Tell me."

Davy clasped her hands in her lap, hesitating. Then she gave Isla a careful smile—*the kind you wear before you deliver unwelcome news that used to be good.* "Well, last night—I guess after you and Aiden had those drinks—you had volunteered to host the whole travel show. And Aiden had agreed to sponsor it. I should have known it was too good to be true. But I told Antony—"

Oh shit.

Isla bit her lip, the full realization of Davy's predicament crashing down on her. "I'm sure you could get a different host," she said softly.

"Maybe," Davy said, not meeting her eye. "Though Antony took a look at your old acting reels and résumé, which I sent him, and thought you were perfect for it. But the funding . . ."

The weight of Davy's words pressed against Isla's chest. A different host would be inconvenient. Finding a sponsorship so quickly? Even if it were possible, it wouldn't make Davy look reliable—or paint her in a favorable light. What was Davy supposed to do—tell her boss that she'd taken the word of two drunk and drugged people?

That may have been exactly what she'd done. But it would probably cost her more than the pitch. She'd likely lose her job.

Davy sniffled and wrung her hands. "I can't believe I'm so stupid."

"You're not stupid. Maybe a little overly enthusiastic, but not stupid." Isla tucked her knees in closer to her stomach. "I'm the one who possibly got drugged and ended up waking up in the bed of one of my brother's best friends, so if stupid awards are being handed out this morning, they aren't going to you."

"Oh God, Isla. I'm so sorry. You see? This is why I didn't want to say anything. This is nothing compared—"

"No, no, no." Isla gave her a steady look. "We're not playing the comparison game. We're going to tackle both these problems. One thing at a time."

Davy nodded, eyes dark with worry. "What now, Isla?"

"I'm going to take a shower and think." She gulped a deep breath, trying to wrap her head around the daunting tasks ahead of her today. "Then I need to talk to Aiden. As soon as possible."

8

AIDEN

The fountains of the Bellagio were already dancing and swaying to the music, lights shimmering amid the sparkling waters on a day of perfect weather—everything insufferably cheery as though completely oblivious to ruined hopes and dreams. The conference had chosen March in Vegas for the weather, and Aiden had to appreciate the mildness of the day, even as sick as he still felt.

He straightened as he spotted Isla approaching with two of her friends—Davy, he remembered, but the other blond beside her was unfamiliar. And even though he'd known Isla all his life, he couldn't help the tension that bunched in his shoulders at the sight of her. She and her friends all wore stern expressions.

Brilliant. He was about to be interrogated.

Maybe he should have expected Isla to call in the late morning like she had, but some part of him had hoped she wouldn't. That they could just chalk this up to a drunken mistake, never to be discussed or repeated.

Of course, she *had* called, though, and asked for a few minutes to talk to him in person. He couldn't tell her no.

Rather than waiting for her to reach him, he left his perch and made his way down the footpath in front of the famous hotel. He'd suggested they meet here because the thought and smell of coffee or any other food or drink was completely intolerable right now. Plus, with this being outside, he could think a bit straighter, even with the synchronized music from the fountain show.

"Isla," he said with a smile. "Good to see you again. You're looking well."

Actually, she looks a whole lot better than how I feel. Which, admittedly, was a low bar.

"The magic of rehydrating intravenously," Isla said as she stopped in front of him.

Aiden swallowed. Of course she was managing to look effortlessly stunning while he felt like death on two legs.

He leaned to kiss her cheek as he might do if this was a normal day—but it wasn't. Faltering, he straightened and nodded toward Davy. "Hello, Davy."

"This is Megan," Davy said, nodding toward the woman beside her. "She's the bride we're here celebrating. The lawyer I was telling you about last night."

Aiden felt his brow furrow, just slightly.

A lawyer? Why had Davy emphasized her profession? He extended a hand toward the blond. "Aiden Camden. A pleasure."

She shook his hand, her grip overly firm, and his mouth dried.

The hell?

"We'll be right over here," Megan said with a curt smile, gesturing a few paces away. "Watching the fountain show."

Ugh . . . her voice absolutely held a warning note to it.

As Megan and Davy stepped a few meters away, Aiden crossed his arms, a defensive feeling growing like a vise around his ribs. "Intravenous hydration?" he asked as casually as possible. "Did you go to hospital?"

"Actually, yeah. I did. A clinic." Isla hesitated, then bit her lip. "Not for the IV, though. That was already planned. But after everything that happened, I thought I should . . . you know . . . check."

"Clinic?" Aiden raised his brows, a growing feeling of discomfort rising like acid in his throat.

"I . . . wanted to have a clearer picture of what happened last night. Just in case." Isla met his eyes for a moment. "But, um, they didn't find any evidence of . . . anything, so I think we're good."

Anything? Her words choked him, and he stepped closer to her, a mixture of horror and anger bristling through him.

"Fuck." The word barely made it past his lips, like something inside him had just cracked. His entire body revolted at the suggestion. "You actually thought I—" He couldn't finish. He couldn't even breathe.

"No, no. I mean." Isla drew a deep, sharp breath. "I thought it was important to find out what I could. Look, it was already humiliating enough, Aiden, and I don't really want to talk about it, but I thought it might be good for you to know."

He rubbed the back of his neck, any anger he'd felt melting away into *just* horror.

"I would never hurt you, Isla." His words were forceful. Hard, even. "You need to understand that. *Never.* Christ, you're like my own sister."

Then why had the memory of her skin against his been haunting his thoughts since sunrise?

He pushed the image away. "We grew up together. I respect Callum and you—care for you, *both.* I-I . . ." He struggled for the right words, then cleared his throat and gave her a look that he knew must be as desperate as he felt. "Do you really think I'm capable of doing that to you? Or any woman?"

Isla's face paled. After a moment that lasted just a few beats too long for his comfort, she shook her head. "No, no. I just, I needed to know. I know you said you didn't know what happened, but then you also lied about Lola—"

"I didn't lie about Lola." Aiden struggled for calm, then raked his fingers through his hair. "Lola happens to be in Vegas —or she was—because of the defense and technology conference I'm attending. She's handling negotiations with a company Camden Enterprises is trying to acquire. Making my life miserable, in fact. I promise you that her turning up at my door couldn't have been more inopportune or unfortunate because she's been hoping to rekindle our relationship, which I don't want to do."

He didn't know why he'd just spilled all of this to Isla, but the words didn't seem to want to stop flowing either. "I don't remember much of what happened last night, and I'm sorry about that. Truly. I didn't intend to bump into you last night. I just intended to get as piss drunk as possible, gamble, and go to bed. But for you to suggest that I would ever—"

"I didn't say that." Isla gripped his forearm. "I just . . . look, it's been a long day." She rubbed her temples. "Anyway, I don't want to talk about it anymore. If you say you don't remember, I believe you. In fact, that might be because . . ." Her brow furrowed, and she chewed on her lower lip, her pretty blue eyes wide with worry. "You know what? It doesn't matter."

"It does matter. What happened last night . . . I could never live with myself if you believed I set out to hurt you or did, in fact, take advantage."

"I don't think that."

"Then why did your friends show up like bodyguards?"

Her eyes darted toward them, and she smiled tensely. "Men don't get it. But yeah, we travel in packs. For safety. Not for intimidation. Not to make a point. Just survival." She held his gaze. "Last night made that painfully clear."

His jaw tensed. *Just what did she tell her friends?*

"Listen, there's another thing I need to talk to you about. Last night, we apparently promised Davy that we'd help her with a program she pitched to her boss at the Travelog Channel. I offered to host it, and . . . um, you offered to sponsor it. I know you might not remember."

Aiden blinked at her, his brows lifting quizzically.

Sponsor a Travelog Channel show?

What the fuck?

"I . . . why in the hell would I do that? What show? That's absolutely not going to happen."

Isla held his gaze as though surprised at his reaction. Then something hardened in her gaze. "Davy already pitched it, Aiden."

His lips parted.

And . . . here comes the blackmail.

There it was. The glint in her eye. The opening move in what he could only describe as a well-executed swindle . . . wrapped in a silky accent and wounded eyes.

Wow.

Just . . . wow.

And here he thought he knew Isla Scott.

This time, when his anger returned, it struck through him with an intensity he hadn't expected. "What exactly are you asking of me?"

"I'm not trying to force you to do anything," Isla said quietly. "Really. But, apparently, we had promised to help, and she needs this. I don't even know how I'll make it work with hosting it—the show consists of six episodes in six separate locations named Paris, most in the US, but the last being in Paris, France."

Not trying to force him? *Laughable.*

Little Isla Scott had grown up to be just as cutthroat as most of the women he knew.

He didn't meet her gaze, his fingers curling at his sides. "And what, if I fund your show you keep quiet? Is that the 'bargain'?"

"God, no!" Isla retreated a step. "That's not what I'm trying to do here. I know it's a big ask. I just was hoping for that . . ." Her eyes grew shiny with tears. "You know what? Forget it. We'll figure something else out."

She turned to go.

Shite. Now she'll be in tears when she goes back to her friends, and I'm going to look even more like a villain.

"Wait." He grasped her wrist. "Wait."

His gaze traveled toward the dancing fountains, calm and peaceful, a sharp, discordant sight contrasting with the turmoil inside him.

Whatever had happened last night had clearly shaken Isla.

He didn't want to be a villain to her. More than just her opinion was at risk because Callum would never forgive him.

He swallowed hard, trying to fight against his initial, ugly instinct at the thought of blackmail.

This is Isla. Someone I know and trust.

Calm the fuck down, Camden.

He couldn't let women like Lola poison his view of other women. Isla wasn't like her, right?

And if she was blackmailing him, maybe she'd earned the right.

He did feel guilty, after all.

Horrible.

"What sort of sponsorship are we talking about?" Aiden asked at last, releasing her wrist.

"I don't know. You'd have to talk to Davy. She's handling the finer details."

Aiden blinked a few times. This wasn't a money thing—God knew he could afford it—it was a question of honor.

And if this was the price it took to redeem himself, so be it. He didn't want another woman out there believing he was an arsehole.

Another thought struck him. Lola hadn't believed him this morning that Isla had been there for business, but what if this was a way to prove it? Cover his tracks? Whatever pitiful threats Lola might make against him could vanish—and this might go a long way to help him with the Ipolymer problem.

He could show Lola—publicly—he was, in fact, in a business deal with Isla. *Lola won't have a leg to stand on.*

And maybe he could prove he wasn't in a relationship with Isla at the same time.

"All right, I'll do it," Aiden said, straightening. "But I have one stipulation. Solo hosting is boring. If I'm going to sponsor, I want you to do it with your boyfriend. A couple hosting would be more interesting."

She gave him a baffled look. "I don't have a boyfriend. You know that."

He shrugged. "I'll leave you to figure that out. It doesn't have to be real. You're a good actress, if I remember correctly."

Isla held his gaze. "I don't even have any men I'm currently friends with. Except for Sergio and Kyle Winnick, and that's only because Sergio works for me and Kyle is down at *La Hacienda* every few weeks to go surfing."

"Perfect. Ask one of them."

She gawked at him. "I can't just ask my sister-in-law's brother to pretend—on a television show—to be my boyfriend.

And it couldn't be Sergio. I'm going to need his help at the inn so I can host."

Aiden lifted his chin. "Sponsorship comes at a price, Isla, and these are my terms. Take them. Or walk away." He didn't like the words even as he said them, but pride had a death grip on his mouth today. Maybe he could explain the whole situation with Lola, but he didn't feel completely in the mood to after this conversation.

A sudden breeze brought the damp mist from the fountain toward them, and he almost shivered.

Then Isla nodded. "Okay." A determined look set in her gaze. "Let's talk to Davy."

9

ISLA

SAMARA, COSTA RICA

Isla had never been so glad to see *La Hacienda Tropical*. If the palm trees could hug her, she might actually cry.

As her mother pulled into the parking spot and turned off the engine to the car, Isla's heart lurched.

Home.

God, it is good to be home.

Even though she hadn't been looking forward to Vegas, she *had* been excited to see Davy and Megan . . . even to catch up with the other girls a bit.

But the past four days had been nothing short of awful.

She'd come back with even more problems than she'd left with, and now she needed to find a way to break it to her mum and Sergio that she'd be taking an even longer trip starting in a month . . . in addition to the one she'd already scheduled for London.

Seven cities.

Would she even have time to come home while she was working on this project?

Three days of filming at each of the Paris locations meant

she'd be back and forth from Costa Rica nonstop. And the trip she'd already scheduled to London was for nearly a week. She would have to figure this out better, or it would be completely exhausting.

"Qué pasó?" Mum asked, glancing at Isla, who hadn't stirred from her seat to get out of the car.

Isla sighed, letting her gaze travel to the overgrown row of pink hibiscus by the car. "Nothing. Just . . . don't worry about it."

"Of course I'll worry about it. I'm your mother." Mum opened the car door. "Didn't you have fun?"

"Yeah," she answered quietly, then opened the car door. She and Mum were close—they talked about most things.

Except waking up in bed with Aiden after possibly getting drugged.

This didn't feel like the sort of conversation she could have with her mum. She'd have to tell her about the job hosting the Paris show, of course, but everything else? Mum didn't need to know. She couldn't know. She just might tell Callum.

Latina mothers weren't the best secret keepers to begin with. Mum would mean well, but she'd call Callum, swear him to secrecy, tell him, and then Callum would feel compelled to keep Mum's secret—leaving them all in a place where they knew the other one probably knew but they couldn't talk about it.

"All I want is to crawl into my own bed, between my own sheets, and maybe get un bolillo de pan and stuff myself with bread and natilla." Bread and sour cream had been her favorite comfort food since childhood.

"I'm sure we can arrange that. Anything for my *Islita*." Mum smiled and helped her get her bags out of the trunk.

They dropped her bags off at the house behind the inn, then went into the front office. Since the renovation, they'd expanded the front office to be much, much larger, with a full-size kitchen, a large and roomy waiting area for guests checking in to the inn, a display area to provide guests with champagne, wine, fruit juices, and water, and a selection of fruit, crackers, cheese, and pastries.

Isla swiped a guava pastry from the display and settled into a comfy chair. Fortunately, no guests were waiting right now.

"You're back," Sergio said, coming out from the back room. "Cómo lo pasaste?" *How did it go?*

"Perfecto." She leaned her head back against the seat, closing her eyes as she bit into the pastry. "Is Kyle here, by the way? I thought I saw his car."

"Yes, he came a few days ago."

Isla gave him a wan smile. *Thank goodness.* It was one less obstacle to deal with. She didn't know how Kyle would react to the idea of pretending to be her boyfriend on a show—or, for that matter, how Liddy and Callum would react—but she'd already decided she would make the boundaries truly clear. No kissing. Maybe some hand holding. And they'd explain to their families it was all pretense in advance.

As far as she knew, Kyle didn't currently have a girlfriend. Asking him was pathetic and ridiculous, but she didn't have a lot of options. And if Liddy and Callum gave her crap, she'd remind them that not so long ago, their whole *relationship* had started with them fake dating.

Of course, in this case, fake dating Kyle was *not* going to lead to anything. She loved Liddy's brother, but he was younger than her by three years—just twenty-five. And she wasn't even remotely attracted to him, or going to cross a line like that.

Sucking in a deep breath, she sat straighter. She may as well get the hard part out of the way while Mum and Sergio were both here. "So, I have some . . . news."

They looked at her expectantly. "Do not tell me you did one of those Vegas *bodas*," Sergio said with a handsome grin.

Damn.

See? Sergio? Sergio she could pretend to date. Even though they were friends and the feeling was mutual, he was closer to her age and exceptionally good-looking.

But she couldn't ask him to fake date her.

She needed him here to cover her shifts. And she needed to maintain a business relationship with him because she relied on him too much here.

"I did not, in fact, get married," Isla said with a laugh. She rolled her shoulders back. "I did, however, promise my friend Davy that I'd be the star in a show for her. You remember Davy, Mum? The filmmaker? She's working for the Travelog Channel now."

Mum's eyes went wide, and she clapped her hands together with delight. "A show? Isla, *qué bueno*."

"Yeah, I don't know how good it is." Isla sighed. "It's not here. It's a travel show doing six stops in separate communities named Paris. Most of them are in the States. But it involves a lot of traveling, starting next month. One trip a week, three days of filming in each place, then traveling and prepping for the next location. I'm not sure if I could come back between episodes, but I could try if you really need me to."

Mum and Sergio exchanged a look.

Damn. She could tell their enthusiasm was already waning.

"I . . . I don't *have* to do it, of course. It would just be really, really helpful to Davy if I do. She pitched it to her boss with me as the host, and her boss was really on board with the idea. And she hasn't been doing the best at work, so it would be a huge relief for her if I can do it."

She wouldn't mention that she'd already signed the contract. She could get out of that if necessary—*right?*

"Did you forget we are going to London for Callum's party in May?" Mum asked softly. Her tone didn't suggest she was a fan of the idea, but she didn't outright reject it, either.

"No, I know." Isla cleared her throat. "I'll have to make plans around it." She appealed to Sergio. "And I know it would be a lot of extra work for you. I'll owe you a month's worth of cocktails and playlist control. Plus overtime, obviously."

"You know I'm always happy to help," Sergio said, setting his forearms on the counter and leaning forward. "But what did Callum say? He likes you being in charge."

Isla's gaze faltered from him.

Callum.

She hadn't brought herself to telling him yet.

In fact, she would love to avoid telling him until everything was set in stone.

"Um, I haven't told him."

"Oh, Isla, *por Dios.*" Mum shook her head. "I know you love acting, but you and Callum made an agreement."

Ugh, yes. The agreement. Give up her life in London—and acting—and come here and run the inn if he bankrolled it.

And now her big brother was her boss. One that she probably needed to ask permission from *before* she signed onto a job jet-setting through the Parises of the world.

She couldn't even tell her mum that she was doing this show because of some great love for acting. That wasn't it at all. She was just stuck.

"Do you think we can just wait until we settle the details? I don't want to ask Callum if I can't get coverage for the dates I need to be gone." Besides, she'd have a better case to make to Callum if she had everything figured out.

Mum shifted with discomfort. "I don't know if that's a good idea."

Sergio nodded. "I think you should tell him. He's the owner."

Isla polished off the pastry, then wiped the crumbs from her lips. Couldn't *anyone* make anything easy on her right now?

Or maybe I'm making my own life too damn hard.

"Yeah, okay," she grumbled. Standing, she grabbed her phone from her purse, then stashed her purse behind the desk. "I'm going to take a walk on the beach. Call Callum."

She left them to head out of the front office and onto the main path toward the beach. From here, she could hear the faint call of the monkeys in the trees and the warmth of the sun on her skin. She loved this place.

It *was* home.

But living here and running the inn permanently?

Was this really what she was going to do for the rest of her life?

She pushed the thought away and made her way down the winding path until she reached the steps to the beach. There, she tossed aside her sandals and headed barefoot down the steps into the sand.

Kyle wouldn't be surfing here—this wasn't the best beach for surfing—but she'd see him soon enough.

God, how am I even going to ask him to pretend to be my boyfriend?

And why does the thought of asking Callum if I can do this fill me with even more dread?

She dialed before she could overthink it.

The call rang, and she blinked out toward the surf, shading her eyes from the sun.

"Isla," Callum said, answering on the third ring. "To what do I owe the pleasure at this late hour?"

"Don't act as though I never call," she teased. She checked her watch. Two in the afternoon here. He was acting like she'd called past midnight. "And it's not *that* late over there. You're only six hours ahead of me."

This shouldn't be hard. It's Callum.

"You don't call *that* much. Not nearly as much as when we lived in London and you were a thorn in my side."

"Aw, so sweet of you." She settled down into the hot sand, stretching her feet in front of her. The ocean brought her an instant sense of calm, and she needed that right now. "But, in fact, I do have a question for you."

"See? I knew you wanted something. That's all you call me for these days. *Callum, we need more money for this idea. Callum, we need more hammocks. Callum—*"

"All right, all right, I get it." Isla rolled her eyes, then combed her fingertips through the sand, letting the grains slip between her fingers. To be fair, she'd enjoyed the part of this whole taking over the inn when they'd been remodeling it. It had brought a different facet of her creativity to the surface, and she'd been surprised by how much joy it had given her. Not only had it been brilliant to give the place a makeover but collaborating with Callum was also fun. They'd never gotten along better, in fact.

"But in this case, it's not just me that needs something. It's Davy. When we were in Vegas together, she asked me if I'd host a new show for the channel she works for. It's a six-episode show in six separate places named Paris, starting next month. I'd need to travel once a week, filming on location for three days, for six weeks."

Callum chuckled. "That sounds like a massive headache. Davy always was good for a laugh. I bet you're glad you quit the business for the inn right about now."

Oh God.

Isla dropped her chin. "Callum, I told her I'd do it."

He was silent for a moment. "You must be joking."

"No, I'm not." She released a sigh that did nothing to loosen the tension in her chest. "She needs me, Callum. Her boss threatened to fire her until this pitch, and she pitched it with me as the host."

"Why in the hell would she do that?" The irritation dripped from Callum's voice.

She cringed. "I *may have* suggested the whole idea to her."

Callum grunted. "Isla, for fuck's sake."

"Cal—I just . . . I don't know. She needed my help. And I don't want to let her down. She's my closest friend."

"And what about the inn? You're just going to leave for six weeks? Who's going to run the place? We both know we can't count on Mum for the job—she's the reason I had to buy it."

"I was thinking Sergio could do it. And anyway, I wouldn't have to be gone the whole time. I could come back between trips."

"And be there what? Two days a week? You'll lose two days a week on travel and three days filming. You can't be flying back and forth like that—it's ridiculous and won't be that help-ful. You're supposed to be running the inn, Isla."

"I *am* running the inn."

"You just need a six-week vacation in the middle of the busy season? For another job? That's completely irresponsible."

Ouch, that was harsh.

"That's not fair. I have someone who can step in. This is a one-time thing. And you know I've done more than my share of the bargain with this inn, Callum. It's not like you're here running it day-to-day, making all the sacrifices. Sure, you write the checks, but the last time I checked the ledgers, you're also *getting* the checks, too. The inn is profitable. At this point, you're just a glorified bank."

As soon as the words were out, she regretted them. She wasn't trying to be cruel—she was just desperate.

Callum sighed. "I wasn't a glorified bank when you came to me begging to buy the inn, was I?"

She released a slow sigh, pinching the bridge of her nose. She didn't want to sound ungrateful. Callum *had* saved this place. For her. For Mum.

"I'm sorry—"

"No, it's fine," he said tersely. "I'm overreacting. I'm just . . . surprised. I know it doesn't seem as though I'm that involved, but I do plenty on the administrative side that you don't even know about. But if this is that important to you, and you've got coverage, and you promise you're not going to make a thing of it, then go ahead. I just want to be certain you haven't suddenly gotten cold feet to running the inn."

She grabbed a fistful of sand, letting the warmth of it heat her palm.

His words hit harder than she wanted them to.

Cold feet?

She swallowed hard. "It's a one-time thing." But she sounded less than reassuring, even to herself. "I promise."

"Yeah, okay. I'm sorry. I'm just a little stressed at the moment." He cleared his throat. "I'm actually going for a run with Aiden, but I'll call you in a little while. We can talk more about this then."

"Aiden?" she repeated, his name jarring her. "Didn't you just say it was practically bedtime over there?"

"Yes, we've been running most days together. But with his schedule, it's either got to be at the crack of dawn or once it's dark. Work is full on for him all the time. Funnily enough, I think he just got back from Vegas, too."

Of course they run together. Because apparently her life was now a comedy being directed by Satan himself.

"Oh really?" she choked out, her throat tight.

"Yeah, I meant to tell you, but I forgot. I'm sure your paths probably wouldn't have crossed anyway. He was there on business. Not quite the hen party scene."

She forced a laugh. "Yes, not quite."

They said their goodbyes, then a flurry of panic raced through her.

Oh no. Why didn't I just tell Callum I saw Aiden?

And what if Aiden told him when they went running? Callum would *know* she hadn't said anything on purpose. And once Callum started wondering, he wouldn't stop until he had an answer.

Shit.

But Aiden wouldn't do that, would he?

10

AIDEN

LONDON, ENGLAND

"Your mail, Mr. Camden," Louise said, setting a stack on his desk.

Aiden looked up from his laptop and glanced toward his assistant for the barest second. "Is it that time of day already?" he asked.

Louise always brought the mail at the end of the day, as he'd directed her to do. Nothing worse than getting a letter in the middle of the workday that could derail him from the task at hand.

"Well, probably not for you, but as for the rest of us . . ." Louise shrugged with a smile. "Good night."

"Good night." He returned his eyes to the computer as she shut the door. A few minutes later, he sighed and shut the laptop, eyes burning. He hadn't been sleeping well the last three weeks since he'd come home from Vegas, and he knew exactly why—the next Ipolymer acquisition meeting was looming.

He knew what he needed to do. He just hadn't done it yet.

Pulling out his mobile, he opened his messages and tapped one out to his brother, Mason.

Aiden: Still here?

His reply buzzed a moment later.

Mason: *Getting ready to head out. Need something?*

Aiden: *A few minutes of your time.*

Mason: *Be right up.*

This was the inevitable. What had to happen.

He'd been mulling it over for weeks since Lola had shown up at his hotel room and announced that her father was handing the acquisition over to her. Maybe Jorge had done it out of spite—or maybe he just trusted Lola that much. But . . . *enough.*

Two could play at that game.

A tap on his door followed, then Mason opened it a crack. His younger brother grinned and stepped inside. "I feel as though I'm being summoned to the headmaster's office."

Aiden chuckled. "Nothing that serious. Take a seat." He gestured toward a decanter on a nearby table. "Scotch?"

"No, thanks. I have dinner plans tonight." Mason unbuttoned his blazer and sat opposite Aiden's desk in the leather chair. "Something wrong?"

"You might say that." Aiden frowned, then slid a leather folio across the desk toward Mason. "I know it's a lot to put on you, but I need you to take over the Ipolymer acquisition. Jorge Salas has put Lola in charge of advising the company on the deal, and frankly, there's too much of a conflict of interest given my history with Lo. I can't handle this deal effectively."

Mason went still, an uncertain expression on his face. "Are you serious?"

"There's no one I trust more, Mason. I know it's not your job, so I won't force you to do it, but I think it would be the best way to move forward." He leaned back in his seat. "We need this acquisition. When I was in Vegas, I heard from Felix Covington that Covington Biotechnics is considering finding a new partner for future contracts. I've bungled the whole thing, and my involvement is now detrimental to the deal."

"I . . . I just don't know that I'm equipped to handle something like this, Aiden. What if I mess it up?"

"I'm still happy to advise you and even do most of the work behind the scenes. But I need you to be the face of the deal. Having a Camden there is important, but it doesn't have to be me. And, sadly, it's down to you and me."

Lola's silence over the past few weeks—considering the bomb she could potentially explode in his life if she wanted—had been disconcerting. He'd tried to simply put it out of his mind, considering he could do little about it. He was swamped with work anyway, but he needed to do something to be certain the next meeting about Ipolymer wouldn't blow up in his face again.

He'd questioned this over and over, whether Lola had been simply biding her time to make him sweat or if she wasn't going to use the ammunition she thought she had after all. But he knew without a doubt that Lola would hold a grudge, and for Camden Enterprises to get the deal, the only option was for Mason to run it.

"Damn Logan and Quinn for getting out of working here," Mason said with a self-conscious laugh, returning Aiden's focus to the conversation. "Maybe we're just more dimwitted than they are."

"That's for damn sure." Aiden palmed his face, the scruff of his jaw rubbing like sandpaper against his hand. "They got out early. Like rats off a sinking ship."

He reached for his mail and started thumbing through it. "But I promise you, I'll make this as easy on you as possible. I'd do it myself, but Lola is determined to make this process as difficult as she can."

"Can't we just acquire a different company?"

Aiden kept his smile to himself. It wouldn't do any good to make Mason feel foolish. "Sadly, Ipolymer holds the patents we need. My bigger concern is that someone else is going to snap them up before the ink dries on the deal we're proposing."

Mason nodded slowly. "Well, better you than me—I . . . I mean . . ." He chuckled. "Could I think about this?"

"I suppose." Aiden leaned forward, tossing a letter into the bin without opening it. "But I do need you to be aware that I wouldn't ask if I didn't find the situation necessary. As I said, I'll do most of the work. But we need to change our tactic if we're going to get this deal done."

Mason nodded, then stood. "Speaking of Lola, how are things with her? You're not back together again, are you?"

Aiden's lips pursed. "Well, when you put it that way . . ."

Mason blanched. He'd always been the shyest and most nervous of the Camden brothers. "I didn't mean—"

"That she's the devil incarnate? No, don't worry, I already believe that myself." Aiden released a guttural sigh. "No, we're not back together. Though, I'll admit, I considered it for all of five seconds—that's how desperate I was. Felix suggested I just date her until the deal was done."

Mason shook his head with disgust. "That bastard would suggest something like that." He offered an encouraging smile. "For what it's worth, I'm glad you've got a backbone. That you aren't just another slimy, greed-driven, corporate arsehole willing to lie and cheat his way to get what he wants. You make Mum and Dad—and the rest of us—quite proud."

Aiden shifted with discomfort. This sort of ebullient praise wasn't something his family offered—or accepted—well. *Not to mention that I don't particularly feel like a man of deep integrity.*

It wasn't like he was beyond lying to Lola. *Or forcing Isla to pretend to be in a relationship in a very public fashion in order for me to lie.*

And every time he ran with Callum, he couldn't help feeling like an enormous hypocrite. Isla had called him in a panic a few weeks earlier, just as he was leaving for a run, to beg him not to tell Callum about even *seeing* each other in Vegas.

He'd gone along with it, but one too many people—Lola included—knew that wasn't true.

The whole situation felt like a bomb waiting to explode.

Turning his attention back to Mason, Aiden gave a stiff nod. "Happy to do my part." Then he tried to get the conversation back on track. "Do you think you could give me an answer tomorrow morning?"

Mason nodded. "I appreciate the time to sleep on it. I have to admit, the whole idea is a bit intimidating. Especially the part where I'd have to handle business with Lola."

Aiden smiled. "Glad to know you're finally free to tell me what you really think of her."

"What did you expect? You two were back and forth so many times we all got whiplash."

"Women," Aiden muttered. "Brilliant at making you feel like you're in charge while they steer the whole ship into an—"

His eyes froze on the envelope he'd just tossed in the bin. His fingers twitched. The logo on the envelope—

The Little Chapel of Instalove. In Las Vegas.

Wait.

Wait.

No.

A cold fear slicked through his spine.

No bloody way.

"What is it?" Mason stepped closer, leaning toward Aiden's desk. "You look as though you've just seen a ghost."

Fuck.

What the hell is in that envelope?

Mason followed the direction of his gaze and reached over, snatching the envelope from the bin.

Aiden lunged for the envelope, which Mason held to his chest, out of Aiden's reach. "Just a bit of rubbish."

Mason frowned at him suspiciously. "What sort of rubbish?"

His heart rate accelerated. "Nothing to worry about."

Mason cocked his chin, no longer an employee but instead an annoying younger brother. "Then let me see it—if it's just rubbish. *The Little Chapel of Instalove.* How intriguing."

"Mason Camden. Hand over that envelope right now," Aiden demanded, voice coming out rough and hoarse. Beads of sweat formed on his forehead.

Mason held his eyes, then a slow smile spread on his face as he tore the seal with a sickening rip. He darted away, just as Aiden dove for him—too late. Mason twisted away, tearing the envelope free. Paper ripped. Aiden's arms caught Mason's calves, and the two men landed on the floor of the office with a thud.

Bollocks. That hurt. His hip smashed against the floor, pain radiating up his side—but that was the least of his concerns.

Not now. Not fucking now.

He and Mason weren't kids anymore, wrestling in their parents' sitting room over the last slice of cake. This was about *so much worse* than losing dessert.

Aiden was still too far to reach the damned envelope as Mason tugged the contents free.

"Why, it's a marriage license," Mason crowed, undeterred

as he tried to read with Aiden clawing for the paper. "Between Aiden Preston Camden and Isla Grace Sco—"

Both men froze.

Aiden saw Mason's mouth open—*saw* the exact moment realization dawned.

"What the actual fuck?"

Aiden groaned.

11

AIDEN

AIDEN'S EARS buzzed so loudly that he could hardly process Mason's words.

"Isla? You married Isla? In bloody Vegas?"

Collecting a deep breath, Aiden sat, panting.

Married. He'd fucking married Isla? What the *hell* had happened that night?

How could this be real?

"Isla?" Mason repeated, unable to comprehend the news.

"Please stop speaking." Aiden held out a hand for the marriage license, desperate to see it for himself. For different reasons now.

I can't believe this is happening.

Mason handed the paper over and peeled himself from the ground, his face a shade of crimson. Wordlessly, he rose and crossed toward the decanter and poured himself a glass of scotch, then swallowed some down.

Aiden's eyes narrowed on the marriage license.

Who in their right mind would let two people as clearly inebriated as Isla and I must have been get fucking married?

No way in hell Isla remembered this.

That night kept getting worse and worse.

Christ, does she even know yet?

Aiden fought the urge to crumple the paper in his fist, as though that would somehow undo any of this. Would a marriage like this even hold up legally? He wasn't a US citizen.

He'd have to get a solicitor involved, though. Expand his trust—and the knowledge of what had happened—to yet another person.

He lifted a sharp gaze at Mason and stood, legs unsteady, pain flaring from the bruise on his hip. "You cannot breathe *a word* of this. To anyone. Not a single soul, Mason. Especially not Liddy or Callum."

"As in Liddy, *who works with me?* Callum, who you see nearly every day? They don't know? Bloody hell, Aiden, what in the world were you thinking?" Mason shook his head. "And *Isla.* I can't believe you're sleeping with Isla. She's like a sister to us."

"I'm not sleeping with Isla. This is all just an enormous mistake," Aiden snapped. Tempted as he was to go over and join Mason in grabbing a drink, he held off, pacing instead.

"How does one get married by mistake? If there's a joke here, I'm failing to see it. Callum won't think it's a joke. Neither will Mum or—"

"Good God, do you ever shut up?" Aiden dug his fingertips into his eyes, trying to think. "You sound like Mum when she opens the paper to the weather report."

Mason ignored him. "The fact that you're not sleeping with Isla might make it worse. I'm not going to lie."

Aiden shot a glare at him. "How could that possibly make it worse?"

"Because it means you likely had a one-night stand with someone we all care about. Callum will murder you for it. And, anyway, Isla isn't a one-night-stand type of girl. She's going to wind up hurt if she hasn't been already."

"Thanks, Mason. If I ever need a therapist with a law degree and a flair for melodrama, I'll be sure to call." Aiden shook his head with a scowl. "How do you know what Isla is or isn't?"

How did it always come back to somehow *him* having done this to her?

"A drunken wedding in Vegas? Because I'm assuming that's what happened. You had to have slept with her at least then. And I hardly doubt Isla would just *marry* you if there hadn't been something going on for much longer. So how long, Aiden? Maybe since Costa Rica? You two were awfully cozy a couple of years ago during Quinn and Elle's wedding, come to think of it. Or maybe at their anniversary party last summer?"

"I had already started dating Lola last summer," Aiden said dryly, unamused at Mason's line of thinking. "But you know that."

"What I know is that I'm unwilling to be your secret keeper on this. Not this. It's too huge, too explosive. I don't want to be guilty by association. When this blows up in your face—because Callum will find out about this—I don't want anyone pointing fingers at me and saying that I knew." Mason swallowed the rest of his whiskey. "Fix this. You've wronged Isla."

"Isla signed it, too, Mason."

"Still a flaming mess. Whether you both signed it or not, you've got to fix this—and tell Callum. Because if you don't, I will."

Mason started for the door.

"Mason, please." Aiden sucked in a shallow breath. "I'm attempting to fix this. I have every intention of fixing it. But I need time. Please don't go running off to Callum and making this worse. Isla wouldn't want Callum to know any more than I do."

Mason paused by the door, hand on the doorknob. "How much time do you need?"

Aiden's jaw clenched. The show Isla's friend had put together was set to start shooting next week. He'd largely been ignoring the emails about the whole thing, though Davy dutifully included him on everything.

But this was the sort of conversation he needed to have with Isla in person. If he met her in the US, he might even be able to file something there to start the annulment process more quickly. He could meet her at the location where they'd be filming, explain the situation, and they could come up with a solution together.

"A handful of weeks," he answered Mason at last. "At least to get the process started for annulment. Then Isla and I can also discuss the best way to tell Callum."

Mason nodded curtly. "Fine. But I'm warning you, Aiden, if you don't make this right with her on your own, I'll make sure you're forced to."

He had to admire Mason's loyalty to the Scotts.

Yet, I'm one of Callum's best friends. The thought only brought a fresh wave of shame.

When his younger brother left, Aiden made a beeline for the personal safe he kept behind a painting on the wall. Moving the frame to the side, he punched the code, then pressed his thumb and forefinger to the fingerprint scanner. The safe unlocked with a beep.

He shoved the loathsome marriage license inside and slammed the safe shut.

If only he could hide away from his problems so easily.

Digging his mobile out of his pocket, he scrolled through

his email until he found Davy's email with the production schedule.

He dialed Louise, who picked up right away. "I've already left, you know."

"Yes, I know, but I need you to get me airline tickets. Immediately."

"For when and where?"

"Next week. I'll need hotel and a car, too. I have no idea which airport, but I'm heading to Paris, Texas."

12

———

ISLA

PARIS, TEXAS

WHEN SHE'D LANDED in Dallas, Isla hadn't quite known what to expect from the small town 110 miles northeast of the city . . . and the reality of it was even grimmer than she'd anticipated.

The Uber Davy had provided for her stopped in what appeared to be a small, run-down parking lot surrounded by brick buildings. At the far end of the lot, two trailers were parked to the side—*A Tour of Paris's* official mobile head-quarters.

Isla gulped a breath, worry mounting.

Maybe she'd given Davy a terrible idea. Not all Parises were created equal, but starting in this one? *This does not seem promising.*

In fact, this seemed like the middle of nowhere.

A bleak, empty expanse of flat streets, square, brick buildings, and a few scraggly trees. The sign to the parking lot, a giant red arrow that announced, *"Welcome to Paris!"* appeared worn and weathered, much like everything she'd seen on the drive in.

With unease clawing at her stomach, she opened the door and climbed out of the car as the driver off-loaded her suitcase. She thanked him, then wheeled the case over toward the first trailer and knocked.

Davy opened the trailer a second later. "Isla!" She threw her arms wide and hugged her. "I'm so excited you're here. Come on, bring your stuff in."

Isla managed a weak smile and pushed away the temptation to ask, *"Are we in the right place?"*

Farther inside the trailer stood Kyle. A crew member was fastening a camera and microphone to him, and Kyle winked. "Hey, Isla."

"Oh, you beat me here," she said, relief settling into her ribs as she caught sight of the third Winnick sibling. Surfing had only improved his good looks—his hair was sun-streaked golden, his skin tanned from days in the sun. Isla didn't entirely know what Kyle did for a living, just that he was a computer genius who worked remotely.

"It was a quick flight from Nashville," Kyle said with a shrug. His blue eyes twinkled with amusement. "How's my favorite girlfriend?"

Isla laughed and set her suitcase in the corner of the cramped trailer. Davy and the rest of the crew knew they weren't really dating, which helped. Explaining the need to pretend a relationship to her family had been . . . *interesting.* Liddy had laughed about it, thankfully, but Callum had looked at her over the FaceTime video like she'd sprouted horns. "I'm good. Slept most of the flight. I didn't realize it would be such a long trip to here from the airport, though."

The crew member straightened. "It's Texas. Every trip takes a long time." He smiled, extending an arm covered with a tattoo sleeve toward her. "I'm Tim, by the way. I'm sound-slash-electric-slash-gaffer on this set."

"Isla Scott," she said with a grin.

"Yeah, I saw you in *Cabaret* on the West End several years ago. You were amazing."

"Oh, thank you." She settled into a chair and rolled her shoulders back. Thankfully, they wouldn't be starting to film until tomorrow, but Davy wanted her to come straight to the "set" after arriving—to give them a final overview of filming.

Tim brought another mic pack and camera over to Isla. "So, here's the deal. We'll be using several types of fully immersive film methods. Besides your on-body camera, we'll also set up and stage typical camerawork that you might expect with a documentary. Think of this as your own reality miniseries. Arms up. I'll fit you better for it later."

"Mic'd at all times?" Isla asked, glancing at Davy as she lifted her arms. Tim tinkered with the camera and mic, strapping it to her.

The idea of having a film crew following her around for the next three days wasn't *that* strange, but in the past, she'd always had a script to work from. While Davy had spent weeks preparing small segments for Isla to memorize and record, the pressure of being filmed without having any idea what she might say was enormous.

"Everything's going to be great," Davy said brightly. "Tomorrow is the annual wine festival, which is why I scheduled this town first. We can spend some time acquainting you guys with most of the buildings and places we want to feature on the show, and then, since it's already quite late, we can wrap for the night and grab some dinner. Sound good?"

"Whatever you say, boss," Isla said with a confident smile.

Davy tugged the walkie-talkie from her belt loop and lifted it to her lips. "Boyd?"

Static answered.

"Dammit. He must have turned his off. He should be in the

other trailer with the crew. I'll go get him," Davy said, then headed out the door.

"Boyd?" Kyle asked, giving Tim a curious look.

"Starling Boyd. He's the director."

"Oh." Kyle's brows furrowed. "I thought Davy was the director."

Tim lifted a coil of wire. "Davy's the producer. Her boss, Antony, is executive producer for the studio. Starling is the director." He closed a case and picked it up. "You'll get used to all the various roles. We run a small production crew, so most people have multiple jobs. You'll mostly interact with the film crew. The editing crew—well, that's all Bartholomew here in the States—will be editing as we travel and while the film crew takes the new location's A-reel. I'll be back in a bit to make some adjustments for you, Isla." He went out the door Davy had gone through, leaving Isla and Kyle alone.

Kyle sank beside Isla. "Is it me or this town a bit . . . um . . . small?"

"I haven't really seen it, but that was my thought." Isla grimaced, then rummaged through her purse for a lip gloss. "Yet Davy seems to still be really excited about it."

"I'm just not sure how we're supposed to be here for three days. I got here around noon and took a look around." Kyle rubbed his neck. "This is the type of town where I'm pretty sure you could see everything in a couple of hours."

"There's an Eiffel Tower here, though, right?"

"Yeah, complete with a red cowboy hat on top." Kyle chuckled. "Unsurprisingly."

Isla reached over and squeezed Kyle's hand. "Thanks for being here with me, by the way. I know it's a crazy ask, but it means a lot that you're willing to be a part of this."

Kyle shrugged. "Sure. It sounds fun, actually. I mean, I can't promise I know how to act, but if it's like a reality show, that shouldn't be hard. Hopefully. They don't *seem* hard anyway."

Even with the uncertainty of diving into a project like this, Isla relaxed in Kyle's presence. They'd become good friends over the past couple of years—and since he was at *La Hacienda* all the time, it was like he was a piece of home.

"Well, I'm sure you'll be sick of me by the time the next few weeks are over. By the way, I think between the Arkansas and Tennessee episodes, I'm going to stay with Elle and Quinn in Nashville for a few days. Callum didn't think it was worth it for me to fly back and forth between Costa Rica."

"Then we can hang there. Though I should point out you're choosing Elle over me." Kyle and Liddy's older sister was the common link between the Camden and Winnick families— Elle and Quinn Camden had met years ago, and, because of that, Liddy had moved to London and started working at Camden Enterprises . . . and met Callum.

A slightly messy circle, maybe, but their families all felt like one large extended family now, celebrating holidays and special occasions together.

"I'm not choosing her over you. I'm choosing her big, beautiful house over your questionable-smelling one-bedroom apartment," Isla said with a smirk.

Kyle put his hand over his heart. "The hits just keep coming. Next, you'll be telling me I have to sleep in a bunk bed with Tim, the tattooed sound guy."

Acting like they were a couple was going to be tough . . . in a lot of ways, as Kyle really did feel like a younger, far less uptight brother.

The door to the trailer opened once again, and Davy came in—without anyone else. "Hey, Isla . . . you have a visitor."

"Visitor?" Isla raised a brow.

"Yeah, he's outside." Davy winked and held the door open for her.

After exchanging a curious look with Kyle, Isla rose and headed toward the door.

Then she saw him standing a few feet from the trailer.

Callum.

Isla's jaw dropped. She hurried down the wobbly trailer steps and across the tarmac. "Callum, what the heck?"

He grinned, then caught her in a tight hug. "Surprised?"

"Shocked." She shook her head and stepped back, grabbing his hands. "How in the world did you know how to find me?"

"I may have asked Kyle to send me some of the production information." Callum gave her hands a squeeze. "God, it's good to see you. I know it's only been a handful of months, but it always feels like too long."

"Well, maybe you and Liddy should come down to *La Hacienda* more often. It's not a half-bad spot for a quick holiday." Her voice was teasing but *hopefully* Callum could hear the genuineness of her words. She really did wish he'd come more. That he wouldn't leave her to do so much at the inn.

And . . . I miss him.

"You know how Liddy's job is—it's a miracle if she makes it home before sunset."

"And you? You still enjoying being a kept man?" Isla poked him in the ribs, once again knowing how easy it would be for Callum to read into her statement.

When Callum had resigned from his job at Camden Enterprises, he'd spent a lot of the first year flying back and forth between Costa Rica while *La Hacienda* was being renovated. But now that the renovation was complete, his trips were often several months apart. She hated that she never saw him now. And Isla wasn't even sure *what* Callum was doing for a job instead.

"A kept man," he repeated with a scoffing laugh. "I've been looking at buying several other properties—mostly in Scotland and Ireland. One in France. I want to make short-term rentals of them. I've enjoyed the administrative side of *La Hacienda*, but I think my next properties aren't going to be quite so difficult for me to get to."

The defensiveness in his tone told her the tension between them wasn't just imagined. He felt it as much as she did. *I hate it, too.*

"So, what *are* you doing here?" She crossed her arms.

"Actually"—Callum cleared his throat, then glanced back at the ride-share car he must have come in—"I've brought someone. An alternative—and more logical choice—for your boyfriend problem for this show."

Boyfriend problem? What?

Isla furrowed her brow as the door to the sedan opened . . . and Tomas stepped out.

Her heart slammed into her ribs as she glanced at the beautiful, tall Black man she'd been dating casually in London right before she'd moved to Costa Rica. A fellow actor. Both had agreed to go their separate ways, and oddly, she'd been fine with that.

So . . . what the hell?

"Isla, darling." Tomas flashed her a smile and sauntered toward her. He pressed a kiss to her cheek.

Isla's lips parted as she gave Callum a hard stare, her heart pounding.

"I ran into Tomas on the Strand the other day. We got to talking about your project . . ." Callum's voice took on a smug note that immediately set Isla's teeth on edge.

"I mentioned you needed a boyfriend for the show, and well"—he gestured toward Tomas with satisfaction—"problem solved."

Isla could barely think straight, her anger mounting. She whirled toward Davy, who still stood at the trailer door, watching.

Does Davy know about this?

She gave Isla a baffled look.

"I spoke to Antony Lugazi. He was thrilled with the idea of bringing on another known actor to the production," Callum said behind her.

Isla's pulse pounded in her ears.

How dare he?

She turned toward Callum, her fingers clenching. "You went over me? Over Davy? I told you we had the whole situation figured out." She flicked a glance at Tomas.

Tomas flashed his easy grin, completely unperturbed, and Isla's stomach twisted. How could he even be here?

"No offense, Tomas—"

"None taken."

Shock barely had time to settle before fury erupted.

Isla stepped closer to Callum, seething. "You had no right to take this into your own hands. Kyle is in there right now, and he's flown from Nashville, interrupted his life—"

"And you should have asked your sister-in-law, your *brother*, hell, anyone in your family how we might feel about you masquerading around in public with a fellow *family* member for a television show," Callum shot back, his face reddening, "before you made the plans. You two are like siblings—you can't act like a couple. I'm shocked you'd even be comfortable with the pretense."

"Kyle's not family, Callum. That's the point." Isla gaped at him. "And I don't need to ask permission for something like that. It's between Kyle and me." She glanced back toward the trailer, hoping against hope that Kyle wouldn't have heard all this commotion.

But he had.

He stood beside Davy, watching the scene, an uncertain look on his face.

"Maybe he's not family to *you*. But he's my brother-in—" Callum stiffened, his gaze locking on something behind Isla. "What is he doing here?"

Isla shook her head. "I told you. Kyle came—"

"Not Kyle." Callum jerked his chin toward the other trailer, and Isla turned to follow his gaze.

Then she saw him exiting the production trailer.

Aiden.

13

AIDEN

Oh . . . fuck.

Aiden's eyes locked with Callum's, and his gut dropped.

No, no, no.

But it was too late. Callum's brows furrowed, and he broke away from Isla, striding across the carpark toward him. "I thought you were going to New York."

Maybe there was a simple solution to this. Confess now, beg for forgiveness, and deal with the consequences.

But those consequences could also potentially end his friendship with Callum.

He wouldn't forgive or forget that Isla had ended up in Aiden's bed.

And Callum definitely wouldn't easily let go of the fact that they were now, technically, married. For that matter, *Isla* wouldn't forgive him for telling Callum without talking to her first.

Aiden cleared his throat and stepped down from the trailer. "I-I am. I just had to stop here first." *How in the hell am I going to explain this?*

But before he could make up an excuse, Isla was at Callum's side. "It's my fault. I told him not to tell you—given how angry you were with the whole Kyle news—and I didn't want you to think I was upsetting the balance of your world too much. The show needed a corporate sponsor, and I suggested Aiden."

Callum looked from Isla to Aiden, frowning. "Why would Camden Enterprises sponsor a travel show?"

Good question.

"Isla isn't completely to blame. I told her over Christmas that I wanted to diversify our ventures—help the everyday person connect better with our industry. See a different side of us," Aiden said smoothly, giving Isla a tight smile.

Callum listened with a look of disbelief, and Aiden counted the seconds as they passed. There wasn't a hint of a breeze, the air still, the tension thick.

Aiden dared a look at Isla, who gave him a worried frown.

"There's no trip to New York, is there?" Callum's eyes narrowed at Aiden.

If only Callum knew how much worse it was than he suspected.

But why exacerbate the problem?

Aiden sighed. "No, there is. But I should have told you about this, and I'm sorry. I panicked because I didn't expect to see you here. Speaking of which, what the hell *are* you doing here?"

Callum frowned, then glanced back at Tomas, who'd drifted off to stand near Davy. "Trying to solve a problem." He sighed and then offered Aiden a nod. "Apology accepted. But in the future, you don't have to lie to me, Aiden. You had a perfectly reasonable excuse for being here."

The words were soft blows that somehow struck like a hammer to Aiden's chest.

"Well, you, darling brother, don't," Isla cut in, setting her hand on Callum's elbow and redirecting his attention. "What the hell possessed you to hop on a plane and fly all the way here from London, Callum? What's worse is that you've dragged Tomas into this mess." She crossed her arms. "Does Liddy know you've done this? Because I'd be shocked if she signed off on this sort of interference from you."

"Pardon," a male voice spoke up from behind them.

All three gazes turned toward Starling Boyd, the director, stepping toward them. He held out a hand toward Callum. "Starling Boyd. Mr. Scott, is it? I believe we spoke on the phone yesterday."

Aiden's eyes drifted from Callum toward Isla. She seemed genuinely angry about Callum being here. It wasn't any of his business. He should stay out of it, considering it appeared to be a sibling spat.

But Isla looked so flustered that his throat tightened, and he moved nearer to her. "You all right?"

She didn't accept the offer of his help, however subtle it was, and instead directed her attention to Boyd. "Mr. Boyd, I'm Isla Scott. I believe there's been a mistake. I've already made all the arrangements with Kyle Winnick to—"

"There's no mistake." Boyd gave her a measured smile, then slipped the tie from his wrist and tied his long gray hair back behind his neck. "Antony had casting in London work out all the details with Tomas Meyer's agent yesterday. It's a fantastic idea—he's got a half a million followers on Instagram alone."

Isla stiffened, her gaze flicking between Boyd and Callum.

Aiden still wasn't completely following, but the situation was starting to grow a bit clearer. Kyle came down from the trailer just then, and Aiden greeted him with a nod before Kyle said, "Excuse me, I'm just trying to clarify. Are you saying you don't need me here for the role of Isla's boyfriend?"

"No, the production team has decided to place Tomas in that role. But, actually, we'd still like for you to remain—perhaps as Isla's best friend? It could make for an interesting dynamic," Boyd said, slipping his hands into the back pockets of his jeans.

Beside him, Isla's hands were in tight fists, her knuckles white. She threw another look back at Davy, then at Callum, then back at Boyd.

Aiden sensed an explosion of anger coming. He recognized that darkening expression on her face. "Excuse us for a second." Grabbing her by the elbow, he pulled her back toward the trailer where Davy stood. He offered Davy and the man beside her an apologetic look as he shoved her past the door and then shut it behind them.

"Sit," he said in a firm voice.

To his surprise, Isla did as he'd directed. She settled onto the trailer's sofa, hands over her face, and Aiden went over to the fridge. He found a case of water bottles and yanked one free, then brought it to her.

"Thank you," she said, then lifted raw, furious eyes at him. "I'm going to murder my brother."

She uncapped the bottle and sipped it, her shoulders heavy with a strangled breath.

"Care to tell me what happened?"

"You. This is your fault." Isla glared at him. "You couldn't just help me on this. It was a tidy little job . . . host a few episodes in a few—apparently ridiculously boring—Parises, then move on with my life. But, no. You had to suggest a couple would be more interesting to follow as a host. And Antony and Davy loved the idea. Except now my idiot brother has apparently decided to interfere with whom I chose to play my boyfriend—"

"Kyle?" Aiden asked.

She nodded. "Yes. Which was fine. I already told Davy—no public displays of affection. But that wasn't good enough for Callum. He dug into my past and pulled out an old ex of mine, dragged him into it."

Ah. That must be who the mysterious Tomas was.

"The fellow who looks like a rugby player?"

"Yes, if rugby players had perfect teeth, six-pack abs, and walked the catwalk for Versace in their downtime." Isla shook her head.

Right.

That would be the type of man Isla Scott dated. Look at her. She was fun and flirtatious. She had pink streaks on the underside of her hair and a golden tan that spoke to her days on the sun-drenched beaches of Costa Rica. And Aiden had seen her in those bikinis she wore.

What the hell am I doing?

He blinked, cutting the thought off, then cleared his throat. "Did things end on a bad note with Tomas?"

"No, no, that's not it." Isla combed her fingers through her hair, a defeated look on her face. "It just ended. I was moving to Costa Rica. He was staying in London. There wasn't enough there to keep us together, really." She took another sip of water. "But that's not the point. Callum had no right to interfere."

"Why did he?"

She avoided his gaze. "I don't know. Because he was apparently that deeply uncomfortable with the thought of me pretending to date Kyle on a show." Their gazes held for an awkward moment.

Not surprising.

And also further evidence of how protective Callum was of Isla—and his neatly ordered relationships.

Isla tore her eyes from his. "And because he's an arsehole."

"Well, maybe not an arsehole. You know how Callum is.

For years, you were the center of his universe. The only person he really gave two shites about."

"Besides the Camden brothers," Isla said with a scoff. "Well, and that wanker Luca Harris. Fucking prick completed the process of giving Cal trust issues when he caught Luca fucking his ex-fiancée in their flat. And we've all paid the price since."

Aiden winced. *That's true.* Callum definitely had valid reasons for being wary of his friendships and mistrusting others. He hadn't even told Quinn or Aiden about catching Luca with Sophia until a couple of years earlier. The admission had been enlightening—and given Aiden a much deeper understanding of Callum's personality.

But it was also another reminder that Callum had experienced *deep* betrayal before from a man he'd considered a close friend. If anything, it made Callum more sensitive to even the perception of betrayal.

Aiden cleared his throat. "Right. Well, it's true. Callum lets few people in. If anything, Liddy has softened him considerably—taken the pressure off you. And now that he's finally talking to your mum again, I'm sure it helps, too."

"I know," Isla said with a roll of her eyes. "And believe me, I thank Liddy for it regularly. But that doesn't mean he had the right to step into not only my *personal* business, but a business relationship, and then walk all over my arrangements. The sheer audacity of it, Aiden." Her eyes grew red-rimmed, and she swiped her lashes with the back of a knuckle.

Gently, he crouched in front of her, then brushed a tear from her cheek away with his thumb. "I'm sorry."

Isla lifted her eyes to his, and unexpectedly, his heart stumbled.

He hated seeing her so miserable, especially knowing he'd caused some of this.

But that was *normal*, right?

He'd known her all his life. Cared about her.

She sucked in a breath, and the moment held for just a smidge longer.

God, it would be so easy to close the distance, brush his mouth over hers, taste the salt of those tear-drenched lips. Comfort her.

She dropped back onto the sofa. "Ugh. I'll figure it out. What are you doing here anyway?"

He gritted his teeth. The last thing he wanted to do was lie yet another time—this entire situation with her was filled with so many lies that it drove him insane—but telling her about being married right now?

The timing couldn't be worse.

He inhaled sharply. "I just came to check on my investment." He settled back onto his heels.

God, I'm such a fucking liar.

"Listen," he continued, not wanting to dwell on it any longer than necessary, "I don't think Callum has handled this appropriately, but the fact that he flew all the way here from London and went to the lengths that he did is good evidence of how strongly he feels about this. I'm not saying he's in the right, but you probably do need to talk to him. Without all the listening ears."

"I know, but I'm not ready." Isla stood and glanced back at Aiden. "To be honest, I'm glad you're here. You probably kept me from having a meltdown in front of everyone. Thank you."

"Of course." He stood, the unease churning harder now. "Ready to go back out there?"

She nodded, then sighed. "After you."

14

———

AIDEN

SETTLING BACK into his seat at the most highly rated restaurant in Paris, Texas, Aiden let his gaze wander over the eclectic decorations—the tin roof that jutted over the kitchen, string lights between the brick walls, and clear lofty ceilings that gave the feel of sitting on a patio rather than inside. Even some of the tables had umbrellas.

Interesting.

He and Callum had left the rest of the production crew behind at the Hampton Inn and headed out on their own for dinner and beer—which they'd grabbed in a jug. Reaching for the center of the table, Aiden refilled his glass as Callum returned from the lavatory. He gave his friend a steady smile as though guilt wasn't eating an acid trail through his lungs. As though this was just another normal night in London.

But it wasn't. And until Aiden managed to have the conversation with Isla that he'd come for, things wouldn't begin to go back to "normal."

Callum sighed and sank into his seat. "I've really made a mess of things, haven't I?"

"I've seen messier situations," Aiden said dryly, sipping his beer. He'd also caused them. But this one felt uniquely catastrophic. "But yes. I'd say walking all over your sister's plans and flying here from London without telling your wife what you were up to are both . . . slightly unhinged."

Callum groaned. "Don't remind me."

"Not that I'm a paragon of advice when it comes to women, but my guess is that you'll be in the dog kennel for a while. Might I suggest you invest in some fine Swiss chocolates?"

"If I could buy my way out of this one with chocolates, I'd probably have to buy a whole factory." Callum poured himself a glass of beer and downed a large swallow. "Speaking of hiding things, I still can't believe you didn't tell me you were a part of this catastrophe."

"You didn't seem too keen on Isla leaving the inn to do this, and I didn't want to have to confess that I helped make it possible." *Funny how fast one lie turns into a dozen.*

Mason's words hung in the back of his mind, though. *"You've got to fix this. And tell Callum. Because if you don't, I will."*

Insane how one drunken mistake had led to this—two best friends, stuck in the dullest town in America, eating burger baskets and drowning in beer.

Yet he was no closer to fixing this than when this had all started.

He didn't have the foggiest idea *how* to fix it, either.

"Would it really have been that bad if Kyle pretended to be Isla's boyfriend?" Aiden asked in a casual tone.

"Ugh, yes. It would have. You have no idea—well, maybe you do, considering that whole Ciara thing—but after my accident, not to mention my parents' divorce, dealing with everyone feeling like they knew my business, gossiping about my family and me . . ." Callum palmed his face. "I hate that sort of attention. Loathe it. I know Isla loves the spotlight, but I can't stand it."

"Because you'd be seen as dating siblings? That happens sometimes. There's nothing wrong with it."

"But I'm not just dating Liddy—she's my wife. And can you imagine at the elopement party? Some people will know about Isla's show by then. Enough of my father's friends are already offended that they didn't get invited to the elopement at Christmas. They'll see this as just another thing to gossip about. They'll ask questions, expecting Isla and Kyle to be a couple. Or we'll have to explain over and over again how it's all a ruse. In which case, they might think it's a bit odd that my sister is so casually intimate with my brother-in-law. They'll either be scandalized or make comments like, '*Ah, Callum. Isla loves keeping it in the family, eh?*' I truly don't want to punch anyone at the party."

Callum had clearly put quite a bit of thought into this, and it was tormenting him.

Aiden reached for a chip from his basket and dipped it in ketchup. "You know you can't control what people say about you, Callum. Or who Isla happens to sleep with, real or pretend. You knew when she got into acting that she might have to pretend to have sex with men on stage or on film. That's part of the business."

The thought of *that* made his skin prickle and his chest tighten.

This would be the perfect segue. The opening he needed, perhaps, to come out with it and attempt to make things right with Callum.

But he'd said it, in part, to gauge Callum's reaction. Test how a conversation like this might go.

"Maybe not, but I don't have to like it. And to be honest, it was a relief when she quit the damn business to focus on the inn. Now it's like that whole can of worms has been opened again." Callum took a bite of his burger and chewed, deep in thought.

"Do you think that's what's bothering you? That she's getting back into acting again?"

"Maybe. I do feel like she has one foot out the door of the inn. Like somehow she sees it as a punishment now. Like I'm *forcing* her when she was the one who begged me to save the place for her. Between you and me, my mum has been telling me over the past few months that she feels like Isla isn't very happy. And that bothers me, too. I wish she would just *tell* me if that's the case."

"It can get complicated, trying to keep friends and family happy," Aiden said, averting his gaze and swallowing another chip. "Admitting the truth."

"Maybe. But if a relationship is worth a damn in the first place, it ought to start with trying to be honest."

Aiden held his breath, the words sharp like a knife.

Callum hung his head. "What am I going to do? I've never seen Isla this angry. And I can't undo it. The production team was thrilled to get Tomas on board."

"Apologize," Aiden said in a strangled voice. "Try to fix it before it gets worse. And maybe accept that there are some mistakes you can't undo." He wasn't sure if he was speaking to Callum or to himself at this point.

Callum nodded slowly. "Yeah, you're right." He picked up his glass and then frowned again. "Isn't that the cameraman?" He gestured to the front window. "Across the street?"

Aiden followed his gaze. Sure enough, one of the camera operators that Boyd had introduced him to was there . . . and appeared to be pointing a camera right at the restaurant.

Are they filming us?

No, that couldn't be it. They must be getting B-roll footage to use as filler shots.

Sure enough, the camera operator continued walking past.

Aiden focused his attention back on Callum. "When do you head back to London?"

"Tomorrow morning. You?"

"Not for another day." He was glad he'd given himself some margin. Hopefully, he could talk to Isla more freely once Callum was gone.

"I'm surprised at your level of commitment to this," Callum remarked with a chuckle. "Still can't see how it makes any sense for Camden Enterprises to bankroll something like this."

Yeah, I haven't figured that part out either.

Fact of the matter was, he'd cut the first sponsorship check out of his own personal savings. He'd reached out to his financial adviser about finding the best way to handle any of this. "I know. On the surface, it all seems a bit illogical. But what can I say? I have a soft spot for the Scott siblings."

"You know, maybe you can help me, too. Since you're such a devoted investor in travel television and all. How involved are you going to be?"

"Not sure what my schedule will allow for. But some, obviously."

"Then can you do me a favor?"

Aiden leaned forward in his chair, the few chips he'd eaten feeling like lead in his stomach. "Anything."

"Keep an eye on Isla for me, will you? She may or may not forgive me tonight, and I could use someone I trust watching over her."

Holding Callum's gaze was damn near an impossibility right now. "Of course," he said with a taut smile. Then more softly, almost to himself, he repeated, "Of course."

15

ISLA

"So, you didn't talk to Callum before he left?" Davy asked as Isla sat in front of the mirror for hair and makeup.

"Nope. I'm not ready to talk to him." Isla shrugged and lifted her chin as Molly, the makeup artist, brushed some powder onto her neckline.

"I get it. I'd be furious too. Boyd and Antony are singing his praises, but that's not necessarily a good thing. Chauvinists."

Isla cut her eyes with disgust. She didn't care if Tomas had two billion social media followers. And maybe, *maybe* if Callum had bothered to suggest the idea to her *first*, she would have considered it.

But for him to go over her head?

That was completely unacceptable. Not to mention unprofessional.

I feel so undermined.

A tap on the door redirected her attention. Boyd poked his head in the trailer. "Ready to go?"

"Give me two minutes," Molly called, reaching for another brush.

"Tim already got the mic and camera on you, though?" Boyd asked Isla.

She nodded, a flutter of nerves going through her. "Yup, I'm all set."

Boyd smiled, then moved out of sight again.

"Hey, hand me that stack of index cards over there," Isla said, pointing at a nearby table. She'd taken the time last night to write down the scripted parts on the cards to help her memorize the facts about the wine festival. "We're starting at the Eiffel Tower, right?"

Davy nodded. "We have about five hours before the VIP reception for the wine festival this afternoon. The town is super excited about the feature on the show, so they're pulling out all the stops. Locals are nice."

The trailer door opened again, and Boyd stepped through, this time carrying a clipboard. He looked straight at Isla. "Quick question. Could you give Aiden these? He's riding over to the Eiffel Tower with you. Just in case he's in any shots if he's hanging around the set, he needs to sign release papers." He winked at Isla and handed her the clipboard. "Thanks, love. I'm heading over there now."

"Why's Aiden staying?" Davy asked as Boyd left again. "I can appreciate the fact that he's interested in seeing what this is all about, but between him, Callum, and Tomas popping in out of the blue—" She sighed. "I know I'm only a lowly producer on this, but I just hate it when I feel so out of the loop."

"I have no idea. It does rather feel like the men have all taken over this show, doesn't it? I'm surprised Boyd didn't tell you about Tomas, though. You'd think he would have done that at the very least."

Davy shrugged, but Isla caught the hurt on her face. "He's the director. If this was a normal film set, I'd outrank him, but our crew is so small that his importance tends to be overplayed.

If Antony gives a green flag on anything, he rarely cares about what I think."

That was such bullshit.

Molly's presence—since Isla didn't know her or her loyalties—kept her from saying that, though. But it was true. Davy had worked so hard not only to develop this idea but also to bring it to life.

For weeks, Isla had been getting daily emails from Davy, who'd gone home from Vegas via towns she hoped to film in, researching and taking the week to scout and take pictures. She'd fast-tracked filming permissions with mayors and sheriffs all over, not an easy feat. She'd worked so hard, and Isla admired her grit and determination.

Only to have Antony and Boyd come along and make a last-minute change without even *consulting* her?

As soon as she stepped out of the trailer with Davy, Isla reached over and gripped her hand. "The audacity of the men in our lives is out of control. I'm here for you; I just want you to know that. You're the *only* reason I'm here."

Davy squeezed her hand. "I know."

Isla climbed into the waiting van as Davy took the passenger seat. Aiden was already in the back. "Good morning," he said with a smile, then held out a cup toward her. "Got you this for the road."

She frowned down at the paper cup, then sipped it. "Chai tea latte? How did you know?"

"You forget I've known you forever," he replied with a smirk. "I remember you begging for chai every time you came to our house for tea when we were children. That and your godawful pronunciation of *croissant*." He handed her a bag with one in it.

"You try navigating the linguistic gymnastics that are required when growing up in so many transatlantic locations. I never quite knew how to pronounce anything." She opened the bag to the warm, buttery scent. "Thank you."

The driver of the van started forward, and she held tighter to her cup to keep it from spilling.

"There's a bakery down the street on a quaint little square called Paris Bakery. They can't pronounce them either. Seemed apt."

"Where's my croissant and chai tea?" Davy asked with a chuckle from the front. "I'm Indian and English, you know. I *love* chai. Actually, it's the only tea that doesn't taste like dirty dishwater to me."

With a deadpan expression, Aiden handed another bag and cup over to her. "As offended as I now am, on behalf of our national drink, I didn't forget you, Davy."

Davy grinned. "Keep this up, and you can be our official craft services for the set. Don't worry, I'll find a way to put you to work if you hang around here long enough."

"Oh! Speaking of which," Isla said, then unfastened her index cards from the clipboard Boyd had given to her. "Boyd wanted you to sign this. Some release form since you're going to be around the film crew."

"Release form?" Aiden took it and scanned it with a frown. "For what? I leave for New York tomorrow."

"I don't know, ask Boyd. I think he was worried you might get in some of the shots, and he wants to have all the legal bits and bobs taken care of. I just sign where I'm told and don't question it, unlike you business types."

"It's just a standard form," Davy said with a shrug. "Boyd is meticulous about that sort of thing. Just fill in the highlighted parts and sign it."

Unfastening the attached pen, Aiden did as Davy had directed, then handed it to her. "What's on the agenda for the day?"

"We're going to film a segment by the Eiffel Tower to introduce the town and get some footage of our stars discussing their honest thoughts about the tower. Then we'll come back to the town square and film in the center of town. Any place of significance, Isla will introduce to the audience. The rest of the time, we'll just be following them. At some point, we'll cut for lunch, and after, we'll move to the VIP reception for the wine festival. The goal is to get as much interaction as we can with the locals but also get to know Isla and Kyle . . . and Tomas."

Isla tore off a piece of the croissant and ate it. "Did you read the emails Davy sent? Most of this was in them."

Aiden's gaze faltered. "I get quite a few emails a day."

A polite way of saying no.

Also a reminder of who he was.

He wasn't *just* Aiden Camden, friend from childhood and man she'd ended up doing God-knows-what with in Vegas.

He was the CEO of a major corporation. And worth *billions*.

The thought made her throat thicken, the realization suddenly overwhelming her. She'd been so bold, hadn't she, going up to Aiden and just treating him like an everyday man. Even Callum was wealthy by his own right—from working at Aiden's family business—but he'd never come close to the wealth or position that Aiden had.

And, as if that wasn't enormous enough, his father was a member of the peerage. An earl.

The sheer ridiculousness of it made her laugh—sharp and breathless, like it had slipped out by accident.

Aiden's brows furrowed. "You all right?"

"I think I've just realized just what it is you do for a living—*who* you are. And it's—"

"Crashed your processing system?" Davy provided helpfully.

His lips pursed. "What do you mean?"

"Aiden! You're the CEO of a major defense contractor." Isla's eyes widened as she stared at him. "What are you *doing* here? Maybe I've been living in Costa Rica too long. It's just . . . so insane to think about."

Aiden gave her an odd frown, then exchanged a look with Davy.

"You spent too long on earth, and now it's hard to remember what it's like to walk with angels?" Davy asked with a laugh. "That's the most ridiculous thing you've ever said, Isla. You don't know what it's like to be around normal people. You've spent most of your life with the upper crust."

Isla sipped her chai, feeling shaky.

My God, I'm having an identity crisis.

Davy wasn't wrong.

Her father had been wealthy from old money in England. That was how she knew the Camdens.

But her mother—a bisexual hippie from Costa Rica who loved yoga and the beach?

When she'd lived with her mother, it was like Isla had a completely different life. Like *she* was a different person. She'd left that, mostly, when she went to boarding school in Connecticut and moved to London, where her friends were actors and models. Film and theater folks. Maybe not as wealthy, but definitely not just average run-of-the-mill people.

And then she'd gone back to Costa Rica, where the people she saw on a daily basis were Sergio and her mum . . . Kyle.

Tourists and locals.

All people who'd lived ordinary lives. Maybe Kyle's sisters lived in more elite circles now, but they hadn't before.

Sergio wasn't wealthy at all. She'd met his family.

And the inn guests? Even though it was a boutique inn, they were just average citizens.

I don't know who I am anymore. Which world I belong in.

I'm not sure I belong in either world.

Before she could say anything—not that she was even sure she wanted to voice any of these thoughts—the van pulled up in front of a sixty-five-foot-tall Eiffel Tower replica with a red cowboy hat on top.

Davy hopped out, already speaking into her headset, and Isla glanced up at Aiden, her heartbeat slow and shallow.

"You look pale," he said in a low voice.

"I'm not sure I feel so well."

"Why don't we step out of the van? Get some fresh air?"

She nodded, and he opened the door, then helped her out. He held on to her elbow gently and, rather than guiding her toward the group for the production, he led her closer to the Eiffel Tower, then released her. "That's . . . *something*, isn't it?"

Isla lifted her gaze toward the cowboy hat, then smiled. "It's kind of sweet, I have to admit. I didn't know if I would like it, but now that I see it, I do."

"Texans know how to put their brand on things, don't they? I saw a shirt in a store earlier with *I Love Paris* on it. Except where there would normally be a heart shape, there was a shape of the state."

"Of course." She smiled, trying to catch her breath, still feeling jittery and out of sorts. Her hand trembled when she lifted her chai to her lips again.

Aiden's fingertips brushed against hers, and she caught her breath, a warm rush of tingles going up her wrist. "Hey. Look at me for a moment."

She swallowed hard, then turned her gaze toward his.

"I'm just Aiden. And you're just Isla."

"But you're not—"

"But I *am*." Aiden gave her a gentle smile. "And I need to be. To you, anyway. I don't want you looking at me the way you did in that van. Quinn was supposed to be the head of the company—he's the one with the title. I just fell into the role I'm in when he abdicated, but that doesn't mean it's how I ever saw myself. Or how I see myself now. I don't live in a penthouse or drive an expensive car. And some days, I wish I could go back to the military, where life was simple and the meals were shite, but at least I had friends who valued my friendship and not competitors who only valued my pocketbook."

"Why does it matter how I look at you?" Isla asked dryly.

Yet something in his words hit her hard.

Like he knew. He *understood*.

He saw her.

"It just does."

She swallowed a lump in her throat and nodded. "I'm not sure where I belong anymore, Aiden. What world I'm really a part of. Living the bohemian, salt-of-the-earth existence on the beach—where I've also worked harder than I ever have in my entire life—has changed me."

"That's understandable." He held her gaze. "I've felt that same confusion before—in the military. Helped me to think about the last time I felt like I belonged. And that led me back to London. And it wasn't a career or prestige that called to me as much as it was my family. I wanted to be a part of them again."

She smiled wistfully, remembering the way Aiden had vanished for a while. How strange it had been when she visited the Camdens with Callum, and Aiden wasn't there. *Like a huge, gaping hole, really*. She'd been so happy when he'd left the military.

The idea that Aiden had needed to go off and *find himself*, though, had never occurred to her.

When is the last time I felt like I belonged?

"I'm not sure if I know when I even stepped off course.

Moving to Costa Rica felt so right—so fun. Fixing up the inn, painting the rooms, and designing the new layout was so exciting. I think I ran on sheer adrenaline for months until reality set in."

"Isla Scott . . . adrenaline junkie. I might have known."

That delicious brush of his fingertips came again, and she held her breath. Then she reached her own fingers toward his, letting the back of her knuckle trail against the palm of his hand.

"Isla, darling." Tomas sauntered toward her, arms extended. "Ready for this?"

Before she could answer, he caught her in a hug and lifted her off her feet, twirling her around before setting her back down again on the tips of her toes.

The action had the effect of setting her off balance, and her cup dropped out of her hand, landing in the grass beside her. She leaned into his broad, strong chest, the spice of his cologne filling her nostrils with its familiarity and warmth. He brushed a kiss against her temple. "This is going to be fun," Tomas breathed.

Fun. She managed a smile, then pulled back. "Can't wait," she forced out, then leaned over to grab her fallen cup. But the lid had popped off, and the tea spilled.

She sneaked a glance back toward Aiden once again.

He was gone.

16

AIDEN

NO DOUBT ABOUT IT—VEGAS had opened a door to *something* Aiden didn't know existed.

If anyone had asked him about Isla before that trip, he would have smiled—probably fondly—and said something nostalgic about the girl he'd known since childhood. Brilliant actress, funny, warmhearted.

But now?

Now I'm sitting at a wine tasting in a coffee shop, wishing I was drinking wine instead of coffee, and every time Tomas touches her, I feel sick.

Aiden swallowed more of his cappuccino and stared at the scene unfolding by one of the tasting stations. Tomas and Isla stood there, chatting with the shop owner, laughing like they were already in on some private joke. Tomas had eagerly assumed his job as boyfriend, his hand a constant presence at the small of Isla's back—territorial, possessive.

Aiden curled his fingers around his coffee cup, knuckles stiff. He forced himself to sip and ignore the irrational irritation gnawing at his ribs. Tomas had every right to touch her.

Yet Aiden wanted to break his fingers.

Tomas even knew how to chum it up with Kyle, who had fallen easily into the role of humorous third wheel when he'd butchered the pronunciations of every wine they tasted.

"Need something a bit stronger than wine?" a deep voice asked from beside him with a chuckle. Aiden glanced over and saw an older gentleman, broad shouldered and wearing a plaid shirt and bow tie . . . and a cowboy hat. He flashed a bright smile framed by a St. Nicholas-like beard.

Aiden returned a polite smile. "Something like that."

The man winked. "I hear you. I'm staying away from the stuff, too. If I'd started drinking wine at five, I would have been asleep by six." He extended a hand. "Name's John."

"Aiden," he said, shaking John's hand. "Are you a local?"

"Yup. Lived here all my life." A proud look filled his eyes. "Wouldn't want to call any other place home. We might be a humble town, but we've made it through a lot of adversity."

"Ah, so you're a native Parisian then?"

John barked a laugh, then cupped his hands around his mouth. "Hey Kathy, this fellow wants to know if we're Parisians," he called to the woman speaking to Tomas and Isla.

Kathy rolled her eyes and grinned. "You asked the wrong man," she said to Aiden with a shake of her head.

John set his hand on Aiden's shoulder. "We're Parisites." He winked again.

Isla's lovely laugh trickled through the shop. "That's clever."

"So how do you fit in with this group?" John asked, lowering his hand from Aiden's shoulder. "You seem to be mostly observing."

"That's apt. My role is more . . . accessory," Aiden said as he set his mug down on a table.

"You're the money, eh?" John gave him a thoughtful look. "From England?"

Aiden nodded and shifted with discomfort.

"You're a long way from home. What do you think of our small town?"

"It's charming," Aiden said in a practiced tone.

"Bet you say that everywhere you go." John chuckled. "Our town has its problems, just like every other town. Young folks leave and don't come back. Not much to do here compared to the bigger cities. But it's a good place to settle down with someone you love and have a couple of kids. Grow old in a place where people actually know you—there's a value in that young people don't always recognize. What's home to you, Aiden? What does it look like? Smell like? Sound like? More importantly, who's there waiting for you? If you can answer those questions, you're pretty fortunate."

Of course he'd get stuck talking to the most gregarious person here. *So un-British to pepper a complete stranger with so many invasive questions.* Aiden restrained a sigh. "So, what are the answers to those questions for you, John?"

John smiled. "Home is that lovely lady over there." He pointed at a woman with short gray hair serving wine at a tasting station. "Been married to her for forty-three years."

"And the rest?" Aiden arched a brow.

John inhaled an exaggerated breath and released it. "Home smells like rolls from Ideal Bread baking on the square in the morning, Speas Vinegar in the air. Crepe myrtle blooms in the summer, and the sounds of kids running through the sprinklers." He gave Aiden a wink that he was increasingly sure must be one of his trademarks. "I don't ask questions I don't already know the answers to, sonny."

As John moved away, Aiden settled into the background

again, vaguely drained by the interaction. His gaze flicked toward Tomas and Isla once more. Tomas had slipped his arms comfortably around Isla's waist, tugging her back against him.

Kyle was laughing with another local. The film crew moved around, capturing their conversations, while other people here for the wine festival sipped on their drinks in various states of attire—some dressed to the nines, some in jeans.

No wonder John had taken one look at him and realized he wasn't at home. Not here. Maybe not anywhere. He was a man who traveled the world but had nothing real of his own. No crepe myrtle summers, no scent of fresh bread on the square, no one waiting for him at the end of the day. Just the cold sterility of offices, boardrooms, and polished steel elevators.

And really . . . I wouldn't be here if I had a choice.

He'd toiled in front of a laptop all night, trying to catch up with all the work that demanded his attention. Tonight would likely be similar.

Yet here he was, standing around and waiting for the appropriate moment to tell Isla they were mistakenly husband and wife.

But he'd spent the entire day waiting for the opportunity to present itself, and it still hadn't appeared.

He checked his watch. Nearly nine thirty. Sidling up beside Davy, he asked in a low voice, "Do you have any idea when we'll be done?"

Davy frowned and then pulled out an iPad. "Yeah, I think we'll probably wrap here in a few minutes. We have more than enough footage for the day. I'm not sure what Boyd is waiting for."

"All right, well, I'll be outside getting some air over in the square when you're ready to head back."

He left the coffee shop, then headed across the street

toward the main square of the town, where bright string lights lit the trees. In the center was a white fountain, which a plaque stated was a gift from a J. J. Culbertson. The fact of the matter was, it really was charming, and the cool evening air and sparkling lights were a refreshing break from the noise and crowds of the people on the wine crawl.

A few lovers strolled hand in hand near the fountain, and Aiden stopped under the shade of a tree and leaned against the trunk, arms crossed. He couldn't remember the last time he'd been out on a date like the people around him were. With Lola, every date had been about status—the fanciest, most exclusive restaurants, the hottest tickets to the best shows, and quick getaways to expensive resorts.

But picking a girl up, a stroll through a quaint town, taking her back to her home, perhaps hoping for a kiss . . . the days of those simpler relationships were far, far behind him. He'd chosen that—couldn't blame anyone but himself—but it hadn't always been that way.

When did life get so complicated?

He couldn't quite understand, either, why it had bothered him so much when Isla had given him a look in the van this morning like he was Aiden *the businessman*. Maybe because he'd always counted on a handful of people to see him as he really was and she was one of them.

But more than that, *her* opinion mattered.

Even as children, there'd been an understanding between them as the "younger" siblings of their respective brothers. But as they grew older, too. She believed in him when others didn't. He could be himself around her.

And now . . . there was this new, unexpected need to *impress* her. Not with his job or money or anything like that. Something else. Something more important. Like he could be in a crowded room with her and they'd still be alone together when they made eye contact—know what the other was thinking. Share something secret—deeper—just with one look.

"Trying to escape?" Isla said from behind him.

He glanced over his shoulder. "Did you wrap that quickly?"

She appeared to be in good spirits with a smile on her face and carried a brown paper bag in her hand.

"Ugh, not soon enough," Isla said, bending down and tugging her heels from her feet. "And I still have to go back to the trailer—give them the mic and the camera." She straightened, dangling her heels from the straps, looping her fingers through them.

"Not soon enough? You seemed to be having fun. You *and* Tomas."

Isla rolled her eyes at him. "It's called acting, Aiden. Maybe learn to do some of it, rather than sitting there all day, sulking and brooding and whatever the hell else you were doing."

Sulking?

Isla held the paper bag out to him. "I got you something. Thought it might cheer you up."

With a frown, he accepted the bag, then reached inside it to pull out a soft, navy T-shirt emblazoned with "I Love Paris."

"You got me one of these?" He tilted his head, his lips curving despite his mood.

"To commemorate our time here in Paris." She backed up, with a grin, toward the fountain.

"What are you doing?" Worry grew in him as she went up the stairs to the fountain, backward. He left the tree and headed toward her.

"What do you think?" She tied her long hair back, some of the pink glittering in the warm, electric light. "Soaking my feet;

they're throbbing. I work on a beach—ask me how often I wear something other than flip-flops and sandals."

Aiden had already reached her, his alarm rising as he drew closer. *Is she drunk?*

"How much wine have you had to drink tonight?" he asked, gripping her arm as she stepped closer to the fountain.

"Don't know. Six glasses? Plus, the tastings? I'm fine. Who knows?" She threw him a breezy smile. "Just a bit tipsy. Contrary to what you may believe, I am *not* an alcoholic. They just kept putting glasses of wine in my hands while the cameras were rolling. I was working."

She teetered forward, and his hands shot out—one firm around her wrist, the other slipping instinctively to her waist. Her skin was warm, damp from the mist, the soft give of her body against his chest sending an electric bolt through his nerves. She smelled like wine and something sweet—strawberries, maybe.

Aiden's pulse kicked up. *Shite.*

"I don't think that's a good idea, Isla." His voice was rougher than he meant it to be.

She arched a brow. "And why not?"

"It might be slippery. Marble can be slick when it's wet."

"By all means, feel free to join me—give me something strong and sturdy to hold on to." She pushed past him and stepped in, holding her skirt up to keep it from getting wet.

She gasped, "Oh it's cold!" but kept moving.

"I'm not sure the production company will want you getting the camera and microphone wet."

She turned toward him, a sultry grin on that perfect mouth.

"Is that just your lame way of getting out of joining me? And here I thought Aiden Camden was the daredevil who liked to jump from airplanes and have adventures across the globe. Or have you been keeping that top button too tight to remember?"

He let her words roll off him. She was clearly inebriated, even if it had been several hours since she'd started tasting wines. Maybe he should have expected this, but he'd avoided drinking all night.

She started to twirl, head back, the mist of the fountain dampening her skin and making it stick to her throat and face. Her skirt was hiked up, revealing the smooth skin of her thighs, her taut belly peeking out from her crop top.

Aiden's mouth went dry.

Beautiful, wild creature.

Near them, onlookers had pulled out their mobiles to film.

Fuck.

He was going to have to go in there after her.

With a groan, he set the bag she'd given him to the side, pulled off his shoes and socks, then rolled the cuffs of his trousers. He glared at her as he stepped in.

Bollocks. She wasn't kidding. The water was frigid.

"Come on, you little menace." He tugged her by the arm.

"Menace?" She gave him a breathless smile. "Didn't you have a different nickname for me when we were younger?"

"Yes, Miss Skye."

She stumbled, and before he could think, his hands found her. *Bare skin. Soft.* A breath hitched between them, a flicker of something dangerous. He should step back.

He didn't.

And then he hated Tomas Meyer because he'd been smelling and embracing her like this all day.

Isla set her hand on his chest and grinned up at him. "Why Skye?"

He shrugged. "My favorite island."

"Aw, Aiden, even with all that teasing and hair pulling you did? Maybe you had a heart after all."

She smiled up at him, and for a second, she wasn't Isla, the woman who could shatter his self-control with a glance. She was Isla, the girl who used to race him across the lawn at his family's estate of Littleton, who once cried on his shoulder when her father forgot her birthday. A lump tightened in his throat.

Aiden swallowed it down. "I wouldn't go that far, Miss Skye."

She trembled with cold. "I suppose we liked each other enough in Vegas. Even if neither of us remembers it."

One can always count on children and drunks for the truth.

His gaze dropped, then flicked toward her lips. "Well, we'll always have Paris . . . Texas, anyway."

She laughed, then gave a shriek as her foot slid hard on the slick marble. He caught her once again, barely keeping her from falling. "Come on," he said, then hoisted her over his shoulder. "Let's get you out of here before you catch pneumonia."

"What are you, Tarzan? This isn't the way you carry me romantically out of the fountain." She giggled, then smacked his arse. "Though the view isn't bad."

"Isla, you're outrageous. And drunk. But I'll pretend I won't remember any of this in the morning." He set her down on the ground and held her upright.

She arched a brow, lips pursed. "Is that what you did last time?"

Touché.

"No," he said flatly.

He reached for both of their shoes and the T-shirt and handed them to her. "Hold these."

Isla gave him a baffled look. "What for?"

"I need you to carry them." He didn't wait—just bent and scooped her into his arms like he'd done it a thousand times before. Like it wasn't rewiring something deep inside him. Like it wasn't the most natural thing in the world to hold her this close.

Like it isn't exactly where I want her to be.

"I'm taking you back to your hotel room. Before you get either of us in any more trouble."

17

ISLA

THE FIRST THING Isla saw as she woke up was an enormous bouquet on the nightstand beside her pillow. She startled, then sat up, frowning at the vase of daisies and English garden roses —her favorite.

"From Callum," Aiden said from the corner of the room.

Isla drew in a sharp breath, her gaze shooting toward him. Aiden sat in a chair, one leg crossed over the other, a laptop poised on his lap.

"What are you doing here?"

"You asked me to stay, so I stayed," Aiden said with the hint of a smile on his lips.

She squinted at him, thinking back at the night before . . .

Her heart sank.

The humiliating way he carried her out of the square.

Aiden helping her to her hotel room.

She wrinkled her nose.

Yet, it was different this time—she remembered it all clearly. She'd been in that fountain, and—for a moment—she'd fantasized about his arms around her. Holding her. Kissing her. Hopefully, she hadn't made it obvious.

Oh God, I really embarrassed the hell out of myself.

"I really need to never drink again," she said, mouth dry. "I swear I don't usually do this."

"You were working. We'll chalk it up to overly eager locals hoping for a moment in the spotlight who kept handing you drinks."

"Did you sit in that chair all night?" she asked, climbing out of the bed.

He closed the laptop and stood. "I thought it was for the best. We don't want a repeat of Vegas, after all."

She flicked a glance at him, something in his tone making her pause.

Vegas had brought nothing but trouble into her life.

Yet the idea that he feels the same way . . . makes me weirdly irritated.

"No, you're right. Thank you for being the sober and responsible one this time. I'll be sure to repay the favor next time," she said with a tight smile, her posture stiff. The more this sounded businesslike and transactional, the better.

That's all this is, anyway. All he's here for. A business arrangement. He knew how to keep things professional, even with her. He'd shown that when she'd gone to him, asking to help Davy, and he'd responded coldly, making demands of his own about a costar.

Her brother's flowers by the bedside were only a further reminder of the boundaries she needed to draw.

Aiden cleared his throat. "Speaking of Vegas, there *is* something I wanted to discuss with you. I was hoping to catch you before I leave to—"

Isla's phone rang. *Davy.* Lifting it to her ear, she said, "Hello?"

"Isla, where are you? Call time was at seven. The driver at the hotel says he's about to leave."

Isla checked the time.

Shite. I'm forty minutes late.

"Oh my God. I overslept. I'm so sorry. I'll be in the lobby in five minutes." She hung up and flew toward the bathroom.

"Everything all right?" Aiden's voice carried from behind her.

"Yeah, I'm just insanely late. Call time was at seven. You should have woken me." She grabbed her toothbrush and squeezed some paste onto it.

"Sorry, I didn't know the call time."

She didn't answer, scrubbing the terrible taste in her mouth away as she ran the water. She spat, then managed, "Not your fault. But I need to get out of here. What was it you wanted to talk about?"

Aiden stepped toward the bathroom door, then hesitated. His fingers flexed at his side as he watched her through the reflection of the mirror, and she sensed . . . something different about him. Something she couldn't quite put a name to. His expression wasn't quite readable.

She threw her hair into a ponytail, dragging foamy cleanser across her cheeks.

"It can wait," he said at last.

"Maybe tonight, after I get done filming?"

"I'm flying back to New York this morning for an important meeting Mason is heading up for me." He let out a short, frustrated breath. "I'd delay, but I promised Mason my support. Turns out the role of CEO is rather important to a corporation."

That's right. He was leaving.

And the thought of him not being here—well, that shouldn't matter. It shouldn't make her feel off balance like she was stepping onto a stage without knowing her lines. He'd just hung around the set scowling anyway.

Yet, I'm going to miss him.

Not in some big, dramatic way.

Just enough that it niggled at her with the unexpectedness of it. Of how much his presence here had mattered to her.

"Yes, it must be difficult being so responsible. So important," she said with a teasing laugh, then washed her face.

After she'd finished, she dried herself. "Will you be coming to some of the other locations?" He couldn't hear the hopefulness in her tone, could he?

"We'll see," he said with a frown.

She shot a smile at him, then closed the door in his face.

"Rude," he called.

"I didn't realize we were at the point in our relationship where I used the loo while you watched," she called back.

"Well, you did vomit in my closet last time and leave me to clean it."

"Don't remind me." She flushed the toilet and pulled herself back together.

Hurrying to the door, she opened it.

"You didn't wash your hands," he remarked with a wry grin.

"Ugh, I was going to, but I figured I'd open the door first since you missed looking at me so much." She turned the water back on, smirking at him through the mirror.

"Much better," he deadpanned. "Now I can *see* the loathing."

She loved this.

These moments with him felt easy and carefree. Like they were an old married couple, in some ways, because they'd known each other for almost thirty years. Teasing came so effortlessly with Aiden Camden.

But there was something new in it, too. A page they'd turned, where she couldn't help wondering—hoping, really—that maybe there was something more to his teasing.

She washed her hands, then flicked the excess water onto his face as she walked past. "Glad we're finally being honest with each other." She grabbed a folded wardrobe bag from her closet, slipped on some sliders, then picked up her phone. "I really have to go, though."

He gave her a look of disbelief. "You're going in your pajamas?"

She shrugged. "I'll get dressed once I'm there."

He nodded, a distant look crossing his eyes. Then he straightened. "Let me just get my things, and I'll follow you out, then head back to my room."

"You can just let yourself out if you want." Isla bit her lip. *What does Aiden want?*

Clearly, something is bothering him.

"You sure you don't want to come down to the lobby? We can talk along the way."

"I'm sure." He slipped his laptop into the case. "You never know, maybe I'll turn up at the next set, and we can talk then."

Her heart stumbled—both with excitement and uncertainty.

What isn't Aiden saying?

The phone rang in her hand, and Isla looked down. *Davy.* She squeaked. "Oh God, that driver is going to leave. I have to go." She dashed past him toward the door, then paused, hand on the doorknob. "See you in Paris?"

He smiled, but it was tight. Hollow. Her least favorite Aiden smile. *Because I love his normal smile.* "In Paris."

18

ISLA

PARIS, ARKANSAS

"Holy crap," Isla breathed to Kyle, edging closer as they approached the Springtime in Paris festival. "I thought Paris, Texas, was small."

Kyle peered over the top of his sunglasses. "Wow."

Like Texas, Arkansas also appeared to have an Eiffel Tower replica.

Unlike Texas, it was part of the town fountain and only about fifteen feet tall.

No wonder Davy's smile had been so overly bright at call time that morning—*forced.*

"How are we supposed to get three days of content out of this?" Isla asked, watching the townspeople as they milled near the Eiffel Tower fountain. Canopy awnings had been set up all around it, along with some inflatables, cornhole games, and a dunking booth.

Close to a brick wall, a chain-link fence was covered in locks—a lovelock fence to commemorate France.

Cute. But still . . . not a lot to work with.

"How are we supposed to get three *minutes?*" Kyle retorted.

Maybe she should have realized it would be like this when she'd shown up to her room last night at a weathered motel like the ones she'd seen in old movies but had never stayed in.

Isla glanced nervously over her shoulder at the crew, who stood in an adjoining parking lot, discussing among themselves. Tomas was still finishing hair and makeup, thankfully, which meant Isla could prepare herself mentally before he started pawing at her again.

Funny how wholly she'd moved on. Tomas . . . was part of a different life.

When Davy had first brought this hosting plan up, she'd thought about that life and that past with rose-colored glasses. Nostalgia about the good, fun moments.

Now, on the second week of filming, she wasn't sure *backward* was what she wanted at all. It had been so easy to forget what she didn't love about acting. Being touched on a film or theater set by her costars—some who were less courteous than others about the state of their breath—and the early mornings and late nights. Hell, even the way her skin hated this amount of makeup.

Stepping back into *acting* was easy enough. Stepping back into the lifestyle, though?

That was entirely different.

She wasn't *that* much older, but she felt older somehow. The problem was that she realized now how much she hadn't known or understood even just a few years ago.

And she was more acutely aware than ever about how unanchored she felt *now*.

"No Aiden and Callum ambush this time?" Kyle asked, following the direction of her stare. "I keep waiting for them to pop out from one of the trailers."

"Thankfully, no. At least, they haven't warned me of an ambush." She kept it light. Casual. Like it didn't matter that she'd sent Aiden a text last night asking him if he was still coming.

And he'd never replied.

"Callum hasn't, anyway," she added quickly before Kyle could pick up on the shift in her tone. "I haven't heard from Aiden at all."

Kyle's brows flicked up over his sunglasses. "Really?"

She shrugged. "He's busy—CEO things. Too important for the likes of me." Her joke was hollow, the words sharp in her throat.

Dammit. She could not let this keep bothering her. She knew he was busy and had been stressed about his work, but it took two seconds to send a text.

"So, you and Callum are talking at least now?" Kyle shot her a worried glance. "I was worried we would get to London for the party, and you'd still be fighting."

"I'm not sure I would have called it fighting per se. I was mad at him, not really the other way around. He's been trying to get on my good side ever since."

Kyle peered at her. "Oh, I don't know that I'd go that far. He was definitely mad at you. Mad enough to dig up an old boyfriend, get me bumped down to third wheel, and hop on a nine-hour flight."

That's true. She cringed. "I didn't mean that—"

"You know I'm on your side. What he did was much worse. If I ever did something like that to Liddy or Elle, they'd probably punch me in the face. But Callum's . . . very protective of the people he cares about. It's what makes him good enough for my sister."

"Listen to you, talking like an old man instead of the spoiled youngest child."

He snorted. "Takes one to know one."

"Look, I'm trying to get over it. But I'm letting Callum squirm for a little bit. He should have thought about that before he forced Tomas into my orbit again."

"Tomas seems like a nice enough guy." Kyle shrugged.

Tomas *was* nice enough, but that was as far as it went. And he'd clearly felt the same way about her, considering he'd let her go just as easily.

"Yeah, he's fine. It's just that whatever spark was there is gone now." She sighed, then looked back at the people gathering at the Eiffel Tower Park for the festival. "I need to find Davy—ask her what the plan is."

"Sounds good. In the meantime, I'm going to go snag something with bacon in it."

"Don't say that too loudly," Isla hissed, glancing at a local man a few feet away holding a pig.

An actual pig. What in the world?

She started toward the crew, looking for her friend, but she didn't see her anywhere. "Any idea where Davy went?" she asked Tim as he passed her.

"I think to grab some coffee and muffins across the street." Tim nodded at a row of shops on what appeared to be the main street. "True Grit Grounds—down that way."

A ridiculously small main street.

Phew.

Isla saw the distant sign and then headed down the sidewalk, hurrying in case Boyd wanted her back sooner rather than later. As she drew closer, she spotted Davy sitting at a small table in front of the café, sipping on a paper cup.

Her hands trembled.

Isla drew a sharp breath, then rushed toward her. "You okay?"

Davy's eyes were red-rimmed and shiny. She blinked at Isla

distantly, then nodded, swallowing whatever she was drinking. "Yeah, yeah, I'm fine."

Isla pulled out the chair beside her, the metal legs scraping against the sidewalk. "What happened?"

"I just . . ." Davy let out a slow breath from puffed cheeks, then shook her head, unable to finish.

Sliding her hand on top of Davy's, Isla gripped it with a tight squeeze. "You can tell me anything, Dav."

"I know." Davy inhaled and exhaled, struggling for calm. Then she glanced at the park and back at Isla. "Is your gear on?"

Isla bit her lip. *Crap—is she that nervous?* And would anyone really be recording anything right now? That was a troubling thought.

Davy leaned over, then reached behind Isla. With a quick tug on her shirt, she flipped a switch on the pack tucked into Isla's waistband, then straightened. "Boyd chewed me out," she said at last. "Said this wasn't what I promised—that this shouldn't even be a stop on the tour."

Hesitating for a few moments, Isla tried to come up with the most positive way to approach this. "It's a small town, sure, but isn't that the point? If every town named Paris was the same, it'd be a boring show."

"Try telling that to Boyd," Davy said glumly. "It hasn't been announced yet, but after last week, they've already decided to nix the episode in Virginia because they felt there wasn't enough there. We're down to five. And now, after this, they might just cut their losses and cancel the whole thing altogether."

Scrap the whole production?

Isla wasn't as familiar with the ins and outs of the business side of film, but Boyd had to be seriously worried if that was what they were leaning toward.

"What happens if they scrap it?" Isla asked softly.

"I lose my job," Davy said, lifting her cup in a bitter toast. "That sort of loss would be enormous for the company. It's a modestly-sized YouTube and cable channel, so absorbing that sort of financial penalty means job cuts, even with Aiden's investment."

The door to the coffee shop opened, and a woman came out, holding a box of muffins. "Here you go, sweetie," she said with a warm smile, then set them on the table. "Hope you enjoy the visit."

Isla watched the woman go, a visceral feeling of helplessness washing over her. Was there any way to make this better for Davy? Sure, maybe Paris, Arkansas, was small, but it was a town full of *people,* and people were inherently interesting with stories worth telling.

Hmm. Maybe that's what the show needs.

Not just a travel focus. A human element, too.

"What if . . . what if we frame this episode a little differently?" Isla asked in a cautious tone.

"What do you mean?" Davy stood and picked up the muffin box, and Isla joined her as she headed back.

"I mean, this is basically a reality show. A travel documentary, sure, but there are three hosts on it now. What if this episode focused a bit more heavily on something like my relationship with Tomas to fill the gaps from the lack of location? Tomas is a good actor, and he and I could play something up and add some drama, which might keep people invested on a different level."

Davy didn't answer for a moment but studied Isla's profile. "I don't know. The Travelog Channel might not approve it."

"Sure they would. They have a handful of other shows that fit the profile. And all the networks do it. Think about it—what made *Fixer Upper?* Not the amazing house flips. It was Chip and Joanna Gaines. Or *The Crocodile Hunter?* Steve Irwin was a god. That's why people tuned in. To see *him*." Isla smiled confidently. "I'm not saying I'm on their level, but between Tomas and me, we could stir up enough interesting *human* dynamics to keep people's interest, don't you think?"

Davy still looked hesitant. "Do you really think so?"

"It's worth a shot." Isla reached over and poked Davy in the ribs. "And I'll even let you take all the credit. Pitch it to Boyd and see what he says. Maybe it can be something like . . . Tomas and I are arguing about something, and the trip is 'wearing on us.' I don't know."

Turning toward Isla, Davy gave her a grateful expression. "Have I ever told you I love you?"

"Thank me if it works," Isla said, then eyed the muffins in the box. "Save me one of those blueberry muffins, by the way. They look amazing."

"You can grab it out if you want." Davy turned toward her and opened the box.

Isla pulled one out with a grin. "I'm going to find Kyle. Let me know how it goes. Keeping my fingers crossed."

Hurrying back toward the festival, she found Kyle near a sign announcing a rubber duck race. "Didn't you get something to eat?" she asked him, holding out the muffin. "I stole this from Davy if you want to split it."

Kyle smiled and pulled a large chunk of it from the liner. "Did you know you can win five hundred dollars if you win this rubber duck race they're doing?"

"Oh yeah? You going to enter?"

"At ten dollars a duck, it's a steal. How many ducks should I get? Ten?"

She shook her head at him, taking a bite of the sweet muffin. "No," she said, then swallowed. "It's a good thing you didn't go to Vegas with me. You're the type of person who gets stuck at the slot machines losing all their money because it's 'only a quarter.'"

Kyle gave a look of feigned insult. "I'll have you know I can play poker with the best of them."

"Don't believe it. You wear your heart on your sleeve, Kyle Winnick." Isla looped arms with him and tugged him toward the crew. "Speaking of which, how good do you think your acting chops really are?"

He let out an exaggerated puff of air, letting his lips vibrate. "Pork chops, I'm good at. Acting chops . . . not so much."

"So clever with those corny jokes." She took another bite of muffin. "The reason I ask is because we might have to actually do some acting here. Make our personalities shine a little brighter, given how small this town is."

"Does that lady have a goat on a leash?" Kyle asked, eyebrows lifting.

Isla sneaked a glance, then pressed her lips together to keep from laughing. "It's not funny. We're here to highlight this town."

"It's *kind of* funny." Kyle tore another piece from her muffin. "I think it's great, too. All towns have their quirks. It's part of what I love so much about beach life in Samara. Different beat of life—people like Juan at the pulperia who knows what I'm going to buy before I even walk up to the counter."

One of the assistant directors approached them with a clipboard. "Boyd wants to talk to you two."

They followed her across the parking lot toward where the production crew had gathered. Tomas was already there, seated in a fold-out chair beside Boyd. Davy stood a few feet away but didn't meet Isla's eyes.

"Glad you could join us," Boyd said, barely glancing up. He tapped his thumb on his clipboard. "Where have you been?"

"We were just checking out the festival," Kyle said with a confidence that Isla didn't feel. Boyd was clearly in a rotten mood. But Isla also knew he'd given Davy a dressing down and made her cry, so she wasn't about to piss him off further.

"Well, don't check it out too much. Given the lineup, you'll have completed the whole festival before we get the cameras rolling."

Ouch.

Davy seemed to wilt more.

Boyd stood, scratching his forehead. "All right. New plan. As suggested by our *trusty* producer, today's segment will focus on the relationship dynamics between Tomas and Isla. I'm going to give everyone ten minutes while I sit and discuss this with the actors. Do not be late coming back."

Isla bit her lower lip. No wonder Davy had been crying. Boyd was unapologetically rude.

As the crew wandered off, Tim snuck over to her side. "There a reason your equipment is off?" He moved around her to check the battery pack.

He *had* noticed. "Oh, sorry about that."

"In general, don't mess with the equipment. Especially on a day when Boyd's ready to blow his top." Tim said it kindly, but Isla shifted with discomfort.

What would a set be without drama, though? That went hand in hand with the creatives she'd always enjoyed spending time with so much.

Though maybe I never noticed it quite as much as I am now.

Isla moved closer to Boyd, then took a chair opposite him. Kyle sat beside her. *Thank goodness Kyle is here.* She appreciated him now more than ever. She'd enjoyed the carefree banter between them this morning, although it had cemented one extremely valid point. And that was that sadly, Callum had been correct. The banter she and Kyle shared resembled close siblings, and she doubted she could have sold their friendship as anything else. Not that she'd tell Callum that, of course.

After a few heavy beats of silence, Boyd looked Isla directly in the eye. "Here's what I'm thinking, but it might take some filming outside this Paris location. You're going to London in a couple of weeks, right, Isla? Kyle, too?"

"Yes, but it's for my brother's and Kyle's sister's post-elopement party. We won't be able to work," Isla said, exchanging a glance with Kyle.

"What type of party?" Boyd asked. "Big? Small?"

Isla frowned.

What is he getting at?

"Something fancy. They had an intimate elopement over Christmas rather than a big wedding, so this is the celebration for the friends and family who didn't attend."

"That's perfect, actually. Do you think your brother would let us bring a camera in? Something small and mobile in addition to the one on you?"

Isla's jaw dropped.

This is not what I suggested.

"I-I have no idea," she stammered. "He's fairly private." *Understatement.* "I doubt he'd want his personal business—"

"The thing is," Boyd said, glancing over at Tomas. "I'm thinking we could start some drama in your relationship here. Something that might not get solved right away, that will make viewers want to come back for more episodes after having been exposed to the dullness we offered them in exploring the town. We'll continue to escalate the drama in the next episode, film a quick segment of you and Tomas in London before the party, then cut to something like the two of you dancing at the party—happy once more—and then move onto the loveliness, *hopefully*, of Paris, Maine—then wrap with the two of you happily ever after in France with all the drama in the past."

Isla's fingers curled in her lap, a flush heating her face.

No.

Not a chance.

Callum wouldn't be all right with that. She didn't have to ask. He would *hate it.*

But Davy looks so miserable.

Then again, Callum owed her. He'd been groveling for the past week, asking *what* he could do to make it up to her. That he'd do whatever it took.

Maybe this might have to be what it took.

"Tomas isn't invited to the party," she managed weakly, her gut already screaming that this was a bad idea.

"The production can probably cover the cost," Boyd said like that was the issue. "And he doesn't need to be there for the whole thing. Just a quick shot of you two happily dancing the night away."

Isla looked at Tomas, who held her gaze. His lips twitched —not quite a smirk, but close.

"I'm fine with it if you are," Tomas said smoothly. "Callum's a good bloke. I doubt he'd turn me out." A flicker of something in his eyes—*anticipation? Amusement?*

Isla's stomach tightened. Was he looking forward to pissing off Callum? Or did he like the idea of playing couple in a setting like that?

"Do we have to decide this right this moment? I think Isla would probably want to ask her brother's permission," Kyle said, leaning forward in his seat. "My sister would want a say in it, too. You know, being the bride and all. I've heard they like some sort of input with things like their weddings."

Thank you. She offered him a grateful look, though both she and Kyle knew that Liddy wouldn't be the holdup here, ironically. Even though Liddy was organized and disliked last-minute changes to plans, Callum was more likely to balk at something so intrusive.

"No, we don't have to decide immediately. But we do need to plan. Whatever we film today will be largely dependent on that plan, so it will be good to have an idea of where we're heading." Boyd crossed his arms.

"Look, I know this isn't exactly what we had in mind, but we need to make this episode *work*. You're the star, Isla. If anyone can make something out of nothing, it's you." He smiled like it was a compliment, but it wasn't. It was a challenge. "So, what's it going to be?"

Isla didn't like the sound of that. Or the way Boyd was making Davy shrink with every word. This wasn't what she signed up for.

Boyd was treating Davy like a child who needed to be disciplined.

I could walk away. Say no. Stand up for myself and for Davy.

But then what? They needed this spring festival to film this episode, they didn't have a ton of material to work with, and this was what Davy had pitched. Isla would ruin the plans, be in breach of contract, the network would frame her as "difficult," and Davy would take the blame.

Boyd had already canceled one of their episodes with the stroke of a pen. Would he really scrap the whole show like Davy believed?

But she couldn't really agree to this without Callum's blessing, could she?

She stood abruptly. "I need a minute to make a phone call."

Without waiting for Boyd to respond, Isla hurried away from the others, a sudden, crushing anxiety gripping her as she pulled out her phone. She unlocked the screen and stared at it, heart pounding.

Gulping a breath, she dodged behind a building, then leaned against the brick facade.

She wasn't ready to talk to Callum.

Not yet.

Whatever line they'd crossed when he'd brought Tomas into the show hadn't really started then, and the truth was she wasn't ready to face the tension that had been creeping into her relationship with her brother. Because he was her only sibling, they'd always been close.

Fixing the inn together had brought them even closer—or so she had thought.

But for months now, she'd been stewing with resentment and unhappiness, and Callum had been an easy target. Whatever anger she had toward him about the Tomas situation was also laced with guilt about *La Hacienda* that made silence between them the easier option at the moment.

Because, deep down, she knew she needed to tell Callum that he was right about her having cold feet about their arrangement.

That she wasn't happy.

And that I have no idea how to move forward.

She stared at the phone, clicking on her text messages as she ground her teeth. As she did, the message she'd sent to Aiden last night—still unanswered—caught her eye.

Her heart fell further.

If Aiden were here, she could ask him to step in. Surely, his money carried some weight, and he'd know how to handle someone like Boyd.

But he wasn't here. And she couldn't quite put her finger on why that bothered her so much. *We're not that close.* Yet, given how fun it had been when he'd come to Texas, she'd felt closer to him than ever before.

Clearly, I have a vivid imagination.

Or maybe something else—twice now, his presence had been an enormous relief, both in Vegas when that man had harassed her, and in Texas when Callum had overstepped like he had.

I can't expect Aiden to hang around and solve my problems. No matter how nice it had been to feel like she had him in her corner.

Leaning her head back against the brick, she closed her eyes.

But would it really hurt to get Aiden involved?

Aiden wouldn't think it was strange if she reached out to him again, would he? He might be able to offer her some advice about this situation with Boyd's proposal since he knew Callum better than most people.

Before she could overthink it, she dialed.

The phone rang once, twice . . . four times.

Then a woman's voice came across the line. "Hello?"

Maybe an assistant? "Can I speak to Aiden?"

"Isla? It's Lola. We're at brunch, and he stepped away from the table, I'm afraid."

Isla's heart squeezed hard.

Oh.

Oh God.

Brunch? Why is he having brunch with his ex?

Unless—*maybe*—they'd gotten back together again? Maybe that was why Aiden hadn't answered her text.

"I can tell him you called," Lola said

Her chest burned as though someone had just stolen the oxygen from all her lungs, and she strangled, "No. No need. Thank you."

She ended the call, face burning.

What the hell? Why had this hurt so much?

She'd seen Aiden and Lola together at Christmas. It hadn't bothered her then, had it? But Lola was tall and gorgeous. Polished and elegant.

Her opposite in nearly every way.

And that's the sort of woman Aiden's into.

She shouldn't care. She couldn't care about it.

Yet her throat felt thick, her heart still encased in a painful grip.

"I have bigger, more immediate things to worry about," she gritted to herself, then peeled herself from the wall. She fanned her face and squared her shoulders, determined to put Aiden out of her mind once and for all.

She had to help Davy.

Striding back toward Boyd and the others, she walked with a confidence she didn't feel.

What's the best foot forward here?

Was there really a choice?

She exhaled, pressing her lips together, then held Boyd's gaze. "Fine," she said, voice tight. "I'm in."

19

AIDEN

PARIS, ARKANSAS

"THIS CAN'T BE RIGHT," Aiden muttered to himself.

He checked the address Boyd had texted him, then slowed and turned his car around on the two-lane road. He went back to the spot the GPS had announced as the pub and frowned.

A large, empty field stood on one side of the road. On the other side stood a nondescript building that looked like it should be a garage for a mechanic—tin roof and all. Windowless. The car park was made of gravel, barely visible due to the dearth of light, and tufts of grass grew between the stone.

The lack of windows was particularly intriguing. Was it a strip club?

Still, an unlit sign in front of it announced some sort of establishment, and nothing else was in sight. And there were several trucks and motorcycles parked in front of the building.

Maybe he should have rented a truck at Clinton National Airport.

He pulled into the car park and killed the engine, then stepped out and checked his watch. Just after ten. Surely, the show wasn't still filming? Scanning the front of the building, he looked for the entrance, which appeared to be one door, near to which stood a couple of gruff-looking bikers, smoking.

Hesitation pulsed through him.

Maybe this was a sign he should just go back.

He shouldn't be here.

Except when he'd been at a business brunch Saturday morning with Lola, Mason, and the president of Ipolymer, he'd made the mistake of leaving his mobile on the table when another acquaintance had come into the restaurant, drawing the three men away for a few minutes.

"Oh, by the way," Lola said as they were leaving the restaurant, "your girlfriend called."

Aiden gave her a baffled look. "Girlfriend?"

"Isla. When you, Mason, and Gerard were over speaking to Lawton Pierce. I promised I'd deliver the message, and I have." Something glittered in Lola's expression, the corners of her eyes narrowing slightly.

Fuck.

Why in the hell had she answered his phone? The audacity of it was unnerving.

But she also had likely seen the caller and couldn't resist the urge to bare her teeth. Just what in the hell had she told Isla?

Mason—close enough to overhear—stared at Aiden with a dark look.

"Isla's a family friend, Lola. She's currently working on a travel show for the Travelog Channel that I'm sponsoring and likely had a business-related question. The information about it is on their website if you don't believe me. In the future, I can take my own calls. Thank you."

And that had been that. He'd finally played the winning card. Perhaps now he could finally and truly put any worry about any leverage that Lola thought she'd had since Vegas to rest.

On the other hand, Lola had created another problem for him to fix.

Isla hadn't answered his calls during his attempts to reach her since Saturday. And now it was Monday.

Though she was probably busy filming.

Or maybe he should have texted her back when she'd texted on Friday night.

But as each second slipped further away, as he'd stared down at his mobile, thumb hovering over the keypad, wondering what to respond, it just seemed easier not to. He needed to tell her about the marriage and be done with it.

They'd get an annulment and put their egregious mistake behind them once and for all.

Yet he hadn't been able to bring himself to do it over the phone. And since he'd called several times without a response, he'd flown here instead.

He'd almost missed his flight from New York City—the meeting with Ipolymer had gone late, and he'd been forced to take the last flight out to Little Rock. Mason had been at Ipolymer's headquarters, handling the negotiations directly with Lola, but Aiden had been at Camden Enterprise's New York offices, just to be on standby.

The grueling negotiations had been just as difficult as Aiden had expected. Just as harried as the last week had been. This was the first break he'd taken.

But the stress of it all was nothing compared to the idea of walking into this pub and facing Isla.

He didn't need this headache, an attachment that would only make his life more difficult. But lately, every time he thought about Isla, the thought of her brought a thrill. And deep down, he couldn't help wondering if he'd put off telling her about the marriage just to give himself another excuse to see her in person.

Yes, it was mad and irrational, but ever since Vegas, she'd been in his orbit in a way that felt like the only thing he was genuinely interested or excited about.

Dammit.

He was a bloody fool.

Even if she were interested in him—which she wasn't—Callum was an obstacle. He wouldn't be happy with the idea of Aiden dating his sister. And he would be even angrier about how things had started and everything Aiden had concealed since.

He sighed, checking his mobile once again as he considered hopping back in the car and leaving. Mason hadn't texted since concluding the meeting, and unfortunately, the negotiations were far from over. They wouldn't resume for another few days, but Mason had seemed encouraged. Like progress was finally being made without Aiden at the helm. In fact, the only time he'd even seen Lola was during that business brunch when the blessed phone call from Isla had come in.

Of all the rotten luck.

The deal was what he needed to be worried about and focusing his attention on.

Not Isla.

He set his hand on the handle of the car.

You owe her the truth.

He swallowed the acrid taste from his mouth, stomach roiling with disgust for himself.

Jumping out of airplanes in the military had been less intimidating than this.

He inhaled, dragging a hand down his face, willing his feet to move. *Just open the damn door. Tell her. Walk away.*

You're a grown man, Camden. Stop acting like a coward.

Then—a sudden scuffle. Raised voices. His head snapped up.

Several people stalked out of the pub onto the gravel. The camera crew from the production he recognized . . . and also *Isla*.

She rushed out toward a car, Tomas in tow.

"Come on, Isla, you know you're blowing this completely out of proportion," Tomas said, reaching for her hand.

Isla yanked her hand from his and turned, face filled with fury. "Am I? Look, maybe this whole thing was a mistake, Tomas. After two years apart, people change. *We* changed."

"Isla, you know how much I care about you, baby." Tomas grabbed her by the shoulders, then kissed her on the mouth. *Hard.*

A flash of heat shot through Aiden—sharp, unbidden, impossible to control. His jaw clenched so tightly it ached.

But something inside him coiled tight, a surge of anger that had no place here. No logic. No reason. Because it didn't matter.

Except it did.

Because Tomas kissed her, and she hadn't kissed him back. Because Isla had stiffened. Because she'd pulled away.

But why did it feel like Tomas was getting away with something? Like Aiden had just stood back and let someone else take what should have been his?

They're just acting, right?

The camera was still rolling. It had to be.

A slap rang out, and Aiden jerked his chin up.

Isla was struggling to get away from Tomas, but he held on to her by the shoulders. "Let me go," she hissed. "I saw you flirting with her—"

"That meant nothing—"

"Seriously, Tomas, you're hurting me. Back off."

Aiden's heart lurched. *Enough.*

Maybe they were acting. Maybe they weren't.

Aiden was moving before he even registered it.

His hands fisted in Tomas's shirt, yanking him backward hard enough that his boots scraped across the gravel. Aiden shoved him away, his body coiled, ready for a fight. "Stay the hell away from her."

"What the—" Tomas landed on the gravel sending a few rocks flying, then lifted his head up, brows raised.

"Aiden." Isla's voice was rough with shock. She grabbed him by the elbow as his hands clenched into fists. "It's fine—"

"It's not fine. She said stop," he said, glowering down at Tomas. "Which means you stop."

Tomas stood with narrowed eyes and dusted himself off. "Why is he here, Isla?"

"And cut." Boyd's voice came through the chilly night air, and he crossed toward them. He offered Aiden a smile. "Sorry, mate, you walked into our shot."

Aiden's jaw dropped, his face flushing as he looked from Tomas to Isla. Tomas had his arms crossed, a smirk on his lips.

But Isla? The look of confusion in her eyes was palpable. *And she doesn't look pleased to see me, either.*

"What is going on?" She scowled, then flicked her gaze at Boyd, a tired expression on her face. "Do we need to do that take again?"

"No, I think we've got enough material to work with." Boyd smiled broadly. "I think we can call it the martini shot and wrap."

Tomas laughed and clapped Aiden on the back as though they were more than acquaintances. "You didn't think that was real, did you?"

No, of course not.

Moron.

"I—" Aiden offered a terse smile. "Sorry about the shove. Are you all right?"

"Fine, fine. Just some dust. Nothing to worry about. Coming in for a drink?" Tomas asked, nodding back toward the pub.

"Maybe," Aiden offered. He gave a hesitant glance back at Isla, but she'd already started off across the car park, heading for the large van that the crew had been using to transport everyone. Excusing himself, Aiden hurried toward her. "Isla, wait."

She didn't slow.

"Isla—"

She turned, her face shadowed by the darkness. "Does Lola know you're here?"

Lola? He slowed. Just what *had* she told her?

At his hesitation, she shook her head. "You know what? Forget it. It's none of my business. You obviously had plans with your girlfriend this weekend, and I should have understood when you didn't answer my text on Friday. I'm not really sure why you've bothered coming here at all, Aiden. We just wrapped, and I'm leaving in the morning. But swooping in and attacking Tomas while we're filming? What the hell even was that?"

"No, look, you're right. I . . . misread the situation. And I should have responded to your message."

She let out a short, bitter laugh. "Oh, you *should have?*" Her arms crossed tightly over her chest. "Yeah, well, I should have known better. Should have remembered that you only ever show up when it's convenient for you. Or aren't distracted by more interesting things."

Aiden stilled.

That shouldn't have hurt. But it did.

He almost said something cutting, something about how she had no idea what his life was like—how much pressure he was under, how many fires he was constantly putting out. But he swallowed it down.

Because she wasn't wrong.

He'd tried to amend that side of himself, of course, but his reputation with his family and old friends like Isla existed for a reason.

But I hoped Isla saw me differently.

"I tried to call you, Isla. I just . . . my life is in shambles at the moment, and a deal critical to the business is hanging by a thread. I've been from London to Texas to New York, all while trying to work fifteen hours a day. But I'm here, aren't I? Would I be here if I wanted to ignore you? Being here *isn't* convenient, and I still came."

Her arms settled to her sides. "I suppose."

He held his breath. *That's it?* He'd expected her to fight him more.

"You're not mad?"

She let out a deep sigh. "No. I was hurt, I guess. I know you called; I just didn't want to talk. But it's stupid. You're busy, and you don't owe me text messages. Our last few interactions have just been confusing. I didn't know you were with Lola again. It threw me off."

A sardonic chuckle left him. "I'm not with Lola. I don't know what she told you, but the only time I saw her was on Saturday at a business brunch. In fact, I went out of my way to *avoid* Lola last week." Her comment about Lola was curious, though.

Why would that throw Isla off? He peered at her. "Then you purposely avoided my calls? I thought you might be busy filming."

She hugged her arms to her chest. "I mean, I *was*. But . . ." She furrowed her brow, stepping closer as she scanned his face. "So, you and Lola aren't back together again?"

He almost smiled. The fact that this mattered to her—that it had worried her . . . felt like an encouragement he hadn't known he was looking for.

And then, a deep stab went through his gut. *I have to tell her about Vegas.*

"No, we're not. I swear it. Ask Mason if you'd like—he's spent the whole of last week in an office handling negotiations with Lola and was at that brunch. I'm here because . . . I had to see you. You wouldn't answer my bloody calls, so I'm here. To talk to you. At the first break I've had in work. And I'm sorry that I didn't text. Truly."

That hint of a smile at the corner of her mouth, the relaxing of her posture . . . *why am I suddenly paying such close attention to her every mannerism?*

"Now you really have me curious. You flew all the way here to talk to me?" A divot formed between her brows.

Admitting that made him feel suddenly *exposed*. He nodded.

She tore her gaze from him. "Okay . . . about what?"

How was he fumbling this conversation so badly already? *Shite.*

He drew a quick breath. "Let's start over. Hello, Isla. I made it to Paris, after all. Is there any good place to eat around here? I'm starved."

She choked out a laugh. "Oh, there's no . . . never mind now, Aiden Camden. You've got my curiosity burning. What is it you want to talk about? No good conversation has ever started with the words *we need to talk.*"

He cringed. "Why don't we go somewhere more private?"

Turning, she glanced around the mostly empty surroundings and probably thought he was a lunatic. But she didn't press him any further.

"Do you have a car?"

He nodded.

"Would you be willing to drive me so we don't have to wait for everyone?"

"I can do that."

She reached into the waistband of her skirt and pulled off her battery pack. "Help me take this off, will you?" She teased the hem of her shirt up, turning her back to him.

Aiden stepped closer, his pulse hammering in his throat as he reached for her. When his fingertips skimmed the bare skin of her waist, he inhaled sharply. Isla shouldn't be having this effect on him.

Yet it was undeniable.

Focusing on the wire to the camera and microphone, he tugged it, but found it threaded under her bra. Deftly, he unhooked the bra clasps. She gasped, hugging her arms to her chest. "What are you doing?"

"Untangling the damn wire."

"By taking my bra off?" She threw a laughing glance back at him. "I swear, Aiden. Every time I'm around you lately, some article of clothing seems to magically fall off me."

Don't think about it.

But dammit. The image of her, gorgeous and half naked in his bed, wasn't that easy to scrub from his memory.

Impossible, actually.

He tore his gaze from her and finished with the wire, then hooked her bra once again.

She turned and grinned. "Thank you." Quickly, she wound the wire around the battery pack, then hurried toward the van. After opening the door, she set the pack on the passenger seat and closed the door. "I'm all yours."

She sauntered back toward him, completely unaware of the weight of her own words.

He tilted his head toward the sedan he'd rented. "This way." A knot formed in his stomach as they went toward it.

Telling her about their marriage was necessary, but he'd let the matter take on its own life at this point. *I shouldn't have waited so long to tell her. Too much time has passed.*

He held the door open for her, then shut the door behind her after she'd slid into her seat.

Moving around to the driver's side, the smell of new leather and car cleaning soap reached him. Yet, somehow, he swore he could still find the trace of her perfume or scent it was that she wore that made her smell so incredible.

God, I sound like a man obsessed.

"Where are we headed?"

Isla laughed lightly. "Back to the glamorous motel. Make a right out of the parking lot. It's only a couple of minutes down the road. Turns out this is an itty-bitty town, hence that scene you saw outside the bar. Boyd is trying to put a bit more filler material into this episode since there isn't much to see in town. Today, we spent most of the day hiking at Mount Magazine. We visited a monastery yesterday, and did the town spring festival on Saturday."

"So, a fight in a pub is filler material?" Aiden gave her a curious look.

"Yeah. Tomas and I are having a fight." Isla leaned back in the seat. "And we're going to make up at Callum and Liddy's elopement party. They'll film a short segment with us happy once again and then move on."

What on earth?

"And Callum is all right with this?"

She grimaced. "I haven't quite worked up the nerve to tell him yet."

"Isla—"

"I know. I'm going to. Soon. And if I can't, I'll just figure out a way to firmly tell Boyd no."

"But you've already agreed to it?"

"Just a verbal agreement. Nothing in writing. Boyd was furious with Davy for falling short with this location. He felt as though we could have explored a different city instead. This kept him happy. Actually, that's what I had called about on Saturday—to get your opinion. But I handled it on my own." She pointed to the left. "That's the motel up there."

He slowed, then turned into the car park, a sinking feeling going through him as he caught sight of the *No Availability* sign. And he hadn't booked a hotel yet because he'd been counting on checking in to wherever the crew was staying. "Are there other hotels close to this?"

Isla laughed and shook her head. "Well, I think there's a bed-and-breakfast closer to Mount Magazine. Maybe." She gave him a closer look as he parked. "Do you not have a place to stay?"

"Not exactly, no."

Isla bit her lower lip.

Dammit.

She had to stop doing things that called attention to that luscious mouth of hers.

"You can stay with me if you want," she said with a shrug. "We *have* slept in the same bed before, with considerably less clothes on."

That's precisely why this isn't a good idea.

But he could have self-control. If Isla could handle it, he should be able to also.

"Yeah, all right. Thanks," he said instead. He popped the boot of the car, then pulled his bag from it and followed her toward the motel room.

They slipped inside, and Isla flipped the light on.

Aiden closed the door behind him, scanning the small but tidy space.

One queen-sized bed.

Brilliant. Just brilliant.

Aiden forced his face into neutrality, but for a second—just a second—her eyes flickered over him, like she'd caught something in his expression.

Isla kicked off her shoes, replacing them with slippers. "You okay?" she asked.

If she only knew the absolute war raging in his head.

"Fine." He adjusted his collar, like that would do anything to loosen the knot of tension forming in his chest.

"Do you mind if I grab a quick shower before we talk? I feel gross."

Another reprieve from the inevitable?

"Of course. I honestly wouldn't mind changing either." He still had his work suit on.

"Good. Give me five minutes. I won't even blow-dry my hair." She grabbed a few things from her suitcase, then disappeared into the bathroom, closing the door behind her.

Aiden stared at the door, a heavy feeling settling on his chest.

I shouldn't be this nervous.

But how did one tell a woman he'd known forever that they were legally wed?

And not just a woman. How had she gone from his best friend's little sister to someone he thought about constantly?

He set his bag on the floor and opened it, his head pounding. Changing, he sat on the end of the bed and closed his eyes, listening to the soft stream of water from the shower, counting the seconds with dread.

He didn't need to be so worried. He'd tell her, and they'd face and fix the problem together. Then move on.

But that was it, wasn't it?

Move on *to what*?

What in the hell was he moving toward?

No one. Nothing.

The soulless existence of making money. Being a business-man. Coming home to an empty house and takeaway.

"What's home to you, Aiden? What does it look like? More importantly, who's there waiting for you?"

John's words might have been a tad presumptuous, but they had been on his mind since Aiden heard them. *Who's waiting for you?*

The water shut off and the slide of a shower curtain told him that Isla was getting out.

Time crawled as he waited for her to dress and open that door. And as he stared at it, he felt himself losing the will to tell her—put it off just a little longer. He'd keep coming back here, telling himself that *he'd just get it over with next time*. Give himself another excuse to see her.

The door opened, and Aiden jerked his chin up as she sauntered out, her hair wet and combed, wearing a nightshirt and matching shorts.

God, she's beautiful. How did I never see it before?

Or maybe he had and he'd ignored it because *that* would be crossing the line. Of course, they'd torpedoed that line in Vegas.

Aiden drew a sharp breath and held her gaze. "I need to tell you something and it can't wait."

He hesitated for one last, useless second.

Then he forced the words out.

"We're married, Isla."

20

—

ISLA

THE SILENCE between Aiden and Isla stretched as thin as wire.

For a second, she thought she'd heard him wrong.

But her ears rang, and she blinked slowly, looking at the ridiculously gorgeous man in her hotel room. The room tilted—just slightly—as her lungs squeezed tight. *Married. To Aiden Camden.*

What?

In the shower, she'd been caught between wanting to take her time and racing back to him. Not that she should be dying to race back to him. But when she'd seen him tonight grabbing Tomas, stepping in to defend her like he had, it had done something to her.

Her goddamned panties had practically melted.

And that wasn't supposed to happen with Aiden. She wasn't supposed to want him. He wasn't supposed to make her wet. His lack of a text message wasn't supposed to make her feel needy and ignored.

She'd been miserable all weekend, imagining him in New

York with Lola. And that had been more telling than anything else.

But now that she'd found out that she'd let her assumptions and imagination get the best of her, she was more aware than ever of his effect on her.

She wasn't supposed to be standing in the shower, thinking about him just steps away. About how they'd be crawling into bed together. About how she'd offered in the first place—*because she'd wanted him to say yes.*

"Isla?"

His voice brought her back to his words. How long had she been standing there, staring at him with a vacant expression?

Then she laughed.

A nervous laugh, filled with disbelief and false hilarity.

It bubbled up her windpipe, choking from her throat. "That's impossible," she managed.

Aiden knelt beside a laptop bag, then pulled out an envelope. Crossing the space toward her, he held out a paper. "This came in the mail to my office in London."

She took the paper from him and scanned it.

A marriage license for Nevada.

A *real* bloody marriage license bearing her name and Aiden's.

What. The. Fuck.

"Oh . . . God." She covered her face with her hand, then lowered it slowly. Then her eyes snapped to his. "Do you remember this?"

"No, I was just as stunned as you are when I found out."

"And when did you find out exactly?"

His lips pursed. "A couple of weeks ago."

"*What?*" She hadn't meant for her voice to come out in a shriek. She shoved the marriage license back in his hands.

"You've known for *weeks* that we're legally married, and you didn't tell me?"

This must have been what he'd been pussyfooting around in Texas.

"I wanted to tell you in person." He slipped the paper back into the envelope, an edge of irritation in his voice. "Don't worry, I've already started the process of annulling the damn thing. We just need to meet with a solicitor and sign some paperwork. Shouldn't be difficult."

She glared at him, his words like blows. "Yes, of course."

He frowned, an uncertain look flickering in his eyes. "That's what you want, right?"

"Yes, Aiden. For God's sake. Yes, I want nothing more than to forget that night ever happened, to be honest, but somehow, it keeps coming back and biting me in the arse. All I wanted was a fun night with my friends, and instead, I ended up drugged, married, and committed to a production that is slowly becoming something vastly different from what I signed up for." She sank onto the bed, suddenly thoroughly spent.

"Hang on a second. Drugged?" Aiden raised a brow.

Fuck.

She'd never told him, had she?

"Yes, I think that man who was harassing me when you first came to my rescue in Vegas slipped something in the drinks you and I had."

Aiden's eyes widened.

He didn't move. Didn't speak.

A slow, eerie silence stretched between them, pressing against Isla's ribs like a vise. His fingers curled tight.

Then he raked his hand through his hair, taking a staggering step back. "What?"

She gulped, and her words came out in a rush. "He gave the drinks to Kelsey and Blair, apparently. And then they went to see the Eiffel Tower and left them on the table without drinking any—which you and I did." Then she added with a stammer, "A-apparently."

Why is he looking at me that way?

He lowered his hands to his sides. "And you've known about this since Vegas?" His voice was a rough whisper.

"Yes, but—"

"And you didn't say a word to me?" His throat bobbed as he swallowed hard. "Do you have any idea how much I've tormented myself, wondering what happened? How could I let myself lose so much control that I'd cross whatever lines we crossed? That you believed—thought it possible—that I took advantage of your vulnerable state? And all this time—you knew? You knew. I was as much of a victim as you were." His hands clenched at his sides, white-knuckled. "Holy fuck, Isla."

A defensive feeling rose from her gut. "Is it any worse than not telling me we are *married* as soon as you found out?"

"Yes, it's worse!" His voice was sharp. "I wanted to do you the courtesy of having this conversation face-to-face. You, on the other hand, didn't intend to tell me at all. You just saddled me with the guilt and moved on merrily with your life, filming and—" He stiffened, his face darkening. "Is that it? Is that why you said nothing? Because you wanted to use my guilt to fund this production for your friend's sake?"

"No!" She stood, the offense hitting her like a physical blow. "That's awful, Aiden. How could you even suggest something like that?"

"It makes the most sense. Why else wouldn't you tell me?"

"Because . . ." She squared off with him, mind scrambling.

Why didn't I tell him?

She'd meant to tell him.

But then they'd been there in front of the Bellagio, and he'd been so hurt when he'd thought she'd accused him of taking advantage, so she'd just shut down the discussion, not wanting to talk about anything.

People talked about this sort of thing like it was romantic—like you could mistakenly get blackout drunk in Vegas and wake up in bed with someone. Married, even. The cliché was so ironically real, and the reality so much less fun than it'd been portrayed.

She drew a slow breath, trying to calm her racing thoughts.

Aiden was legally her husband?

"I'm sorry," she managed at last, forcing herself to meet his gaze. "You're right. I owed you the truth about that—or what I suspect is the truth, anyway. We did talk to security at the casino before I met with you, to tell them about what we thought had happened. I was just exhausted, Aiden. The whole ordeal was awful—not *you*, of course—but I just didn't expect to have this happen."

His jaw worked for a moment as he considered her words, flexing with tension. At last, he nodded. "I understand. And I apologize also. I should have told you about the marriage license as soon as I found out."

She took his hand into hers and squeezed it. "It's fine. You're right. We'll just face this together, annul it, and go on with our lives before Callum finds out and murders us both."

He grimaced. "Don't remind me. God, I feel like such a liar right now. How am I supposed to face him after all this?"

His thumb brushed against the back of her hand, gently, and her breath stilled.

And there it is.

That. *An innocent touch that shouldn't feel like a current that sets my pulse racing.* Yet it did.

But it was dangerous and stupid, and she wasn't about to put herself through the temptations Aiden offered when he was so clearly trying to keep things platonic between them.

She pulled her hand back, then smiled and headed toward the vanity near the bathroom. She'd made the mistake of not bringing her own hair dryer, and the one provided at the hotel was ancient—but it was better than nothing.

"You know, you're not the worst choice for a husband. I could hold out for a *really* good divorce settlement." Isla sighed dramatically. "Maybe a vacation house. A yacht. Some nice jewelry. I *do* like Cartier."

Aiden's lips parted with shock. He came closer and crossed his arms, leaning against the wall beside her. "You wouldn't."

She smirked. "I don't know, Aiden. I could retire to a beach, live my days getting tanned and reading books. Oh wait, that's already what I do."

"Unbelievable." He shook his head, exhaling. "Most women would have at least *pretended* they weren't interested in my sizable bank account."

"Oh, I'm not *most* women, Aiden. Your sizable . . . *um, bank account* is definitely one of your best assets." Isla winked, then turned toward the mirror. She glanced at him through the reflection.

He watched her with a mix of astonishment and amusement, a grin on his lips. "Isla Scott, are you flirting with me?"

"And if I am?" She grabbed her brush, feeling a little bolder. "Is it so wrong for a woman to flirt with her own husband?"

She turned the hair dryer on, which screeched. A burst of hot air shot her hair across her face, and when she pushed it off, Aiden was still watching her with a look that didn't *quite* say enough . . . except that he appeared to be enjoying her antics.

That was a relief. They'd threatened their entire relationship with lies, misunderstandings, and behavior that might be considered downright toxic from the outside, and the whole thing had made her feel off like they needed to pause and find their footing again.

"I'm just Aiden. And you're just Isla." His words from that day in front of the Texas Eiffel Tower returned as she stared at him through the reflection.

Her heart squeezed. In moments like this, she understood exactly what he'd meant. It was so easy to be herself around him. To tell him anything on her mind, free of judgment and fear. Vegas had only deepened that aspect of their relationship, in a way, because he was the only one besides Davy who *knew* about that. Like in the space of their shared secret, they had grown closer and more open with each other in a way they couldn't be with others.

A spark shot out from the hair dryer.

Dropping it and jumping back, Isla watched as the hair dryer clattered to the carpeted floor, a shower of sparks firing from it. Smoke and flames followed, filling the air with the tang of acrid, burned plastic.

Springing into action, Aiden peeled off his shirt and covered the hair dryer with it, then took a step toward the wall and yanked the cord from the outlet.

"What the hell was that?" Isla asked with wide eyes.

Aiden put his hand on the small of her back, concern in his face. "Are you all right?"

"Fine, I think." She touched her cheek, her skin still stinging from the spark.

Aiden leaned closer and examined it, then touched a section of her hair. "Looks like you managed to escape without burning your hair. This skin here is a bit red."

As he lowered it, she caught sight of the redness of his own fingers and reached for his hand. "Aiden, you burned your fingers."

"It's nothing." His fingers intertwined with hers. "I'm just glad you're okay."

She wet her lips, stepping closer to him. "Aiden . . ."

God.

Why did they keep ending up like this? The attraction was tangible, even if they both had tried to resist it. It felt as though whatever had drawn them together that night in Vegas had been real, even if they hadn't been in the right headspace.

Maybe she'd refused to let herself see him this way before, but now that they'd opened that door, there was no going back. He was handsome. Sexy.

And they clearly had chemistry.

She reached for him, and his arm encircled her waist, drawing her closer to his bare, muscular chest. As she stood on her tiptoes, his mouth crashed down on hers, their kiss hot, raw, and filled with desire.

Isla slid her arms around his neck, letting her weight sink against his as she kissed him back, a soft moan of pleasure leaving her.

His tongue slid against the seam of her lips, and she parted them for him. As one of his hands tangled into the hair at the nape of her neck, holding her close as his tongue clashed against hers, robbing her of breath.

And sanity.

God, this is incredible.

And incredibly stupid.

Yet she didn't want to pull away. Didn't want to stop. She wanted to be wrapped in his arms, pressing against him, feeling him harden like this.

Then Aiden's hands slid to her waist, and he lifted her, setting her on the vanity and stepping between her knees.

Fuck, yes.

They were really doing this, weren't they?

A deafening, shrill alarm pierced the quiet of the room.

Isla and Aiden yanked themselves free from one another, glancing around for the source of the noise. The smoke alarm, a few feet over.

"Oh shit," Isla breathed, hopping down from the vanity. Her lips still throbbed, wet from their kiss. She drew a deep breath, then started to climb the dresser to reach the smoke detector.

Aiden was steps behind her and caught her by the waist, lowering her to the floor. "What are you doing?"

"I was going to turn it off."

"Not sure we can do that in a hotel, darling."

A knock sounded on the door, and they exchanged a look. Aiden grabbed his suit jacket from the nearby chair and held it out to her. "Here, put this on."

Isla shrugged into it, catching the subtle scent of his mascu-line cologne clinging to the collar, then she crossed to the door and opened it.

A motel worker stood there. "You all smoking?" he asked with a lift of his gray brows.

Isla held the door open. "No, the hair dryer burst into flames."

The worker didn't flinch but peered over her shoulder. "I'll need you all to come on out here for a moment. Just to make sure. We have a strict no-smoking policy."

Isla glanced back at Aiden, her stomach knotting. Did the worker think she was lying?

She sighed, then stepped out, followed by Aiden, who was still shirtless. The hotel worker stepped inside, and Isla hugged her arms to her chest, shivering in the cool night. "You must be freezing," she told Aiden.

He didn't answer, his eyes tracking the worker as he moved through the room.

The sound of tires caught Isla's attention, and she glanced over her shoulder.

The crew van had just pulled in, headlights flashing against the gravel as it parked a few spots away.

Isla froze. Her stomach plummeted.

The doors opened.

First Kyle stepped out. Then Davy. Tomas. Then *Boyd*.

They all stopped in unison, staring. At *her*. At *Aiden*. At his bare chest and her wearing his suit jacket.

A horrified silence stretched between them.

Oh . . . fuck.

21

———

AIDEN

Isla froze at his side, but from the sharp intake of breath, he understood exactly what she was thinking.

Fuck.

Davy raised a brow at Isla, then hid a smile and pulled out a key to her own room.

Kyle sauntered toward them, a wide grin on his face, while the rest of the members of the crew went in other directions. "Hey, Aiden, didn't know you were coming to town. Today was the last day here."

Aiden cleared his throat, his mind drawing a complete blank on how to respond. At last, he managed, "I had to—"

Kyle cut him off with a laugh. "Listen, I'm not going to tell anyone. You heading to Quinn and Elle's tomorrow too?"

Dammit. That would have been a decent excuse. "Yes, I actually came to pick Isla up."

"I'm sure you did." Kyle winked. "See you in Nashville."

Kyle continued past them, his chuckle carrying in the wind. "Did I make that worse?" Aiden asked once Kyle slipped into his room.

Isla shook her head, not meeting his gaze. She hugged his jacket closer around her. "I'm not sure it can get any bloody worse."

God, he wanted to pull her into his arms and kiss her again.

That damn smoke alarm had ruined his foray into a lack of restraint that he'd desperately wanted—needed—with her. And she'd wanted it, too.

Now what were they supposed to do? Crawl into that bed together and act like it hadn't happened? Pick up where they'd left off?

He felt like an inexperienced adolescent, questioning his every move.

The motel worker stepped back outside, holding the burned hair dryer in his hands. "Sorry about that, and I apologize about the mess. Probably need you to vacate the room, though, so we can get it all cleaned up."

Isla lifted her brows. "Vacate? But there aren't any other rooms—"

"Sorry, ma'am. It's just a motel policy after something like this. I'll be back—gotta go get my manager." The man shuffled off without a glance back.

Isla groaned and gave Aiden a helpless look. "I guess maybe I could ask Davy if I can crash with her. Maybe Kyle would let you sleep in his room?"

Aiden pinched the bridge of his nose. The last thing he wanted was to face Kyle right now. As much as he liked Elle's younger brother, he was one more person, now, who knew something about him and Isla. This was starting to spiral out of his control.

"How far is Nashville from here?" Aiden asked.

Isla pulled out her mobile and opened Maps. "About seven hours."

"So that would put us in around—what—six in the morning? If you want to come with me, of course."

"You're not seriously thinking of driving all night to Nashville, are you?"

Was he?

They could stop, of course, somewhere along the way. Get a proper hotel with separate rooms.

But the way he was feeling right now, he could see himself knocking on her door, unable to resist that temptation that had been choking him for the past week.

The temptation to fuck his best friend's sister.

Goddammit.

Maybe that smoke alarm had been a blessing in disguise.

He released a slow breath and met Isla's gaze. "I think that might be the best idea, yes. Elle and Quinn will probably be awake. Tara gets up early." And once they were in Nashville, it would be easier to stay away from Isla. Quinn might be the only person as close to Callum as Aiden was. Which meant Quinn was the last person Aiden would want to know about Isla.

The disappointment in Isla's eyes was clear. Her fingers curled tighter around the lapels of his jacket like she was holding herself back from arguing. From demanding he stop overthinking. Stop ruining this before they even had the chance to begin.

She nodded, then looked away. "If you don't mind me sleeping in the passenger seat, yeah, I guess that works." She chewed on her lower lip, looking toward the door Davy had gone into. "I really should talk to Davy, though."

"I wouldn't mind a shower before we go. It's been a long day, and now we've got a long drive ahead of us."

"Why don't you go ahead back into the room? I'll go talk to Davy, come back and pack, and then we'll head out."

Within thirty minutes, they were in the rental car, pulling out of the inn, the silence between them tense and thick.

"You can put some music on if you'd like," Aiden said quietly, desperate to lighten the atmosphere. A seven-hour drive would be interminable like this.

Isla picked up her mobile and connected it to the car stereo, then turned on a quiet, mournful song. She set her phone into the side pocket of the door. "Are we going to talk about what happened back there?"

Maybe I should have just let the silence continue.

"What do you want to talk about?"

Isla released a frustrated groan. "I don't know, Aiden. We were making out, for goodness' sake. We can't just ignore the fact that we're clearly attracted to each other because it's inconvenient."

"I think we can," he said in a flat tone.

"No, we can't."

He felt the weight of her glare.

"Yes, we can. To begin with, I'm English. I'd rather ride strapped to the bonnet of this car naked than talk about this sort of thing. You should know this about us, even if you're some strange, American mutant version of us now."

His attempt at humor didn't work. She didn't even crack a smile.

Then he sighed. "Isla, you know this can't go anywhere. Callum—"

"I don't give a shit about what Callum will think, Aiden."

"Well, I do. It took him nearly ten years to tell Quinn and me about how Luca stabbed him in the back with his ex. The last thing I want him to think is that he's been betrayed—in any way—by another close friend."

"Being with me is not a betrayal. Will he be annoyed? Probably. But why shouldn't we pursue something if we're both interested? We're two consenting adults. And frankly, his opinion doesn't matter when it comes down to it. I've never known you to be a coward, Aiden."

Oof.

Her words hit him hard.

"Isla, it's not that simple."

"It *is* that simple. Unless there's another reason like . . . Lola? Are you still hung up on her? Because if that's it, then fine. I understand. And I'd rather know that now. I know you had something intense—"

"*No.*" His tone was hard. Forceful. "God, no. That's not it at all. I told you. We're completely, totally through."

"But she answered your phone the other day. I'm not saying I don't believe you, but that's a massive overstep."

"I left my mobile on the table for a few minutes while I was saying hello to a friend. She saw the call come through and—I don't know what she said—but I wouldn't put it past her to try to chase you away after what she witnessed in Vegas. She was a controlling and jealous girlfriend, Isla. And she suspects that we're together."

"Actually, she didn't say anything," Isla admitted softly. "She just said you'd stepped away, and she'd give you the message. I filled in the blanks myself since she picked up the call."

"Which is what she probably wanted." He sighed, settling deeper into the soft leather of his seat. "Lola doesn't hold a candle to you, Isla. You're brilliant and beautiful and . . ."

She smiled, and his heart squeezed.

"And you're all I can think about," he choked out at last.

The soft strains of the song she'd put on filled the quiet space in the car.

Isla reached over and slid her hand onto his, letting the tips of her fingers brush against the sensitive skin between his fingers. Goose bumps rose up his arm.

"Isla—"

"Shhh . . ."

His eyes shifted toward her, and she held his gaze as she leaned over farther, sliding her hand onto his thigh, her hand tantalizingly close to his groin.

Fuck. He was already hardening at her touch.

"You know," Isla said, her fingers brushing closer to the inside of his thigh. "Friends aren't supposed to lust over each other the way I've been thinking about you."

He nearly groaned. This side of her, the wild side, had always been appealing. But now that he knew that side was sexually adventurous, too? Not to mention the delicious taste of her lips and the softness of her skin.

He was a goner.

Then her hand slid onto his cock, the flat of her palm rubbing against him with firm but gentle pressure. A rasp of a breath left his throat. *My God. She's driving me insane.*

"Here's the thing. I'm not going to stop until you admit that you've been thinking about me, too. Until you get over that fear of my brother and stop pushing me away because it's inconvenient."

He didn't want to admit it. He wanted to let her carry on and do whatever the hell she had in mind. Wanted to reach over and push those panties to the side, feel how wet she was. Maybe that was why she'd done it this way.

She leaned closer, fingers gently tugging his zipper, dangerously close to the hardness of his length.

His breath hitched. *Christ.*

"This is a dangerous game, Isla," he growled, his grip tightening on the wheel.

She just smiled, that wicked little smile that made his blood heat. "Then admit it."

He exhaled, staring at the road, his hands clenching on the wheel. A muscle ticked in his jaw. He wanted to resist. He wanted to stop this before it went too far.

But fuck, she felt good against him.

He should be fighting it. Fighting her.

And then he lost.

"What do you want me to admit? That I want to pull this car over, bend you over the bonnet, and fuck you until we're both senseless?" His rough voice was thick with need. "Fine. I admit it. I want you, Isla. If that smoke alarm hadn't stopped us, I wouldn't have wanted to stop. But, maybe, thank God it did. Destroying my friendship with Callum worries me, and I don't know how to navigate these new, unchartered waters with you."

He snuck a glance at her, taking his eyes off the road in time to see her grin, apparently satisfied.

Tricky little vixen.

"I'm going to have blue balls tomorrow, you know."

"Look, we have to talk about this. I can't go back to the unbearable lack of communication between us. I know you weren't looking for this complication in your life, and honestly, neither was I. And I don't know what any of it means. Maybe it's just lust, and maybe nothing will come of it. But don't we owe it to ourselves to find out, Aiden?"

"But find out what? God, Isla. This is more than a complication. Let's say we have sex. Then what? We just keep having sex until we decide we want to have a relationship? You're in Costa Rica. I'm in London. Our lives are set for the foreseeable future."

"Do you want me to ask you for a lifetime commitment?" Isla raised her brows. "Why do we have to have everything figured out now? Can't it just be sex? Two people who are attracted to each other enjoying the moment—what little time they get to spend together."

He shook his head, amazed that he was even having this conversation. The irony wasn't lost on him. He'd broken up with Lola because she *wanted* a lifetime commitment. Now, here he was, and the idea of not defining everything . . . *mattered* somehow.

Because *she* mattered. Callum, too. He wasn't about to just screw her and not think of the consequences.

"So, we'd be what? Friends with benefits? You think Callum wouldn't murder me for that? Too many people know that something's happened between us for him not to eventually find out, Isla."

"And like I said, it's none of his business. Or how about this? Let me handle telling Callum—he's *my* brother."

"And he's my best friend. He'll expect me to be honest with him."

"It's not *dishonest*. It's just not his business," she repeated. "He started dating your sister-in-law's sister—one of his employees—without asking permission, didn't he? Of all people, he has no room to judge us. He didn't care about the chaos he created when he got together with Liddy, did he? He just saw what he wanted and went for it."

She has a point.

He released a slow sigh. "But I'm not Callum. Believe it or not, I didn't become CEO of my father's company by being irresponsible and throwing caution to the wind."

"I know that," she said softly.

He gave her a sidelong glance. "Do you, Isla? Do you know how often I'm awake in the middle of the night, unable to breathe with the weight of everything on my shoulders? Quinn stepped aside because he couldn't handle the pressure. Quinn

—the dependable and responsible one. I'm not half the man my older brother is."

She leaned her head back against the seat-rest. "To begin with—and I say this with all the love in my heart toward Quinn —I would take you a thousand times over Quinn. He never knew how to let loose and have fun. Never carried me on his back out to the yard so I could see the glowworms at dusk like you did that summer I broke my leg. You don't have to be Quinn. The man you are has grit and tenacity. Creativity and determination. I like that man, Aiden."

His hand tightened around the steering wheel. "Maybe I did once. These days, I just feel exhausted. Uninspired. Like I'm drowning, and there's no lifeboat in sight." He leaned forward as he pulled into the heart of the small town, the replica of the Eiffel Tower looming from a street corner up ahead.

"Hmm. I don't believe that. Pull over."

Aiden shot her an incredulous look. *Does she want to have sex? Now?*

She must have caught the question in his eyes because she laughed. "No, I didn't mean that. As much as I would love to be bent over a bonnet, I had something else in mind. Right there. At that Eiffel Tower Park."

At the park? What could she possibly want to do there? The park was tiny . . . not much besides the Eiffel Tower replica and a few benches. But he did as she requested, pulling the car off the road. Flicking a wary gaze at the fountain, he said, "I'm not climbing in another fountain if that's what you have in mind. I'd rather not drive through the night with soaked trousers."

"It's *not* what I have in mind, but that could be interesting." Isla's eyes practically twinkled. "Do you have any ribbon? Rope?"

"You're not succeeding in diverting my thoughts from adult

activities with those suggestions," he said dryly. "What do we need those for?"

"You'll see. What do you have that we could tie?"

Tie? "I have a tie."

"Perfect. Grab it." She opened the door, then stepped out onto the footpath beside the parked car.

Baffled by her, Aiden shut off the engine and went around to the boot for his suitcase. He pulled out one of his silk ties and joined her on the footpath. He held it out to her. "Here, Miss Skye."

She grinned and took it from him. "Follow me."

"Was there any other option? I suppose I could leave you here on the side of the road—that might prove my impulsiveness."

Her pace was brisk as they passed the fountain and the unimpressive Eiffel Tower, heading for a chain-link fence . . . covered in locks. "Is that—"

"A love lock fence," Isla said with a wide smile. She stopped in front of it. "Cute, right?"

Cute was one word for it. "Because this is Paris. I get it."

She lifted her chin. "I think we should commemorate our marriage. When in Paris, you know."

He guffawed, finally following her train of thinking. "You want to tie my tie to that fence?"

"Together. In the absence of a lock, this is the best I could come up with. And anyway, it's a good symbol. Not permanent, like a lock. Easily undone, like our marriage. Just the two of us, passing through, and having a fun memory together."

He didn't comment on the fact that it wasn't just a tie, but an expensive silk one.

Yet . . . this was so Isla.

At his hesitation, she added, "You came all this way to

Paris, Aiden. You may as well do something to remember your time here."

He searched those blue eyes of hers, heat flaring through him. As though he wouldn't remember that kiss from the hotel room. It would probably haunt him—as would their conversation from the car. "All right."

She turned toward the fence, and he came up behind her, her back resting lightly against his chest. This should feel awkward and silly, but somehow, it didn't.

Somehow, it feels perfect.

Like she's meant to be in my arms.

His hands brushed hers as they tied the necktie through a link in the fence. "At least we'll remember this," Isla teased as they finished. "We should probably take a selfie with it, don't you think?" She fished her mobile from her handbag, then squatted to be at eye level with it.

Helpless to do anything other than follow her lead, he squatted beside her, then smiled as she pointed at the tie. "This is ridiculous, you know that."

She kissed his cheek and took another picture. "It's adorable, and you're going to smile every time you think about it."

She's probably right about that. He stood, then helped her to her feet.

"We should probably go. We have a long drive ahead of us," he said, squeezing her hands gently.

She nodded, her lips parting as though she wanted to say something. Then she thought better of it and walked with him in silence back to the car.

The air between them had shifted as they pulled back onto the road—to something comfortable. Friendly. Isla didn't speak for a while, clearly lost in thought, playing her quiet music instead.

At last, when they pulled onto the highway, she said, "You know, I may not run a multi-billion-dollar business, but I actually understand what you're going through. I didn't set out to be the manager of an inn in Costa Rica—whether or not I love it." She rolled her head to the side, then tilted her seat back, setting her feet up on the dash.

He tried not to let himself be distracted by the smooth, bare skin of her svelte legs.

"Pop your legs down, love. I've heard of terrible accidents associated with people putting their legs up there." Aiden *heard* her eye roll, but thankfully, Isla listened. *And removed her gorgeous legs from my sight.*

"Do you want to go back to acting?"

"I thought I might. But after doing this the last couple of weeks, I'm not sure what I want. Or where I'm supposed to be. And the worst part is, I can't even tell Callum that I'm not sure I want to do this anymore. Because he bought *La Hacienda* for me. And if I don't want it now, that would make me the most ungrateful sister on the planet."

Just like fooling around with Isla makes me a terrible friend.

He let her words fade. Maybe she was right. Talking about everything somehow made it better. *Easier.* They weren't talking around things now or pretending.

He reached across the center console of the car and slipped his hand into hers, as though it were perfectly normal for them to hold hands.

They were no closer to figuring out how to deal with their attraction to each other.

No matter what Isla said, he knew what Callum would want. How Callum would react to any perceived betrayal from a friend.

Aiden knew what he *should* do.

Walk away. Shut this down. Forget the way her lips felt against his, the way her touch burned through his clothes.

But the thought of never having her again felt like a slow kind of death. Like condemning himself to an existence of obligation, loneliness, and nights staring at the ceiling wondering what could have been.

He couldn't have both. He couldn't reject her without hurting her. Without it becoming a source of tension between them.

But he wasn't sure he could let go of her, either.

"So where does that leave us?" he asked at last, his voice rough.

Isla didn't answer. She still held his hand, but her grip had slackened—she was asleep.

Aiden sneaked a glance at her. *Beautiful, tempestuous, sexy Isla.*

She'd turned his world upside-down. And for the first time in ages, he felt something other than exhaustion. Other than obligation. Life kicked within his heart, a pulse in his veins, raw and insistent.

22

ISLA

NASHVILLE, TENNESSEE

"Do you remember what sleeping in until eleven was like, Q?" Elle asked Quinn with a wink as Isla settled on the couch with a mug of fresh coffee.

Quinn looked up from the floor, where their eighteen-month-old Tara sat on his lap looking at a board book. He shook his head. "No."

"You're selling this whole 'getting married and having kids' thing so well," Isla said with a grin as she sipped her coffee. "Is Aiden still asleep?"

From across the living room, Mason lifted his head from where he'd had it buried in his laptop. "No, he got the three hours he requires as a robot and went out for a run."

The fact that Mason had also been here had been a surprise to both Aiden and Isla when they'd pulled in a little after six in the morning. If Isla didn't know any better, Aiden had appeared annoyed to see Mason—but that also might have been because he'd driven through the night and was clearly exhausted. Isla had slept on and off, uncomfortably, but it had helped lessen her fatigue.

"I still don't know what Aiden was thinking driving through the night like that," Quinn said with a shake of his head. "I know he puts us all to shame with his work hours, but he's going to collapse if he keeps going with so little sleep."

"Remember that time he tried to see how many days in a row he could go without sleeping?" Mason said with a chuckle, raising a brow at Quinn.

Quinn palmed his face with a laugh. "Bloody moron."

Elle set down the watering can she'd been using for some of her houseplants and crossed toward Isla, then sat beside her. "Oh good, we've already reached the part of the Camden brothers' reunions where they sit and reminisce about times long since passed while making fun of each other nonstop."

"Oh, believe me, I know. It's even worse when Callum and Logan join the mix." Even though her brother wasn't one of the brothers, they'd always treated him like one.

Elle gave her a sympathetic look. "I can't imagine what it must have been like as the only girl among these guys."

Isla sipped her coffee. "Oh, they weren't so bad. It helped that I was every bit as eager to join them, even if Quinn was constantly scolding the others for not taking it easy enough on me. The summers I got to escape to England, especially as a teenager, were my favorite." Partially because her grandparents, whom she'd loved dearly, had still been alive.

God, I miss them so much.

"Choo," Tara babbled happily, pointing one chubby finger at the picture of a train in her book.

"Oh, we should get a video for my mum," Quinn said, pulling out his phone. "She was so disappointed Tara didn't say any words during the last FaceTime call."

"Wait," Elle said, popping up from the sofa. "Let me change her outfit first. She's got some drool on her neckline."

"God, you two are such stereotypical firstborn, first-time parents," Mason said with a snicker.

"Oh, shut it," Elle said as she grabbed an outfit from a nearby basket and sat beside Quinn. "Mark my words, you'll be the next one of the Camden brothers to marry and settle down with children."

Quinn helped Elle with the buttons on the back of Tara's little dress. "Well, that's a bit obvious. Logan's too young, and Aiden's not likely to ever marry."

Mason's eyes darted to Isla.

Isla's throat went dry.

Does Mason know?

Then Mason's gaze flicked away, and he shrugged. "So sue me for being more domestic. Doesn't mean I still can't make fun of you."

Her heart squeezed, and she focused her attention on the caramel-colored brew in her mug. Would Aiden really have been so foolish to tell Mason about their Vegas marriage? He trusted Mason, obviously, but that was explosive information. Recovering, she said, "Quinn's not wrong, Mas. Make fun of them all you want, but you're definitely going to be as big of a sucker with your kids as they are."

"You never know," Mason said, eyes boring into her. "Aiden could surprise everyone and find someone to elope with."

Oh, he definitely knows.

But this felt like a challenge.

One that made her pulse speed.

Surely, he didn't want her to admit the Vegas situation in front of Elle and Quinn?

So Isla threw her head back and laughed. "Well, we all know that's never going to happen."

Something in Mason's eyes glittered, but before he could

speak, one of the French doors to the expansive back patio opened, and Aiden slipped inside.

The sight of him, coated in sweat, athletic shirt stuck against the hard muscles of his torso made her core twist, and she fought to keep a smile from her lips. How she'd wanted to continue what she'd started in the car—*feeling how hard he was for me was thrilling.* She was like a schoolgirl with a crush, and dammit, she had it bad. But the frankness of their conversation in the car the night before had only increased her desire, if she was honest. She couldn't get his words out of her head.

"What do you want me to admit? That I want to pull this car over, bend you over the bonnet, and fuck you until we're both senseless?"

Yes. That. That was what she'd wanted him to admit. Because she wanted it, too.

Aiden didn't look her way, though, clearly wiser than she was. "Morning," he said, then flashed a smile at Tara. "How's my favorite niece?"

"They're changing her to make a video for Mum," Mason said as Elle dragged the onesie off the baby's head. Then Mason stood. "Can we have a word?"

Aiden raised a brow. "Right now? I was heading toward the shower."

"Preferably now, yes." Mason's face was serious. He didn't wait for Aiden, then walked past him and went back out to the patio.

"What has his knickers in a twist?" Aiden asked Quinn, who shrugged. With a sigh, Aiden followed, shutting the patio door behind him.

A nervous feeling fluttered through Isla, and she stood, taking slow steps toward the patio, acting like she just wanted to look out at the gorgeously landscaped backyard. "When do you all open the pool for the season?"

"In a few weeks. If I'd known Aiden and Mason were going to drop in at the same time as you, I would have pushed Q to open it early. It's heated, so we could have had it ready for you all." Elle tied her long blond hair into a messy bun, then returned to a squirming Tara, who was trying to run away in nothing but a diaper, giggling.

"It is funny how we all ended up here at the same time," Isla said, glancing over her shoulder at Elle with a hesitation. "I hope we're not putting you out too much."

"Are you kidding? She lives to host." Quinn smiled. "Besides, my brothers are the ones who came uninvited. We *knew* you were coming."

"Why is Mason here, by the way? I didn't expect to see him here," Isla said with a curious look.

"Yes, well, none of us expected Aiden to be involved in the project you're working on," Quinn said as he stood from the floor, gathering the books he'd been reading to Tara and setting them on the coffee table as Elle changed her diaper on a changing pad. "Apparently, I need to call my brothers more."

"To answer your question," Elle said with a roll of her eyes, "Mason has been in New York working on some big acquisition deal with Aiden. Apparently, the talks took a break last night, so he decided to take a red-eye flight and spend a few days here, rather than go back to London. He's got to be back in New York in a few days anyway, and he figured this was a shorter trip. At least, that's how he explained it."

Isla set her lips on the rim of the mug, scanning the back-yard for Mason and Aiden. They were several feet from the door, near an arbor that marked the entrance to the flower garden.

And they appeared to be arguing.

She shouldn't intrude. They worked together, and they were brothers, and she really had no business intruding.

But, somehow, she couldn't help feeling like this involved her. Mason had been testing her with those comments. And he didn't seem happy with her responses, either.

She didn't want to be so obvious by heading out there in front of Elle and Quinn. On the other hand, she was staying in the guesthouse on the other side of the pool. "I think I'm going to go get dressed and ready for the day. We still planning on going to lunch?"

Tara zoomed past Isla unsteadily, fleeing from her mother, laughing with a big, toothy grin, blue eyes sparkling.

"Yeah, I have this cute little place I thought we could go," Elle said with an exasperated look. "Get back here, you crazy child. Don't just sit there, Q. Help me out here."

Isla left them chasing Tara and slipped out onto the patio. She sneaked a glance back toward them, but they were obviously occupied with Tara.

Then she marched up toward Aiden and Mason. "What in the hell is going on?" Isla demanded to Mason.

"I don't know. What *is* going on?" Mason shot back, eyes narrowing slightly.

"Were you *trying* to announce to Elle and Quinn about that mistake in Vegas? Because you weren't exactly subtle." Isla crossed her arms.

Aiden tossed his hands into the air. "Thank you," he said in a clipped tone to Isla and shifted his body back toward Mason. "You see? I told her. She knows. Now, will you kindly stop trying to shove your nose into our business?"

Mason's face flushed, his mouth parting as he looked from Isla to Aiden. "Oh. Um . . ."

The situation became instantly clearer. Mason *had* been testing her to find out if Aiden had told her about the marriage license. He hadn't been trying to get a rise out of her, but instead, he was trying to make certain Aiden did the right thing.

Of course.

Mason was like a mini-Quinn. Responsible. More serious.

"How did you find out?" She didn't imagine Aiden had told him willingly.

"He happened to be there when I received the license at the office. Practically stole it out of my hands trying to read it," Aiden said with annoyance. "Then he demanded I tell you and Callum immediately, which is why we were arguing out here. He's still threatening to call your brother."

What?

Isla's eyes widened. "Oh no, no, no," she gasped, gripping Mason's arm. "No, Mason, you *cannot* tell Callum *anything*."

"He's my friend—Aiden's friend. He's going to find out about this, and then we'll all look like a bunch of liars," Mason argued, tugging at the collar of his polo shirt.

"He might not find out if you don't say anything," Isla argued, edging closer to Aiden.

"But if he does? I'm not comfortable lying to him. And I work closely with Liddy. That could make things exceptionally uncomfortable."

"God, you're a fucking prude, Mason," Aiden seethed through his teeth.

"Like I said in London, it's your obligation to tell Callum. I won't have to resort to saying anything if you just do the right thing and tell him yourself," Mason said, the flush in his face deepening.

She cringed. Mason had a good heart and was a loyal friend, but she wanted to smack him.

"Mason, I say this with all the kindness in my heart, but this really doesn't involve you. Or Callum. It's no one's business but

Aiden's and mine. We're getting an annulment, and then the whole thing will cease to be an issue. Callum won't know that you knew because we won't tell him—either about the marriage *or* you knowing. And that will be it. Life will carry on as normal."

Mason tensed, looking from Aiden to Isla, then back to Aiden. "I—"

"Don't you think Isla should have the final say in all this? It's *her* family, mate. You're threatening her privacy with her own brother," Aiden said, crossing his arms.

A few more tense beats of silence as the three of them squared off, Mason twisting with discomfort.

Then a French door opened, and Quinn popped his head out. "Everything all right?" he gave them a curious look.

"Brilliant," Aiden breathed under his breath, then offered Quinn a disarming smile. "Yes, why wouldn't it be?"

"You all look like you're having a serious discussion, that's all." Quinn held a dirty diaper in one hand and leaned against the door handle with the other. "Not to mention you're all out here."

"Oh, they just distracted me on the way back to the guesthouse," Isla said, taking a few steps away. "I'll be over there in a few."

Quinn nodded, then glanced at the diaper. "I should throw this out," he said, then slipped back inside.

"We'll talk about this later," Isla said to Mason with a sharp look. "But I'm warning you, Mason. Don't you dare think of telling Callum anything. If anyone is going to talk to him, it's going to be me, understood?"

Mason raised both brows as though startled by this side of her. Then he nodded. "Fair enough."

She didn't give Aiden another glance as she stalked away. She couldn't afford to. Mason already knew too much. If he caught even the slightest hint of flirtation between them, it would only make things exponentially worse.

But as she slipped into the guesthouse and closed the door behind her, she caught the tremble of her fingers against the doorknob.

Mason wasn't entirely wrong. Too many people knew enough about her and Aiden—Callum could find out.

And somehow, that still didn't make her want Aiden any less.

But she needed to figure out a way to break this to Callum —if there was a way. How could she tell Callum that she no longer saw one of his best friends, someone they'd both known since childhood, as a platonic friend? That she'd crossed that line and wanted to keep crossing it . . . *over and over?*

She closed her eyes, the sizzle of hot lust curling through her as she thought of Aiden's kiss the night before. Her thighs clenched, her jaw squeezing tight.

Maybe it was a crush.

Maybe one taste, *one night*, would be enough to satisfy whatever attraction kept pulling them together.

But one thing was for certain: staying away from Aiden wasn't an option.

23

———

AIDEN

"So, you lasted one class?" Mason asked Elle's friend Taryn across the large, farmhouse-style dining room table.

Taryn laughed, shifting her weight forward as she lifted the glass of red wine beside her plate. "I lasted *ten minutes*, Mason. I went into that one class, decided I'd rather stab my eyeballs out with a fork than listen to an entire lecture on statistics, and walked right out." Taryn shrugged. "Went right over to the guidance office, switched my major to dance, and never looked back."

"What I can't understand," Quinn said as he leaned back into his chair, "is how you possibly thought you could have done economics in the first place. You're a natural performer."

That was putting it mildly. Aiden had seen Taryn dance on more than one occasion—both on stage with Elle, when his sister-in-law still performed in public—though that was getting rarer these days—and at private functions like Elle and Quinn's wedding in Costa Rica. The beautiful Black woman owned any stage she walked on. She had presence in spades.

Taryn set her napkin beside her plate. "Maybe, but my parents wanted me to do something in STEM. They thought a degree in the arts was useless and gave me hell for it. Now they've come around." She winked at Elle. "Helps that Heartbeats has grown so much. They don't worry about me not being able to pay the bills anymore with the steady income of the dance studio."

"Not to mention that you're a co-owner of a highly successful business," Elle said with a proud nod.

"I'm jealous, I have to admit," Isla said from her seat beside Elle. "I miss the performing arts so much. Of course, in my case, no one really fought me when I tried to pursue them, so I suppose I had it easier."

"Maybe there's a theater troupe you can get involved with in Costa Rica?" Elle asked, reaching for the video monitor beside her. Tara had fallen asleep for the night a couple of hours earlier, but Elle seemed to check the monitor every few minutes as though to make certain she was still there.

"Yeah, I don't know," Isla said. She looked down at the empty plate in front of her, then absentmindedly reached for another piece of garlic bread to sop up the remains of the marinara. "Weirdly, it's hard performing in Spanish. Even though I've spoken it since birth, it doesn't feel like my native language. Even my mum and I default to English most of the time."

Aiden's stomach clenched as he caught the look of sadness in her eyes. He'd replayed their conversation in the car so many times all day. He wanted more than anything to be alone with her and dig deeper into the wounds that were clearly weighing her down.

"I'm not sure where I belong anymore, Aiden—what world I'm really a part of." She'd been so sad when she'd said that to him. And he wanted to help her through it—especially because he knew what she was feeling.

Give her the room to talk to him the way he'd been able to talk to her.

"I always forget what you are," Elle's friend Hunter said from the other side of the table. "You and Callum are *Amertinoish*."

"I can confirm she has every bit the Latina temper," Kyle said as he pushed his chair back from the table. "Almost broke my surfboard because it was in the way of her supply closet one day."

"Yeah, well, maybe you shouldn't leave your junk lying around my office," Isla shot back with a smirk.

Kyle laughed. "On that note, I'm going to head out and take advantage of being home to see some of my own friends instead of hanging out with the same losers I see all the time." He winked at Isla, then went over to his sister and kissed her cheek. "Tara excluded, of course. Thanks for dinner, guys."

"Hey, I resent that," Elle said with a look of mock outrage. "You can't come to my house, eat my homemade lasagna, then call me a loser and Irish goodbye me."

"Technically, it's not an Irish goodbye if he says goodbye," Aiden said dryly.

Mason snorted. "And believe me, Aiden would know. He's the master of slipping out sight unseen from every family event."

Elle stood and hugged her brother. "Let me walk you to your car at least. Who knows when I'll see you next. You're home so rarely that I'm beginning to feel like both my siblings have abandoned me."

As Elle and Kyle left, Aiden glanced at his own brothers. It's funny how, even though they all got along, he wouldn't entirely characterize their relationship as close. Certainly not the sort of friendship that Elle seemed to have with her siblings. Or even the way that Callum and Isla were.

Maybe it was because there was four of them. Or maybe because Quinn and he had fallen out for years until Aiden had left the military and started at Camden Enterprises, giving Quinn the freedom he'd longed for to leave the family business and start a nonprofit organization.

And, unfortunately, Mason was three years younger than Aiden, so while they'd grown up together, they'd never been *friends*, per se. Logan was even younger. Maybe more like Aiden in personality—funny as hell, too, and a more natural rebel—but too young for them to have gotten in the sort of trouble Aiden had gotten into with Quinn.

"Are we pulling out a board game?" Hunter asked with a waggle of his brows. "I brought a few good ones."

Oh God. Aiden couldn't think of anything worse.

"Sure. Go ahead and set one up," Quinn said with an affable smile. "I'll join you in the living room once I take care of some of these dishes." He rose from his seat.

Isla pushed her chair back and grabbed his plate before Quinn could. "Actually, let me. The cook shouldn't have to clean, and you guys have been working your tails off all day to host us. I can do the dishes."

Dammit, why didn't I think of that?

"I'll help," Aiden said, gathering his own plate.

Mason and Quinn both shot him a quizzical look. "This from the man who used to regularly pay us to do his chores?" Quinn asked.

"Wouldn't be right to leave Isla to it on her own," Aiden said as casually as possible. Had he seemed too eager?

He gathered more empty plates before anyone could question it and followed Isla to the kitchen. Setting the dishes beside the enormous farmhouse sink, he watched as Isla turned on the tap and reached for the sponge. "Not much of a board game player?"

She laughed, her eyes twinkling as she met his gaze. "No, I love board games. I just genuinely wanted to help—unlike *you*. Covering up your dislike for their fun activity with *my* good deed."

"You wound me," he said with a look of feigned outrage.

"Yeah, yeah. I *know* you is more like it. Not to mention, I have solid memories of you cheating at every board game we played as kids."

"It's only cheating if you get caught," Aiden said with a shrug, then headed back to the dining room. Even though the others had made their way to the dining room, he hid his smile as he reentered the room. He didn't want anyone else to catch the expression he was certain must be on his face.

Because Isla made him smile. She made his heart instantly lighter.

He balanced several more plates in his hands, then carried them back over to the kitchen.

After he'd cleared the table, he set to putting away the leftovers. "I don't know how Elle and Quinn find anything in this kitchen. It's bigger than the one at Littleton, and that's saying something."

He opened a drawer to reveal neatly organized utensils, then shut it.

Going over to another drawer, then another one, he frowned. No storage containers. He opened a cabinet and smiled. "Quinn would have every spice organized alphabetically," he said in a deep voice and chortled.

"What makes you think it's Quinn? Maybe Elle likes things neat and tidy." A smile played on Isla's lips as she looked over her shoulder at him.

They both laughed. *Not a chance*.

Another thing to like about her. She knew his family and their quirks.

Even though he and Lola only saw his family a few times together, she'd felt like a stranger in their midst, clinging to Aiden's side, forcing laughs and smiles.

At last, he found the container he was looking for and put the leftovers away. Carrying the empty casserole dish toward the sink, he held on to it, looking for a place to set it. The counter beside the sink was already filled with dishes. "Where should I set this?" he asked at last.

"You can just put it in the sink," Isla said, shifting over slightly to give him room.

He reached around her and set the dish down, his forearm brushing against hers as he did, his hips pressing against her backside with the barest touch.

But it was enough.

Enough to make every inch of him alert at how close she was, his body intoxicated with her instantaneously as he held on to a breath, chest tight.

Isla stiffened too, then she relaxed, leaning against him, her weight pressing harder against his hip, the smooth curve of her arse fitting against his thigh.

Aiden didn't move his hand from the stream of water or the sudsy water swirling around their fingertips.

God, I want to touch her.

Taste her.

He reached for her fingers, letting his hand brush against hers. Then he leaned closer still, his lips grazing her ear. She'd worn a sexy little dress at dinner—black with a daring halter top neckline, her shoulders bare. "I could barely keep my eyes off you at dinner, you know."

She smiled. "And why's that?"

His lips nipped her earlobe. "Because I kept imagining taking this dress off you," he growled.

Her breath caught softly, something warm and sexy in the sound. Turning her face toward his, her lips tilted toward his and caught his lower lip, soft and firmly between her own.

Fuck. Me.

Just a gentle nibble of a kiss, but enough that he didn't pull away like he should have. His heart slammed hard into his ribs, and he returned a kiss. Then another.

A longer kiss now, unyielding, insistent, raw with hunger as he withdrew one hand from the sink and slipped it around her waist, dragging her arse tight against his hard cock.

She returned each kiss for kiss, and his body burned as he felt himself spiraling, control slipping quickly from him. Then her sweet, delicious tongue darted against his lips, urging them to part.

And he was helpless.

He tilted his head, angling it better as their mouths opened to each other, their tongues colliding with need. His grip tightened at her waist, the edge of the sink pressing into her stomach as he pushed her closer—

"You know you guys can use the dishwa—"

Elle's voice came through the doorway as they sprang apart.

Oh, Christ.

Isla bit down on her lip, looking down at the running water, her cheeks already turning pink.

Aiden stepped away from Isla and turned to glance at Elle, who stood in the doorway, her mouth still open in shock.

She held Aiden's gaze, then closed her mouth, swallowing. "Um," she stammered. "Um . . . the dishwasher."

Elle continued into the kitchen, not saying a word about what she'd seen. She didn't meet Aiden's eyes again, either. "We have two of them," she continued, opening one, then the other. "Just throw everything in here."

Holy fuck, what do I even say?

If he knew Elle, she wouldn't be against it—or even judge them. But she might tell Quinn. Probably *would* tell Quinn.

She'd be *dying* to tell Quinn.

The awkward silence continued as Isla set a plate into one of the dishwashers. "That's great, thanks," Isla said quietly.

"No, no. Thank you. Both of you. I really didn't expect . . . um, for you to do the dishes." Elle paused, looking between them again, then gave an overly bright, forced smile. She turned to hurry back toward the door.

Aiden followed Elle and caught her in the dining room. "Please don't," he said, his voice edged with a rough scrape.

Elle froze, then turned and glanced at Aiden. She gave him a good, long stare, then squeezed his forearm. "You know I'll never judge. But you're playing with fire, Aiden. You're going to get burned."

"What if I already am burned?" he asked, stepping closer. "And I still can't stop?"

"I don't know," Elle whispered, her eyes wide and filled with sadness. "But I know you're a good man, Aiden. And you're tough. I just hope this doesn't blow up in your face because you don't deserve that. But it might. Please be careful."

She hurried off, leaving him standing alone in the dining room.

Aiden released a breath, his chest aching with the effort. He couldn't very well go into the living room now and sit with Elle and Quinn, acting like nothing had happened.

But he couldn't go back to Isla, either. Not yet. Not when his hands were still tingling with the memory of her skin. Not when her taste still lingered on his tongue.

This wasn't just a mistake anymore. It wasn't something he could laugh off or walk away from. He knew it, Isla knew it, and now Elle knew it too.

And soon, Callum would know it. One way or another.

He needed to think.

To figure out what he wanted.

And what he was willing to lose.

24
———

ISLA

I HAVE *to stop doing this to myself.*

Isla slid into the bed of the guesthouse wearily, the faint pulse of a headache at the edge of her senses. She was thankful for the luxurious king-sized bed all to herself.

Elle and Quinn were such incredible hosts, with a beautiful home she knew they'd paid off from the money from Elle's music career. They'd chosen a place off the beaten path that afforded them privacy and security, and despite it all, they were still both so humble. So normal. She'd always appreciated that about Quinn.

In that way, he and Aiden were different.

Aiden was arrogant. A full-of-himself *asshole* that she had to stop allowing to toy with her.

After a sizzling kiss that had made her weak in the knees, he'd left her in that kitchen tonight, doing dishes by herself. Because *why?* He wasn't willing to face her after Elle had caught them kissing? She hadn't wanted to face Elle, either, and definitely not alone.

But that was precisely what she'd had to do. She'd put the

dishes in the dishwashers, then gone back out to the living room to play a board game with Mason, Elle, Quinn, and their friends. No Aiden in sight.

Asshole.

Ugh.

Maybe he was a bigger coward than she'd believed.

"Why do I have the worst taste in men?" she muttered, flipping onto her back and staring at the ceiling.

She couldn't keep doing this. She'd practically thrown herself at Aiden—three times now. And, sure, maybe he'd expressed interest, but it wasn't like he initiated anything beyond those encounters. He hadn't even gone out with them today, choosing to stay at Elle and Quinn's and work instead.

"*Work-a-holic* asshole."

Yet none of the verbal slings made her feel any better.

It was like all sense went out the window when she was near him. The barest of touches set her skin on fire and made her want to find a way to fuck him right then and there. Take risks.

Stupid, stupid risks.

And that was the exact opposite reaction Davy had the night before. *Man, that feels like so long ago now.* Davy had naturally been giddy at the idea of Isla and Aiden together. Isla felt a little guilty because she hadn't come out and told Davy the whole truth about the marriage. *Maybe because I'm still processing that myself.* And she'd downplayed how much she was feeling.

"*It's not a big deal,*" she'd told Davy. "*We kissed. That's it. It's nothing, really.*"

"*Girl, just climb that delicious man like a tree. You're clearly into each other,*" Davy said.

Just the thought of "climbing Aiden like a tree" made her wet, her thighs clenching, her body begging for fulfillment.

She hadn't had sex for so long—since she and Tomas had broken up because one-night stands weren't usually her thing—and maybe that was what was driving her crazy. She *wanted* "one night" with Aiden. She didn't want to think about what it could mean or where they'd end up. She was sick of rules and all the adult bullshit.

For once, she wanted to return to being irresponsible and free. Eating takeaway at three in the morning after a long night on stage, followed by drinks.

Yet, the last time she'd tried to let loose was in Vegas, and look what happened.

With a heavy, strained sigh that did nothing to release the tension from her body, she slid her hand down to her waist, then slipped it between her legs. *God, I'm fucking soaked.*

Sliding one finger deeply inside her, she closed her eyes, her heartbeat speeding as she imagined Aiden kissing her by the sink. The taste of his tongue, the firmness of his cock against her ass.

Oh fuck. I need this.

She drew a shattered breath, then slid her hand back, rubbing the wetness over her clit. Her body jerked in response, desperate for release.

A soft knock sounded at the door.

"Shit. You have got to be kidding me!" she muttered.

She climbed out of her bed, adjusting her panties as she walked toward the door.

She grabbed a zip-up sweatshirt from the suitcase just in case—her nipples were hard and visible under the satin fabric of her pajamas—and she wasn't about to open the door this turned on without something to cover her if necessary.

Opening the door a crack, she peeked out.

Aiden.

She swallowed hard, then opened the door a bit more. "Did

you get lost on your way back from the kitchen?" Her tone had more bite to it than she'd intended.

Aiden gave her a pained, tortured expression, his hands in the back pockets of his jeans. "Can I come in?"

She opened the door farther, and he stepped inside, closing the door behind them.

He stood there for a few seconds, staring at her, his eyes traveling over every inch of her, focusing on her breasts, her nipples, then going down to her waist. "You took the dress off," he said, his voice almost hoarse with strain.

"Aiden, that was hours ago."

Isla hugged her arms to her chest, goose bumps rising on her skin.

Aiden closed the gap between them, something darkening in his eyes. Lust. *Need.*

He lifted her chin in his hands, the pad of his thumb brushing over the soft flesh, then dragging it down, just slightly, eliciting a shiver from her. "What do you want?"

"The same thing you want," he answered, eyes boring into her.

"Well, maybe I don't want it anymore," Isla said with a glare. "Maybe you blew your chance."

The hint of a feline smirk tugged the corners of his sensual mouth, and Aiden dragged her closer to him. Rounding his palm over the curve of her ass, he slipped it below the waistband of her pajama shorts, then her panties, then farther still.

She moaned as he slid two fingers inside her. "Doesn't seem like you don't want it."

Her senses swam with the feel of him there, stroking her clit. Then he pulled his hand away, and she swallowed hard and held his gaze. "Maybe you interrupted me."

Aiden raised a brow. "Interrupted you?"

She narrowed her gaze. "I can take care of myself if you can't, Aiden."

A muscle flexed in his jaw. With a smooth motion, he lifted her, then carried her over to the bed and set her on the very edge. He knelt on the floor in front of her, then reached for the waistband of her shorts once again and peeled them away.

She watched him, her heart slamming into her chest, as he pulled a chair over in front of her, then pushed her farther onto the bed, so that her head rested against the pillows. He lifted one foot, then the other, and set them flat against the fabric of the mattress so that her knees were bent. "Show me," he demanded.

"Show you what?"

"What I interrupted." He sat back in the chair.

Oh my God.

She'd had sex plenty of times before.

But this? With Aiden? She felt out of her depth. And, somehow, more daring. She didn't even send sexy pictures because she'd been an actress, and she knew how that could end up.

But the boldness of his stare was hypnotizing. She drew a shattered breath, body twitching, then pushed her panties to the side, baring herself to his view.

"Fuck, you have a perfect pussy," he said, drawing a sharp breath.

"You sure you don't want to feel for yourself?" she asked, then slid her fingers down, circling her clit. It took every last bit of her effort not to hop off this bed and straddle him. Her body was swimming with desire.

"I do. And I'm going to. But first, I want to watch." Aiden cocked his head to the side. "You've been toying with me, Isla. I told you it was a dangerous game."

She licked her lips, her chest heaving as she leaned her

head back, closing her eyes as she touched herself. "I want your hands on me, Aiden," she gasped as she pushed her fingertips deep inside her. "I want to feel your cock."

"Not yet, baby." Aiden's voice was a throaty growl. "Fuck, I love watching you like this. Take your shirt off. I want to see your beautiful tits."

She tugged it away as though under his spell, unable to do anything but what he wanted.

His eyes zeroed in hard on the peaked pink nipples, and he swallowed as though barely restraining himself. "Keep going." He didn't move, didn't touch himself, just watched her with an intensity that made her feel like his sole pleasure was in watching her. Like he was memorizing every inch of her.

"Aiden," she breathed, then returned her fingers to her clit. Slow circles became steadier, faster. More intense. As her hips rose against her hand, her face heated. Her thighs trembled now, her body begging for release.

"Aiden, please."

"I want to see you come, Isla. You gorgeous fucking woman."

"Help me," she managed at last.

With a smile, Aiden climbed onto the bed beside her, then slid two fingers inside her, stroking against her. He pulled them out, then pushed inside her again.

Again.

The feeling of him there was enough to undo her. She let her head drop back as her body released, the frantic circles against her clit faster as it pulsed against her fingertips. "Oh God," she moaned, the cascade of her orgasm slamming against her as her thighs went taut, then relaxed completely.

Aiden's other hand caught her waist, keeping her upright as she finished, panting.

Then he closed the space between them and caught her

mouth in a fierce, open-mouthed kiss. When he pulled away, he whispered against her lips, "You're incredible. God, I want you, Isla. You have no idea how fucking beautiful you are when you come."

She let out a soft groan. "Thank you. I needed that."

"I know you did." Then he kissed her hard, his tongue lashing against hers.

A sharp laugh from the patio, passing by the window of the bedroom, stilled them both.

Aiden froze, then pulled away as his eyes focused on the window.

"You're nuts . . ." Taryn's voice came, laughing, then faded.

Aiden climbed off the bed and went toward the window, peeking out the curtain. "They're still here?"

Isla frowned, then propped herself up on her elbows. "Yeah . . . Taryn and Hunter were hanging out with Quinn and Elle down by the firepit."

Aiden turned away from the window. "Fuck. I thought they'd gone. I didn't see anyone when I snuck over."

Then annoyance flared through her.

As though we're fucking teenagers. Sneaking around.

As though I'm a dirty little secret.

Isla reached over and grabbed her pajama top, then pulled it back over her head. Then she tugged her panties back into place. "So it's fine to come over and have sex? So long as no one finds out about it?"

Aiden adjusted himself, guilt flashing across his face. "I came to say goodbye, Isla. I didn't expect . . . I didn't come to—"

"What?" White-hot anger surged through her, and she shot to her feet.

"I have to go back to London. I have a business to run, but I'm unable to stay away from you. I can't keep saying this will be all right, that I don't have to tell Callum anything and then start fucking you in secret, like a side piece who doesn't matter to me."

"Don't you think I should have a say in this?" Isla scrambled for her discarded shorts and yanked them on. "You were fine with the idea of fucking me five seconds ago."

"I know. And I still want to. I want you with every inch of my body—"

"But you didn't come for that. You came to say goodbye and to walk away. I just provided too much temptation, so you were willing to let me be your dirty little secret so long as you got your jollies? What was the plan after that?" Hurt and frustration spiraled within her.

"I don't understand what you want from me, Isla."

"I don't know!" she exploded. She couldn't get his words out of her head. *He'd been planning on saying goodbye.* "But at the very least, I'd like to be a part of the discussion."

"Okay." Aiden held her by the shoulders. "Then move to London. Have a relationship with me—a real one. Be my girlfriend, in public, out in the open. We tell Callum, everyone. No more secrets and lies."

"I-I can't move to London, Aiden. You know this. I live in Costa Rica."

"Exactly." He moved away. "Exactly. This is why we can't do this. We aren't on the same side of the ocean, and I work almost eighty hours a week. Long-distance isn't an option. You're not going to have any time off after this show to come back and forth, and I can't either. I'm already so behind on *everything* that I feel like I'm falling apart at the seams. And I can't ignore how that would complicate things with Callum, either."

"And this?" Isla glared, gesturing toward the bed. "This is something we can be open to everyone about? This is just another secret and lie, Aiden. How did this make anything better between us? We can't come back from the lines we've crossed, and you fucking know it. Which means you're choosing everything—your work, your friendship with my brother—*all of it*, instead of me."

"You're right, we can't. And I'm sorry. I don't blame you if you don't want to see me again for a while after this."

Tears misted her eyes, and she clenched her hands into fists, then she strode from the bedroom into the small adjoining living room. "I really hate you right now. I'm not sure I'm ever going to want to see you again."

"I don't want to hurt you—"

"But you are. And you don't care. God, I'm such an idiot. I shouldn't have expected any less from the guy who broke up with his previous girlfriend over and over again. Who was infamous in his town for getting a girl pregnant and then walking away the instant she lost the baby."

His face flickered with pain. "You know that wasn't true."

"Maybe. Maybe not. Ciara never said any differently, so who knows if we can believe a habitual liar."

His posture went rigid, his expression closing off to her. "All right. On that note, I'll see myself out." He headed toward the door.

Isla wiped the tears from her cheeks. How dare he? How *could* he?

God, was this it? All the longing and angst, and he was just going to walk away like she meant nothing to him?

Because that must be the truth.

He wouldn't discard her so easily if he cared.

Aiden paused at the door, turning his head at the sound of her tears.

Then he set his forehead against the door, closing his eyes.

His breath came rough and uneven as he stared at her. "If I leave, I'll regret it," he whispered, more to himself than her. He exhaled sharply as if he'd just made a decision he couldn't undo.

Aiden left the doorway again, heading straight for her. When he reached her, he lifted her, cradling her against his body as he carried her toward the bedroom. "What are you doing?" she asked.

"Putting my wife to bed, apparently," he said in a gruff voice. But he set her down gently on the mattress with a look of anguish that made her heart squeeze tightly.

Wife?

She searched his eyes. "That's not funny, Aiden."

"Yet, it's true. We're married right now, and our lives are tied together in a way that isn't as easy as shaking hands and going in different directions." Aiden rubbed his eyes. "I don't know what to do, Isla. I can't leave you like this. I care about you too much. You've turned my entire world on end."

She reached for his hand. "I told you last night. We don't have to have everything figured out right now, Aiden. We don't have to solve this all immediately. Stop asking yourself what makes sense. What do *you* want?"

"You," he answered without hesitation. He brushed the tears from her cheeks. "I want you, Isla."

She reached for his hand and kissed his knuckles. "Then where are you going?"

Aiden blinked at her, a muscle in his jaw flexing.

Please choose me.

She didn't want to beg—that felt too pathetic—yet his uncertainty didn't come from a place of insecurity about what he felt for her. They were just in a terrible position.

If he leaves right now, I don't think I can ever let myself trust him again.

After a few more moments, Aiden exhaled like the weight

of the world had just come off his shoulders. Then, with a quiet determination, he reached for her.

He didn't rush. He didn't pounce. He gathered her slowly, carefully—like she was something fragile, something breakable. And maybe she was. Perhaps they both were.

His hands slid around her waist as he guided himself into the bed, her body molding against his like they had done this a thousand times before. His fingers wove into her hair, tilting her face toward his. A kiss. Slow. Lingering. Less about desire, more about something deeper. A promise. A vow.

"Nowhere," he murmured against her lips. "I'm not going anywhere, Isla. If you want me to stay, I'll stay. If you want to figure this out together, then that's what we'll do. Even if I have no idea what I'm doing."

She closed her eyes, tears continuing to slip from her eyes, but slowing.

She wanted to believe him, but how could she? He'd walked away from her several times already. It almost seemed as though Aiden had walked away from everything difficult in his life. His family. The military. Their marriage—although at least that one made sense. *And he was about to leave me.*

And now she was supposed to believe he'd suddenly stay?

Her throat ached, her hands still trembling against his chest, even as he held her. "You always leave, Aiden." Her voice was barely a whisper, but the words cracked something inside her. "What makes me any different?"

Aiden pulled her tighter, his lips brushing her temple. "Because seeing you hurting is more painful than anything else I can imagine," he said. "Because if I lose you, I lose myself."

Wow. That's . . .

"Can I just stay? Hold you?"

Isla squeezed her eyes shut. God, she wanted to believe

him. He knew how to say the right things. But trust wasn't given—it was earned. And Aiden still had a long way to go.

After all the back-and-forth, she wasn't sure of anything anymore—except that if this was all the time they had, *just tonight*, sex or no sex, then she would take it. Take his promises at face value. Because somehow, *he* mattered to her in an indescribable way. Having him here with her *mattered*. And that was truly terrifying.

25

———

AIDEN

FOR THE THIRD time in several weeks, Aiden had woken up in Isla's room—but this time, she was in his arms.

They'd slept—only slept—which seemed like a miracle, considering he had the image of her pleasuring herself seared into his memory like a brand.

Holy hell, how can I ever erase that from my soul?

But they'd needed to sleep, apparently. Maybe it was just exhaustion or perhaps they'd both needed the comfort—a break from the push and pull that had been drowning them both.

Now, though?

Now he was hard as a rock, and he needed her. Needed to put an end to the torment that was Isla Scott.

Her body was already molded tightly against his, her arse tucked in tight against his groin, their legs entangled. His hand rested against the bare skin of her flat belly, and he grazed her skin with the barest touch until he palmed her breast, fitting it into his hand. Her nipples were silky smooth, *fucking incredible*, and he was on fire for her.

The sharp rasp of her breath told him she was awake now,

and she snuggled into his touch. "Good morning to you, too," she murmured, then shifted against his cock. "Is it morning already?"

"Unfortunately." He kissed her shoulder with a featherlight kiss.

"Mmm . . ." Isla tilted her head back against his throat. "Did you sleep well?"

His palm made a circle over one nipple. "I was horny as fuck. But yes."

She wiggled her hips against him, teasing, taunting.

"God, Isla."

"You know," she said, her voice light and teasing. "For someone who says he wants me as much as you do, you certainly seemed determined to take your time with it. Putting every obstacle in our way."

Her hand moved between them, then she pushed it under his waistband, fingertips grazing the head of his cock.

Fuck. Yes.

"I don't know what I was thinking."

"Hmm." She enclosed her hand around his shaft. "I don't know what you were thinking either." She gave him a firm squeeze, then pulled away. "Because our first time isn't going to be sleepy sex when I'm worried about morning breath. Besides, I don't have a condom here, do you?"

Oof. He reached for her as she slipped free of his grasp and crawled out of the other side of the bed. *Shite.*

He raised a brow at her. "No, but what would we have done if I hadn't stopped us last night?"

She gave him a pretty, sultry smile. "I guess you'll have to wonder. But I guess we'll never know."

He hung his head. "Are you trying to torture me?"

"No." She went over to the bathroom and turned the sink on, then came back with a toothbrush in hand. "But since you keep flipping the script on me and making me feel like I want you more than you want me, you're going to have to earn your way into my pants, Aiden Camden."

His lips parted for a few beats, then he groaned. He tossed the sheet to the side, gesturing to the bulge in his boxer briefs. "And this isn't proof enough?"

Her eyes focused on him for a long moment—*God, I love how she doesn't hide what she wants*—then she shrugged casually. "Like I said. Earn it. But if you don't want Quinn to find out about us, you might want to head back to the house now anyway." She winked. "I'm going to hop into the shower and get all wet and naked. I'll see you at breakfast."

Aiden growled as she closed the bathroom door. "Don't think I don't know you're punishing me," he called.

"So what if I am?" she called back from the other side. The water turned on. "You made me cry. You're going to have to prove you really want me now, Aiden."

Dammit.

He dropped his head back against the pillow. Trust Isla to be unpredictable. She knew how to turn him into knots.

"You always leave, Aiden. What makes me any different?" She made everything different, but she wasn't wrong either.

Her tears? He wasn't sure if he could forgive himself for those tears she'd shed last night. Staying was insane, but he'd been helpless to do anything but after that.

He got out of bed and dressed, checking his mobile. It was early still—just after six—but that was late for him. And Quinn rarely slept past four.

"Fuck," he breathed, then scrambled for his shoes.

He shoved his mobile into his pocket, then left, hurrying across the patio. Maybe if he went for a quick run, he could just convince Quinn he'd been out running—

Quinn and Mason stood near the French doors, watching him.

Oh, goddammit.

They had to have seen him leave the guesthouse.

Sucking in a sharp breath, Aiden gave them a tight smile, then went inside the house. "Morning," he managed, moving to scoot past them.

Quinn already had a fistful of his shirt in his grasp. He shoved Aiden roughly back against the door, the glass vibrating, and loomed intimidatingly, despite the fact that Quinn was a few inches shorter than him. "She's like our sister," he said through clenched teeth.

"But she's *not* actually our sister," Aiden snapped, resisting the urge to push back. A physical fight wouldn't help matters right now.

"It doesn't matter. She's Isla. And you're . . . *you.* Callum would be furious."

Mason gave him a look as though to say, *told you.*

"I didn't touch her," Aiden said, shoving Quinn off him at last. It was *almost* true.

Quinn gave him a skeptical look.

"All right," Aiden corrected. "I may have touched, but I didn't have sex with her. We just slept. She was sad, and I comforted her."

"So . . . you're friends who sleep in the same bed? Kiss? Because I really don't know what the hell you're thinking, Aiden. This is a new low for you in terms of stupid, bullheaded obtuseness."

"It's a bit worse than that," Mason muttered unhelpfully.

He really was going to murder his younger brother.

Quinn's eyes shot to him, then widened. "You knew about this?"

"Shut your mouth, Mason," Aiden said, drawing himself to his full height.

Mason hesitated, looking from one to the other.

"Tell me," Quinn demanded with all the authority of an older brother.

"Don't you dare—"

"They got drunk and married in Vegas," Mason spilled.

Aiden's stomach bottomed out.

The thunk of a gavel. The whisper of an executioner's sword.

He barely heard Quinn's curse over the ringing in his ears.

And there it was. *His death sentence.*

Quinn paled, staring at Aiden with such shock that Aiden could practically see the wheels of his mind turning. Quinn's hand clenched into fists at his sides. "You irredeemable bastard," Quinn growled.

Why did everyone seem to think this was somehow *his* fault? As though Isla was some sweet, innocent young maiden who had been taken advantage of by a hungry wolf?

"Thank you, Mason," Aiden breathed, throwing the full weight of his glare onto his younger brother. "We're in the process of getting an annulment."

Quinn drew a slow, measured breath, then took one step closer to Aiden. "Tell me the truth, for once and for all. Are you and Isla involved in some sort of intimate relationship?"

Were they? Not *exactly*, but he also had every intention of being in one. He couldn't back away from her yet again. Not after last night. Not after he'd promised he'd do it her way.

Not when he was trying to earn the right to be with her. Prove how much he wanted her.

"I don't think that's any of your bus—"

"Yes or no, Aiden?"

Aiden felt a deep, unbearable weight settle on his chest. "Yes," he said, at last.

"And does Callum know about this relationship? Or have you lied to him and concealed it?"

His throat burned. "Callum doesn't know. And I have lied some."

"Then get out." Quinn pointed toward the door.

What?

"You're kicking me out of your house?" Aiden's brow furrowed.

"Yes. You're my brother. And that's the *only* reason I haven't punched you in the face. The only reason I haven't already called Callum and told him what's going on. He's been my best friend all my life."

"He's my friend, too, Quinn."

"Yes, then you should remember how another former friend destroyed him, Aiden. How Callum took you into his trust—one that he doesn't hand out lightly. You have put me in an impossible situation, in my own house, under my own roof. I can't control what you do, but I can control where you do it. Get out."

Even Mason seemed surprised by the forcefulness of Quinn's reaction, and he stepped back hesitantly.

"Right. Because I'm the villain here, aren't I?" Aiden shot Quinn a scathing look. "Always the villain. Oh, it's fine to let me *be* the villain when it's convenient. Or to let me suffer the weight of burdens that you don't want to bear. Then you can slip away and have your fairy tale with your nonprofit and your perfect wife and beautiful baby while I'm stuck slaving away at the job you didn't want."

"No one forced you into that job," Quinn said. "You just refuse to accept responsibility for the decisions you make that come back and bite you in the arse, rather than just admit that maybe you had no idea what you were doing. Or that you took too much upon yourself."

"*You* forced me into it." Aiden's tone was biting and loud. "You were constantly complaining that I never did enough. That I was forcing you to do too much. That I was *enjoying* my life too much while you were dealing with Mum and Dad and being too afraid to tell Elle, *for years*, that you loved her. Well, I'm not you, Quinn. When my brothers need my help, I do step up. And when I see a woman I want, I don't take years to decide whether she means enough to me to actually do something about it."

Quinn's fist was in his face before he could duck.

Aiden staggered, stars bursting in his vision. Pain flared in his jaw, sharp and immediate. He clenched his fists, his first instinct to hit back—but he didn't. Quinn had a right to be furious. Yet it didn't mean he'd just stand there and take it.

"Feel better?" Aiden spat, rubbing his jaw. "Or do you want another go at it?"

Quinn flexed his fingers, eyes burning. "If you weren't my brother, I'd break your fucking face."

Instinct took over, and he barreled forward, heading straight toward Quinn. Mason leaped in the way, grabbing him by the shoulders and pushing back. "Hold on, hold on, steady now."

Quinn flexed his hand, shaking it. "I want you out, Aiden. Now."

Footsteps sounded, then Elle hurried into the room, Tara on her hip. "What in the hell is going on out here?" she asked with a frazzled look as she reached Quinn's side. The sight of her, though, was enough to cool Aiden's temper. He pulled back from Mason, yanking himself free from his grip, then straightened his rumpled shirt. His cheek stung like hell.

"He's been fooling around with Isla, and I want him out," Quinn said, his face red.

"Oh." Elle grimaced and looked down at her bare feet. She didn't glance at Aiden, then set a hand on Quinn's forearm. "They *are* adults, Q."

Quinn scowled at her, studying her for a moment before his brows lifted. "You knew, didn't you? Oh my God. My own wife knew and didn't tell me."

This time, Elle met Aiden's eyes, and she gave him an apologetic look. "I just found out last night. I was going to say something, but it wasn't my place. And anyway, he's family, Q. I don't think we need to be kicking your brother out of our house."

Quinn's eyes narrowed on Aiden, his eyes hard. "He knows what he said. Knows what he's done. And don't expect me to keep your damn secrets."

The words hung between them, final and absolute. Quinn's face was harder than Aiden had ever seen it. But his hands were still shaking.

Then he turned and walked away.

"Happy with yourself?" Aiden muttered to Mason. "You see what happens when you don't keep your damn mouth shut?"

Mason had the decency to look chagrinned, at least. "We'll figure this out—"

"I don't need any more of your help. Not here. And not with the Ipolymer deal, either. I can't fire you because it would only cause me more issues that aren't worth it, but I won't be putting something so critical in the hands of someone I clearly can't trust." He nodded his head at Elle, then leaned over and gave his sweet niece a kiss on the cheek. "Thanks for your hospitality, Elle. I'll see you in London in a few weeks."

He fled out of the room before he could say anything else

he might regret. His jaw clenched, his stomach sick, acid burning in his throat. He'd had fights with Quinn before—plenty of them—but this time, he didn't feel so certain that he was in the right.

What he'd said to Quinn had been awful, even if it was true.

His temper had gotten the better of him, and now the mess he'd created had only gotten worse.

He packed quickly, regret churning with anger as he repeated his conversation with Quinn over and over again. None of it surprised him. He'd known his brother would be mad. Maybe not this mad—mad enough to kick him out of his house—but he couldn't entirely say he blamed him either.

A soft tap at the door drew his attention as he zipped his bag shut. "Come in," he called.

The door opened, and Isla stepped inside, closing the door behind her. Her eyes were filled with worry. They grew wider as they settled on his cheek, then she rushed toward him.

He folded her in his arms, holding her close. "I'm so sorry," she breathed into his chest.

"Don't be," he said, resting his chin against the top of her head. *God, she smells good. That sweet scent of her shampoo that was so strangely intoxicating. Her.* "They didn't kick you out, did they?"

"No, no, nothing like that. But I'm going to leave anyway. I can stay with Kyle—"

"You don't have to do that," Aiden said, pulling back and lifting her chin with his thumb and forefinger. "They love you."

"I'm so embarrassed," she admitted, tearing her gaze from him.

He forced her to look at him. "You have nothing to be embarrassed about. We hardly did anything, to begin with."

"I told Elle that. But I don't think that's what Mason and Quinn believe."

Beneath that mournful expression and the flush of pink on her cheeks, anger flickered in her eyes.

"I love them, but I'm not a fucking family secret," she muttered. "They don't get to decide what I do with my life."

Aiden traced a thumb along her cheekbone. "No, they don't."

"Good," she said, standing straighter. "Yet somehow, here we are. With everyone weighing in about what we're doing like it's their business."

"You're right. They shouldn't have a say."

She lifted her chin. "Then stop letting them."

He stared at her for one long, hard moment.

How had he reached this point? He'd relished his independence as a youth. In being the one who was different from the rest.

Until it had bitten him in the arse, and he'd found himself alone and the outcast of his family.

But what had trying to work his way back into their good graces gotten him? A miserable existence and an eighty-hour workweek.

And it had almost cost him Isla.

He exhaled slowly. "Done."

Something shifted in her eyes. Like he'd passed a test he hadn't even known he'd been taking. Maybe she didn't even know it'd been one. But the look in her eyes was a mixture of relief . . . and *want*. Happiness.

"I don't care what any of them think," Aiden said, then dropped a kiss to her lips. Although he wasn't sure exactly how or when it happened, Isla Scott had become everything he wanted. He couldn't imagine going another moment without claiming her.

I can't frame my answers around what Callum thinks either. "Even Callum. Fuck it. I want you, Isla. And I don't care who or what it costs me."

She slid her arms around his neck, then kissed him, eyes closing tightly. He returned her kiss, which was warm and sweet, filled with unfulfilled longing. Then he pulled away and traced his fingertips gently against her jaw. "I'm going to New York for a few days as I have a business deal I have to work on. I'd invite you, but I won't really be around to spend time with you. But the show goes to Paris, Tennessee this weekend, right?"

Isla nodded, giving him a curious look.

"Then I'll be there. Wherever you are, Isla. I'll be there."

26

ISLA

PARIS, TENNESSEE

As a parade of classic cars rumbled down the road, Isla scooted closer to Kyle on the picnic table bench, grinning at Tomas, who watched the cars with excitement in his eyes. This he didn't have to fake for the cameras. Ever since she'd known him, he'd loved classic cars, especially American ones.

"So, apparently, springtime is definitely the right time to come do a tour of Parises in the States, at least," Isla said with a grin to Tomas. She licked the barbecue sauce from her fingers. "I have a feeling we're going to the car show," she told Kyle.

"We are definitely going to the classic car show," Tomas said with an emphatic nod as he took a swig from his Pepsi.

"And cut, that's perfect," Boyd said from behind them. He approached with the camera crew. "How lucky was that shot?"

Isla elbowed Kyle. "Hand me a napkin, will you? I feel like I'm covered in barbecue sauce."

Kyle laughed and handed her a stack. "I think it's on your nose."

She tossed him a mock glare. "Don't make fun of me. It was *your* idea to eat barbecue for this part."

Boyd dropped into the seat beside Tomas and reached for a French fry from the tray in the center of the table. Whatever foul mood he'd been in last weekend had vanished. It helped that the festival they were attending in Paris, Tennessee, was a bigger affair, though. The World's Biggest Fish Fry was a week-long event, with daily happenings including a large carnival, rodeo, demolition derby, and bike and car show, among other things—not to mention lots and lots of fried catfish.

Isla wrinkled her nose at the thought. She hated catfish.

"So, what's the plan?" Tomas asked, rolling his shoulders back.

"Lunch for the crew, then we move to the car show. Today probably won't be too long of a day. Tomorrow, we'll do a bit more on the square, then do the carnival and rodeo at night. Monday's the country dance."

"Holy crap," Kyle breathed. He still wore athletic gear, having participated in the town's Hushpuppy 5K in the morning. "This Paris doesn't let up with the activities."

"It's because of the fish fry," Davy said, setting her clipboard on the table as she sat beside Isla. "Which is also why we're having to stay a few towns over."

"Speaking of accommodations, will Aiden be joining you tonight?" Tomas asked Isla with a smirk.

Boyd's gaze flicked between them intently.

A flutter of nerves crept up her belly. "Not tonight," she said with a breezy smile. "But maybe tomorrow."

At least, that was what Aiden had said. He'd promised, actually, to be here today when they'd last seen each other in Nashville—but he'd called her after she'd arrived at the hotel the night before and told her the negotiations for his deal had run long and would be continuing today.

Which meant he'd had to delay his flight out of New York, and he'd be here tomorrow.

She hoped.

This time had been different. They'd texted often and called each other a few times. Almost like a real relationship.

Her fingers curled around her phone in her lap. No new messages. He said he'd be here today. He promised.

She forced herself to set it aside before anyone noticed.

But it bothered her that he wasn't here when he'd said he would be. Deeply. Maybe it wouldn't if it hadn't been the first time they'd planned to get together since making things more out in the open. But it was the first time, and he was already pushing plans off with her for work.

Any awkwardness she might have felt in discussing Aiden with Tomas, though, quickly vanished as he reached across the table and squeezed her hand. "That's too bad. I was looking forward to him overreacting while watching our scenes again."

Scoundrel. She rolled her eyes and pulled her hand back. He was a shameless flirt, really. Maybe she'd never realized it before, but now, without the cloud of attraction hanging over her, or the easy forgiveness that came with dating, Tomas's flaws were easier to spot. "Oh stop," she said. "You didn't have to take the scene that far, either. We might be adding some personal drama to the show, but it's not suddenly the *Real Housewives of Paris.*"

Boyd laughed. "Maybe we should reframe it that way in editing. I cut the first episode this week, and Antony really loved the personal segments. He wants more of those."

"What he loves is Isla and Tomas." Davy leaned over and looked at Kyle. "You too, Kyle. He thinks the dynamic between the three of you is fantastic. And he's interested in having you shoot more travel shows for us like this."

Isla tore her gaze from her friend. Davy knew she'd only done this as a one-time favor. That she couldn't continue taking time away from *La Hacienda* to pursue this.

Is she really suggesting I keep doing this?

"I'd be game," Tomas said with a broad smile.

Of course you would be. His entire personality seemed to exist to annoy her right now. But she was also being hard on him. If she was still acting, a steady work opportunity like this would have been thrilling.

"Wouldn't that be fun?" she said noncommittally.

"I have loads of ideas for other places we could do a series out of, like Paris," Davy gushed, either oblivious or ignoring the lack of enthusiasm in Isla's tone. "Do you think you would be interested, Kyle?"

He laughed, then flicked a cautious look at Isla. "I don't really know if I'm much of an actor. Or influencer, reality TV guy—whatever this is. But, sure, why not? Could be dope."

Isla's lips pursed, and she wished she had the telepathic ability to tell Kyle *no, not you, too.*

"One step at a time. We have to see how this one is received. We premier in three weeks, and Antony upped the spending on advertising," Boyd said, then stretched back in his seat and stood. "But I think it's going to be brilliant. I have a good feeling about it." He winked at Isla, then moved away toward the rest of the crew.

"So, Aiden really is coming this weekend?" Davy asked with obvious interest. She leaned closer to Isla. "I thought you said it was *nothing.*"

Because it was nothing. When Davy and she had talked before Isla and Aiden had left for Nashville, it had been nothing.

But now he'd promised to be here. For *her.* For *them.*

"We're just talking at this point," Isla said with a shrug even though a wave of guilt went through her. If Tomas weren't here, maybe she could be more open about it.

Then again, hadn't she told Aiden that she was tired of

being treated like a secret? That they had nothing to hide or be ashamed of?

"Just hooking up with a billionaire?" Tomas said with a gleam in his eyes. "Sounds like you're moving up in the world, Isla."

The way he said it made her whole relationship with Aiden feel cheap. Dirty.

She shot him a sharp look. "What's it to you, Tomas?"

"Nothing at all." He lowered his sunglasses and shrugged. "I think it's great. What does Callum think of it? They're best friends, aren't they? I remember you dragged me to the Camdens' enormous estate for Boxing Day a few years ago."

Dragged. She shook her head, irritated with his comment for more than one reason. "It's none of his business. Or yours." She stood and lifted the tray of food. With as much gracefulness as she could muster climbing over the bench, she moved away and found a nearby trash can. The contents of the tray slid into the trash with a *thunk,* then she banged the tray on the pile on top of the trash can with more force than she'd intended.

Dammit.

She shouldn't let Tomas get under her skin. He set her teeth on edge, though, and it didn't help that she was already feeling insecure about this whole thing with Aiden. But then mentioning Callum was even worse because she still hadn't worked up the nerve to tell him anything.

Instead, she'd been ignoring his phone calls. Barely responding to his texts.

Dreading that Quinn might tell him first—or someone else would—all while trying to figure out the best way to tell him that wouldn't make him feel like he'd been the last person to find out.

Which, considering the number of people who knew now, he might end up being.

She'd asked Aiden to allow her to be the one to tell him, both because it would probably come better from her but also because she owed him the conversation. He was her brother. And she *hated* the fact that Aiden was already having issues with Quinn and Mason because of her. Of course, she was angrier with Quinn for punching Aiden and kicking him out, but that didn't keep her from feeling like all of this was her fault.

Even Aiden hadn't been sure if being with her was worth this trouble.

But she had pushed.

Isla fanned her burning face with her hand, then started away, heading down the sidewalk that framed the main square of Paris, Tennessee. The whole town screamed *small town* but not in the way the other ones had. This one was bigger, with more boutiques and a larger population. Ironically, the Eiffel Tower here also seemed to reflect that. At seventy feet, it was larger than the other two had been and a true-to-scale replica. *Kinda funny how the various Eiffel Towers all seemed to match the towns like that.*

She was grateful for the larger square right now, though, because she needed some space.

Tomas, however, didn't seem to get the hint. "Isla." His voice rang out behind her.

She sighed, considering just walking faster—but they still had to work together. Act like a couple. *Thanks, Callum.*

Tomas jogged to catch up with her, and for a split second, she caught sight of the guy she'd had a thing for. His smile. His energy. And, of course, he was easy on the eyes.

Yet . . . *nothing.* She'd moved on so completely that the image was gone in a flash.

"Hey, I'm sorry," Tomas said as he slowed and stopped in front of her.

She raised a brow. "About what?"

He crossed his arms, with a more serious look than she'd previously seen. "I clearly upset you, Isla. And don't pretend I didn't." He leaned toward her. "I don't know if you remember, but we once used to be friends and lovers. I know you a little."

"Tomas—"

He straightened. "I didn't come to try to reclaim you, if that's what you're worried about. Genuinely. Callum mentioned the project, and I thought, *well, that'd be brilliant—* seeing you again. Working with you was always fun, too. But I have to admit, you took me by surprise, Isla. You're not quite the same girl I knew in London."

I really don't need Tomas, of all people, psychoanalyzing me.

She started back down the sidewalk again without waiting for him to follow. He did, though, as she'd suspected he might. "How's that?" she asked, her voice dry and humorless.

"Well, it's that, right there. You seem a bit muted. As though you've lost your spark. Still comes out from time to time. Like when you had a few drinks in you at that wine festival. Or when you look at Aiden Camden."

She studied his profile, trying to make sense of what he'd said.

Lost her spark?

"I haven't lost any spark, thank you very much."

"I'm not saying it as an insult, but let's be honest, you were always a bit cheeky. Wild. Endlessly laughing and smiling. You draw everyone to you like a moth to the flame. God, I remember that disastrous trip we took to Dover. You had the whole car in stitches despite everything."

"Maybe there's not as much to laugh about now." Her throat tightened despite her protests.

"Or maybe something has happened that's taken the sparkle out of your eyes. The Isla I knew would have been bursting at the seams if someone suggested a job like Davy did. And considering the man in your life doesn't seem to be related to the problem, I can't help but ask, is there something I can do to help?"

She flinched and looked away, letting her gaze drift over the faceless mannequins in the shop windows. The smell of coffee from cafés mixed with the grease of hot frying oil from the restaurants busy for lunch turned her stomach.

Had she really lost her spark? Or had she been pretending with her over-the-top behavior at times? It couldn't be denied that she worked hard at *La Hacienda*. There was rarely any space to "step away" from her job. Even on the days off—which were rare—she never truly switched off.

And she was lonely. Her world had gotten so much smaller, with few friends and no time to make new ones. And no Callum, either. She hadn't realized how much she relied on her big brother's company until he was across the Atlantic, several time zones away.

But all of that would be easier, on some level, if she still had a creative outlet. She hadn't noticed it while she'd been fixing up the inn because that took care of that need. But now?

She had no place to be and feel *herself*.

At last, she said softly, "It's not *one* thing, Tomas. Nothing that can be fixed either."

"Well, can I offer a listening ear?" Tomas gave her a genuine smile. "I have it on good authority you used to like me. And I'm still just as boring and uninteresting as I used to be— haven't changed a bit, actually—so maybe you'll find that I'm still happy to listen to anything on your mind."

She gave him a closer look. Maybe he was right. Perhaps he was the same—and she'd changed.

Maybe, if she went back in time now, the person she was now would find him just as annoying and irritating as she had then.

But why?

Her life hadn't been *bad*. She'd had so much fun with Mum and Callum when they'd renovated the inn. Watching it all come together had been thrilling. And then when the first guests had arrived, the rush had been incredible. For months, she'd buzzed on that energy, loving every moment of it. Even working with and getting to know Sergio better had been entertaining and refreshing.

So, what had happened? Where had she become dissatisfied? And why?

"I don't know what it is, if I'm honest. If I can even find the right words to talk about it." She sighed, then gave him a grateful smile. "But I do appreciate your offer to listen."

"The offer stands. I'm happy to help whenever you need it, Isla. Honestly." Tomas leaned over and set his arm around her shoulder, hugging her toward him. "And even though you don't seem to be enjoying this show, I've been having fun. It's good seeing you again."

She smirked. "Even when I'm being dull and sparkless?"

He ruffled the top of her head. "Even then. You're still a force to be reckoned with. Look, even the production team is dying to have you back. Between you and me, Boyd told me he thinks Antony would get behind more of these. He's really liked what he's seen."

Tomas probably didn't mean to add to her stress, and he couldn't know how much she didn't want to hear that.

"I don't know if there will be too much more of this in my

future. I have an obligation to the inn in Costa Rica—and to my family."

"I know. But it's still nice to be wanted, isn't it? Better that than to be rejected and told never mind."

She grimaced, Aiden's face flashing in her mind.

He was coming, wasn't he? This wasn't just another way to put her off?

You have to trust.

But trust was so hard, especially when the past few weeks had been filled with so much uncertainty.

The worst part wasn't just that he'd delayed their plans. It was that she wasn't even sure she had the right to be upset about it.

They hadn't defined their relationship, but that was mostly her own fault, and she couldn't let that bother her. She'd told Aiden she didn't need things defined. And he'd said that he wanted her. Whatever the cost.

So why did this sting so much?

Somehow Aiden had become the person she wanted to call with her news—both good and bad. The first person she told anything to.

But deep down, she was also aware that he wasn't completely free, and maybe never would be. Even if she became his girlfriend, he'd never be the type of man she could call at any time of the day and expect him to answer her.

He was already committed to something else. A role that would take precedence . . . even to her.

"I think I'm going to pop in that boutique. See if I can't find a good hat. It's awfully bright today," Isla said, heading for the first store that looked like it had women's clothing.

Tomas seemed to sense that she was done talking and nodded, leaving some space between them. "Remember what I said. Anytime you need to talk, I'm right here."

"Thanks," she called over her shoulder.

He meant well. And, in some ways, it was good that he'd followed her, offering an olive branch. She felt strangely better about *him* now. Like they'd settled something from the past she hadn't realized needed addressing.

On the other hand, she felt worse about other things.

". . . it's still nice to be wanted, isn't it? Better that than to be rejected and told never mind."

Her heart squeezed hard, then she pushed the echo of Tomas's words away and headed into the shop.

27

AIDEN

NEW YORK CITY, NEW YORK

AIDEN SLID the thick stack of paperwork into a case, then checked his mobile.

Dammit.

He was already heading out later for the airport than he wanted to be.

Worse still, Isla hadn't called the night before. And the tone of her texts had shifted since he'd messaged her to let her know he wouldn't be able to leave yet again. Almost as though Lola somehow knew he had plans for the weekend, she and her team had insisted on meeting all day yesterday and then this morning to finish reviewing a few items.

Instead of spending the weekend with the only woman he wanted, he'd spent it across a boardroom table from his ex, going over numbers and facts and figures until a migraine pounded at his temples, and his eyes burned with exhaustion.

He downed the rest of the coffee he'd grabbed this morning, wrinkling his nose, and glanced at Lola. "This has been produc-tive. Thanks for your time this morning," he said, as though somehow *she* was the one doing him a favor.

Lola stretched her shoulders back, graceful in her tailored dress as she stood. "I'll walk you to the lobby."

It was the last thing he wanted, but everything in the past few days had been an exercise in patience. They were so close to the finish line on the Ipolymer deal that now he had to be wise. He wasn't here for himself—but for the company. "Thank you," he said with a curt smile as he nodded his goodbyes to her team.

He held the door to the office open for her, and they went through it, walking side by side. When he'd taken this job back from Mason earlier in the week, he'd been filled with regret and hesitation. Working with Lola was a challenge he hadn't relished.

Yet she'd been on her best behavior. The whole thing had gone more smoothly than expected, with their every exchange polite.

Or maybe it was easier now because of Isla. Any hold Lola had on him before was now gone, evaporated completely. That included her ability to get under his skin as easily, too. Each time he checked his phone and found a waiting message from Isla, it brought a feeling of eagerness that he hadn't felt in ages.

"You see?" Lola said as they arrived at the lift and pressed the button for it. "We're capable of working together. We make a great team, Aiden. No need to send Mason."

Discussing the deal out of the office and away from others didn't feel entirely safe. He gave her a polite smile as the lift *dinged*. "I'm glad of it."

She followed him inside the lift, then selected the button for the lobby. "Where are you heading now?"

"The airport. I have a flight to Nashville that leaves in an hour and forty-five minutes." Hopefully, traffic in the city wouldn't be as brutal on a Sunday morning.

"Oh, I love Nashville. It's a fun town. Are you visiting Quinn?"

The thought of his brother made Aiden's fingers curl into his palms. "No." He didn't particularly want to expand on the subject, but he added, "There's a film production I've invested in. I'm going to check on it."

"Oh, the one with Isla Scott?" Lola gave him a knowing look.

What in the hell? How did she know about it?

She caught his expression and smiled. "We still have a lot of mutuals, Aiden. Don't forget, my father is friendly with Frank Scott. They golf together and go to the same tournaments. He saw him at the Masters last week and mentioned Isla was filming something you'd funded. So I asked Callum about it when I called to RSVP for their party. Frank invited us when we were in Georgia."

His pulse speeded. *Called Callum.*

Holy fuck.

The speed with which the lift dropped to the lobby made him dizzy—or was that Lola's words? His mouth dried as the lift slowed and stopped, the doors opening.

"Yes," he said, forcing a calm he didn't feel. "That's what we were meeting about in Vegas." He left the lift, then turned to face her in the lobby.

"I assumed," she said with a catlike smile. "So I told Callum about how I'd run into you *both* there. Funny, he seemed to think you hadn't seen each other."

Oh shite.

He shrugged it off, pretending he couldn't hear his pulse in his ears. "I've barely seen Callum the last few weeks or been in London."

"Yes, he did say that." Then Lola crossed her arms. "But, you know, I got to thinking about how the whole thing just looked . . . *off*. So I did a little digging of my own. Did you know that Las Vegas marriage records are open to the public, Aiden?"

He stiffened, his grip on his bag tighter now.

Bloody. Fucking. Hell.

His eyes bored into hers, and the look of smug satisfaction made his blood boil with fury.

"I guess you aren't *completely* opposed to marrying, after all." Her voice hardened.

"That's my private business," Aiden snapped coldly.

She tilted her head. "You'd think her own brother would know—"

"Don't you dare tell me you shared that information."

Her lips pursed. "Don't worry, Aiden, your sordid little secret is safe with me. For now." She took a step closer. "Because it is sordid, isn't it? The head of Camden Enterprises marries a floozy *actress* in what can only have been a *charming* Vegas ceremony. Prenup? Doubtful. Sounds like a man who makes sound decisions. Not to mention you're clearly screwing your best friend's sister. Trustworthy lot."

"What do you want, Lola?" Sweat formed on the back of his neck.

She shrugged. "To humiliate you, Aiden, the way you've humiliated me. But the truth is, it's not worth it. You had your chance . . . *chances* to keep me, and you threw me away. You chose an *actress* over me. You're a fool. I thought I still loved you, but you clearly don't return those feelings, and right now, I can't say I'm sorry."

His mind raced for the right response.

No matter what he said, he might piss her off further. If he told her the marriage was fake and meaningless, that would only hurt Her because he'd denied her that when they had been in a relationship. And it might hurt Isla, somehow, if it got back to her.

But telling Lola that he *had* moved on? That he'd found someone who he genuinely cared about and interested him? That was just as dangerous.

"I don't know what you want me to say here," he said at last, feeling foolish and unprepared. She'd thrown this at him in a well-planned, conniving sneak attack.

"I guess there's really nothing to say. Anyway, the person I feel sorry for here is Callum. Maybe Isla a little, too, because she's probably infatuated. Doesn't know how easily your affection can turn to cold disinterest. When it comes down to it, you're incapable of genuine *anything*. Clearly not friendship or love. You're just going to break her heart—like you did mine—and lose your best friend in the process."

She stepped back, letting her guard down for a moment. She broke eye contact and blinked quickly as though tears threatened. "But don't think I won't get a good laugh when this all blows up in your face, Aiden, because I will. And you deserve everything that's coming to you. It turns out I don't need to destroy you, Aiden. You'll do that on your own."

"Lola—" he started, but she turned and strode away, heels clicking in the vast, empty lobby.

He palmed his face, trying to think. If he went after her and tried to fix this, he'd miss his flight to Nashville.

Maybe there wasn't anything to fix.

But the fact that she knew left him unsettled. Deeply.

Somehow, the ripple effect of this kept widening, stretching into places and moments he hadn't expected. Like with Quinn.

The ground beneath him felt shakier than ever.

End it. Own your mistakes with Callum.

Get ahold of this before it destroys everything.

Clicking through his mobile, he tapped on a text thread between Isla and him. He was about to type up another message about how he wouldn't make it today when he paused, glancing up at a selfie she'd sent the night before of her in front of an old Austin Healy, like the one his father owned and taken them for drives in on warm summer nights when they were children.

The fact that she'd remembered had made him smile.

She wasn't just another woman.

She was . . . *her*. *The woman*. The only thing his heart wanted.

Closing the text, he clicked over to a ride-share app and opened it instead, then requested a drive to the airport.

Lola was wrong.

He'd never hurt Isla. He wouldn't just protect her, he'd choose her. Every damn time.

Because that was what Isla deserved. Even if he didn't know how to approach talking to Callum. Even if their marriage was hanging over his head like a cloud—something they still needed to figure out how to deal with now that they'd decided to be together—he'd stick by his choice.

Isla Scott was his.

28

———

ISLA

If Isla dreaded one thing, it was being stuck in the air, suspended by a swing and spun in a circle.

She squeezed her eyes shut as the carnival swings slowed, starting their descent to the ground. This had been Boyd's idea —he'd thought it would make a fantastic martini shot—but now all she wanted to do was hurl.

Roller coasters she could handle. Spinning—nope.

Grinding her teeth, she gripped the chains of the swing and waited for the ride to still. She blinked, the neon lights somehow less charming than when she'd been strolling through the carnival with Tomas and Kyle earlier. The sweet aroma of cotton candy mixed with buttery popcorn and oil for funnel cakes and deep-fried Oreos—all of which they'd sampled while shooting various scenes.

By now, her stomach felt like a sickly mess, and she needed water. Not sweet tea. Not soda. Not beer. Just plain old water.

As soon as she was able, she unlatched herself from the swing and jumped out, grateful for the firm ground under her feet.

Kyle came up to her and took her by the elbow. "You okay? I looked back while we were on those swings, and it looked like you were going to be sick."

"I feel like I'm going to be sick, but it'll pass. I don't love things that spin," she said with a grimace.

They made their way out with Tomas, then found the crew standing nearby. "That was a fantastic shot," Boyd said with a smile. "Perfect way to end this segment. Give your equipment over to Tim, then you're free to go. We'll be sticking around to get some more B-roll for another hour or so."

Davy sidled up to Isla. "If you hang around, maybe we can hang out for a bit? It could be fun."

Isla gave her a reluctant smile. She didn't want to be a killjoy, but she also knew Davy was just trying to make her feel better. Aiden hadn't shown up last night, saying he'd catch a flight out of New York this morning.

And now? The entire day had passed, and he still hadn't arrived.

So much for him being where she was.

Tomorrow was already the start of a new workweek.

"Thanks, but I think I'm going to turn in early. Get some sleep."

Davy's eyes were sympathetic. She gave Isla a tight hug. "Listen," she said in a low voice. "Don't let any guy become the reason you're happy or sad. They should add to it, not make or break it."

Is that what I'm giving the impression of doing?

Letting Aiden control my happiness?

Isla didn't answer but squeezed her back, then pulled away. "You sticking around?" she asked Kyle.

He nodded. "But I can walk you back to the van if you want," Kyle offered.

"Nope, I'm good." She winked at him. He'd bumped into

some college friends while they'd been filming earlier, and she wasn't surprised he was staying—this was only about two hours from his hometown, after all. "Have fun at the carnival."

She left her equipment with Tim, then grabbed her purse from one of the production assistants. Weaving her way through the carnival grounds, she let herself slip into the noise and the throng.

Davy was wrong—wasn't she? Isla wasn't so fixated on Aiden that she was letting him control her happiness. Sure, she was bummed out right now, but she had a right to be. Once again, he'd shut them down before they'd had a chance.

As though he knew she'd been thinking of him, her phone buzzed in her purse. She lifted it to her ear. "Aiden?"

"Hello, beautiful," he said, a smile to his tone.

Despite her irritation, a flutter went through her stomach. "If you think compliments are going to get you off the hook, you're sorely mistaken, Mr. Camden."

"I must be in trouble if you're being so formal. That's too bad. You look so delicious under the glow of that neon ice cream sign."

She whirled around, scanning the fairgrounds for Aiden. Her pulse quickened. "Are you here?"

"Yeah, right over here. By the kissing booth."

She frowned, searching the signs. *Nothing*.

But he had to be here if he'd seen her standing by the ice cream booth.

"Where?" she asked, peering closer at the signs.

"Look for the giant stuffed tigers in the dart booth. I'm just past the haze of orange."

Her lips curled in a smile as she hunted for him. Leave it to Aiden to turn this into a game. Then she saw the dart booth and the tigers. And just a few feet away . . . *him*.

Isla's heart throbbed.

Dammit but that man was freaking gorgeous.

He wore jeans and a gray Henley, one hand in his back pocket, his stance relaxed. The other hand held a single sheet of white paper. As their eyes connected, a slow, seductive smile played at his lips, and she hung up the call, walking toward him with deliberate ease. *Don't be overly eager.*

As she drew closer, she saw that he'd scribbled something on the paper in his bold script: *Kissing Booth.*

She raised a brow, hiding a smile. "So now I have to pay for a kiss?"

He leaned toward her slightly, lowering the paper. "You don't have to pay for what's already yours."

Oh . . . man. How did he do this to her so easily? She hadn't even touched him yet, and somehow, he'd already managed to raise goose bumps on her skin, a flush of pleasure going through her.

"That's either very smooth or wildly presumptuous."

Aiden stepped closer and hooked a finger through the belt loop of her jeans, tugging her nearer. "I was going for both."

"Ah, I see." She tilted her head, setting her hand gently on his chest. "You like to live dangerously, Aiden Camden."

"Sometimes."

She grinned. "Lucky for you, I like dangerous men."

His hands slid into the back pockets of her jeans, and he tugged her closer still. "I'm trying to be a safe man for you, Miss Skye." His lips grazed her jawline, then the soft spot of her neck, just below her earlobe.

She wanted nothing more than to sink into his arms and relax into his realness. He was late, but he was *here.* That counted for something. For a lot, really. But the last time she'd been hurt about him not calling and texting, she'd let him off the hook easily. Maybe too easily. Perhaps she needed to be clearer this time.

Drawing a sharp breath, she stepped back and set her hands on his shoulders. "So, I guess you didn't catch that flight this morning? Did your phone stop working, too?"

"No. Well, the phone did die at one point, but that was partially because I missed my flight and then was on it for a while. I tried to get a standby on commercial and then I decided I'd had enough obstacles trying to get to you. So, I called the firm that handles our jet and then had to wait for the chartered flight out here. And then I had to drive from Nashville. I would have flown to a regional airport, but it wasn't much closer, and the rental car selection was better in Nashville."

She searched his face for a moment, her brain trying to put all the versions of him together. He was the wealthy CEO, the boy she'd known since childhood, son of an earl, military officer. In the blink of an eye, he could go from formal attire and look just as natural and suave in jeans and a T-shirt.

And he just chartered a flight on his private jet to get to me.

Maybe that deserved a kiss.

Her lips twisted for a moment. Or maybe she was looking for a reason to let him off easily.

She stepped back, guilt sloshing in her stomach as he quietly folded the kissing booth sign and slipped it into his pocket. "Did the negotiations go well?" she asked, forcing distance between them—not only physically, but with their discussion. She didn't want him to suffer, but the last two days hadn't felt safe—not even close.

"They . . ." Aiden sighed, then glanced around the carnival. "They were fine. Boring. Tedious. But they went well enough. Were you leaving?"

She nodded. "Boyd cut us out early and told us to enjoy the carnival."

"If you're tired, we can go," he said gently.

"No, it's fine. You just got here. I don't want to pull you away from something fun and interesting."

"The fun and interesting part of this carnival is standing right in front of me."

She swallowed, reminded of what Tomas had said the day before. "Really? Tomas practically called me boring yesterday."

"What does Tomas know? He was foolish enough to let you go, wasn't he? The man's judgment is clearly flawed." He glanced around the booths. "What's good to eat here? I'm starved."

"Depends. Do you like your food slick with oil or covered in powdered sugar?"

Aiden's lips twitched, and he gave her a wicked side-eye. "If you're trying to tempt me to think about something other than food, you've succeeded."

"Oh, stop." She elbowed him in the ribs. "I'm serious. It's carnival food. The options either come with the potential for a heart attack or diabetes—there is no in between. Don't make it sexual. You keep talking a big talk anyway and then don't put out." Then because she couldn't resist, she added, "Of course, maybe you prefer hot dogs. Maybe a good kielbasa or Polish sausage?"

He laughed and caught her by the waist, tucking her back against him. "I'll show you a sausage, you lunatic woman."

She squealed with laughter, squirming to get away from him, but he held her fast, the scruff of his jaw nuzzling her cheek. "You won't be proving anything. You, sir, have not yet earned your way back into my pants."

"Oh no?" Aiden released her and slipped his hand into hers. "What do I need to do? Win you a stuffed tiger? Offer myself as the victim at a dunking booth? Buy you some candy floss?"

"Mmm, I'll take all of that and more." She gave him an

exaggerated wink, thrilled by the feel of his hand in hers. It felt so normal. So natural. So real.

"What does Tomas know? He was foolish enough to let you go, wasn't he? The man's judgment is clearly flawed."

Truthfully, Aiden knew her better than most people, except Davy. He was also trying to look past their obstacles, and even though it took longer for him to get here, it was only due to circumstance, not choice.

Maybe I am being too hard on him.

"Did you ever imagine this? Us?"

He gave her a sidelong glance, his eyes both gentle and filled with a frankness that warmed her. "I imagined you. In fact, I've been imagining you quite a bit since that night at the guesthouse. But us? Not quite."

A thrill passed through her at his words, and she felt herself growing wet.

"So how did you imagine me?" She traced her thumb against his, awed by how much larger his hands were than hers —his practically engulfed hers. But she'd never compared her hands to Aiden's. Never walked anywhere with him, holding his hand.

Like a couple.

"Untouchable. A very bad idea."

She slowed, hesitation curling through her. "And now?"

"Still a bad idea." He raised her hand and kissed the back of it. "But worth every obstacle."

She couldn't quite bring herself to meet his gaze, but a warmth filtered through her body, surrounding her heart and peeling back some of her walls.

They came to a food booth and stopped. "Don't laugh, but I'm going to get a hot dog. Only because the other options sound too sweet. Do you want anything?"

"Water. I've had so much sugar today that I feel like I can't get enough of it."

"You may be the cheapest date I've ever taken out." He grinned and ordered.

Once he'd paid, she turned her back to the booth and leaned against it, looking up at him. "Is that what this is? A date?"

"Well, as close to one as we've ever been on. If you don't count our night of obliterated, drunken vows."

"Still hard to believe we skipped the dating part and went straight toward lifelong commitment," she said with a shake of her head. *Or that, for now, Aiden is still technically my husband.*

That thought did something funny to her.

Just like when he'd called her his wife in Nashville. "So what do you want to do after this, husbee?"

He choked out a laugh. "Husbee?"

"Yeah, I don't know. Husband sounded too stiff. Though maybe that would suit you more."

"Whatever you want, *wife.*"

God, why do I like the sound of that so much?

It was completely ridiculous. She wasn't looking to get married, and they were barely in a relationship or whatever this was.

Yet the word wrapped around her, grounding her with a sense of security and comfort. Of something that she couldn't name. Something—someone—that was hers. Of belonging.

"I think maybe I'll take a tiger after all," she said, accepting a water bottle from the man working the register. "I've heard— supposedly—Aiden Camden is a crack shot with a rifle. At least, that's how he used to brag when he was in the military. Before he became a stuffed suit. Maybe he's lost his skills now, though. It has been years since he probably even held a gun."

He took the paper food tray with a hot dog, French fries, and soda and balanced it on one hand as he walked toward the condiment table. "You make me sound ancient. But fine—you're on. I'll win you a stuffed tiger. Your curse will be having to carry it around this damned carnival."

"Like I said, you're awfully cocky for someone who's a lot of talk." Isla looked around for a game booth with rifles. Finding one, she tugged him by the elbow toward it, a girlish feeling of enthusiasm starting to move toward her.

"Hang on, impatient wife. Your husband is eating."

She threw her head back and laughed. "I'm going to have fun with these nicknames until our divorce."

"*Annulment,*" Aiden said, then took a bite of hot dog. "Meaning technically, the whole thing never happened."

She frowned, not loving the way that sounded. Of course, they needed the annulment, but it all *had* happened. Maybe they could erase it on paper, but otherwise? That was impossible.

That night in Vegas had changed both of their lives.

Sobering, she looked away. A group of teenagers passed, laughing and shrieking. Despite the cold, the girls wore high crop tops, and the boys—pimple-faced and lanky boys clutched their hands or had their arms around them. Maybe not *so* innocent but free. Without anything really weighing them down.

"I still haven't told Callum yet." She cleared her throat. "Honestly, I think I held off because I wasn't sure if there would be anything *to* tell. But now that you're here, we have to think of a way to tell him."

"Maybe we can tell him together at the party next weekend. In person. I don't want you to have to do it alone, Isla." Aiden sipped through his straw. "But I can't say I've been the best at answering his texts recently."

"Neither have I." Isla stared down at her feet, twisting the toe of her shoe into the dusty ground.

And now, after all this time, it almost felt ridiculous to be so concerned. What's done in Vegas was just that. And it could be annulled.

Why have we made such a big deal out of that? Considering a relationship . . . okay, that merited a conversation. But if Aiden was Callum's best friend, then that suggested he was someone Callum thought highly of, right? Had they potentially made a mountain out of a molehill?

Maybe it was because they'd felt the need to lie in the first place. Owning those lies would be a tough admission. And considering that she'd been so angry with Callum after the whole Tomas situation, she hadn't wanted to yield the moral high ground.

Not to mention the fact that she *needed* to talk to Callum about how unhappy she was at the inn.

But now, the longer they waited to tell him, the more it felt like they were making a mess of something that could be solved with a simple conversation. Yet avoidance was easier. Less intrusive to the tenuous happiness she'd found with Aiden after weeks of angst.

Aiden reached for her, then kissed the top of her head. "Why don't we get that tiger?"

She nodded, pushing away the worries she'd allowed to creep into that moment. Aiden finished his hot dog, ate a few fries, then tossed his tray. He wiped the salt from his fingertips, then took her hand once again and headed toward the game booth.

"Two," he said, reaching for a few bills.

"That's twenty bucks," the teenager at the booth said, pointing at two seats, worn with age. "You get three shots. If you hit the target three times, you win."

Aiden raised his brows. "For a stuffed tiger?" He handed over the money, though.

"See, I could very quickly become an expensive date," Isla teased. "Though I thought you only needed one try."

"One is for me. The other is for you." Aiden pointed at one seat. "You first."

"I don't know how to do this," she protested but sat regardless.

"It's easy," Aiden leaned in close to her from behind, setting her hand on the trigger. "Look down the sight, pull the trigger."

"Mmm . . . nothing like sexy mansplaining." She let her cheek brush against his jawline, though, and her body tingled at his nearness. "If I win, you owe me a real date."

"And if you lose?" He hadn't moved, and the scent of his cologne made her want to lean over and kiss the smirk off his lips.

"Same thing."

"You know how to drive a hard bargain, Miss Skye. Maybe I'll drag you into my office with me next time I need to do business negotiations."

She leaned away from him, smiling as she looked down the sights. "Oh yeah?" Her finger tightened against the trigger.

He pressed closer still. "Of course, if I had you in my office, I'd sit you on my desk like on that coffee table in the guesthouse. Except this time, it would be my mouth doing the work."

The rifle went off, and the teenager at the booth ducked.

Aiden chuckled. "Nice aim."

"Asshole. You made me miss."

"Why?" His voice was silky in her ear. "Because I said I'm dying to eat you out?"

Another miss.

She glared at him. "You are a brat." She took the last shot as he laughed, this time at least hitting the paper target.

As he sat for his turn, she sidled up beside him. "I'd return the favor," she said. "But then I wouldn't get a tiger."

"Fine. But if I win, I get a kiss." Aiden took the rifle in his hands, with practiced ease.

Goddamn.

"And if you lose?"

His eyes glittered. *"Same thing."* He held her gaze. "But not here. Come back to the hotel with me."

She gulped a breath. "That won't fix everything."

Aiden's face relaxed, just slightly, as though he'd believed she'd say no. "This isn't me fixing. This is me choosing you. Every second. Every messy, unplanned, impossible second. And hoping you choose me back."

Every inch of her wanted him. Wanted to kiss him. Wanted to throw her arms around him right then and there and forget that she'd spent the past two days questioning everything.

"You're making it really hard not to, Aiden. You keep saying all the right things, even on the heels of actions that worry me. How am I supposed to resist when you give me lines like that?"

"Don't. Not tonight."

She felt herself slipping, falling further under his spell. So she stepped back and crossed her arms, giving him a daring look. "Win me the damn tiger, and we'll see."

Three shots later, she picked a tiger from the shelf.

29

———

ISLA

Leave it to Aiden to get the nicest room in the hotel where the production crew was staying.

Isla hesitated at the door to his suite, hand gripping the backpack she'd packed as an overnight bag. After he'd driven them back, she'd gone to her room to shower and change, and packed some things to stay in his room with him.

Like she was showing up for sex, not for him. And she hated that.

The moment was gone, the energy of their playful banter and chemistry at the carnival no longer clouding her judgment.

Yet, wasn't this exactly what she'd asked him not to do? Overthinking hadn't gotten them anywhere so far.

She knocked before she could chicken out.

Aiden let her in, and she stepped through to the modestly sized room. Probably nothing like he was used to. He'd flown here in a private jet, after all. She grinned, setting her bag down. "Well, it's no Vegas luxury suite," she teased nervously. The bad joke didn't help her feel any more at ease.

He gave her a curious look. "Is that what you want? Because Vegas is only a short flight away."

"No," she said, then looked around the room for a place to sit. A small seating area was just past the foyer. She moved past him and sat on the sofa. "I'm not sure what I'm doing here."

His expression softened, and he sat beside her. "If you weren't filming tomorrow, I'd whisk you away to France tonight—take you to the original Paris. Spend the week with you there, doing whatever we want to do. No rules. No agenda."

No agenda.

And . . . then, it all clicked.

"That sounds perfect," she admitted, resting against him. She slipped her hand into his, feeling instantly grounded by his touch. "Better than anything I've done in . . . two years."

Swallowing hard, she fought the wave of tears that threatened her.

Aiden's hand tightened against hers. "What's wrong?"

Isla blinked back tears. "Dammit." She sniffed. "This is going to ruin my makeup." Pulling away, she reached for a nearby tissue and tugged it free from the box.

He turned her to face him, searching her eyes. "Did I say something—"

"Yes. But don't worry, it's nothing bad. Not really. I'm just so tired, Aiden. So tired of living on a schedule. Every single day of my life over the past few years has been filled with plans, places to be, a to-do list. It's always *what's on the agenda.*"

She dabbed her lashes, not wanting to smudge the mascara she'd carefully applied before coming over. "When I left London almost two years ago to go to Elle and Quinn's wedding, I never imagined that it would be for good."

Hell, she'd been in the middle of auditions for a show. She'd gotten the part, only to turn it down.

"I appreciate what Callum did in buying *La Hacienda*—I

really do—it's just that I went from one extreme to another. A life where I never knew what my next job would be, where I was barely scraping by, despite the wishes of my father. Where I would wake up and do whatever the hell I wanted, free of responsibility."

She gulped a breath, appreciative of his watchful gaze. How silently he listened.

Then she said, "And, instantly, it was like . . . I grew up." She gave a sad shrug. "I know it sounds stupid, but every single day of my life since then has been relentlessly planned. It's never *what do I want to do today?* It's always *what do I have to do today?* I'm tired, creatively spent, and I feel like I've hopped on a hamster wheel for a life I'm not even sure I want."

Aiden stood, then went over to the mini fridge and pulled out two small bottles of wine—the sort that came in four packs with screw tops. He uncapped them, then brought one to her. "It doesn't sound stupid. I understand more than you might believe."

She accepted the wine from him with a sad smile. "I know. I know you have it worse. I'm no CEO of a company I didn't want." With a shaky breath, she swallowed some white zinfandel. "Nice touch, by the way."

He chuckled. "It was all I could find at the store nearby." He sat beside her again. "But you're wrong. You are the CEO of your company. Callum may be bankrolling the inn for you, but you're the one on the ground doing the everyday work. It's grueling, soul-sucking, and unending. I get it."

Aiden took a sip and set the bottle down on the table beside him. "The first few years I was at Camden Enterprises were more of an adjustment to me than any of my training in the army. I thew myself into it—much the same way you did—and found myself burned out and ready to set the place on fire after about a year."

Isla frowned and scanned his eyes. She'd gotten the impression that they were in similar places in their lives—neither completely satisfied with their jobs. But that didn't really sound like it was the case for Aiden. Or maybe she hadn't been listening. He *had* felt like that. But didn't now? "So, what stopped you?"

"Besides the fact that I didn't want to serve a life sentence for arson?" Aiden drew a slow breath, and a muscle flexed in his jaw.

She didn't get the feeling he talked about this much. If at all.

"Quitting would have been the same as failing. And I realized that if I failed, I'd rather fail trying than by quitting." Aiden leaned back against the seat, studying her. "So I do understand, Isla. This isn't my dream life. It's not the worst job in the world either. The perks and money are nice—I'm not going to lie. It's just all a bit empty. For me."

"But you're going to keep doing it, right? You won't quit?"

He shook his head. "Not unless the board asks me to. Which, at the rate I'm going, who knows. That possibility always seems to loom over my head, real or imagined."

She looked away, wrapping her hand around the bottle. "I think about quitting. Every day. But then it seems crazy because I don't know what I'd be doing instead. And if I don't want the inn, then what was the whole point of Callum saving it?"

"I think you discount the fact that maybe Callum didn't entirely save it for you alone. He thought about your mum a good deal. Not to mention that he may not admit the fact that he needed it for himself, but that doesn't mean it wasn't true."

Talking about her brother brought another wave of guilt. Because Aiden *did* know Callum well. He was his friend. He might be able to give her better insight because of that—yet it felt wrong to be here, like they were forming a relationship that could supersede that.

Like she was stealing her brother's friend away.

Ugh. Why is this all so complicated?

"I just can't see myself living such a scheduled life forever. I know it appeals to so many people, but it's like poison to me. Even my trip to Vegas—which was supposed to be fun—had been planned with every single thing scheduled. I'm so tired of doing what's expected. You know the only thing that's unexpected in my life right now? You."

He raised a brow. "So, I'm the pool boy?"

She wrinkled her nose, then climbed closer to him, straddling his lap to face him. "No, that's not what I meant."

His hands slid onto her thighs gently. "I'm not offended. People get together for all sorts of reasons. Boredom included."

"So, I'm bored and you're looking for meaning to your empty life?" She quirked a brow.

One hand smoothed around the curve of her ass, tugging her closer. "Could be. And if it is—what's wrong with that?"

She set her arms around his neck. "Seems like we'd be risking an awful lot if it's just about scratching those itches, Aiden."

Aiden searched her eyes. "I never said it was *just* about that. Not for me, anyway. For me, it's that you've consumed my every thought, Isla Scott."

He kissed her forehead, and her eyes fluttered close, her throat tightening at his words.

His lips lowered to her eyelids, and he kissed one, then the other. "You're the brightest spot in my life, yes, but not because there's nothing else."

With a deft but gentle touch, he lifted his hands to her face, cupping her head gently, his hands digging into the hair just behind her ears. "I've seen what else is out there, and *nothing* comes close to making me feel what I feel when I'm with you."

She held his gaze, mesmerized, unable to speak, her body slowly coming alive at his every touch, with each soft kiss.

His mouth hovered near the corner of hers, lips grazing, nuzzling. "You're my past and my present, and I want you to be in my future."

A soft brush of his lips across hers, then he pulled back, searching her gaze. "So badly that I'm here, without a single fucking clue what I'm doing, because even if it means less sleep and more on my *agenda*, I'll do whatever it takes to be with you in whatever way you'll have me right now."

She had to give it to him. Aiden had a way with words that made her completely want to melt into his arms. She kissed him, her heart speeding as she released a tiny moan because *this* was what she'd been dreaming of and denying herself. The taste of him, the way his pliant lips sank against hers, molding, fitting perfectly to her own.

As though he'd been at the edge of his patience too, their kiss deepened instantly. He broke the kiss to tug her shirt from her body, then pulled his own away, and they came back together, a tangle of mouths and tongues and arms around each other.

Every inch of her burned for him, and she gasped for breath. "I want you," she breathed, reaching back and unsnapping her bra. "Right now, Aiden. No more waiting."

He swallowed hard as his eyes focused on her breasts. Then his hands were there, cupping her firmly as his mouth skimmed her neck, then lowered to one nipple. The feel of his mouth against her hardened her nipples to tight peaks, and she groaned, head dropping back as his tongue made a slow circle over her, then drew her nipple fully into his mouth.

The slow pull into his mouth, the soft lashing of his tongue, then his teeth set her blood to a boil. She ground against the hard bulge of his cock between her legs, her clit pulsing with need.

"Please, Aiden. We can spend the whole night fucking, but I want you now. Hard and fast," she managed. "I need your cock inside me."

"Fuck, I love it when you talk like that." He moved his mouth to the other nipple. "But you're going to have to be patient, my greedy little wife."

As though he knew the way that term turned her on.

Two can play at that game.

She reached down for the buttons of his jeans. She unclasped it, pushing her hand down to graze the head of his cock.

She'd been smart enough to wear a skirt, which meant she didn't have to climb off him to slide her panties to the side and press the wetness between her legs against him. And that close, that *bare* was like lava. She made a slow circle against him.

"Absolute fucking torture," he breathed.

"I want what I want," she teased back, grinding harder against him. She lifted herself enough to tug the zipper down, then pulled him fully free.

"Isla," he warned, holding her gaze.

"Aiden," she returned, pushing the head of his cock against her slick entrance.

He groaned, then drew her up into his strong arms, standing. Her legs wrapped around his waist as she steadied herself against him, the absence of him making her ache with need.

"I want you, Isla. I want to fuck you," he said, carrying her over to the bed. "But we started something last week, and I have every intention of finishing it. I've been daydreaming of you ever since. And it starts with stripping you naked."

He set her down gently and then pulled her panties and

skirt off. She stared as he removed his own clothes, her heart hammering.

God, he was so beautiful.

It was almost unfair for him to be this good-looking.

His well-muscled arms and chest were chiseled and defined, broad shoulders tapering to a narrow waist. He clearly groomed, too, and his hard, thick cock seemed impossibly big.

"How do you have time to look like a supermodel while working so much?" she managed, her mouth drying as he climbed onto the bed.

He knelt between her legs. "Running and lifting weights are the only hobbies I have left. The only place where I can set my mind straight."

"Lucky me," she said with a grin. "I fully appreciate the benefits of those hobbies."

He chuckled, then pushed her knees farther apart. Kissing her inner thigh, he traced his way closer to her clit, and she trembled with anticipation. "I've been dying to taste you," he murmured, his breath hot against the sensitive spot. "And watching you come was the highlight of my year, Isla. But this time, I want to feel you against my tongue when you do."

A shallow moan hitched from her throat as his mouth sank against her clit.

"Oh yes," she managed, gripping the comforter below her.

He made a slow circle around her clit with his tongue, sending an electric pulse shooting hard through her, her thighs clamping hard around his head. He pulled away, just slightly. "You're absolutely delicious," he growled, before returning his mouth to her.

He's fucking incredible with his mouth.

Her body started to quiver, and as she grew even wetter, he pushed his fingers inside her, satisfying—enough for now—the aching need she had to be filled by him.

"Aiden," she panted. "I need—"

She couldn't finish the statement. The waves of pleasure grew stronger, and the pressure of his tongue against her clit increased.

"More," she managed, then gripped his hair, holding him tight against her. Her hips rose to meet his kisses, an intense feeling bubbling within her, threatening to boil over with explosive force.

"Come for me, Isla," he demanded, his fingers pushing deeply inside her.

She buckled, then her orgasm ripped free, tearing through her with force as she moaned loudly. Her ears rang, waves of pleasure tingling down to her toes as she fell slack against the bed.

He waited until she'd completely stilled, then lifted his head to meet her eyes. "Good?"

"Mm-hmm," she moaned. Then she drew a deep breath, a wild, feral feeling coming over her.

"Come here," she said, beckoning him farther onto the bed.

He climbed toward her, then she pounced, flattening him against the mattress. She straddled him, dragging her swollen clit over his hard length as she held his gaze. "But I want more." Then she sank down on him in one fluid motion, taking him deep inside her. *Hard.*

Their groans were both loud and breathless. The feeling of him buried deep inside her made her pant, and she pulled back, holding his gaze.

Aiden was inside her.

Fully, deeply.

Inside.

"Oh God, Aiden," she whispered.

Their mouths came together once again, the kiss deep and

fast as she rocked her body against him, nothing slow and lingering as they fucked.

Right now, she just needed him. The feel of his cock buried deeply inside her, his hips pushing against hers, connecting with every grind of her body.

"I love fucking you," she whispered, pulling away just enough to slide up and down his shaft.

"You're a fucking goddess, Isla."

She sank her lips into his neck, biting and sucking the skin there. She'd never wanted to mark anyone so much in her life. *Claim him.*

All for me.

"I'm yours. And you're mine." She ground harder still, a wave of pleasure beginning to swell to a crest.

"Yours, baby," he growled back, bucking harder inside her.

Oh my God.

She rode each wave of pleasure that came with him, filling her to the hilt, then withdrawing slightly but never fully pulling out.

Deep. Intense. Intimate.

The way this had been since the second they'd gotten involved.

His hands gripped her hips tighter. "Isla, I'm going to fucking come inside you if we don't change positions."

"I can't," she gasped, grinding harder, her thighs clenching against him. She was so close to coming again. "Just come inside me."

"Are you sure?" he asked.

"Yes." She returned her lips to his for another hot, frenzied kiss. His fingers dug into the bare skin around her waist, and he rocked her against him as a loud moan left her. Then she came with a cry, her body releasing as her core clenched around his shaft.

"Fuck," he groaned, then she felt his cock pulse hard, his cum filling her.

After a few moments, they both stilled, panting against each other.

Her heart continued to pound, the sweet relief of the orgasm still flickering through her with gentle warmth. Maybe not how she'd intended their first time together to be—*at all*—but still *fucking incredible*.

"Are we okay?" he asked in a deep voice against her. "I know we hadn't discussed it, but I did test after my last relationship, and I'm clean. But I came—"

She kissed him lightly. "Same. It's fine. I've been on the pill for years." She rested her head against him. "I hope it was okay. I didn't mean to stress you out."

"Isla, that was amazing. You're amazing. We can have sex however you want to have sex—bare, with a condom, with or without foreplay. I may even let you tie me up if you're a good girl. Anything. I'm happy to oblige." He dragged his lips to her temple and kissed her.

She nipped his earlobe. "You mean you want to do it again?"

"I wouldn't be a particularly good pool boy if I wasn't willing, ready, and able. Your wish is my command, darling wife."

She laughed, then climbed off his lap, reaching for tissues. "Pool boy or genie?"

"Both. I take it I earned my way back?" Aiden took the tissues from her, then gently wiped the mess he'd made. Her throat tightened at the gesture, and she sent her hands on his shoulders, her heart squeezing in her chest.

Aiden, who'd gone to blows with his brother over her.

Who would sacrifice his friendship with Callum for her.

Who'd kept his word, after all.

Who knew her well—*had known me for years*—and still wanted her.

He'd never know how much that meant to her.

She nodded, not wanting to get teary-eyed at his comment about earning his way back. "You did. And you have me . . . *husband*." She kissed his forehead, closing her eyes.

Maybe neither of them knew what they were getting into, but maybe it didn't matter.

But one thing she knew for certain—she was falling in love with Aiden Camden.

30

———

AIDEN

THE SHOWER WOKE Aiden from a deep sleep, and he rolled onto his back, blinking in the darkness of the bedroom. A faint flow of light around the edges of the black-out curtains told him it was morning but a glance at his watch confirmed it. Already six.

Call time was at seven for Isla—no wonder she was up.

But the fact that she'd been able to get out of bed without waking him surprised him.

He couldn't remember the last time he'd slept so soundly that the slightest movement didn't rouse him. Not since leaving the military, that was for certain.

Then again, they'd been up several times during the night. *Up. Down. Sideways.*

He smiled to himself, stretching a hand over the tangled sheets, which still smelled like her. Gorgeous, *delicious* Isla. He'd promised to kiss every square inch of her beautiful body, and he probably had.

No way out of this now. No parachute or back-out plan or excuses.

His friendship with Callum would be changed forever.

Yet . . . the more he thought of the idea, the more comfortable he became with it. After all, *why not?* Why couldn't he be the man in Isla's life? Callum would have to accept someone in that role, so why not Aiden?

Yes, maybe when he was younger his reputation hadn't been stellar, but so much of that had been blown out of proportion compared to his stiffer, more reserved brothers. They'd all thought he was a reckless rebel. Daring to blow off Oxford and his father's carefully constructed plan for the military. When he'd shown up with his first tattoo—the family crest on the back of one calf—and his father had seen it on holiday, he'd never seen his father so enraged.

Of course, Father hadn't said a word when Quinn tattooed an "L" on his skin as a symbol of his wife.

Yes, maybe he'd dated more women than his brothers—who seemed to *only* go from one serious relationship to another—but he hadn't been a playboy or cruel to women, either. And that was when he'd been younger, anyway. Callum knew that. He knew that Aiden's relationship with Lola had ended over her behavior, not because of something sordid.

But it was one thing to tell Callum he'd decided to date Isla. Quite another to tell him they'd also gotten married, and now the annulment they'd discussed hadn't come back up again.

Were they tabling that for now? Neither of them had really mentioned *staying* married, but last night, they called each other husband and wife.

And that felt so . . . unexpectedly *right*.

Because he wanted to keep her.

The thought of her being with anyone else was unacceptable.

Aiden pushed the memory away and climbed out of bed.

Straightening, he went toward the bathroom and cracked a door.

Steam streamed out, and he smiled, pushing the door open a bit wider at the sight of Isla on the other side of the see-through glass enclosure of the shower. She was covered in suds, hands kneading into her hair, eyes closed as she leaned back into the stream of water.

Fuck me. As if he didn't already have one too many memories of her beautiful naked body seared into his mind. He wanted to capture the image and tuck it somewhere he could pull out and admire whenever he wanted.

Already naked, he crossed toward the door and pulled it open. "Morning, beautiful." Stepping inside the shower with her, he came up behind her, tugging her back against his chest.

Why is being with her the easiest, most natural thing in the world?

She sank back against him, the suds of her shampoo running down his chest. "Hi, sleepy." Her voice was roughened by sleep, and she shivered against his chest. "You're cold."

"Compared to this scalding water you have on, lava would be cold."

She laughed, shrugging. "My shower, my rules."

Aiden's forearm crossed over her fucking amazing tits, one hand settling on her shoulder. The other hand slid around her waist, then slipped down between her legs. "Technically, it's *my* shower." His fingertip traced a slow circle around her clit, then traced lower still. "So *my* rules."

She released a throaty moan. "I have to be at call—"

"In an hour. We have plenty of time for at least one or two rounds together." Aiden pushed her gently toward the tiled wall, then turned her to face him so her back rested against it.

Gliding his hands down her, he knelt on the hard floor, hands grazing her hips. The water splashed softly against them from here, misting them both with warmth. Leaning forward, he pressed a kiss at her belly, just below her navel, watching her thighs quiver with anticipation.

"I'll need time for breakfast," she breathed, her hands dropping back against the wall as she steadied herself.

"You need some unscheduled moments, darling. To relax and be taken care of." His lips grazed lower.

"I know, but—"

He lifted one leg carefully, setting her thigh on his shoulder. Slowly, he traced slow nips and kisses to the inside of her thigh. "When was the last time you just let go and did something that didn't fit with the day's agenda? You need this. Let me give it to you."

Her fingers tangled into his hair as he parted her better for his view. Glistening, slick pussy, swollen clit that begged to be kissed. "You taste fucking delicious," he said, sinking his lips against her.

"God, Aiden," she whispered as his tongue traced around her clit. His fingers slipped inside her tight pussy, stroking her as her body relaxed against him.

The water striking against the hard surface of the tile filled the air, broken only by the soft groans of pleasure that curled from her throat, her thighs beginning to clench around his head. Her hands tightened against his hair, and he increased the pressure of his kisses.

Her breath came in short, shallow pants now. "Oh . . . yes."

Then her thighs clenched tight, her body beginning to peak. He held her hips as she tilted them against him, rocking with a steady rhythm that matched his strokes. Then she gave a strangled gasp, and she cried out, her pussy clenching around his fingers.

He waited until she'd stilled, then gave one last kiss and stood. "Good?" he asked, looking down at her.

She gave him a heavy-lidded gaze and nodded. "Mm-hmm."

"Good. Now turn around. Hands on the wall and spread your legs for me, sweetheart."

With a sumptuous, flirty grin, she did as he said. His cock, hard and ready for her, found her slick entrance immediately, then he pushed inside her. "God, I love fucking you."

"I love it, Aiden," she whispered in a throaty moan. "I love you."

He almost stilled. Almost stumbled.

As though realizing her mistake, Isla turned her face, eyes widening.

His heart squeezed, cutting him off from oxygen, then he leaned over and caught her lips in a kiss. "I love you, too."

And he meant it. Dammit, but he meant it.

Did it matter that they'd only been fooling around for a few weeks?

No.

This wasn't just some girl he'd met in Vegas.

It was Isla.

Maybe he'd been half in love with her all along and hadn't realized it. Or perhaps it had just taken him this long to see that she was everything he'd ever wanted. Either way, when it was someone like this, who he *knew,* who he only wanted to protect and be there for, who he was willing to risk *everything* for . . . it wasn't hard to fall in love.

And I know with absolute certainty that I've never felt this before.

His movements increased as he pounded into her, every ounce the emotion speeding through him.

God, I love this woman.

Then he came, pouring inside her, her body quivering against his.

With a ragged breath, he kissed her, heart slamming into his ribs.

He pulled out, and she turned, slipping into his arms.

For a few minutes, they stood there in the stream of the water, saying nothing. Nothing more *needed* to be said right now, really. This impossible love had taken them both by surprise, but that didn't make it any less real.

At last, he kissed the top of her head. "I'm going to wash up quickly, then leave you to finish."

She nodded, though still unable to speak.

He washed quickly, then grabbed a towel and left the bathroom.

Wrapping the towel around his waist, he heard his mobile ringing at the bedside table. Going over to it, he saw Callum's name flash across the screen.

Aiden ran a hand through his wet scalp, staring at the screen.

You fucking coward.

He should answer.

He needed to answer.

But Isla and I agreed to do this together.

Callum didn't usually call. He texted. He might actually need something.

The call was about to go to voicemail.

Aiden swiped the call to answer and lifted the mobile. "Callum," he said with a friendly tone.

"Hey mate, you doing all right? I called a couple of times."

Aiden cleared his throat, moving to his suitcase to look for a fresh change of clothes. "Yeah. Good. Bit full up at the moment. Just got out of the shower."

"Right, I know—the acquisition. Listen, I won't keep you, but you haven't heard from Isla, have you? I've been trying to get in touch with her for days, and she won't return my calls or messages."

Aiden froze, his gaze flicking toward the bathroom door, which remained shut. "Isla?"

"I was hoping since you've been a part of that production, you might know what she's up to. I'm starting to worry she's angry enough that she's skipping the party this weekend. She hasn't really responded too much to Liddy, either, which is unusual. They get on pretty well."

"I told you, Callum. You should just fly over wherever she's shooting and beg for forgiveness," Liddy said from the background, her voice distant. "You go to the airport right now, and you could still probably catch a flight out there today."

Bollocks. No, absolutely not. "Hi, Liddy," Aiden said as casually as possible.

"She made me turn the speaker on," Callum explained.

That wasn't a bad idea—he needed to get dressed. Aiden turned his own mobile on speaker.

"Tell him I'm working from home today—in case he's worried. I'm not slacking just because he's holed up in New York," Liddy said.

Aiden pulled on a pair of boxer briefs, scrambling to think. He didn't want to outright lie to Callum, but what could he say? He *was* supposed to be in New York. He'd told Lola he couldn't meet again until late this afternoon just to make sure he had the morning with Isla. Liddy knew how important the acquisition was. His dropping everything to come to the middle of Tennessee to check on a production that didn't need him present would make no sense.

"I haven't seen her," he said at last, a stab of guilt going through him. The words came out too smoothly. Too practiced. And they didn't just taste like betrayal. They tasted like cowardice.

He's going to hate me for this if he ever finds out.

"That's it. I'm calling her to find out where she is. You can be at the airport in an hour, babe," Liddy said in a determined tone.

"No, I don't think that's necessary, I can—"

Isla's mobile rang loudly from the other side of the bed.

Fuck!

Aiden dove for it, scrambling to silence it, heart pounding.

Then he whirled back toward his own mobile, which lay face-up on the bed. He whisked it up, turning the speaker off.

The door to the bathroom opened, and Isla stepped out, a towel wrapped tightly around her. "Was that my ph—"

Aiden lifted a finger to his lips in desperation to silence her, then turned back to the mobile.

Please don't have heard that. Please.

"Went to voicemail," Liddy said.

"Callum?" he managed, his throat feeling strangled.

Silence.

"What are you doing?" Liddy asked Callum, a tone of surprise in her voice. "Why'd you take my phone?"

Then Isla's phone rang once again.

Aiden's eyes flew to Isla's. He held a hand out to her, then hit the mute button on his mobile. "It's Callum. He heard your phone ring beside me."

"Oh my God," she gasped, eyes flaring with worry.

"Aiden?" Callum's tone was measured. Deadly calm. "Is Isla there with you?"

What the fuck was he supposed to do here?

He wanted to tell Callum, not have him find out like this.

Unmuting his mobile and putting the speaker on once again so Isla could hear, Aiden drew a deep breath.

"What in the hell is going on?"

Isla bolted toward him, then snatched the mobile out of his

hands. "All right. Stop. Yes, I'm hanging out with Aiden for breakfast this morning."

Oh, bloody hell. This just keeps getting worse.

Lying about things wouldn't help.

"Really? Then why did Aiden say he had no idea what you might be up to? And why the fuck is Aiden wherever the hell you are rather than in New York?" The questions came out as furious demands.

"Because I saw you calling, and I told him I wasn't ready to talk to you," Isla said calmly, sitting on the edge of the bed and hugging the towel to her chest. Her poise, given the situation, was incredible, which Aiden imagined had to do with her acting skills.

Her answer silenced Callum for a moment.

Aiden finished dressing, watching her with caution. Isla didn't look at him, her gaze firmly fixed on her free hand.

"Isn't it six thirty in the morning there?" Callum asked at last.

"Yes, but call's at seven. Look, Cal, the truth is that I'm still pretty angry with the way you went over my head and interfered with Tomas. You had no right to go digging up an old boyfriend or to interfere with my production in any way. If I had ever done anything like this to your professional life, you would have been justifiably furious with me."

"I told him all this, by the way," Liddy sang in the background.

"Isla, look, I don't know how else to apologize. You're right; I shouldn't have interfered. I freely admit that I was in the wrong, and if I could go back and do it all again, I wouldn't repeat that mistake. But how long are you going to continue to hold on to that?"

Isla sighed. "It's not that easy when I'm the one who has to pretend I'm my ex's girlfriend for several days. Each time I work, it's just another reminder of how little you trust in my decisions. I'm fully capable of choosing what's best for me—and for our family—without your permission, Callum."

Aiden sank into a chair opposite the bed and leaned forward, clasping his hands.

She was right, of course. And if they weren't hiding something massively more important, Isla was justified in making Callum grovel.

But now? This would just be another fissure in an already strained relationship.

And I feel so much worse because of my part in all this.

"I'm sorry," Callum said at last. "I won't ever interfere like that again, I promise. Am I still picking you up from the airport on Wednesday?"

"I'd like that," Isla said. "I'm still going to be there."

"Good. Hand me back to Aiden, will you?"

Isla gave him a smile that spoke of relief and brought the mobile back to Aiden. Aiden took it, his stomach clenched in a tight knot, and turned the speaker off. "Yes?"

"Sorry, mate. I didn't mean to get testy. I know I asked you to watch over Isla. I just want everything to be settled by the party, you know? No lingering stress."

"It's fine," Aiden said, the words settling in his gut like rocks. "I'll see you in a few days." He hung up, staring at the mobile. "We have to tell him."

"I know," Isla said in a quiet voice.

"He's not going to forgive me. Not after that." A simple truth. He wasn't trying to hurt Isla—she'd made the decision to deepen the deception, and the fact was that he'd already decided before this that his loyalty lie with her. He'd made that decision when he'd agreed to be with her.

Isla released a slow exhale, then met his gaze. "I couldn't tell him, Aiden. Not like this. He won't understand or realize how much I care about you. He won't think of this as anything but the two of us fooling around behind his back."

"Then what is this, Isla? Because we talked about not having a plan, taking this day by day, which is the definition of fooling around, really. But I'm falling in love with you in ways I didn't think were possible."

Isla held his gaze for a few beats longer, her gaze unreadable, then stood abruptly. "I can't talk about this right now, I have to get ready for call."

She dressed quickly, and Aiden watched her in silence, unable to form the right words.

He didn't want to demand anything from her because she'd said she didn't want commitment.

Maybe that was what had even drawn her to him. *But we're married. Legally.* And maybe, in his heart, that was what he wanted.

But this situation was spinning wildly out of control, threatening every important aspect of his life. He felt like a man standing on a frozen lake, cracks spidering beneath his feet—and no clue when the ice would give way.

It would. The ice would give way.

He couldn't stop it.

But when it did—would he lose her, too?

31

ISLA

LIDDY: *Are you and Aiden hooking up?*

The text message had come in while she'd been filming, which gave Isla an excuse not to answer for a while. But now that they had wrapped for the day, she had to figure out what to do about this.

If Liddy was this suspicious, then Callum probably was—even if he hadn't said anything. He couldn't believe her brother would be so obtuse that his mind wouldn't go there.

Unless he just entirely trusts that Aiden would never cross that line.

She sank onto a park bench at Eiffel Tower Park beside Davy, watching the sun setting. Boyd had decided they had enough scheduled filming for the day and let them wrap early. The entire production crew would be heading to the country dance—this time, for some fun—though Boyd had hinted the camera operator might get some candid footage.

And that all would have sounded exciting—if Aiden was still in town. But he'd left the hotel shortly after she had and gone to the airport.

"What's wrong?" Davy asked, studying her face. "You seemed pretty happy this morning."

Isla rested her head against Davy's shoulder, taking a few moments to think about what to say. Everyone knew, somehow, that Aiden had arrived last night—even though most of them hadn't seen him.

They also all understood that Isla and Aiden were dating. Of course, Kyle had already known about it—since Nashville— and he'd simply winked and said, *"I kinda figured that one out."*

So really, outside of their parents, Callum, and Liddy—and Aiden's brother Logan, who wouldn't care—this wasn't a secret anymore.

They were just intentionally lying to Callum.

Or really, I'm lying to him. Because Isla was 99 percent sure Aiden would have told Callum the truth this morning if not for her.

"Do you remember in high school when Megan started dating Blair's brother?" Isla asked, instead of answering the question.

Davy furrowed her brow. "Yeah."

"Blair didn't get angry. Didn't threaten to punch Megan. She was happy—excited, even. Kept talking about how they were going to be sisters."

"Okay, yeah, but what's your point?"

Isla sighed and sat straighter. "My point is that women don't do this crap to each other. If their friends date their siblings, they're usually cheering for them. I just don't get what the big deal is. Why are men such morons about this sort of thing? Why is it such a huge deal if you date your brother's best friend?"

Davy leaned down and plucked a dandelion from the grass in front of them, blowing soft gusts of air at the globe of feathered seeds. The seeds took flight, dancing in front of them as

Davy said, "Lots of reasons. To begin with, women think about the fairy tale of having a best friend that becomes a real sister, while men think about the fact that their best friend is now fucking their sister—and they don't want to think about *anyone* doing that. Or really think of that."

"I guess that's true."

"It also depends on the brother. In your case, Callum is rather protective. He's the definition of a protective older brother in the dictionary, actually."

"You're lucky you're an only child."

Davy shook her head and gripped her hand. "I have you. I haven't thanked you enough for what you're doing for me here, Isla. You gave me the idea, went to bat for me with Aiden over the financing, and rearranged your whole life to film with me." She gave her a sad smile. "It's almost like those days we spent in London eating curry takeaway and ramen are finally paying off. Especially given Antony is considering extending the series." Davy's eyes misted with tears.

Pressure tightened around Isla's chest. "You know I can't do any more of these, right? I have to return to my life, Davy. To the inn. This has been fun—the martini shot to my own career as an actress—but I've moved on to other things."

"I know, but you don't really want to run an inn for the rest of your life, do you?"

"I don't know. I don't hate it. I think I've just felt burned out." Isla lifted her gaze at the towering structure in the distance. "And all these trips to Paris have been fun, but they don't really fit with the life I committed to. I gave Callum my word."

"Speaking of Callum—" Davy tilted her head. "Everything is all set for us to film in London at the party, right? Boyd already has the whole schedule laid out for the week, but I haven't gotten back the release paperwork I sent you to give to

Callum. I really need to get it back to Antony. We're sort of flying by the seat of our pants with this segment."

Oh . . . shit.

A deep, sinking feeling went through Isla.

Oh my God. How could she have forgotten? Davy had sent paperwork—the day Boyd had suggested the filming in London at the party—but Isla had procrastinated on it, not wanting to think of one more thing she needed to discuss with Callum. She'd seen the email in the hotel room in Arkansas, meant to forward it to Callum, and then Aiden had shown up . . .

And everything else had faded.

She'd totally, *completely* forgotten.

"I forgot," Isla whispered, barely able to move. She met Davy's eyes, the terribleness of it all crushing the oxygen from her lungs.

Davy stared at her with a mixture of alarm and shock. "What do you mean you forgot?"

"I forgot to ask Callum if we could film there. Forgot to tell him what Boyd had requested." She tried to steady herself, gripping the scarred wood of the bench. "I-I forgot about the whole damn segment in London."

"What?" Davy stood, her eyes going wide.

"I didn't mean to—"

"Isla! Are you kidding me? This is all supposed to be happening in five days!"

"I-I . . . why hasn't it come back up again?" Isla asked, brows lifting. "Why didn't you ask me for the paperwork sooner? I've had a lot on my mind, Davy."

"Are you joking right now? Your boyfriend problems shouldn't prevent you from being a competent professional. I sent you all the paperwork. Detailed paperwork that I took hours to draw up. I emailed everything that we'd come up with for timeline and the types of footage we'd need. All you had to do was run it by Callum and get his signature. You agreed to it."

Hurt enclosed around her heart, and she stood, not wanting to have to look up at her. "Yeah, well, maybe cut me a break for once, Davy. Because the last time I said yes to something for you, I was obliterated. Possibly drugged. And I still kept my word."

Davy flinched. "Are you suggesting I took advantage—"

"I'm suggesting I'm your friend. Which you know I am—because you just were thanking me two seconds ago. And I'm doing everything I can to help you. So maybe when I mess up, cut me a break for a fucking moment. I'm not just having *boyfriend problems*, as you call them. My whole life is in absolute crisis. I didn't just hook up with Aiden in Vegas—we got married. And the catastrophe to my life has been spreading ever since."

Davy's jaw dropped open. "You and Aiden are *married?*"

Isla crossed her arms, the wound from Davy's words still cutting her deeply. "Yeah. We're getting it annulled. I think. But yeah."

"Oh my God. What do you mean, *you think?*"

Isla held her breath.

What are we doing?

She and Aiden hadn't discussed the whole marriage thing. Yet calling each other husband and wife hadn't seemed strange. Not like a fetish. But *real*.

They needed to hash this out.

"I don't know. That's the plan. But yes, we're married. But we're also in a relationship now."

The two of them stared at each other in silence, the discomfort between them growing.

Then Davy blinked away tears. "Look. I'm not saying that you're not dealing with a lot right now, but this is my career.

You don't even want to be part of the show after this," she said, her voice wavering. "That's fine. But don't act like none of this matters just because your life is a mess. I know you don't care about this like I do, but it matters. To me. To my life."

Isla didn't answer, for the first time understanding her father's business advice, many years earlier, about not doing business with friends.

Isla looked at her best friend—the same girl who'd snuck her tequila at her twenty-first birthday party, who'd cried with her during Isla's first breakup, who'd slept in the hospital room chair the night Isla had gotten viral pneumonia and Callum had been out of town on a job.

Yet, at this moment, Isla felt like she was staring at a stranger across a fault line she hadn't even realized they'd crossed.

"I'll talk to Callum."

"And if he says no? At this point, it's going to really mess up our plans."

Something snapped inside Isla. Exhaustion from being held accountable for 'way too much that wasn't her fault, maybe. "Maybe then you shouldn't have made plans without important documents in hand, Davy. You've got to take responsibility, too. You can blame me all you want, but this one is on you. I saved your ass last time. Next time, don't confuse verbal agreements with commitment."

She walked away, anger and frustration rankling her. She didn't want to be fighting with Davy. They'd been best friends for so long.

But it wasn't fair, either.

She was putting Isla in an impossible situation.

Callum was going to *flip* at the idea of having a camera crew at his party, especially with so little warning. The guilt he'd been harboring because of everything with Tomas would probably be enough to help her convince him, even if she felt horrible for being so manipulative and using it against him.

But how could she go to her brother and say, *hey, I need a huge, intrusive favor* and also, *by the way, I've been sleeping with Aiden and lying to you?*

She wouldn't blame Callum for saying no to the film crew after feeling hurt and betrayed by Isla and Aiden. And that was exactly what would happen.

Which means I can't tell him about Aiden yet.

Or Liddy.

She wouldn't ask Callum's wife to lie to him. That wouldn't be fair. She loved her sister-in-law and considered her a friend —lying to her wouldn't be easy. Liddy would be hurt, and it would just make everything so much worse when they learned the truth.

Isla clenched her jaw, tears threatening her as she pulled her phone out. Her hand shook.

Then she texted Liddy.

Isla: *!!! Hilarious. Gross, no thank you.*

32

AIDEN

LONDON, ENGLAND

The CHAMPAGNE BOTTLE POPPED, and Aiden looked around the crowded boardroom at the smiling faces. He should feel happy. Proud even.

But the celebration just felt . . . empty.

He'd sat through enervating meetings Tuesday through Thursday, then caught an early-morning flight to London today —in time for Callum and Liddy's party tomorrow.

Days of bone-numbing weariness that had allowed him to close the deal with Ipolymer.

"To Aiden," James Swale, the chair of the board, said, raising his champagne glass.

The group in the boardroom toasted him and he gave a thin-lipped smile, avoiding most of the smiles and gazes directed at him. Mason was noticeably absent from the meeting —not that he was required to be here. But he should have been.

And not just because he oversaw a department.

But because he'd worked hard on this, too. Aiden had put him up to the task, Mason had gotten them over the toughest part, and then Aiden had closed the deal.

Without Mason, he might not even be here.

Aiden downed the champagne swiftly as the crowd in the room turned to relaxed mingling rather than a formal meeting. Within a few minutes, Aiden had let himself out of the room and headed toward his own office. All he wanted to do was go back to his house, call Isla, and crawl in bed.

"Aiden," Liddy called, following him.

Dammit. As much as he loved Liddy, he didn't really want to face her right now.

He turned and forced a smile he didn't feel. "You caught me," he joked. "I was hoping to escape without notice."

"Yeah, not likely. You're head of the company, so people notice when you're gone." Liddy grinned. Funny how much she looked like Elle right now. She'd lightened her hair color recently—which always seemed to be what distinguished the two the most. Their faces were like two different versions of the same flower.

"Is there something you needed?" he asked. "I'm looking forward to the party in a couple of days."

"No, well, sort of. I was hoping you might be able to take Callum out tomorrow for brunch, before the party. I know it sounds like a ridiculous favor, but he's been so stressed. I wouldn't normally go behind his back, but I think he's struggling with depression. He hasn't quite found his footing since he stopped working here. But between buying new investment properties and the fact that his parents are both going to be in the same room together this weekend—his dad got into town today, his mom arrived yesterday—plus all the drama with Isla, I think he could just use some time out with the guys. Grab a drink or something."

A lump formed in Aiden's throat. "You all don't have family get-togethers planned for tomorrow morning? I'm surprised."

"Ha—no. I was lucky that I could get Callum to agree to a post-elopement party. He was happy with the wedding just being us. You know how he is with his parents. But Quinn and Elle arrived yesterday, and I'm going out with our sisters for manis and makeup. Maybe you can plan something with the guys?"

"Leave it to me," Aiden said with a nod. Then because he couldn't help himself, he added, "There hasn't been *more* drama with Isla, has there?"

Liddy sighed, then nodded. "Yeah, and don't pretend you don't know about it. You can drop the act. Callum is fine with it now, though it took a few of us talking him down about it all."

Aiden froze, staring at her.

They know?

Why in the hell didn't Isla tell me?

Then again—he'd barely talked to her the past few days. He'd worked, swallowed some coffee, tea, and sandwiches, and slept. If the company jet hadn't been equipped with a shower, he would have raced for the one in his office upon arrival—not that he would have had time for it.

But still . . .

"And Callum's fine with it?" Aiden asked, voice strangled.

"Yeah, but like I said, I think it would help if you took him out."

Aiden ran a hand through his hair, relaxing slightly. "I thought he'd murder me, if I'm honest. I'm shocked Isla told you. We wanted to tell you together, especially because Callum has always been so protective of her and who she dates."

Liddy's brow furrowed with confusion. Then she inhaled a sharp gasp, her eyes growing wide. "Oh my God, are you and Isla dating?"

Fuck. A thousand miserable fucks. Aiden, you absolute wanker. How could you be so idiotic?

Redness crept up Liddy's neck as she continued to stare at him, disbelief and anger clouding her gaze. "My God, you *are!* Oh my God, Aiden. I knew it! I knew you two were sleeping together. I could tell from the phone call that you were both hiding something. And then you *lied. Both* of you."

"Liddy, I'm so sorry," Aiden said, reaching for her forearm.

She stepped out of his grasp. "You know, I don't even care that you're dating. Like, good for you. I love both of you, and I think you could make a fabulous couple, but why in the hell did you lie to us about it?"

"Christ, Liddy, I'm sorry. This whole thing has me absolutely gutted. But think about it. You've been there. You know what it's like to get involved with someone who might rock the boat and—"

"Don't you dare bring my personal history into this," Liddy said, crossing her arms. "This is not the same thing."

"But isn't it? Didn't you fall in love with Callum while lying to Elle and Quinn?"

Liddy's lips pursed, and she looked away.

God, if I lose this battle with Liddy, what hope do I have with Callum?

Isla is going to kill me before Callum gets a chance.

Then Liddy's expression suddenly softened, and she peered at Aiden. "Wait, are you saying you're in *love* with Isla?"

Aiden glanced around the hall, suddenly more aware than ever that they weren't entirely in a private space. It was after work hours and most of the people left were in the boardroom, but this wasn't just a casual conversation. He nodded. "Yes. I love her."

Liddy frowned. "When did you guys get together?"

This isn't going to sound good.

"Officially? A couple of weeks ago."

Liddy threw her hands up in the air and started to walk away. Then she turned and came back, jabbing a finger at him. "You're not in love. You're in lust. You're in those first glorious weeks of a relationship when the other person can do no wrong."

"I am in lust, absolutely. Not that I could ever admit that to Callum. But I also *love her*. I didn't just meet her two weeks ago, Liddy. I've spent a lifetime getting to know her."

He stepped closer. "She's smart. Quirky. Hilarious. You think Isla is a force to be reckoned with now? Try Isla at five, trying to keep up with all of us playing rugby. Or better yet, at ten, jamming herself into the sitting room sofa to play video games or watch horror movies that would give her nightmares all night—just to prove she was tough enough. I don't just know that her favorite color is pink, I know that it's because her grandmother died of breast cancer and that's why she often dyes her hair like that—to remember her. I held her hand at the funeral."

And maybe I didn't realize the way her tears back then broke me, but they did. God, the way she cried hurt my heart so much.

Taking a deep breath, he went on. "I know her favorite animals are tigers because she thinks they're her so-called *spirit animal*—except she would never use that term because she doesn't love it—and I know she can't decide if she's Costa Rican, or American, or English but swears perfectly three ways now."

His voice grew softer. "And she didn't have to tell me those things. I just knew them. I won't pretend I spent a lifetime pining after her because that's not what I'm saying. But maybe I never understood what I felt for her until I really saw her for the woman that she is. Not a sister I never had. Not my friend's sister. But a beautiful, spectacular woman whom I love."

Liddy looked away from him, her body rigid. Tears welled in her eyes, then she nodded. "You do love her." She paused, taking a deep breath. "I'm happy for you, Aiden, but I hate that you both lied to me—to us—about this. *That* I don't understand. And you can't expect me to lie to Callum about this."

"I'm not expecting you to. Maybe just to give us a chance to tell him? Together? I just got back today and haven't even seen Isla, so we'll tell him tomorrow."

Liddy rubbed her eyes. "I won't make any promises, Aiden. If it comes up, I'm not lying to him. He deserves better than that from me. Please don't cause drama at the only wedding celebration we're having with our friends and family."

That was fair. Liddy deserved a peaceful wedding celebration—not one filled with potential ugliness. He hated that she was worried about that at all. She didn't need that stress.

Aiden nodded. "I can't ask for anything more than that."

She walked away before he could say anything else.

Damn. He'd never seen Liddy so angry.

Not that he blamed her.

Deciding to abandon his bag in his office, Aiden left. He didn't want to be here another minute if he could avoid it. His bag would be here in the morning.

He called a car on his way to the lift—it would be there by the time he reached the building's lobby. These were the perks that had made the job so appealing, at first. Instant command.

But he'd sworn he'd never become like his father. Stiff. Detached. So busy working that he rarely made time for his family. He couldn't name a single hobby his father had maintained while he'd been growing up. He was always just working. Not that he was as ruthless as other businessmen around him—which, thank goodness, he hadn't been—but just wholly consumed by his work.

And now . . . with these lies to his closest friend, he felt as though he'd morphed into something else, too. God knew enough people saw him as a callous, unfeeling arsehole. His own brother had so little faith in him that when the time had come to choose between Callum and Aiden, he'd chosen Callum.

Mason, too.

It didn't matter what he did. How hard he'd tried to recoup his reputation or the countless hours he spent working. They all still saw him the same way—the unredeemable black sheep.

And he was so damn tired of trying.

Within minutes, the car picked him up from in front of the building, and he was on his way home, crawling through the London traffic. He pulled out his mobile, dreading the thought of telling Isla what he'd done.

God, what if I lose her, too? She'd said she loved him, but she was also the one who wanted a commitment-free relationship. To figure it out as they went. The risk felt more enormous than ever now that he was facing reality.

Thumbs hovering over his mobile, he tapped out a message.

Aiden: *Liddy knows about us. I fouled up and let it slip.*

The "Read" message popped up almost immediately, followed by dots showing she was typing.

With each passing second, Aiden felt the pressure around his chest increasing.

At last, the mobile buzzed in his hand.

Isla: *I'm on my way over.*

Bollocks.

What did that mean? Was she angry?

She was staying with Liddy and Callum. What if Liddy had already told Callum?

By the time he arrived at the terraced house he'd bought when he'd first become head of the company, nausea gripped him thoroughly. He stepped out of the car, then waited on the pavement for Isla despite the light mist of rain that had started on the drive over.

At last, he saw her walking toward him, coming from the direction of Callum and Liddy's.

Her eyes met his, and a slow smile spread across her lips.

Isla took off at a sprint toward him, closing the gap between them. When she reached him, she threw her arms around his neck, standing on her tiptoes as she lifted her face for him. "Hi, lover," she whispered, breathless.

Aiden's arms went tight around her waist. "You're not angry? I thought maybe you'd come to have it out with me."

"No, I came because I thought you might be having a full-blown freak-out. And I was right, wasn't I?"

The pressure around his chest eased, and his lips met hers, the connection between them powerful and passionate, as though they'd been apart for months rather than a few days. As though they weren't standing in the middle of the footpath in front of his house, kissing in the rain, where anyone who passed could see.

Liddy, Callum—*everyone else*—could accuse him all they wanted.

He would never apologize for loving Isla.

He could only hope that Isla shared his determination . . . and could also see forever with him.

33

—

ISLA

STANDING in the middle of Aiden's kitchen wearing the dress shirt he'd discarded on the floor earlier, Isla lifted the kettle from the counter and poured the boiling water into her teacup. Steam warmed her face, the fragrant scent of tea leaves filling her lungs. She smiled as she heard Aiden's footsteps approach from behind her.

Aiden slid his arms around her waist, smelling of soap and aftershave, and then he nuzzled her neck. "I could get used to the sight of you in my kitchen wearing nothing but my shirt."

Turning, she found him wearing an undershirt and gray joggers, his hair still damp from the shower they'd taken together. He'd stayed behind in the bathroom to shave while she went to make tea. But between having sex immediately after coming in the doorway, then showering, they'd barely talked.

She lifted her lips to receive his kiss. "I'll have you know, this is about where my culinary skills end. I can boil a kettle and make decent scones, but I survived primarily on takeaway until I moved back with my mother, who does all the cooking for me now."

"I can't remember the last time I turned on my stove if I'm honest. There's never enough time to eat here."

Isla let her gaze wander over the modestly-sized kitchen. For a man worth billions, Aiden certainly didn't live like one. The kitchen was clean, not a speck of food or clutter on the counters. He'd barely had anything in the fridge when she'd opened it earlier to look for milk.

She got the feeling this wasn't a home—not really. A place to sleep, yes. To shower.

To pass through.

Aiden moved her teacup and the kettle to the side, then lifted her onto the counter. Pushing her knees apart, he stepped between her legs and slid his hands up her thighs. He leaned toward her and pressed a kiss to the curve of her throat. "Spend the night with me tonight."

She gave a moan of approval. "I can't. I walked out on my mom and Callum when you texted earlier. I told them the production team needed me for an emergency meeting. They didn't question it, but they'll definitely think it's strange if I stay out all night."

"The irony of you keeping this hidden isn't lost on me— especially considering you didn't want to be a family secret." Aiden pulled back and searched her eyes. "But I promised Liddy I'd tell Callum tomorrow. It has to happen."

She furrowed her brow, ignoring the guilt that came with his words. She *had* prolonged the secret.

She'd had to.

"We can't tell him tomorrow. It has to be on Sunday." Then she shook her head. "I don't understand why you told Liddy—"

"She said that there had been some drama with you. That I shouldn't pretend I didn't know about it. I just assumed that—"

"That it was about us." Isla grimaced. "No, that wasn't it." She drew a deep breath. "Do you remember how I told you Boyd wanted to film at Liddy and Callum's party? I forgot to ask him even though Davy sent me all the paperwork to get his release, and the production team planned around it. Davy asked me about it on Monday. We got into a fight, and I realized there wasn't any way to get Callum to agree to it—which I barely did—*and* tell him about you. So, it has to be Sunday, after the party. Besides, it would be so much drama if we tell him beforehand."

Aiden pulled back, his brows raising. "Isla, that's going to make everything so much worse for us."

"I know, but the production is a more immediate issue—"

"I don't care about the production." Aiden's blue eyes flashed with anger. "I care about *you*. About trying to salvage my friendship with your brother. If we wait to tell him until after the party, he's going to not only feel lied to but also taken advantage of. Not to mention, I promised Liddy."

She stiffened at the intensity of irritation in Aiden's tone.

A defensive feeling uncurled in her gut. "Well, it's done already. If I tell him tomorrow, he could back out of allowing the production team into the party. I didn't know what else to do—"

"Well, to begin with, you could have talked to me about it." Aiden stepped back. "Considering this affects us both. You can't just say *it's done*. How would you like it if I said the same thing about promising Liddy to tell Callum tomorrow?"

Her jaw dropped. "You've got to be joking. You're the one who told Liddy in the first place. How is that my fault?"

"I wouldn't have *told* Liddy anything if you'd just communicated with me about the situation with the production crew—not that I would have supported it. We can't do that to Callum, Isla."

She threw him a glare, reaching for her teacup to calm down. "And when was I supposed to tell you? You've been working nonstop, Aiden. I barely hear from you once you go into work mode. That's all you have time for."

She'd aimed the barb well enough—he flinched.

"You knew who I was when we started this, Isla. I've been working on the most important business deal I've ever done in my life for the past few weeks. A deal vital to the company. Yet I've taken the time to visit Texas, Arkansas, and Tennessee—for you. In the middle of everything. I can't give any more than that. Take it or leave it."

Isla closed her eyes, gripping the edge of the counter. *What are we doing?*

This was exactly how things would always be between them.

Her getting the scraps of his time.

Resentment and worry bubbling in the background.

She could see it now.

And if this was how they were starting, wouldn't it only get worse?

What hope did they have?

Yes, they had chemistry. The sex was incredible.

But new love couldn't withstand so much opposition, could it?

Drawing a shaky breath, she hopped down from the counter, then scooted away from him.

She headed straight for the bedroom, where she'd left her clothes scattered, and started to gather them from the floor.

Aiden followed her. "You're leaving?"

Isla didn't look at him. She could barely think straight, let alone respond yet.

I don't know what I'm doing anymore.

Aiden was supposed to be a soft place to land.

I love him. But would that be enough? The last they'd discussed it, they were getting their marriage annulled, he was always going to be busy . . . *and our lives don't naturally intersect.*

"Take it or leave it." The blunt way he'd just said that sliced through her heart. No room for the communication he claimed he wanted.

"Isla."

"Look at us, Aiden," she said in a strangled voice. "We're already fighting. How can you draw a line in the sand like that and expect me *not* to leave?"

She straightened and started unbuttoning his shirt, not particularly wanting to get naked around him now. But she also didn't want to be in his shirt for one second longer.

Aiden crossed the room toward her, then scooped her into his arms.

She struggled against him as he lifted her. "What in the hell are you doing?"

"You can't leave in the middle of an argument like this." He set her down on the bed gently.

As he sat beside her, tears formed in her eyes. She blinked rapidly, not wanting him to see her crying, but he was already there, cupping her face in his hand with an aching tenderness, swiping just below her wet lashes with his fingertips. "I don't want to do this. I can't stand seeing you cry."

His forehead pressed softly to her own. "I'm sorry, Isla. I'm sorry I wasn't available to talk to, *and* that you felt alone in deciding all this with the production. God, darling, I'm sorry for all of it. You make me want to leave everything behind for you."

Her heart ached so deeply at his words that she wrapped her arms around his neck, holding on to him as though he was a tether keeping her steady.

"No, you're right," she said with a sniffle. "I've made everything so much worse for you with Callum. We'll do it your way and tell him tomorrow. About everything—being together, the marriage in Vegas. What you want is more important that the production."

A soft, sad smile crossed his lips. "It's almost ironic that Callum always joked I'd never marry. I doubt he'd ever expect my wife to be his sister, either."

He cupped her face. "You're the only woman I want, Isla. And I don't know what you want anymore, but you need to understand that. You're it for me."

Her throat clenched and she lifted her mouth, kissing his neck softly. "Keep calling me wife and I'm going to think you want it to be real, *husband*."

Aiden released her face, setting his hands on either side of her on the bed as he stared down at her. He searched her eyes for a moment. "I do want that."

Isla's mouth opened with a gasp and she held his gaze.

Is he serious?

"I don't know what happened in Vegas, Isla, but I know that something brought us together that night. Maybe something deep within both our subconscious. And at that moment, we picked lifetime commitment, of all things. To each other."

She swallowed, trying to process his words.

Is Aiden asking me to be his wife?

"You want to stay married?" she whispered, barely daring to voice the question.

"We don't have to decide right now. But we also don't have to rush to annul it." He added quickly, "If you don't want to."

Is that what I want?

To be married to Aiden?

And why wasn't she freaking out about the possibility more?

Instead, the thought made her strangely *happy*.

She searched his eyes, her heart racing. "I think . . . I think I do want that."

He smiled. "Really?"

"I know it's crazy. But I don't want to annul our marriage either, Aiden. Being with you feels like the part of my life that was always missing. Nothing has ever felt more natural. It's like breathing. But are *you* sure?"

"I love you, Isla. I've never been more certain of anything— or *anyone*—in my life. I know our lives will be difficult to mesh, but I'd rather face all those obstacles with you as my wife than to face the possibility of you not being with me."

She smiled, locking her wrists behind his neck. "Call me your wife again."

His mouth drew closer to hers, until his lips brushed hers with the barest pressure. "My gorgeous wife," he whispered against her mouth.

Oh God.

She shivered with delight, then consumed his mouth with a deep kiss, holding him firmly down against her.

Marriage had never sounded *sexy*, so why in the hell was this turning her on so much? Was this some secret fantasy of hers she'd never realized she had and they were just role-playing through it?

But they weren't—were they? He really was her husband.

She wrapped her legs around his hips, pulling his body down on top of hers. Tearing her mouth from his, she drew her lips to his ear. "I need you naked. Now."

"I couldn't have said it better myself," he said, pulling back. Heat simmered in his eyes as he stared at her. He removed his joggers and shirt, then leaned over her. Gripping the lapel of the shirt, he gave it a sharp tug, and then buttons popped off, flying across the room.

"God, you're so fucking hot," she breathed, drinking in the sight of the hard planes of his chest, the military tattoos on his strong biceps, the lean, ropy muscles of his forearms.

He smirked. "You liked that trick, did you, darling wife?"

He fucking knows he's riling me up with that word.

She bit her lip. "I swear to God, you're going to make me come just by calling me that."

Aiden knelt before her, pushing her legs apart, then reached down to glide his fingertips over her wet entrance. "You really do like it, don't you? Horny little wife."

Isla let out an appreciative moan as he flicked her clit.

He pushed his cock inside her, the sensation robbing her of all rational thought. "*Oh* yes, Aiden—please. I need you so much."

Aiden leaned over her, and she wrapped her legs tightly against his ass, pinning him deep inside her. As his lips found hers once again, he pulled his hips back, pulling out most of the way, then sank deep inside her again with a thrust that made her scream.

Fuck.

"Yes, baby, like that. Deep inside me," she groaned.

He pulled out again, then thrust harder, deeper, faster. Her hips rose to meet each thrust, receiving him as deeply as she could, their bodies moving with a rhythm that was perfectly in sync, her orgasm starting to build deep within her core.

They panted against each other, their mouths consuming one another's in a full-throated kiss, his hands grabbing hers, fingers intertwining. As though they wanted to meld their bodies into one.

Together.

Maybe it was the argument, or the fact that he'd opened a cataclysmic door for them, but her body flushed with heat, the intensity of her need like never before. Her legs trembled as the waves of pleasure built to a scalding point, each thrust, each moan, each whispered word of praise sending her higher and higher into a heaven of bliss unlike she'd ever experienced.

Then, as though a dam had broken, white-hot bliss broke through her, curling her toes, making her thighs fall slack. Then Aiden groaned, releasing deeply inside her, his arms tight around her as he slowed, then stilled.

Their bodies were slick with sweat, their chests heaving for air.

Isla pressed her cheek into the curve of his neck, relishing in the feeling of his heartbeat pounding against her own. "I love you," she whispered at last.

"I love you, too, Isla." Aiden breathed hard, then pulled himself free of her and rolled to his side. "Fuck, I'm exhausted."

She took a moment to return to earth, then climbed out of the bed, went into his bathroom, and took care of herself. Running the warm water on the sink, she looked around for a washcloth, soaked and wrung it out, then returned to the bed.

Aiden still lay there, half asleep. She crawled onto the bed, then cleaned him off with the washcloth.

His eyes popped open. "Thank you," he said, surprise in his voice.

"You take care of me. I take care of you," she said with a gentle smile. "It's the least I can do."

She returned the cloth to the sink, then went back and got under the sheets beside him.

"What are you doing?" he asked, folding her into his arms.

The hell if I know.

But she didn't say that. Wouldn't say that.

She loved him.

"You asked me to stay, so I'm staying. Good night, Aiden."

And even though everything felt like such a mess right now

—and tomorrow would likely be a disaster—tenuous hope about the future sang through her heart.

This is where I belong.

34

———

AIDEN

THE KNOCKING on Aiden's door roused him, and he blinked hard, his mind foggy with sleep.

Beside him, Isla gave a soft groan. "How is it morning already?"

But somehow, it was morning—sunlight streamed in through the curtains of his bedroom. He closed one eye as he stared at them sleepily. He was usually gone before the sun came up. Even on the weekends, he usually ran with Callum to start the day.

Shite. That couldn't be Callum, could it? They hadn't texted about running today.

But he *had* told Liddy he'd do something to take Callum out for brunch and hadn't. He'd gotten completely sidetracked with Isla.

Isla grappled with her phone, then sat bolt upright. "Oh my God. Callum's on his way here."

Fuck.

Aiden scrambled from the bed, his heart pounding. "What?"

Isla continued scrolling through her phone. "I have a bunch of missed calls from Elle and Kyle—and my mum, apparently. Oh God. He must have found out." She jumped out of the bed. "Dammit, where are my clothes?"

Another loud knock.

Aiden yanked on a pair of trousers and a shirt. "Stay in here. Close the door—just in case."

"Well, I'm not going to greet him naked—"

He was already out the door and on his way through the hall. Hurrying down the stairs toward the front door, he braced himself as he unlocked it.

Sharp relief sank through him. *Not Callum.*

Elle and Kyle, instead.

Out of breath, apparently, with red faces.

They pushed past him like a SWAT team, Kyle slamming the door behind him like they were dodging sniper fire.

"Nice to see you too," Aiden muttered. "Make yourselves at home. Raid the fridge. Hide the evidence."

"What the hell is going on? Why are you and Isla both ignoring our phone calls?" Elle asked with wide eyes.

Aiden almost cringed. They already knew she was with him, but the assumption that they'd ignored them spoke to the breach of trust.

"We weren't. We were just asleep."

"Told you," Kyle said with a smirk at his sister.

"Oh, save it." Elle rolled her eyes and turned back to Aiden. "Callum's on his way here. He texted you to find out if you wanted to run and then when you didn't answer, he decided to run here to ask. Kyle and I had to book it to beat him, but he'll be here any second."

Goddammit.

As if on cue, a key scraped into the lock behind them.

Aiden shoved them both toward the stairs. "Go!" he hissed. "In my room."

"He has a key?" Elle asked with wide eyes.

He didn't have time to explain. They had barely vanished from sight as the door opened behind him. Aiden whirled around as Callum stopped in the doorway, surprise on his face.

"I thought I heard someone at the door," Aiden said as smoothly as possible. He'd given Callum the key years ago in case he ever needed someone to check on things while he was out of town.

Callum withdrew it from the lock, a sheepish expression on his face. "Sorry about that. I tried texting and calling. Didn't know if you wanted to go for a run. I could use a moment out of the house. Between my mum in one guest room, Liddy's parents in the other, and Kyle crashing on the couch, it's been a lot."

That explained Kyle's presence here—but Elle's? Elle and Quinn maintained a house in London in addition to Littleton, which was closer to Oxfordshire. But since Quinn had started renting Littleton out to film crews and for parties a few years earlier, the house wasn't always available when they wanted to come to England.

Aiden checked his watch.

Then again, it's almost nine. Goddamn jet lag. No wonder he hadn't woken up. Between an exhausting night with Isla and still being accustomed to the East Coast time zone, he was a mess.

"Yeah, I can grab my trainers." He almost added, *wait here,* but would that seem oddly suspicious? He'd never made Callum wait in the foyer before.

Callum followed him up the stairs. "You doing all right? Liddy said you closed that deal with Ipolymer."

"Yeah, it's great," Aiden said, summoning what little enthusiasm he could fake as he came to the main level.

Shite. Isla's knickers still lie on the floor beside the sofa, from where they'd been discarded the night before. He stopped abruptly, his hands clenching by his side.

Oh God. What was he supposed to do—shove them in his pocket and pray Callum didn't ask why he'd suddenly developed a fondness for lace accessories?

He glanced down the hall toward his bedroom door, which remained shut. "Can you see if I have any bottled water in the fridge," he blurted, sweat breaking out on his neck.

Callum gave him an odd look, then nodded. "You going to run with it?"

"Thinking about it. I'm parched."

Callum rounded the island and froze, gaze snagging on the edge of the boots poking out from beneath the barstools. He glanced around, then his eyes focused on the knickers.

Fuck. Me.

"You have company?"

Aiden's mouth went dry. "Not right now."

Callum's gaze flicked to the boots. "Huh. She leave in a hurry?"

That eyebrow lift. That smirk. He knows—or he thinks he does.

"I had someone over before New York. I didn't even know those were still there. Got in late last night and went straight to bed."

If I rot in hell, it will be in whichever circle holds the liars of the world.

The words tasted like acid. Aiden had told lies before—he'd grown up in a house where evasion was an art form—but not to someone who mattered like this.

Not to *him*.

He kept his face still, but inside, something cracked. Because this wasn't just a lie. This was betrayal. Of Callum. Maybe Callum had been Quinn's friend first, but since Aiden had moved back to London? This friendship that had carried him through every bad moment. They'd become closer than Aiden had ever imagined, despite already being like an honorary brother in his family, and Callum had always believed in him—until now.

No wonder his family had no faith in him. Maybe all this time the only person he'd been deceiving about any goodness he possessed was *himself*. Had he always been so selfish? So willing to be so cold and detached to get what he wanted?

He used to think he was different from his father—used to pride himself on it. But now he was hiding the woman he loved in a bedroom while lying to his oldest friend with a straight face.

What would Isla say if she saw him now?

No. He didn't want to know. Because maybe, deep down, he was exactly the man they all believed him to be.

The moment held, and Callum's eyes continued to focus on Isla's shoes as though he was lost in his own thoughts. Then he gave Aiden a tight smile. "For a moment, I figured that you had taken back up with Lola again in New York and flown back with her."

Aiden went over toward the knickers, then gathered them from the floor.

Right. Because Callum wouldn't assume his own sister had taken that place in Aiden's life.

Of course, Lola would be a major obstacle to convincing Callum that he loved Isla. Callum had been there through that entire debacle. No way he'd easily accept that in the span of a few months, Aiden had not only moved on so wholly but also fallen completely and utterly in love with someone else.

Aiden barely believed it himself.

But it was also true. He loved that woman.

Hated that he had her hidden away in his bedroom, though.

"No, it's safe to say Lola will not be returning to my life," Aiden said, at last.

Callum set his hands on the island, then nodded. "Good. She was terrible for you. Though I have to warn you, my father invited her to the damn party tonight. He got a little carried away talking to her and her father at the Masters. I nearly wrung his neck for it on your behalf."

Guilt had a way of making everything so much worse. Every comment Callum uttered, however innocuous, ripped through him like battery acid clawing its way through his gut.

When he didn't answer, Callum frowned. "You sure you're all right? You look pale."

No, I'm not all right.

Every fiber of his body was screaming at him to just tell Callum already. Because that was what he'd promised Liddy he'd do. That was what he *should* do. That was what needed to happen. This thing had become such an awful, toxic secret burdening him down, threatening to tear his world to shreds. And he didn't want it to be. God, he wanted to shout from the rooftops how much he loved Isla.

But their argument last night had worried him, too. If they were a team, *partners* in this—or at all—telling Callum without her wasn't fair either.

"Actually, you caught me at a bad moment," he admitted at last. He cleared his throat. "I was planning on coming over and stealing you away from the women for a while later this morning while they get ready for the party. Just trying to finalize the plans."

Before Callum could respond, he added, "But let me grab my trainers. We'll run first, then we can go afterward."

Congratulations, Camden. You've officially hit rock bottom: hiding your best friend's sister from said best friend in your own bloody bedroom. What's next—tax fraud?

He headed down the hallway and slipped into his bedroom, locking the door behind him.

Elle, Kyle, and Isla all hung by the bathroom door, close to the door to his bedroom, watching him. Isla was dressed, thankfully, and he held out her knickers. "These are yours," he whispered.

A faint blush lit her cheeks, and she took them. "Sorry."

"Not your fault." He moved past them and went toward his closet.

"Geez, you guys," Elle breathed with a shake of her head.

"Eh, this isn't my first sibling scandal. But it's definitely the most naked one," Kyle hissed.

Isla gave Kyle a look of indignation. "What the hell are we going to do?" Isla whispered as Aiden reached for his trainers.

"I'm going for a run," Aiden said simply. He glanced at Elle and Kyle. "How did you know to come warn me?"

"Callum's mom called me," Elle said with a grimace. "I called Kyle and got him to delay Callum, then ran out of the house. Quinn has already texted me twenty times."

"My mum knows?" Isla asked, eyes wide.

Elle nodded with sympathy on her face. "I think Liddy told her last night."

This was completely, utterly out of control.

Aiden closed his eyes, trying to think. At last, he said, "I think we should tell him."

"No!" Elle hissed. "Not before the party. It might ruin the day."

"I agree," Kyle said with a wince. "I mean, not that I want to be in the middle of this, but maybe just wait until tomorrow?"

Aiden rose, his heart thrumming at a quickened pace. He went over to Isla, then kissed her gently. "We need a plan."

That did nothing to erase the worry from her face, but she nodded wordlessly, as though afraid of being overheard.

He turned to Kyle and asked quietly, "In the meantime, can you all call some places and make a brunch reservation for us and Callum? Call my brothers. Maybe the fathers, too. Liddy had asked me to last night, and I . . . forgot."

He saw the flinch in Elle's face.

Yes, I know I'm a terrible friend.

"I can ask Quinn—"

"No, I'll handle it," Kyle said, nudging his sister with his elbow.

Aiden nodded his thanks, then slipped back out the door.

If Quinn knew about Elle being here, it would only be one more thing his elder brother wouldn't want to forgive him for. He'd pulled Elle and Kyle too deeply into this now.

This day was one giant disaster waiting to happen.

35

ISLA

"THEY REALLY SHOULD HAVE JUST GOTTEN married today rather than elope and wait to celebrate it five months later."

Isla stiffened at the familiar sound of her father's voice as he came up behind her at the cocktail table. Dad set a plate of canapés on the tablecloth with a frown. "This is a wedding reception without a wedding. Wouldn't have taken much to just allow us to witness the nuptials."

Isla leaned over and kissed her father's cheek. "Honestly, Dad, what difference does it make? Receptions are the only part of the wedding worth attending."

He scowled at her. "*That's* a sad statement about your views on marriage, Isla Grace."

She grinned. "You know I'm just purposely ruffling your feathers." She looped her arm through his. They didn't see each other often, but she'd always had an affectionate—but distant— relationship with her father.

God, this party was giving awkward family dinner energy but with nicer clothes and fewer carbs.

She'd planned on hiding in the loo until dessert, but now

she was stuck making small talk with her father about the sanctity of marriage. Fantastic.

He hadn't been a bad father, just a brokenhearted one—left humiliated when Mum ran off with another woman. It had wrecked his self-esteem, hurt his pride, *and* broken his heart. Diana had been the bandage: cold, poised, and conveniently uninterested in her stepchildren.

Maybe that was why Dad had chosen another wife so opposite from Mum. Mum was a warmhearted Latina—a carefree, beach-loving free spirit. Whether or not Dad had been aware of his choice in a stepmother as Callum and Isla had been at the time, it had put a wedge in their relationship.

Unintentionally having slipped into silence, Isla shifted her weight. "So, you're not having fun?"

Dad shook his head. "I didn't say that. I'm just saying that when you get married, I expect a proper wedding. At least one of my children could grant me the honor of being there when they wed."

Isla grimaced, her gaze flicking across the crowded room toward Aiden.

God, he looks so sexy in his suit.

There was something impossibly unfair about him looking that good and feeling this distant from him. How could he look like her safe place and still feel a thousand miles away?

They hadn't talked once since the beginning of the party. She'd purposely avoided him, and he appeared to be doing the same. It didn't help that there were at least six people here who knew the truth about them—and once Tomas and the film crew got here, there would be even more.

Isla was dreading that, to be honest. Callum and Liddy had agreed to allow Tomas and one cameraman in after the dancing had begun, though Boyd was setting up in an adjoining room to watch live. But none of that messiness compared to the thought of seeing Davy.

Boyd had wanted to film some footage of Tomas and her walking in the streets of London on Thursday—and the interaction with Davy had been stiff. Awkward.

The rift between them seemed like a chasm.

She needed her best friend right now. The fact that Davy wasn't there, and the wound from their argument, hurt deeply.

To make matters worse, Liddy was also being cool. And while Elle had tried to help Aiden and Isla in the morning, Isla hadn't gotten the impression that Elle wanted to get pulled any further into the middle of it while they'd been getting ready earlier. Not that Isla blamed her.

And then Mum gave me an earful about it.

So here she was, stuck talking to her dad—and Kyle, when he drifted by—feeling like an outsider in her own family.

Like Dad probably did, ironically. Of course, Dad had Diana to attend to occasionally. Diana had parked herself next to Aiden's parents and hadn't moved since.

"You should come visit me occasionally," Dad tried again, his voice softer. "I miss seeing your face at the house."

Isla reached for her cocktail. "Well, I would, but I don't really know if Diana would like that, Dad."

At least they'd reached the point in her life where they could talk about this openly.

"Whether she does or not is irrelevant. She enjoys enough of my money to keep her happy. Come for your old dad, instead. I'm sure you can always stay at Megan's if you'd prefer, like you did last time."

"I'm not sure about that. She's busy planning her own wedding in a couple of months." She sipped the gin spritzer, the tangy lemon flavor making her mouth pucker. "But I'll do my best."

"I tried to be a good father, you know," Dad said, face reddening as he attempted to eat a canapé in one bite.

Oh God, the wine is probably going to his head. Just what she needed—feeling like a loner with an extra side of family recrimination.

"You are a good father, Dad. Love and marriage just have a way of fucking us when we least expect it."

He frowned at her language. "Isla."

She rolled her eyes. "I'm just teasing." *Nope. Not getting pulled into a mid-party therapy session.* She grabbed her drink. "I'm going to make the rounds. Catch you in a bit."

She passed by her mum as she left Dad's side. "Que estaba diciendo?" Mum whispered too loudly. *What was he saying?*

"*Nada.*" Nothing. She really wasn't about to get caught in her parents' perpetual stand-off. "I'm going to get some air."

"*Ten cuidado,*" Mum warned behind her.

Yeah, yeah. She'd be careful.

Isla left the elegant room being used for the cocktail hour and slipped out onto the adjoining balcony. The venue was an old bank that had been converted into an event space and hotel —most of the guests were staying here tonight, including her. She'd checked into her room earlier when she'd come with Elle and Liddy and now all she wanted to do was flee to it.

The balcony had an impressive view of London, including the dome of St. Paul's, and Isla walked toward it, glad for the break from the chatter and the soft lyrical strain from the string quartet. Nothing added to the chaos of a party quite like classical music being played over the sound of emotional implosions.

Glancing at the few people out on the balcony, she shouldn't have been surprised to find Callum there. Yet there he was.

Of course he was there. Where else would a brooding older

brother lurk if not on a balcony with a beer like a Victorian ghost haunting his own elopement party?

He caught her eye and smiled as she came up beside him. "I completely understand why you eloped," she said with a groan. "And why Liddy had to talk you into a party."

"I saw you caught over there with Dad. Sorry." Callum grimaced, his gaze refocusing on the cityscape. "Though usually you're able to rise above it all with a smile. Not today, though. Something on your mind?"

Isla focused her gaze on the dome of St. Paul's. Like her heart wasn't thudding in her chest. Like talking to her big brother—who'd always been a safety net for her, the only one who understood everything she'd been through—wasn't somehow painful now. "No," she said brightly. "You? Just avoiding your guests?"

"No," Callum said. A muscle in his jaw flexed, then he sipped on the beer. "Just trying to figure out why everyone I'm close to—including my own wife—is lying to me."

Isla drew a sharp breath, and her gaze collided with her brother's.

He flicked his eyes away from hers again. "I'm not stupid, Isla."

Oh God. What does he know?

Her heart slammed hard against her ribs. "Callum, I—"

"I'll admit, I was angry at the thought at first. Angry because I worry about the implications of you and Aiden sleeping together and what that might mean in the future if it ends badly. I don't want my little sister getting hurt, especially not at the hands of one of my closest friends."

Oh fuck.

Her mouth went dry, and she sipped more of her drink, letting him continue talking for now while she gathered her thoughts.

"But then, my anger faded, and it occurred to me that there also wasn't anyone I trusted as much as Aiden—except for Quinn, of course—even though he's lying to me, too. But really, you're both adults. And he's responsible. Wealthy. He's always cared about you, and I couldn't think of someone I'd be happier to see you with."

Isla's throat clenched. If this was where the conversation ended, it would be a good thing.

She hadn't expected this. Calm. Mature. Like maybe, just maybe, she hadn't given Callum enough credit.

The whole situation with Tomas had skewed her perspective too much.

She'd spent weeks dreading this moment, expecting fury or disappointment. But here it was—something worse. *Resignation.* It didn't slam into her like a door. It seeped in, slow and sad, like rain under a cracked window.

Somehow, that hurt more.

But from the manner of Callum's delivery, he *wasn't* happy about the fact now.

Because we lied to him.

"Callum, we wanted to tell you." Isla turned toward him and gripped his elbow. "And you can't be angry with anyone else who knows. We didn't try to tell them and leave you out of it. It was all accidental, and both of us asked them for the chance to tell you ourselves."

"It's a sad day when the only person who tells me the truth about my own sister and best friend is Lola Salas."

Isla's eyes widened. *Lola? She knows? How in the hell had she found out?*

Of all the people to break the news, it had to be Lola.

Not Aiden. Not me. Not even Elle.

The woman who'd once torched Aiden's heart and still

somehow held the match to hers. The shame hit hard and fast like she'd swallowed a mouthful of glass.

"How . . ."

Callum gave Isla a cool look. "Of course, she didn't do it out of goodwill. She let slip that she'd seen you and Aiden in Vegas —after a long night of drinking, apparently. Said something about how you threw up on her suitcase after leaving Aiden's room in the morning."

Humiliation burned in her cheeks. She couldn't really say nothing had happened that night even though she was tempted to. Because something *had happened*. Something bigger than hooking up.

"And then there was that morning I called, and you were clearly waking up together. Or this morning, when your boots were lying on the floor of Aiden's kitchen. And *knickers*. Have to admit, that wasn't the most pleasant way to start the day. And for Aiden to suggest they belonged to some stranger from before he went to New York? That burned, Isla."

She wanted to laugh. Or cry. Maybe both.

Of course he'd noticed.

Of course he'd been paying attention—because that was what Callum did. He protected. He saw what others missed.

And she'd treated him like he was blind. She couldn't imagine how much it must have hurt him to *know* Aiden was lying to his face. How he wasn't raging right now showed a side of him that neither of them deserved.

Tears pricked her eyes. "I'm so sorry, Callum. We were going to tell you. We just didn't know how you'd take it and wanted to wait until after the party." She swallowed hard, then added, tenuously, "But, I mean, it's a good thing you know now, and we can talk openly about it. And it's a relief to know that you're not opposed."

Callum chuckled without mirth. "I might not have been

opposed. *Before.* But now? Now my enthusiasm is . . . definitely tarnished." He leaned closer. "That sort of thing happens when you realize everyone around you is lying."

Her hand tightened on his sleeve. "It's not their fault, so please don't blame them. Most of them are angry with us, actually—which is why this party has been so awkward for me."

"Wonderful. Just the sort of drama I love." Callum released a strangled sigh. "I just don't understand. Am I a terrible brother? A monster who would resort to caveman antics of beating his best friend? Or is there something I'm not seeing here? Are you just hooking up? Is he blackmailing you into sex or something more nefarious?"

Isla dropped her hand to her side. "No." At least he clearly didn't know about the marriage. He might be angrier if he did, though.

"Maybe I deserve this after what I did with your production and Tomas."

Isla set her glass down on the balcony ledge, then slipped her arms around him. "No, no. That's not it. And I'm so sorry, Callum. I truly am. You've always been the best brother in the world, and I hate that I've put such a horrible damper on your happy day." She wiped her cheeks.

She should tell him about the marriage now and be done with it. The only way to get over this *thing* she and Aiden had created—this monstrous lie—was to go *through* it.

And now that Callum had admitted he knew, the news about the Vegas marriage was a ticking time bomb that anyone might let slip.

Her hand trembled at her side. Tell him now. Rip off the bandage. You already jumped the first fence—what's one more confession?

Aiden might not be right beside her to tell him together, but

Callum was her brother, and this was the only way forward now. "I have to tell you something—"

"Callum! There you are," Brenda, Liddy's mother, stepped out onto the balcony. She waved him toward her. "The event planner is looking for you. They're moving the party to the dining room, and she wants you to be introduced with Liddy."

Callum held Isla's gaze for a moment, then looked away and nodded at Brenda. "Coming," he said. He squeezed Isla's hand. "We'll talk soon. I'm going back to all the pretenders. Liddy deserves a nice day, and I don't want this to be the focus."

Isla watched him go with a heavy heart.

Dammit.

Abandoning her drink, she rushed into the cocktail hour room and scanned the space. Aiden wasn't hard to find—thank goodness he was tall—but he was already moving toward the dining room beside Logan, the two of them laughing at some joke as though they didn't have a care in the world.

Like the last few minutes hadn't happened. Her heart had cracked open and spilled the truth all over a balcony railing. But Aiden hadn't heard it yet.

Hurrying in her long evening gown and heels, Isla came up behind Aiden and grabbed him by the elbow, eliciting a look of surprise from Logan. "I need to talk to you. *Now.*"

Aiden gave her a curious look but said nothing as she dragged him away down the hallway toward the toilets.

"What is it?" Aiden asked.

They appeared to be alone, thankfully, and she stopped at the end of the hall, between the two doors for the men's and women's rooms. "Callum knows the truth," she whispered.

Aiden stilled. Completely. No breath, no blink—like the words had frozen him mid-thought.

"What?" he asked, voice low, almost hoarse.

"He's known for a while apparently. Lola told him something about seeing us in Vegas."

Aiden closed his eyes and turned slightly away, exhaling through gritted teeth. "Fuck." His hand went to the back of his neck, massaging the skin like he'd suddenly developed a deep headache. For a long moment, he said nothing.

"How did Lola find out, exactly?"

"After that phone call she picked up. I think it set her over the edge. She couldn't stand the thought that I'd picked you. So, she started digging and found the public marriage records in Vegas."

Oh shit.

Isla shifted her weight, nervous energy ticking through her limbs. "He doesn't seem to know about the marriage. At least not yet."

That got his eyes back on her—blazing now, but not with anger. With something else. Dread? Shame? Regret? All of it?

"He must be furious with me," Aiden said, barely above a whisper. Isla softened, especially as she thought about Callum's thoughts on Aiden and her.

"But then, my anger faded, and it occurred to me that there also wasn't anyone I trusted as much as Aiden . . . He's always cared about you, and I couldn't think of someone I'd be happier to see you with."

"He's hurt, but not in the way you think. He said that he couldn't think of anyone he'd be happier to see me with." Aiden smiled at that, although it was a reluctant smile. Isla's heartbeat was erratic. "He's upset because everyone has been lying to him, which is fair. We should make sure he learns about *our marriage* from us."

"Tonight? Here?" Aiden hesitated, his face lined with worry.

Isla nodded. "I think so."

Aiden was silent, as though allowing the news to sink in. "All right. I'll follow your lead." A determined look crossed his eyes, the type that she imagined he must have in the office when closing a deal.

This was the side of him she loved. The one that wouldn't back down. Who'd hold her hand even if they were walking through fire.

He seemed to catch the moment her gaze turned lusty, and a smile curved at his lips.

He bent, then pressed a deep, scorching kiss to her mouth, his hand grazing her breast. "It's taken every single ounce of my control not to do that all evening," he whispered, heat blistering through his gaze.

Funny how a kiss from him could make her instantly feel better. More grounded.

"Get out of here," she whispered with a roll of her eyes. "Before you get us both in more trouble."

He winked and turned to go, and she reached out, playfully smacking him on the backside.

His step faltered just slightly, then he tossed her a wicked grin. "Don't tempt me with ideas for later."

Settling back against the wall as he left, Isla closed her eyes, trying to still her heart.

We can do this. Together. The hard part was almost over, and it might not be so bad after all.

36

AIDEN

THE ONLY THING worse than lying to Callum, Aiden had discovered, was knowing that Callum knew about it.

That and watching Isla snuggle with Tomas for the goddamn travel show.

His throat burned as he sipped his glass of scotch, tearing his eyes away as Tomas's lips nuzzled Isla's neck.

"Might want to relax your grip on that glass," Kyle said from beside him. "Squeeze it any harder, and it might shatter in your hand."

Aiden slammed down the rest of his drink and sat back in his chair at the long, elegantly decorated dining table. Thank God for younger brothers right now—both Kyle and Logan were the only ones who were keeping him sane during this blessed event.

Quinn and Mason, on the other hand, had barely uttered two words to him.

Kyle reached into his pocket and pulled out a flask. "I was saving this for later, but it looks like you could use this more than me." He handed it over to Aiden. "Nothing fancy. Jack Daniel's. I am from Tennessee."

Aiden chuckled and uncapped the flask, then took a swig. "You'd be surprised, but I'm not the liquor snob. That's more of an elder Camden trait." He flicked a glance at Quinn, who stood by the bar, surrounded by friends from uni, including Callum. Quinn and Callum had more friends in common—as they were the same age.

Maybe I've only ever been the stand-in. The convenient one. The one who was around when Quinn wasn't.

The pathetic, jealous thought snuck in before he could stop it—and he swallowed it down with another swig of whiskey.

But wasn't there truth in it? Hadn't it always been true?

When push came to shove, Quinn had picked Callum over his own brother. And if Callum had to choose a friend between the two of them, Aiden was certain it wouldn't be him.

Especially not now.

Now that I can't look Callum in the eye.

Now that I know he knew I was lying to his face.

"They are *such* a handsome couple," Mum was saying across the table, a few seats down as she spoke to his father. "And he's fairly famous, isn't he? Marlene was telling me she's seen him in a magazine."

Aiden followed the direction of his mother's gaze. She was speaking about Isla and Tomas. Tomas took a moment to give her a twirl, then led Isla onto the nearby dance floor, where the music was still soft and slow. Exactly the kind of shot Boyd had wanted. Intimate. Romantic. Made-for-TV magic.

Oh perfect. A spin. Maybe they'd do the tango next. Or a dramatic lift, *Dirty Dancing*-style.

Tomas's arms wrapped tightly around Isla, his hands grazing dangerously close to her arse. And of course she looked incredible—her gray dress hugged every curve like it had been stitched on by sin.

Tomas's hands smoothed lower on Isla's backside.

Aiden bit down on the inside of his cheek.

He focused his gaze on the cameraman, who stood discreetly to the side. For all the rest of the guests knew, he was just there to film the reception.

It's just an act.

She's an actress.

"How long is this production going to be hanging around for?" he hissed at Kyle.

"I think like an hour or two."

"How much fucking footage do they need?" he growled.

"You know, I think Logan mentioned something about cigars on the balcony. Why don't we see if he's still out there?" Kyle asked, pushing his chair back.

Probably not a bad idea.

Whatever superpower was required to watch the woman he loved be groped by another man—acting or not—Aiden didn't seem to possess it.

Every touch, every smile, every comment about how *fucking perfect* they were together sank like gravel through his stomach.

"I'm just going to get a refill," Aiden said, grabbing his glass from the table. "I'll meet you out there."

Kyle gave him a hesitant look. "If it helps, she's talked about you nonstop. Even when she thinks she's being subtle. Between shots while filming, or on the plane ride over here, all she did was find a way to sneak you into the conversation. It makes me wish I had someone, too. You don't realize how lonely you are until you see everyone else around you happy."

Aiden gave a grim nod. "Don't get too romantic, Winnick. I don't need any more rumors starting at this party."

Kyle chortled, then left him at the table.

Making a beeline for the bar, Aiden held his breath as he passed Callum and Quinn. Neither of them looked his way, though he didn't doubt they both noticed him.

A suffocated feeling closed in around him as he stood in line at the bar. Isla was busy, obviously, and she'd meant well in telling him about Callum, but this was sheer misery. Every second since then had felt fraught with the potential for error. A powder keg that could erode the relationships he valued the most even further.

"Aiden," a man said beside him. One of Callum and Quinn's friends who had pulled away from the group to stand in the line for the bar.

"Ah, hello . . ."

Michael? Ben?

Something biblical.

"Philip," he said with a grin. "You're looking duly miserable. What are you drinking tonight?"

"Bell's," Aiden said, groaning inwardly. The last thing he wanted was to get caught in a conversation with one of Callum and Quinn's friends—especially when they were just a few feet away.

"Of course you are. Moved away from pints and onto the whiskey, have you? God, I think I remember the first time you drank with us all in uni. You were up from"—Philip snapped his fingers at some vague recollection that Aiden had no memory of—"I can't remember now. Anyway. You were green around the gills the entire night."

Aiden gave a bare nod, still trying to decide whether it was better to feign interest or to be flat-out disinterested. One would make him look even more like a prick—the other would only keep him here longer.

Philip, either too drunk to notice Aiden's dilemma or

feeling particularly chatty, kept right at it. "Of course, lots changed since then. You're the big shot in the family now, I hear." He clapped Aiden on the back.

Please, God. Let the line fucking move.

Only one person remained in front of him, though Philip had sidled up beside him, rather than stand behind. Aiden focused his gaze on the bartender as he strained a drink into a glass.

"Wouldn't be Camden Enterprises if a Camden wasn't in charge," Aiden replied dryly, his gaze darting away.

That was a mistake. His eyes landed on Tomas and Isla, who continued wrapped in each other's arms on the dance floor.

Still? How many bloody shots does Boyd need?

A pulse beat at his temple, slow and brutal. Laughter rippled from a nearby table. The clink of cutlery. Someone toasted Liddy and Callum. Meanwhile, he stood there, pretending not to notice Tomas's hands on the woman he loved.

Philip followed his gaze. "Oh yeah. That's changed too, right?" He lowered his voice. "Little Isla's all filled out now." The sod had the audacity to lick his lips. "Girl's got a reputation, too. I'd pay good money to see what she's like on her knees. Bet she's wild with that mouth. Wouldn't mind getting a turn."

"What?" Aiden asked sharply, his voice booming louder than he'd intended. Rage curled through him, and he turned, towering over the sniveling moron as he grabbed him by the collar. But he couldn't control the fury. "What the *fuck*?"

Philip's eyes widened. "I-I . . . meant no harm. Isla—"

"Get her name out of your fucking mouth," Aiden growled, leaning closer. His grip tightened. "Don't you *ever* think of talking about her that way again, you pathetic little fuck."

Quinn was at Aiden's side. He gripped Aiden by the elbow. "Whoa, there, what the hell is going on?"

Philip's face was a deep shade of crimson. "S-sorry," he sputtered.

"This sod just insulted Isla," Aiden snapped, not bothering to look at Quinn.

Quinn put his hand on Aiden's shoulder. "Maybe we just let it go right now, Aiden."

Callum had joined them, a circle of onlookers gathering around them. "What the fuck, Aiden?" His eyes narrowed as he stepped between Philip and Aiden, shoving Philip out of Aiden's grasp. "This isn't the place for this."

"You wouldn't be saying that if you knew what a sorry excuse for a friend this arsehole is," Aiden said, meeting Callum's eyes for the first time in the past couple of hours.

Callum's expression flickered, then cooled. He lifted his chin in a challenge. "And you would know what it means to be a friend, would you, Aiden?"

Aiden fingers curled, his restraint already spiraled so far that he wasn't certain he could rein it in anymore.

"I didn't say I was perfect—"

Callum barked a laugh. "Not perfect? You've been sleeping with Isla for what? Weeks now? And lying to my face."

As though the accusation wasn't bad enough, everyone—absolutely fucking everyone—appeared to have heard it. Conversations had gone silent. The entire room appeared to be staring at them.

Heat rose on Aiden's face as he stared at Callum, his chest tight with pressure. "It's not like that," he whispered hoarsely.

Footsteps hurried toward them as both Liddy and Isla reached them. Isla came up beside Aiden and slipped her hand onto his elbow. "Aiden—"

"How dare you?" Callum went on, his eyes narrowed and

piercing through Aiden. "How dare you make a scene like this during our party? You *know* how much Liddy put into this. And I was willing to let it all go, watch you sit there and pretend to be my fucking friend, and now you pull this?"

"I *am* your friend," Aiden said, his voice a rough scratch. He straightened, pulling his shoulder free from Quinn's grasp. "I was just defending the reputation of the woman I love from that sod." He gestured toward Philip.

Liddy bit her lip and took Callum's hand. "I think maybe we should all just step back. Cool down. Talk about it later."

Aiden flicked his gaze down at Isla, who squeezed his elbow. "Aiden, please," she whispered.

Drawing a sharp breath in through his nose, Aiden nodded, trying to dig deeply for a single strand of calm.

Then Callum shook his head. "Love, Aiden? That's rich. She's been your girlfriend for what? Three weeks? Just stop lying. To everyone. Including yourself."

Everyone stared at him.

With fucking judgment in their eyes.

His family. Workmates. Acquaintances. All of them looking at him and believing the worst—because he was so easy to believe the worst about.

Something deep inside him snapped. For *once*, for one bloody time, he wanted to come out on top. Prove to everyone he wasn't the villain they all believed.

Just fucking win.

Aiden lifted his chin. "My wife, actually. For almost two months." As Callum and Liddy's faces registered shock, Aiden stepped closer. "And you know, for someone who claims to value privacy as much as you do, I appreciate you airing our private business to everyone. But go right on defending that arsehole, Philip, if you want, but I'll defend my wife."

Then he turned, not waiting for anyone—even Isla.

Let them all think what they would.

He was done.

37

ISLA

GREENWICH, CONNECTICUT

"I can't believe you're leaving already," Megan said as she came into the guest room where Isla had spent the past few days.

Isla zipped up her suitcase, then went over toward her and gave her a tight hug. "I know. It's crazy how quickly time flies, right? But Paris is calling. One of them, anyway."

Megan pulled back, searching her face. "You sure you're gonna be okay?"

Am I?

Isla had asked herself that question hundreds of times over the last week.

The truth was, she still wasn't entirely sure how she'd gotten here. After Aiden had announced to everyone that they were married—then left her to deal with the fallout—the next day and a half had been a blur.

She'd argued, shed tears, tried to sort the whole situation out and restore whatever fragile balance to the world she'd taken a wrecking ball to. She wasn't entirely sure Callum would ever forgive Aiden—and Mason and Quinn seemed equally infuriated by him, too.

And then there was Liddy, the sister she'd never had, who'd been a *close* friend the last two years. Isla would never forget the hurt in her eyes from the scene at what had basically been her wedding reception.

Mum had been surprisingly unsupportive—maybe because Isla hadn't confided in her—or maybe because she worried about what Isla's marriage might mean for the future of *La Hacienda*.

Of course, Isla and Callum weren't exactly on speaking terms either.

But in the middle of all that, Dad had thrown Isla a lifeline —bought her a plane ticket to go spend the week in Connecticut. Less than forty-eight hours after the whole fiasco had unfolded, Isla had boarded a plane and fled here, where Megan had offered her a listening ear and a bed to sleep.

And, God, she'd needed it.

Needed to get away from everyone and everything—especially Aiden.

She didn't want to think about him now, though. He'd called and texted that night, after Callum's party, and she'd pushed back. Told him she needed time. Not to contact her in the meantime.

Now that time had stretched to five days.

"You sure you don't want me to drive you to the airport? I don't mind. I can call work and tell them I'll be late today," Megan said as Isla pulled the suitcase upright.

"No, it's fine. The flight to Maine doesn't leave for another couple of hours, so I think my dad wants to take me to an early lunch."

Megan bit her lip. After hesitating for a few moments, she ventured, "I know I said I wouldn't interfere, but I think you might want to try to smooth things over with Davy while you're in Maine. You can't fight battles on all fronts, Isla. You need your friends sometimes. And we're here for you—if you allow us to be."

Allow.

That was the sticking point, wasn't it?

Isla let her gaze wander over the bedroom. Comfortably furnished—not by a designer—but by Megan. With her touches. Her taste. She'd only ever stayed here once before this, because she made it a point to avoid Connecticut even though she'd spent part of her life here.

And, other than Diana—who just wasn't interested—it wasn't as though anyone from here was *mean* to her. The *Squad* had even taken her out to lunch this week.

She'd just thought she was so much better than them all.

She sighed. "Megan?"

Megan lifted her chin. "Hmm?"

"In an effort to differentiate myself from the snobs, I think I've been a snob. Including to my own father."

Her words elicited a soft laugh from Megan. "I'm not going to *argue*." She grinned. "Look, I'm not going to lie. The *Squad* can be a lot. Even that moniker makes me want to stab someone. But they're just women at the end of the day. Women with deep-seated insecurities, Daddy issues, boyfriend and husband problems, bullying traumas that no amount of money can erase. You can't Botox a wounded heart."

"Well, you could, but it might stop," Isla said wryly. She swallowed hard, flushed with guilt. Guilt she needed to let go of to move forward. "Maybe you're right. But I can't pretend that what Davy did didn't hurt. I put my whole life on hold for her."

"Isla, if you're willing to believe that you married Aiden Camden that night in Vegas out of some subconscious desire to be with him, it's worth considering that you agreed to do that production for Davy because you *wanted* to. Maybe even needed it."

"Maybe. Or maybe I was just romanticizing the whole decision-making process about Aiden to make me feel better about what happened." Isla sighed, then lifted her purse onto her shoulder as it buzzed. She dug through it to find her phone and checked it. "My dad's here."

"I'll help you with your suitcase," Megan said, taking the handle.

They left the room and headed through the small rancher toward the front of the house. "Thanks again for letting me stay here on such short notice," Isla said as they reached the front door.

Megan held the door for her, and Isla squinted into the bright, sunny day. Perfect crystalline sky. The scent of cherry trees blossoming in the air. Connecticut shone in May.

Dad climbed out of his idling BMW and hurried over, taking the suitcase from Megan. "Let me get that. All set to go?"

"Think so," Isla said, handing him her carry-on. She turned toward Megan as Dad wheeled her luggage toward the trunk.

"I wish you could come back here and watch the premiere of your show with us tomorrow night," Megan said. "We'll all be watching. The Squad wants to throw you and Davy a watch party when you guys have a chance."

"It's just the first episode on YouTube. The next one won't drop for a few more weeks—I'm sure the editing team in London is still working on it."

"Either way, it would have been fun to see it with you."

"Ugh." Isla laughed. "I make it a habit to never watch myself in anything. I can't stand the way I sound. Makes me shudder." Besides, Megan was acting like the premiere was some sort of big deal. The episode would be releasing to the YouTube Channel and hadn't even managed to snag a spot on the cable lineup—which wasn't great for Davy—but Isla doubted many people would be watching.

"Text me from Maine," Megan said with another hug. "And let me know what's happening with Aiden. I won't ask, but obviously, I'm dying to know."

Isla's throat clenched, and she nodded, smiling sadly. "I will."

She climbed into the passenger seat, running her hands over the soft leather. Her father always had a thing for BMWs. Now they reminded her of him, no matter where she was.

"Diana couldn't join us?" Isla asked, hiding a smile as Dad climbed inside. "What, did she have an unbreakable spa appointment?"

He shook his head. "You're terrible, you know that?" But he smiled anyway, light blue eyes twinkling with laughter. "Dog grooming appointment, actually. She told me to tell you how crushed she was over the conflict in schedule."

Isla laughed as her father pulled out of the driveway. "Long as she makes you happy, Dad."

Dad shrugged. "Happiness is a state of mind. She suits me, I suppose. We're both content to let each other live the lives we want to live. She never wanted to be a mother, and I guess I took it for granted that you would still want to come visit me once you got older with her around."

Maybe when she was younger, it had bothered Isla more, but what could any of them do about it now? Her father carried enough guilt about it.

Isla leaned over and squeezed his hand. "It's all right, Dad. Honestly, I have enough mothering from Mum. The woman has called me five times a day since I left London. I think she's worried I'm not going back to Costa Rica in a few days like I promised."

Dad gave her a look of surprise. "I thought you still had to go to France after you film this coming episode?"

"I do, but not for another couple of weeks. We've got a short break in the schedule with the show premiering tomorrow, so I'm heading home in the meantime." She set her hands on her lap and scanned the passing buildings. "Where are we heading?"

"The house, actually. I had Carla make tiramisu and fix those caprese sandwiches you like so much. And I want to give you something while Diana's out." Dad scratched the scruff of his jawline as though he hadn't shaved this morning. Her father had always been clean-shaven. His sandy-blond hair had long since gone white, and he wore glasses now. Callum got his height from him.

Both of them had inherited his blue eyes, much to Mum's delight. Her own father had had blue eyes.

Isla gave him a curious look. "You secretly handing me the deed to the house?"

Her father laughed. "No, nothing like that. Though, I already told you, I'm more than willing to loan you whatever you need if you need it. Or pay for a good lawyer for this mess you're tangled in with Aiden. I gave Arthur an earful about it, you know. It's one thing for you two to quietly annul something like that when it wasn't splashed around publicly. But for him to soil your reputation and walk away—"

"I don't want Aiden's money, Dad," Isla said more seriously, dread pooling in her stomach. "And it's hardly a real marriage. I'm still fine with an annulment."

Saying that, though, was the farthest thing from the truth.

She wasn't fine with an annulment. Not anymore. Not after what she and Aiden had discussed.

But telling her family that?

This, perhaps, had been the worst part of what Aiden had done by leaving her to explain everything to their families. And it hadn't just been that night, after the party—when she'd had to sit up with Dad, Mum, Liddy, and Callum and make explanations—but the next day too, to the Camdens. Aiden hadn't even bothered returning their calls.

Telling her family about Vegas was humiliating enough—but *his*?

And then explaining that when Aiden called her his wife, it was only in the technical sense? That had infuriated Callum, of course. Dad, too. Didn't help that they'd been sleeping together, which for some reason became the focal point for the parents as they discussed—aloud—whether consummating a legal marriage would have an impact on the possibility of annulment.

Like they were back in the 1800s.

Isla had wanted to crawl under the rug and stay there.

Thankfully, Dad did her the favor of not going further into the topic for now and pulled into his circular driveway several minutes later. As a young girl, the first time he'd brought her to the stone and clapboard Georgian estate was when she'd realized her father was a wealthy man—she thought he'd bought the White House.

The glaring difference between this and the teeny three-bedroom beach house where she lived with Mum was enormous. Two hugely different worlds that could never really be reconciled. Mum's whole house could fit in Dad's foyer.

Yet Isla had *always* been more at home on the beach.

Dad parked out front, then came around and held the door open for her. She had to give him credit there—her father was a gentleman. A well-mannered Englishman who'd never forgotten his roots.

"We'll just leave your luggage in the car," he said as they went toward the side door he always used instead of the front.

The smell of *clean* hit her from the glass storm door, and Isla smiled, blinking at the bright white *everything*. Diana used color sparingly—unlike Mum, who'd hand-painted a mural in the living room at home. But the house was beautiful, light cascading into the high ceiling rooms of the first floor, walls designed with extensive custom millwork, vases of sweetly scented white peonies on the tables.

Lunch was already set at the breakfast nook table. Probably Dad's effort to be casual—as one could be with expensive service ware. "Here we are," Dad said, holding the chair for her.

Isla sat, automatically pulling her napkin onto her lap as Dad sat across from her. "I have to admit, I feel a bit intimidated," Isla said with an arch of her brow. "Lunch at a bistro—easy enough. Lunch at home while Diana's out with some mystery hanging over the whole affair? You're not planning on giving me bad news, are you? I'm not sure I can handle anything difficult right now, Dad."

Dad chuckled, then stood once again. He went over to a nearby cabinet and opened it, then took out a box labeled "Frank" in his handwriting.

"I don't want to keep you in suspense." Dad slid the box onto the table beside her, then sat. "I dug this out of the attic for you. Thought you might want it."

Isla furrowed her brow then opened the lid. A neat stack of pictures and papers were inside, and she scooped some up, peering closer at them.

Of her and Callum as children.

And the Camden boys.

Isla's mouth went dry as she flipped through the pictures, her heart beating painfully. Callum and Quinn standing in bathing suits in front of a pool on a trip they must have taken somewhere.

Aiden carrying Isla piggyback over a lawn.

Her heart squeezed hard, and she set the pictures down, then glanced through the papers hand-drawn on white printer paper with the labored, unskilled crayon efforts of a child. Stick figures with circles for eyes and wobbly smiling lines. Of six children, standing on a green crayon field, rainbows and clouds in the sky.

"Is that . . .?"

"You and the Camden boys, of course. And Callum."

She flipped to the next one. Just two figures in this one.

Her and a boy.

She didn't have to guess who it was—the way he was drawn taller than her, even in crayon. The A above his head gave it away. She traced the wobbly line of his hand holding hers, her thumb brushing faintly across the crayon.

God, was it really always him?

The thought came and went like a heartbeat, too fast to chase.

"You always did like Aiden Camden, you know," Dad said gently. "Your mum and I used to joke about it. He was a few years older than you, so you'd follow him around a good deal, but he was patient with your antics. Much more so than Callum was, to be honest. We thought you might be keen on him."

Isla swallowed hard. She didn't remember having a crush on Aiden as a girl, but then again, after Mum and Dad's divorce, she'd only seen him on an occasional summer's day. Hardly with the regularity that they had been used to when she and Callum had lived in England as children.

Reaching for the glass of water set in front of her, Isla sipped it, then returned the pictures and drawings to the box.

She covered them with the lid, fingertips shaking. "Thanks, Dad, but it might be safer if you keep these for now—while I'm traveling."

Dad's mouth drew to a line. "I've upset you, haven't I?"

She shook her head, forcing a smile. "No, that's not it."

Dad sighed. "Listen, Isla. I know you have a great deal on your mind, but I hope you'll think long and hard before you decide about Aiden. You have *history* to consider. Memories. Be a pity to throw it all away."

What is he saying?

She gave him a baffled look. "You want me to stay married to him?"

"It's worth considering."

She couldn't believe what she was hearing. Of all the people, she never would have expected her serious, practical father to propose this. Mum had wanted her to get the annulment *yesterday*.

"Dad, you do realize that we only got married on a whim, under the influence, and neither of us remembers it? That's hardly the start of a marriage, let alone a *partnership* requiring a lifetime commitment."

"Can I be frank?" he asked.

She smiled despite herself. The pun had always amused her. "Go ahead, *Frank*."

He shook his head at the joke. Then he sobered and went on, "I never wanted a divorce, but your mother gave me no choice. And, goodness, but I loved her. Loved her laughter. Her joy. The way she drew everyone in the room to her. She put feeling into my veins."

"And you think that's what Aiden does to me?" He did make her feel alive, but that was beside the point. She wouldn't be admitting it, and Dad *certainly* couldn't say he'd seen any sort of interaction between them that gave that impression about how she felt about him.

"No, I'm saying that's what *you* do to Aiden."

She stilled.

Dad held her gaze. "I was close enough to hear a lot of what happened at Callum's party. And Callum may be too angry to see it, but I'm not. The man is clearly in love with you. I'm not sure if you feel the same for him, but if there's a chance that you do, it's worth considering that the way he loves you is extraordinary. Trust me. I know a thing or two about falling head over heels for a fiery woman who might not be good for you."

She looked away, blinking rapidly.

Dad looked down at his hands. "When your mum left, it took years to feel anything again. Not because she was cruel but because I'd never known anyone like her. She made me feel . . . alive. I see the way Aiden looks at you, and I think he's in danger of the same kind of loss . . . if you leave."

If this was a case of history repeating itself, then that would make Isla *her mother*—the woman who didn't quite know what she wanted. Who was willing to betray her marriage when she figured it out.

Yet, somehow, I do feel like Mum.

Adrift. Unsure. Unable to fully commit to any of the worlds I'm in.

Her dad probably hadn't meant to extend the comparison to *that*, but there it was.

And I have no idea how to move forward. With anything.

"Thanks, Dad," she said at last, then reached across the table and squeezed his hand. "It's something to think about, for sure."

"Well." Dad released a sad sigh. "Let's eat. You have a plane to catch . . . and maybe a future to decide."

38

AIDEN

ISLE OF SKYE, SCOTLAND

SWEAT DRIPPED off Aiden's brow as he leaned down by the cottage gate, trying to unwedge a pebble from the tread of his trainers. He'd pushed himself hard this morning, running over twelve kilometers down the country roads and back again to the small cottage he'd bought a few years earlier.

Meant to be a place to escape to, it had sat mostly empty since the day he'd bought the damned thing on an impulse. He'd hired a local gardener to look after it, make sure that it remained cared for, but the truth was, he'd only actually come out here three times since purchasing the damn place.

He dug the pebble out, then straightened, squinting from the glare of the morning sun. Then he frowned.

A Range Rover Sport was parked beside his at the cottage.

Wiping his face with his shirt, he started toward the cottage, then stopped mid-step as the doors to the car opened.

Callum stepped out, then Mason.

Then Quinn.

Aiden stared at them, his pulse burning slow and steady.

Fuck. The time away had been absolutely bloody necessary, but he knew he'd cocked up every relationship he was in. It hadn't taken long, and he'd mostly felt shame. But then there was the pain he still felt from Isla's last message, asking for space. *Again.*

So much for a peaceful interlude.

There was only one reason they'd come all this way, and it wasn't for tea. But he was too tired to keep running—both figuratively and literally—and they'd already spotted him anyway.

He strolled toward them, taking his time as he stretched one arm, then the other. Like their presence here didn't rattle him.

Like the last time he'd seen them, they hadn't all been looking at him as though he was an unforgiveable villain.

"Morning," Quinn said first, unsmiling.

"Morning." Aiden furrowed his brow, trying to read their expressions.

He didn't have much to say. A part of him already knew why they were here, so he nodded and gestured toward the cottage, then walked past them and went inside.

Quinn and Mason followed.

Callum did not.

Smashing.

Aiden went toward the small kitchen and poured himself a glass of water, then downed it in a few gulps. He barely lifted his gaze toward his brothers. "Tea?"

"Yes, thank you," Mason said, then sat on the small sofa that took up most of the adjoining living room.

Aiden filled the kettle, then plugged it in. He set both hands on the counter, bracing his weight against it, then leveled his gaze at Quinn, who was busy staring out the window.

"Nice view," Quinn said in a deep voice.

"May was always my favorite month here," Aiden said. "Rain's not quite so unbearable."

Thank goodness for stereotypical English behavior. He could always count on a nonthreatening conversation about the weather.

But that would do nothing to end the awkwardness, so he cleared his throat. "Why are you here?"

Quinn glanced at Mason, who clasped his hands, leaning forward. "Everything's running smoothly at work, you should know. In case you were worried."

"I wasn't." Aiden poured another glass of water. "I think I've earned a bloody holiday, wouldn't you say?"

"You have," Mason said with a grimace. "You absolutely have. And Dad told us to remind you that the best CEOs should be able to take leave or holiday and know that everything will be in good hands. Which it is. Because you do a good job, Aiden. Better than good—excellent—"

"I know I do." Aiden's eyes narrowed at him. Maybe he shouldn't be such an arsehole about accepting a compliment.

Quinn sighed, then turned fully toward Aiden. "What Mason is doing a piss-poor job of telling you is that we've all been a bit hard on you, mate. Don't worry, we're not here to interrupt your well-earned holiday, and we won't be staying, even if it did take us a bleeding long time to get to this remote part of the world. But both of us owe you an apology. Not only for interfering in your personal business but also for putting so much on you."

They were here to apologize?

Aiden held Quinn's gaze, unable to fully comprehend what he was hearing.

He'd spent the week certain that the only way to bridge this chasm between him and his brothers was if he groveled. Came back on his hands and knees.

He hadn't expected this.

"But I'm the one who insulted you."

Quinn sighed. "Look, I'll admit, I was angry in Nashville. But you weren't entirely wrong. I almost lost the woman I love by being a fool when I was younger. I don't love to be reminded of the fact, of course, especially by my obnoxious younger brother, but it's true."

"That's a hell of a way to give an apology," Aiden said in a wry tone.

Quinn smirked. "I'm trying, you know." He approached the other side of the counter. "You shocked me. Maybe I shouldn't have been surprised that one of us might fall for Isla—I've always seen her like a sister—but I was still shocked. And I suppose a protective side of me reared its ugly head. It was wrong of me to kick you out of my house, and Elle's been upset with me ever since. I just didn't want to see Isla get hurt or for things to get messy. But it wasn't my place to interfere or judge you so fiercely. Retrospectively, I can see how I made everything worse."

Aiden blinked at him.

Am I dreaming?

When Aiden didn't answer, Quinn's eyes flickered with regret—and resignation. He exhaled sharply and turned toward Mason. "Your turn," he said, walking over toward the couch and sinking beside him.

"Right. What he said," Mason said with a frown.

Quinn elbowed him in the side. "Well, you've got to do better than that."

Mason rolled his eyes. "I shouldn't have interfered," he said in a flat voice, with considerably less enthusiasm. Then he lifted his chin. "But I maintain I was barely involved."

"You were a bloody snitch," Quinn snapped. "Made everything so much worse."

"That's for goddamn sure." Aiden chuckled.

Mason sat back on the couch and crossed his arms. "How

was I to know that they loved each other? It's Aiden. Stirring up scandal is practically a hobby."

"Tosser. That's the worst apology I've ever heard." Quinn scowled.

Aiden almost smiled. Shaking his head, he relaxed his shoulders, feeling slightly less wary. "And that's what you've come all this way for? To apologize?"

The idea was ludicrous.

To begin with, Aiden was the one usually having to issue apologies—it'd been that way for all his life. Broken window? He got the blame. A fight between them? He'd be punished.

Not that he hadn't usually deserved it.

Not always, though.

That was the trouble with being the second born, though.

"Mason and I have, anyway. Callum has his own reasons and, sorry, but he hasn't quite told us what they are. We left London last night and stayed in Inverness so we could be here first thing. You didn't, by any chance, happen to watch the premiere of Isla's show a couple of nights ago, though, did you?"

Aiden shook his head. Even the sound of her name cut through him like glass. He'd tried to reach out, but she'd asked for silence. Time to think. And he'd given it to her. Every aching second.

That had been the hardest thing of all. He'd wanted nothing more than to send her a message. Had typed them out and let his thumb hover over the *send* button. Only to force himself to delete the message and turn his phone off.

He wanted to respect her wishes, but it was killing him.

And it had been a week. He didn't think he could handle watching her on that show. Not right now. And depending on how things went between them, maybe not ever.

"My service is a bit spotty here," he answered truthfully. "But also, no."

"You should watch it," Quinn said quietly. "It might . . . help. Maybe. It helped us anyway to see your side better."

What in the hell does that mean?

Aiden lifted his brows. "My side?"

Mason gave him an impatient look. "Just watch the damn thing."

The kettle clicked off, and Aiden gave it a scant glance, then pulled a box of tea from the cupboard. "Not much of a selection here, I'm afraid."

Quinn came back over and took the box. "We can handle it. You should go talk to Callum."

Grimacing, Aiden flicked his gaze back out the window. He didn't particularly want to talk to Callum, but it wasn't as though he could avoid him forever.

"Fine." He grabbed a jumper he'd left on a chair and pulled it over his head.

May as well get it over with.

Aiden strode out of the cottage. Callum wasn't where they'd left him—not that he'd expected him to be. Instead, he'd wandered off toward the cliffside. The view was the reason Aiden had bought the place to begin with. The cottage itself needed updating, but he doubted he'd ever get around to it.

Pushing his way through the gate that led toward the tall grass on the cliffside, Aiden made his way toward Callum. The grass was still wet from last night's shower, so it soaked his legs and trainers, seeping into his socks by the time he stopped beside him.

Somehow, he doubted this conversation would go as painlessly as the one with his brothers had.

Callum's jaw was set, his eyes focused on the water. "It's beautiful here," he said without looking at Aiden.

"I always loved Isle of Skye," Aiden said, his voice a rough scratch.

"Isn't that what you used to call her? Isla of Skye, I think."

He remembers.

Aiden's shoulders tensed. "Yes. Or Miss Skye. She didn't get it, though."

Callum nodded. His hands slipped into his pockets, his frown deepening. "You know if you had told me that you were in love with her—"

"And you believe that now? That I love her?" Aiden crossed his arms. "Because I'm not certain that she does. Not after last Saturday."

Callum turned toward him. "I'm not here to fix things between you and Isla."

"Then what?"

"The hell if I know." Callum looked away again.

"I didn't set out to fall in love with her, you know. Or to lie to you. I don't know if Isla told you, but we don't remember anything about the night in Vegas except that we didn't have sex. I had no clue that we were married until I received the papers once I was back in London, but I had to talk to her first, and at that point, I just wanted to have it annulled. But then the show happened and with the Ipolymer deal and Isla's filming . . ."

It was utter chaos, and I handled everything poorly. "Look, I'm sorry, Callum. I hated every moment that this was hidden from you. That we were hiding it *from* you. It's not who I am. She's . . . Isla. The easiest thing about the last month was falling in love with her. She's—" He couldn't get the words out.

God, talking about her hurts so much.

"She told us about Vegas—how it all happened. So, I don't think any of us can hold you responsible for that. And I can't be angry with you for falling in love with her, either. Or defending her at the party. You did nothing wrong in either case."

"But I did lie to you."

"Yes, you did." Callum flinched, and a muscle in his jaw worked.

"Callum, I'm sorry. I truly am. And not because I got caught in a lie—I wanted to tell you long before I was able and definitely *before* you found out. But everything just got so . . . complicated. And my loyalty—"

"Belongs to her now. Yes, I understood that, too."

Why does that sound so godawful?

Callum squinted at him. "To tell you the truth, I'm less worried about you breaking her heart than I am about her breaking yours. Isla . . ." He sighed. "Isla's difficult to keep happy. She has a restless spirit. Mum used to call her an old soul, one that couldn't quite rest easy. I thought it was all bull-shit, but I have to admit I see it now. When she's interested, she's unstoppable. But when that interest dies . . . no one and nothing can motivate her."

What is he saying? Aiden frowned. "So, are you giving me your blessing to be with her?"

"You can try." Callum held his gaze. "And it probably will change some things between us, regardless of what happens."

That didn't sound promising—especially with Isla refusing to speak to him.

Aiden nearly ground his teeth, the whole conversation feeling painful and vague. "But you and I—"

"I think our friendship will survive. If you're willing to accept my apology for not believing you about Philip. One of my father's friends was in line ahead of you at the bar and heard what he said to you. He took me aside after the scene and let me know what had happened. Amazingly, Philip had made himself scarce by then."

A lump rose in Aiden's throat.

He nodded, then turned his body away to look at the sea as Callum had been doing. The slightest hint of blue peeked through the clouds, birds flying in the sky, the salt spray in the air.

I can appreciate that Callum, Quinn, and Mason came to see me, but somehow, the ache in my heart hasn't dissipated. Not fully, anyway.

Settling things with his brothers and Callum was a relief, but it meant nothing if he couldn't have the woman he'd put it all on the line for.

Maybe they'd rushed everything. They'd gone from childhood friends to lovers to spouses all within a matter of a couple of months.

Had he scared her away?

"I really should sell this place." He sighed. "I don't make it out here often enough. Someone should get to appreciate this view occasionally."

"You know, if you're interested, we can discuss some sort of partnership in the business I'm trying to get off the ground. With some updates, this would make a fantastic place to rent out as a short-term holiday house."

Aiden studied Callum's profile, recognizing the full weight of his words. A tenuous olive branch, offer of trust.

Both of them had been raised with caution when it came to doing business with friends.

And Callum needed this business to find his footing. He didn't need the money—just to find his way again after he'd idled, trying to settle into something after resigning at Camden Enterprises.

After a moment, Aiden nodded. "That might be something to consider."

They stood shoulder to shoulder, neither of them saying

much, but the silence between them was more comfortable now. Friendly, even.

Another beat passed, then Callum chuckled. "You really do love her, don't you?"

The laugh that escaped Aiden sounded as though it choked out of him. "I do."

"Then why the hell are you here? Hiding in Scotland?"

"She said not to contact her. To leave her alone to think. So I've done that, even though it's been torture."

Callum shook his head. "You've got a long way to go when it comes to understanding women, especially Isla. If you want her, you're going to have to learn what she *needs*, not just what she says she needs. And you, my friend, are standing on the wrong side of the ocean if there's a prayer she'll ever take you back. That show was filming a lot more than you might think."

All right, fine. They'd piqued his curiosity, and now it burned impatiently.

Just as soon as he was somewhere with decent reception, he'd watch. He'd force himself to watch the woman he loved and try to be the man she needed.

Pray that she'll still want me after all this.

As the waves crashed beneath the cliff, Aiden turned to his friend and set a hand on his shoulder. "Thank you, Callum." He cleared his throat, hopeful but still discomforted.

At the very least, he had his brothers. His friend.

And tea. There's always tea. He drew his hand away. "Fancy a cuppa?"

Callum chuckled. "Sounds good, mate."

39

—

ISLA

PARIS, MAINE

THE SWEET SCENT of lilacs filled the air as Isla strolled through the McLaughlin Garden & Homestead with Kyle and Tomas. They were about a week too early for the lilac festival—Davy's original plan for this episode—but it didn't matter. Boyd had sat them down after they'd arrived on Thursday to shift the show's dynamic yet again.

"We've made some changes to the way we're framing the show," Boyd had said. *"Tomas and Isla, you can keep it platonic and friendly from here on out. This is yet another incredibly small town, so we're going to focus on the personal angles. The three of you in the distinct places the town is known for, just having fun."*

So that was what they'd done.

Somehow, it didn't matter that there wasn't a festival. They'd found plenty of locals to chat with about the lilacs and the founder of the gardens here. Yesterday, when they'd gone mining for gems in West Paris, Kyle had everyone there in stitches with his jokes.

Tomas had done a fantastic job of interviewing a theater

troupe at a local barn theater—a reminder of the fact that Isla had gotten to know him as a classically trained theater actor. They'd met after having been cast together in Othello, and he'd even taken to the stage the day before to recite some of those lines with her. *Almost like we were old friends.*

And they'd even forgone a hotel this time. The whole cast and crew stayed instead in a campground twenty minutes outside of town. At least for the duration of filming.

Four episodes in, and it finally felt as though they'd hit their stride, learning to live and breathe in these towns more naturally, as they were rather than the way they might have hoped or intended them to be.

The only significant difference? No Aiden lurking in the shadows.

She felt the absence like a bruise. She still reached for her phone sometimes, half expecting a message. An apology. Something. But there'd been nothing. Maybe because she'd told him not to call. Maybe because he'd finally listened . . . and that hurt even more.

And this time, I haven't had my best friend to turn to.

Davy had stayed in the background once again, barely meeting Isla's eye. And Isla hadn't worked up the courage to bridge that conversation.

Maybe once I leave here today. She just had one short take left, and this whole episode might be over.

Isla lowered a fragrant bough of lilacs toward her face and grinned at Kyle. "If there's anything I'm going to suggest to people, it's that they do Paris in the spring." She inhaled a deep breath.

"Paris or Parises?" Kyle asked wryly.

"Definitely Parises. Though the smells here beat the fried catfish, got to be honest. Even if that was a brilliant trip," Tomas interjected.

"Yeah, if by brilliant you mean when you decided to try to do something in the rodeo." Kyle shook his head and laughed.

Isla rolled her eyes, then looked straight at the camera. She'd already fumbled these lines a couple of takes now, so hopefully, she'd get it right this time. "So, I hope you'll join us as we leave the Parises of the USA behind and hop across the ocean to the city where it all began. See you next time, in Paris, France."

"And cut," Boyd said.

Isla grimaced. "Did I seriously say hop?" The line was supposed to be jet, *dammit*.

"I think it works," Tomas said with a hopeful look at Boyd. "Hopping. Jetting. Practically the same thing."

She gave him a playful smack. "That's just because you and Kyle have run out of material to improv."

"There's only so many wonderful ways to wax poetic about lilacs," Tomas said with a chuckle.

"All right, all right." Boyd shook his head. "I think we have enough to wrap this episode and all go home. We're going to devote part of this episode with some of the London footage anyway."

Isla frowned and glanced toward Tomas. "I thought the romance wasn't going to be as important in the show."

Boyd nodded. "That's right." Then he gave her a curious look. "Didn't you watch the premiere?"

Isla shook her head. "No. I usually avoid watching myself in anything if I can avoid it. Besides, where was I going to watch it? In my tent?"

Boyd shrugged. "Could be. That's where I watched it."

That didn't surprise her. He'd overseen the whole project from start to finish and approved the final edits. Of course Boyd would watch it. He'd probably spend the whole time critiquing it, too.

"I didn't watch it either," Kyle said.

"Neither did I," Tomas admitted with a chastened smile.

Boyd shook his head. "I should fire all three of you for mutiny or lack of support. Imagine if everyone just said *never mind*. We need the views, goddammit."

Tomas protested, "But I did make a live about it for my Instagram. Told people to watch. I've been plugging it."

Yikes. She should have done that, at the very least. Not that she was regularly active on social media anymore. She ran the page for *La Hacienda* now, which usually meant she was out of steam for her personal page.

No wonder Davy didn't seem to think she cared.

Boyd scowled at Isla once again. "Well, *you* especially should watch it. Davy went to bat for you over the final cut, you know." He stormed away in the direction of the crew.

"What is he talking about?" Isla asked, peering at his receding form.

"Beats me," Kyle said, then pulled out his phone. "What's the name of the show again?"

Isla chortled, her shoulders shaking with mirth. "*A Tour of Paris*," she said. "How do you not know this? It was on the paperwork we signed."

"I'm just along for the free food and the escape from unemployment," Kyle said with a shrug. "And I can't remember the last time I read anything I signed."

Jerking her chin at him in surprise. "Unemployment?"

Kyle grimaced. "Yeah, turns out that when your boss finds out you're doing your work-from-home software support job all over the country while filming a cable show, they don't like that so much. I got fired two weeks ago."

Ouch.

Dammit. "Oh God, I feel so responsible now." Especially because Kyle hadn't said anything. She'd been moping around him for weeks, carrying on about her troubles, her problems—and he'd had a problem of his own and said nothing.

Did I even give him the room to talk about it?

"It's fine. I'll figure it out." Kyle didn't look up. His brow furrowed in concentration as he continued to scroll.

"You never know. Maybe this show could turn into something," Tomas said hopefully.

Isla bit her lip and then looked from one to the other. She had a set life waiting for her after this and maybe had forgotten what it was like to *need* something to work out. Tomas had a following and recognition, especially on stage, but if she'd learned anything from the entertainment industry, it was how easily replaceable they all were.

An acting coach had once told her that. *"You think you're important? You're not. That role you want? You step aside, and they'll find a hundred girls in less than an hour who want it, too."*

Maybe that was why acting didn't really appeal any more. Nothing was permanent. Nothing stayed.

A lifetime of sacrifice, hoping it all would mean something, *but it just didn't.*

"Why am I not finding this show?" Kyle asked, giving Isla a baffled look.

"Oy, you know what? Did you say *A Tour of Paris*? Didn't you read the email? They changed it. It's *One Time in Paris*," Tomas said.

Really? What could have provoked the name change?

"Found it," Kyle said with a grin. His eyes widened. "Whoa. We're already closing in on a million views."

That was enough to get Isla to lean over toward his phone. Kyle clicked on the first episode, and the sound of her voice came through the speakers of his phone. She grimaced, still remembering every word she'd recorded for the introduction in the trailer in Texas.

"You sound fantastic. Stop being so hard on yourself," Tomas said with a knowing, friendly smile. No flirtation. No agenda. She liked this side of him.

"We're here in Paris, Texas," Kyle's voice drawled from the phone as the camera panned to a shot of the three of them, sitting in front of the Texan Eiffel Tower.

And just like that, she was back there with them. It hadn't been *that* long ago, but it felt like months earlier. Like she had been a different person then.

Another narrator cut in, one that Boyd had mentioned had been hired to make the episodes more seamless. "But as the crew settled into explore this historic Texas town, they were off to a bumpy start—"

Then came footage Isla hadn't expected: Aiden. Her brother.

The argument outside the trailer when Tomas showed up.

She gasped, gripping Kyle's sleeve.

What. The. Hell.

She blinked hard, dizziness cresting over her as she thought back to that day. She *had* been wearing a camera—Tim had started fitting her for it when she'd first gotten in . . . but *they were filming?*

Shit.

Aiden's face filled the screen. Unfiltered. Unscripted. And the sound of his voice—angry, protective, real—hit her straight in the chest. God, she missed him. Missed the way he looked at her like she was impossible and brilliant all at once. Missed the way his arms felt around her in the dark.

She hadn't been ready to see him. Not when her heart still twisted at the memory of him walking away from her at Callum and Liddy's party—without a backward glance to see how *she* was doing. When she'd asked for space . . . and he'd given it to her a little too well. What if that was it? What if he'd taken her silence as his answer?

And now, this would do nothing to help the frayed relationship between them.

A glance at Tomas's and Kyle's faces revealed their surprise, too. "Did you know?" Kyle asked.

"I had no idea. I—"

How was this even legal? Callum and Aiden would have had to agree to this footage of them being used, wouldn't they have? They would have had to sign release forms and—

"Boyd!" Isla nearly screeched, her voice so sharp that both Kyle and Tomas shrank away.

Isla broke away from them and stormed through the gardens toward where Boyd stood. A few feet away, Davy wrapped an extension cord into a coil. Her head jerked up, eyes meeting Isla's for a split second before she looked away again.

"What the hell is going on?" Isla demanded.

Boyd's demeanor was so unperturbed as he tapped on an iPad, not bothering to look up, that she wanted to punch him. "What is it now?"

"The first episode! Why are Aiden and Callum in the first episode?"

Boyd sighed and slid the cover over his iPad. "There was a romance blooming in this show. Drama. The sort of thing that viewers crave to see. We needed real tension, Isla. Not the G-rated fluff you and Tomas came up with."

She felt the blood drain from her face. "I-I don't understand. This is not what I agreed to. I did not give you permission to go rooting around my personal life for footage."

As Tim passed by with a plastic storage box in hand, she jabbed a finger at him. "And you! How dare you not tell me you were recording me—"

"You might want to take a second look at the contract you signed with us, Isla. It stated very clearly that we could use any and all footage from the entirety of this production for whatever creative purposes we saw fit."

Kyle's words echoed hauntingly, *"I can't remember the last time I read anything I signed."*

Even Aiden, whom Isla was certain was usually more discriminating before putting his signature on a piece of paper, had signed the release form without looking at it in detail.

Because of Davy.

Acid rose up Isla's throat as she looked at the woman who was supposed to be her friend.

Her hands trembled as she crossed the path toward her. Davy's back was to a grove of trees, giving her little space to escape—unless she backed into the trees and shrubs. Which, from the look on Davy's face, it appeared she might be considering doing. "Davy?" Isla's voice was hard.

"I—"

"Did you know they were filming all the time? Even when we weren't aware?" Isla asked, hurt and betrayal pressing deeply against her heart.

But her eyes confirmed it. And if that wasn't enough, the memory of Davy crying outside that coffee shop in Arkansas, then reaching over and switching off Isla's camera, came back with sickening force.

God. She had known. She'd known they were recording all those private moments.

And if they had enough footage of Aiden to weave it into the show in a natural way . . . who knew what the camera had captured? Or when they'd decided to start using this unscripted, raw footage for the show itself?

"It wasn't meant to be malicious," Davy said in a quivering voice. "We only kept the cameras on to get some of those natural moments to supplement. But then there was such a good storyline there that Boyd caught it while reviewing dailies. And then Antony loved the idea."

"My *life* is not a storyline, Davy." Her voice cracked on the last word, fury and heartbreak coiling in her throat.

"I know," she whispered, her voice raw and filled with emotion.

Isla rubbed her temples, a pulse pounding there. "Do you, though? Or was it, once again, just another chance to push your own career forward at *my expense*? Because that's what it feels like. God, this whole time since Tennessee, I've been trying to come up with a way to apologize and mend things between us because you're supposed to be my best friend. No wonder you haven't bothered to try. You threw away our friendship a long time ago."

"I didn't. I swear I didn't." Davy gripped Isla's arm. "I didn't know how to tell you, and Boyd didn't let me because he felt like it would ruin the organic feel to the footage we were getting. But Isla, I swear. I never meant it to hurt you. And Antony wanted to take a much more salacious, edgy tone for things, but I fought for you. To show both you and Aiden in the best light possible."

She didn't want to know what people were seeing. What version of her and Aiden they'd edited into something palatable. Romantic. It was easier not to look. Not to feel that ache return full force just from the sound of his voice. But not only that. *They'd set me up to look like I was cheating on Aiden with Tomas at every turn.* The shots when *they* were meant to look in love with each other, and then viewers would see Isla with Aiden. *Fuck.*

And worst of all, they'd made a story out of the one thing that had felt real. Him. Aiden. Whatever they'd had, however messy or brief—it had belonged to her. Not the audience. Not a production team looking for ratings.

"Oh, and I'm supposed to thank you for that?" Isla shook her head, yanking her arm away. "I don't care which way you presented me. What you think you did—"

Kyle was at her side suddenly. "Isla," he whispered, his mouth beside her ear. "They're filming this, you know."

Isla whirled around to find the camera operator pointing his equipment right at her.

Her heart dropped.

Everything she'd done the past two months—from going to Vegas, marrying Aiden, hiding from Callum, working on this show, fighting with Davy—the *whole time* she'd felt so out of her depth. Like she was fumbling in the dark, trying to find her way, trying to find herself again.

And Davy had turned her life into a plot twist.

Davy, of all people, had suggested she shouldn't find her sense of self through another person. But that was the thing . . . when had she ever fit with anyone? Yes, she'd had Callum growing up, and she knew her parents loved her. *But I've always just felt like the outsider.*

The only girl among a group of brothers.

The stranger without a true home in boarding school.

The replaceable actress, not to mention the replaceable girl-friend. *Tomas didn't pine for me when I moved to La Hacienda.*

And Aiden, who had told her he loved her and had suggested they stay married? How long had he waited before he'd made a move? *And how easily did he walk away from me without a backward glance . . . without truly fighting for me?*

Perhaps that was why he was somewhere else now—free of all this, free of her. The thought made her stomach turn.

She thought the life she'd had made her tougher, somehow.

Isla blinked a tear away, determined not to cry, then turned toward Kyle. "Can you help me grab my things for the airport? I want to go home."

"Isla, I'm sorry. I really am—" Davy's voice broke.

Isla couldn't meet her eye. "It doesn't matter. If there's one thing I've learned in the past month, it's that I hate lying. I hate lying to others, and I hate being lied to. Maybe this is also proof that friends shouldn't work together."

Davy gasped at that. She started to speak, but Isla cut her off. "No, you had your chance to speak to me, to be honest with me, Davy, and you chose your career over our friendship. I don't care if I'm in breach of contract, but today was the last Paris you'll have with me in it. This was never supposed to be the story, and you know that. I *trusted* you, Davy, but I won't make that mistake again."

She turned to go, tears trailing from her eyes as she tore through the garden, not caring if the lilacs hit her as she passed. Kyle hurried to keep up, but she didn't wait for him.

She just wanted to leave.

God, I'm so stupid.

Maybe she wouldn't feel so alone in this pain if she hadn't told Aiden to go away.

Maybe I should've told him I didn't mean forever.

She reached the main gate to the garden, shoving her way through it as she swiped her tears away. The soft crunch of tires drew her attention as a car turned into the parking lot, then sped toward her and stopped.

The back door opened, and her knees nearly gave out.

Aiden.

40

AIDEN

AIDEN ROLLED his shoulders as he stepped out of the car, stiff and sore. He'd left Skye with his brothers and Callum, flew from Inverness to London, then immediately climbed aboard a private jet and flown to Portland, Maine, which was still an hour south of Paris.

He'd been traveling for almost fifteen hours straight.

But he would have traveled fifteen months if that was what it took to get to Isla.

His heart slammed into his chest as his eyes focused on the trails of tears on her cheeks, the redness of her eyes, and the heartbreak on her face.

I never should have waited to come.

He grabbed the only bag he'd brought with him—a rucksack—and set it down, then closed the car door. The Uber drove away, leaving the faint trail of exhaust in the air as Aiden turned his focus to Isla.

She was motionless, a slight divot between her brows as she stared at him—as though she couldn't quite believe if he was real or she'd imagined him.

Was she upset with him being here?

She didn't *appear* happy.

"You came," she whispered at last, looking like she might crumple.

He didn't hesitate. Closing the space between them, he pulled her into his arms the way he'd been imagining doing this entire trip. "I should have come sooner. I know you didn't want me to, but—"

"I wanted you to," Isla said, her voice thick with tears.

What? His breath emptied, and with it, the tension he hadn't realized he'd been carrying finally broke loose.

She sniffled and pulled back just enough to look up at him, her breath broken and uneven. "How did you know I needed you?"

The sight of her tears made a lump rise in his throat, and he cleared it before answering, "Callum, actually. He came to see me."

He caught sight of Kyle just past the gate to this place. Davy had texted him the address when he'd landed in Portland. Kyle gave a faint smile, stepped back, and turned to walk away.

Isla wiped her cheeks. "You talked to Callum?"

He nodded, the spark of hope in her eyes helping him feel more settled. "I did. We've still got a way to go, but things are on the mend. He didn't threaten me, so that's a good start." Cupping her face, he brushed away her tears. "Where were you heading off to in such a rush?"

"I just wanted to go home." She looked away, something sad and wounded in her tone. "The show used our business as a focal point for the episodes, and I'm so mad at Davy for it. They had no right. And she knew about it."

"I know." One of his hands slid into the hair at the nape of her neck as he cradled her close to him, his other hand firm around her waist. "I saw the episode. Callum had me watch that, too."

The cameras, it turned out, had caught a substantial amount of time between them.

His discussion with Isla in the trailer that first day he'd arrived in Texas.

The way he'd watched her during the wine festival.

Carried her out of the fountain.

And thanks to Callum's surprise appearance there that first day—and the fact that he'd also signed a release form—they'd even managed to touch on the tension that had formed by hiding their relationship from him.

Sure, it was only bits and pieces woven together with the more substantive tour of the town.

But it was compelling. *Interesting*. Personal.

Even romantic.

Their love story as captured by an impartial observer.

Of course, there wasn't any way that it would have his favorite parts. But even Aiden, who had lived the damn thing, had to admit it made for a hell of a plot.

Isla stilled, her breathing growing more even, then she pulled back, confusion filtering through her face. "It didn't make you angry?"

Aiden chuckled softly. "No, Isla, it didn't."

"But they exploited the situation—lied to us. It can't possibly be legal, can it? They used our relationship to sell their show."

"That's true, except for the legalities. I had a substantial amount of time on my hands today, actually. Read some of the waivers and paperwork I signed for the production. But if that worries you, I can have someone else take a closer look."

The tension in her face relaxed. "No, I was worried about how you might take it."

Aiden set his hands on her shoulders and gave them a soft squeeze. "Isla, I love you. I don't care who knows, and I'm not ever hiding it again. From anyone. If anything, I'm ready to shout it from the rooftops. The past week has been torture without you. I don't think I've ever checked my mobile so many times in my life, just *hoping* you might call."

She swallowed, her eyes scanning his, no longer tearful but still wary.

God, please let her forgive me.

"You walked out on me the night of Callum and Liddy's party, Aiden. Left me to face everything . . . *alone.*" Her voice trembled at the last word.

That was his biggest mistake and regret. He shouldn't have left her to face it all alone.

He kissed her forehead, then brushed his lips tenderly down to hers. Pulling his mouth a fraction away from hers, he murmured, "I never meant to leave you alone, Isla. I just felt like everything I touched turned to ash. Incapable of protecting you and preventing myself from torching everything around me. But I am sorry. I'm here now, and I'm not going anywhere."

A soft sob broke free from her. "You keep saying that. But then you go away again—"

He kissed her again gently, his heart aching at the pain he'd caused her. He'd failed her despite his best efforts.

"I'm here," he repeated, his voice scratching through his throat. "I'm here, Isla."

Her fingertips combed up to the nape of his neck, gripping him as she returned his kiss, first timidly, a kiss desperate for comfort. For the security that had felt so threatened. Then slowly, her kisses deepened, the intensity growing as the familiar hum of electricity sizzled between them, tearing through him with a ferocity that made his chest throb.

"I love you, Isla," he whispered, pulling back to cup her

face in his hands again, staring at her deeply. "It may have taken me years to find my way to you, but once I realized I'd been looking for you this whole time, falling in love with you was the easiest thing I've ever done. You're all I want. Tell me what you need, and I'll do whatever you ask to be with you. It's that simple. You want me to resign? I will. To tattoo your name across my chest? Happy to. You're already inked much deeper anyway."

She gave a tearful laugh. "I don't need any of those things. I love you too, Aiden. I know we had an unconventional start to our relationship, but I have to admit you scared me. One night, we were talking about staying married and being together forever, and the *very next day,* you were gone. And not for work this time."

He brushed a tear from her cheek. "I wanted to respect your wishes for space. God, Isla, the last thing I wanted was to hurt you more. Just tell me what you need."

She scanned his gaze, her eyes bright with tears, lashes wet. Her kisses had given him hope—but maybe he ought not to expect it.

They loved each other—but was it enough?

They hadn't even started to face the many obstacles between them.

Maybe I'm too late. Maybe the damage I've done is already too deep.

"I need . . ." She drew a slow breath as though she hadn't fully fleshed out the thought herself.

What was it that Callum had said?

"Isla's difficult to keep happy. She has a restless spirit . . . when she's interested, she's unstoppable. But when that interest dies . . . no one and nothing can motivate her . . . if you want her, you're going to have to learn what she needs, not just what she says she needs."

Yet how could he give her what she wanted if *she* wasn't even sure what she wanted? A desperate feeling curled within him. Was he beating his head against a wall? Had she lost interest in making this work?

"I need . . . a *home*," she said at last, her voice barely above a whisper.

In an instant, something clicked in his heart.

Isla, his beautiful Isla, strong, fiercely independent gorgeous woman that she was—*just needed him.*

She was the tide, restless and wild, and he would be her moon—always steady, always pulling her back home.

He dipped his forehead against hers. "I promise you this: I may not always get it right, but I will always try to do right by you. I'm not going anywhere, my love. And if you still want me —this marriage—then I will never stop trying to be the man you deserve. Or your home."

Isla blinked back more tears, then smiled and said in a cracked voice, "I want you, Aiden. And this marriage."

He smiled, then stepped back, holding her hands. "Then where are you running off to?"

Isla glanced over her shoulder, back toward the lilac-filled garden. She blinked. "I probably should've taken my mic off," she said, tugging the battery pack free and winding up the wires with a sigh. "I don't know where I'm going, to be honest. I just needed to get away."

"Well, I may know a bloke with a jet to fly you anywhere you want—so long as you don't mind me taking a nap and a shower along the way."

She raised her brows. "You have a bed on your jet?"

He grinned, then kissed the curve of her neck. "One I'm more than happy to show you."

She squirmed, a smile lighting her features. "Aiden Camden, are you proposing I join your Mile High Club?"

"Considering I skipped the proposal part of the other significant parts of our relationship, it only seems appropriate." How they moved forward with *that* was an entirely different conversation. But one that somehow didn't feel necessary to rush. He drew his head back. "How about Paris? I hear it's a lovely place for a honeymoon."

Isla wound her arms around his neck and kissed him again. "Paris sounds perfect," she said, pressing herself tightly against him. Then she drew her head back sharply. "But what about your job? You—"

"I'm learning to delegate. To make time for the things that matter. And you, my love, are at the top of that list. Forever."

The way her eyes warmed sent his pulse skittering, and his lips curved. "Have I earned my way back?"

She gave a low, throaty moan of approval, her lips finding his. "I love you, Aiden. Now and always. Let's go."

41

ISLA
PARIS, FRANCE

THE STONE STEPS of the Square du Vert-Galant disappeared into a fringe of willow trees, their branches trailing in the slow current of the Seine. The air was sweet with the scent of rain-washed leaves and river moss, and somewhere across the river, a street musician played a lazy, lilting tune on an accordion. The city rumbled beyond the island's edge, but here, tucked into the shade of the old plane trees, it felt like the world had folded in on itself.

Isla held tighter to the picnic basket as she and Aiden descended toward the river. The last week here had been so peaceful.

So perfect.

Café crème or chocolat chaud with macarons and pain au chocolat for breakfast. Slow, meandering days spent strolling the city hand in hand. Wine and cheese and incredible dinners beneath the Parisian stars.

And sex.

Loads of incredible, earth-shattering sex with her ridiculously handsome husband.

But she also knew they couldn't stay.

Aiden had been away from his job for two weeks now, and she'd all but abandoned her mother and Sergio in Costa Rica—not to mention her obligations to Callum.

She'd talked to her brother—briefly—about it all over the phone. To her surprise, he'd done her the favor of flying to Costa Rica after visiting Aiden in Scotland, in order to make certain that Mum and Sergio had help.

And though she hadn't outright quit yet, she knew now that she had to. She'd told him she and Aiden needed time to figure out how to make their marriage work, and Callum had said he'd understood.

But now it was clearer than ever: her time at *La Hacienda* was at an end.

It had to be.

And for some reason, that made her sadder than she expected. But even worse was the fact that she might need to be away from Aiden for several weeks—maybe even months—until she sorted the situation.

As though he could read her thoughts—which sometimes she wondered if he could—Aiden squeezed her hand. "You all right?"

"I'm just thinking about how much I'm going to miss this impromptu honeymoon we've had. And you." She leaned against him. "I'm not looking forward to the flight out of here to Costa Rica tomorrow morning."

"Neither am I," he said, then leaned over and took the basket from her. "I do have a few small surprises for you this evening, though, and I hope you won't be angry with me for them. But there was unfinished business I thought we needed to take care of before we left here."

She gave him a curious look. *Surprises?*

Normally, she'd welcome them.

But Aiden hadn't presented them like a good thing. "What sort of surprises?"

Aiden nodded, gesturing with his chin for her to look ahead.

Then she saw them—standing on the grassy area where she and Aiden had been heading for a picnic—Callum . . . and *Davy.*

Isla drew a sharp breath.

Callum . . . she was happy to see.

But Davy?

She paused mid-step. "Aiden—"

"Before you say anything, Callum brought Davy. I didn't know she was coming. But this time, I agree with his ambush, Isla. I think you need to talk to her. You've been friends for half your life. Even if you choose not to continue that friendship, it might help you to hear her out."

Isla let herself breathe slowly, listening to the distant chatter of a couple on a bench. Her gaze fell to a man reading a book, and she focused her mind, thinking.

Is he right?

She knew he was.

And maybe this was yet another thing she appreciated about Aiden. He gently but firmly challenged her to be a better version of herself.

She nodded, then let go of his hand, heading toward her brother and Davy. She greeted Callum with a hug. "This is a surprise," she said, her voice tight before she turned to Davy. "Hi."

Davy's eyes were pained. "I tried to call and text you—"

"I know," Isla said softly. She'd ignored Davy's attempts to reach out over the last week. She cocked her head to the side as Aiden greeted Callum. "Why don't we take a stroll?" She'd deal with Callum later, but she did *not* want to have this conversation with Davy in front of Aiden or him.

Davy nodded, and they moved away from the men. Neither woman spoke for a few moments, their gazes focused on the Seine. At this time of the evening, before sunset, Parisians often came here to read and spend quiet time in the square.

"I know I shouldn't have tagged along with Callum. I just didn't know how else to get you to talk to me," Davy blurted out at last.

"Maybe . . ." Isla started cautiously, "you should have given me some time to decide I was ready to talk to you, Davy."

Davy gave a sorrowful nod. "I know."

She looked so miserable that Isla felt sorry for her.

With a sigh, Isla said, "Davy, you violated my trust. And not just about something insignificant. You filmed something private and made a television show of it. *My life.*"

"I know." Davy gripped her forearm. "And it's not excusable. I know that, too. It wasn't what I planned, though. I had no intention for the show to ever be about your life, you know that. But Antony and Boyd steamrolled me and my objections at every turn. The only win I had was that I refused to let them twist what happened between you and Aiden into something ugly. They wanted a whole cheating storyline, and I made sure it didn't happen."

Isla pursed her lips. She'd watched the first episode—at Aiden's urging—and at least that was true. The show had painted it instead as Isla being pursued by *both* Tomas and Aiden—leaving the question as to who might end up with her as a point of tension.

In fact, the show had been pretty interesting.

Even I didn't completely hate watching myself.

"You still should have told me what they had planned—"

"I know. And honestly, I didn't even find out about it until Tennessee. And then we had that argument when you forgot to tell Callum about the London segment, and—I don't know. I let my anger and hurt get the better of me for a while. And then you had so much going on in your life." Davy stopped and shook her head.

"I'm so ashamed, Isla. I love you. You're my best friend. I should have said something, and I don't blame you if you don't forgive me."

I love you too. And I've missed . . . us.

Isla felt so conflicted. Davy *seemed* truly sorry, and she could acknowledge that she had been steamrolled by Antony and Boyd. Both men seemed so misogynistic. But a breach in confidence like this?

Her gaze flicked toward Callum, who stood chatting in the distance with Aiden.

What type of hypocrite will I be if I can't forgive someone who lied to me when they're acknowledging it and apologizing?

"It's a good show," Isla said at last. "You did a good job, Davy. And you should be proud."

Davy's face fell. "But . . .?"

Isla smiled. "But nothing. Maybe I'm the idiot who needs to learn to read the paperwork a little better." She reached for Davy's hands. "Listen. I forgive you. I can't say that it won't take some work to figure out where we go in our friendship from here, but I love you, too. And I hope you'll forgive me, too. Not only for the things I said in Tennessee and Maine, but also because you were right about me being self-centered the last couple of months."

Davy sniffled. "Really?"

Isla nodded. "Really."

With a laugh, Davy hugged her tightly. "Isla, I'm so sorry. If it helps, I'm planning on quitting my job at the Travelog Channel as soon as we figure out how to wrap this show. I shouldn't have—"

"You must be joking. No, absolutely not. You've worked too hard to get where you are, Davy. I won't allow it. Besides, that channel needs some fierce, kick-ass women breaking the glass ceiling and contending with the likes of Boyd."

Davy sniffled and wiped her face. "I guess that's true."

Isla linked arms with her and tugged her back in the direction of Aiden and Callum. "It's absolutely true. You need to represent us all. If you quit now, it'll be a blow for women everywhere."

Davy laughed lightly. "Leave it to you to be dramatic."

They reached the men with smiles on their faces. And Isla felt amazingly, surprisingly better. She hadn't realized how much the conflict with Davy had been weighing her down. So she cut her eyes at Callum and set her hands on her hips. "We're better now, you happy? But no more ambushes, big brother. The next time I see you and you're surprising me, I don't want to feel like I should have prepared for a therapy session. And bring Liddy, occasionally."

Callum chuckled. "Actually, she's back at the hotel. And once you and Aiden are done picnicking on the Seine, if you all want to join us for dinner, she's dying to see you. You too, Davy."

Isla sidled up to Aiden. "What do you think?"

"I think that would be a fantastic way to spend our last evening here," Aiden said, slipping his arm around her waist.

"Good. Because I have one more thing to surprise you with," Callum said, crossing his arms.

Isla's jaw dropped. "Is Liddy pregnant?"

Callum's face colored. "Good God, no." He choked on a

laugh, then gave Isla a sharp look in the eye. "No. The surprise is that you're fired, Isla."

What?

She stared at him, stunned.

Aiden stiffened. "I don't know if that's the best phrasing."

Callum chuckled. "Of course, if you still want the job running *La Hacienda*, it's yours, but otherwise, I took the liberty of hiring Sergio as the full-time manager. And do you remember Marco? He'd been interested in working at *La Hacienda* three years ago but decided to study tourism and marketing at uni first. He applied for assistant manager, and I feel he's perfect for the job. And, in the meantime, I'd like to hire you—if you're interested—in helping me renovate a few properties I've bought for short-term rentals. You did such a fantastic job with *La Hacienda* that I thought you might enjoy it. Plus, it would keep you in the country and—"

He didn't finish. Isla cut him off with a hug, a surge of emotion flooding her. She squeezed him tightly, pressing her face into his shoulder, blinking back the tears that threatened to spill over.

God, she loved her brother.

He'd always been there for her. Helping her when she needed it.

And now . . . what he was offering?

It's perfect.

Tears stung her eyes, and she squeezed him tightly. "How did you know?"

"That you wanted to quit? Or that you might be keen to help me with the renovations?" Callum returned her hug and then pulled back, grinning at Aiden. "A friend of mine might have supplied me with some inside information."

"You're not mad at me for quitting *La Hacienda*?"

"You know . . . funny thing. That same friend helped me to

see how saving the place wasn't just about you. Useful people, those friends."

She could kiss Aiden for it.

Having a husband who was best friends with her brother might turn out to be the best decision she'd ever made.

"And Mum? How did she take all this?" Isla asked.

Callum chuckled. "Have you met your mother? She carried on in the only way our mother knows how. And then she hugged me, knowing that her baby girl *Islita* would be happy."

Isla smiled, so at peace. *Finally.*

He set a hand on her shoulder. "Is that a yes?"

"Yes," she said tearfully. "To all of it. The quitting. The renovations. And dinner with you and Liddy . . . and Davy."

Callum smiled. "Good." He winked at her. "Then we'll see you at dinner. Come on, Davy. We don't want to interrupt the honeymooners."

As they left, Isla turned back toward Aiden, her heart so full that she could barely form a sentence.

"Happy?" Aiden asked, setting his hands around her waist.

"I—" She couldn't get the words out and kissed him instead. "I love you with all my heart, Aiden Camden."

"Good. Consider it a wedding present. You still probably have to go to Costa Rica tomorrow—get your things—but I want you coming back to me as soon as possible, darling wife. Turns out the thought of having you away makes me profoundly cranky."

Isla sighed happily, then leaned against Aiden, tucking her head against his chest. "I love you, Isla Camden," he whispered.

"I love you, too. And I can't wait to spend my life with you."

Willow branches swayed above the water, their shadows dancing on the worn stone benches tucked beneath them. The scent of fresh peonies floated on the breeze, twining with the earthy tang of grass and river stone. Somewhere upriver, the low chug of the engines of the bateaux-mouches teased the evening air, and the sunlight dripped gold over the slow, shining skin of the Seine.

It was the kind of place made for whispered promises. For choosing forever.

EPILOGUE
ISLA

Paris, France

"Remind me why I agreed to this whole spectacle again?" Isla asked, eyeing herself in the full-length mirror. "I feel ridiculous."

Mum came up beside her and made a small adjustment to the birdcage veil pinned into Isla's hair. "To make me happy," she said with a wide smile. "Estás bella. No te preocupes." *You're beautiful. Don't worry.*

"Actually, it was because millions of viewers demanded it," Callum said dryly from his perch by the balcony. "And because getting out of that Travelog contract was a nightmare."

At his side, Liddy rolled her eyes, poking him in the ribs. "You're so romantic."

"I'm *honest*," Callum said with the hint of a grin, then kissed his wife on the cheek. "Which is something to be said among this group."

From the other side of the room, Elle dropped her mouth open in mock offense as she fixed the white headband that Tara had pulled off her head again. "I resent that," Elle said. "Tara did nothing to be lumped in with the rest of us."

Megan came into the room then with a bottle of champagne in her hand and Davy at her heels. "Can I get one of the guys to open this for me? I'm always afraid I'm going to break something when the cork pops out." She looked hopefully at Callum and Kyle.

"Megan's not a liar either," Isla pointed out as Callum took the bottle.

Megan laughed. "What's that?"

Callum sighed. "Apparently, Megan, it turns out that you and I are the only ones in this wedding who don't struggle with the truth."

A loud pop sounded as the cork flew across the room, landing harmlessly on the floor. Kyle snapped it up. "In my defense, I was barely involved. No one bothered to ask me anything, so I didn't really *lie*."

Davy cringed. "Do we really have to have this conversation now?"

Isla left her mother's side and went over, holding a hand out for Davy.

The first time they'd talked in Paris—a month ago—had been tough. But things felt almost back to normal now.

Isla knew how much she needed her friendship. And despite not being completely honest, Davy had fought with Antony and Boyd about the final cut of the show—resulting in the romantic version that had enraptured viewers so much that a larger network was now streaming their little travel show.

Davy had been promoted—which she'd only accepted under the condition that she be moved to executive producer for future episodes of the series—and Tomas and Kyle had been offered a contract for more cities and spinoffs.

Isla had turned the offer down.

Acting would always be there if she wanted it, but the truth was that she had moved on. Maybe an occasional job would be fun to keep her creatively energized, but she didn't want to pursue it full-time anymore.

As Davy slipped her hand into Isla's and squeezed it, they shared a smile. "You look beautiful. The perfect bride."

Isla glanced back at her reflection. Rather than a traditional wedding gown, she'd chosen a tea-length white dress with a soft, floaty skirt and off-the-shoulder ruched sleeves. Delicate pink silk flowers trailed the hem like something from a dream. She felt—finally—Parisian. And just a little chic.

A tap sounded on the suite door, and Elle hiked Tara onto her hip, then went over to it and opened it. "Can I come in?" Aiden asked.

"No!" the women in the room—except Isla—all called collectively.

"Oh, it's fine," Isla said, rolling her eyes at them.

"It's bad luck," Mum said with a warning look. "Wait until after the wedding."

"Is it any worse luck than not actually even remembering the wedding?" Isla asked with a laugh, then crossed the room despite their protests. She nudged Elle to the side and opened the door fully.

Aiden stood there, her dad and Quinn with him. "We've come to collect the women," Quinn said flatly. "Everyone is ready and waiting."

Isla's eyes collided with Aiden's, and her heart skipped a beat. *God, he's so sexy.*

And he was hers. Her *husband*.

The love of her life.

Aiden ignored everyone else as he stepped into the room, slipping his arms around Isla. "My God, you look beautiful," he whispered as though she was the only one there.

The group gathered their things, filing out past them. Isla glanced over Aiden's shoulder and caught her father's eyes. "Be right there, Dad. I just want to talk to Aiden for a few minutes before the wedding."

"As long as I get to walk you down, I'll wait," he said with a wink, then closed the door behind him, leaving them alone.

Isla bit her lower lip as her arms tightened around Aiden's neck. "You like the dress?"

"Once again, *you* make the dress. And much as it's lovely, right now all I can think about is taking you out of it," he whispered huskily, grazing a kiss along her jaw.

"We cannot have sex minutes before the wedding." Her body betrayed her words, though, her mouth tilting back to meet his as he consumed her with a kiss.

"Wouldn't take long," he said between kisses, edging her back toward a wall. He pressed himself against her eagerly. "I could be quick."

"Don't tempt me." She kissed him back hungrily, then pushed him back. "Dammit, now I have to fix my lipstick." She wiped the remnants of it from his mouth with a grin. "I promise, there will be plenty of time for sex after the ceremony. And, um, for the rest of our lives." She gave him a mischievous grin. "*Husbee.*"

"That's ghastly, you know. *Wife.*"

Isla shivered with delight, loving the way it sounded in his voice, even if he was pretending to cringe. "That's not fair."

Aiden gave her a roguish smile. "What can I say? If I'm going to say wedding vows in front of a camera, beside the Eiffel Tower, *with* a hard-on, I may as well make sure you're completely wet, too."

Isla groaned, then headed toward a small table for her lipstick. She went to the mirror to fix it. Through the reflection, she watched as Aiden adjusted himself, then stepped out onto the open balcony, and she grinned.

I love him so much.

She reapplied her lipstick, then joined him on the balcony. They'd gotten a hotel that could not only accommodate everyone they'd flown over here for this last-minute wedding ceremony but one that also had a spectacular view of the Eiffel Tower.

Below them, the streets of Paris bustled with life—tourists and Parisians in cafés, delighting in coffees and chocolate, vendors making crepes, couples laughing and smoking. Cyclists everywhere, racing through the streets somewhat recklessly. And a street violinist, too, playing "La Vie en Rose," on a spectacular, cloudless, warm day.

Even from here, Isa caught sight of the production—the chairs they'd set up on the grass—the small group of her family and friends walking toward them.

"We should go," she said, slipping her fingers through Aiden's. "Wouldn't want to be late to our *second* wedding."

He chuckled, then turned and pulled her into his arms. "I don't know. I sort of miss all the neon and flashing lights from the background of our first wedding." Regret hinted at his voice. "I wish I could remember it, though."

"I know. Me too. Though, if we remembered it, we might not have gone through with it. I do have a faint memory of you kissing me that night, though. We were by the Eiffel Tower there, I think."

"Really?" He set his head on top of hers. "How's that for irony? All roads lead to Paris, apparently."

"Maybe not irony. Maybe destiny." Isla stepped back, still holding his hands. "You know what? I have something for you. I was going to give it to you later tonight, but this seems a better time."

He gave her a curious look as she left him and hurried over toward her suitcase. Digging into it, she pulled out a rectangular package wrapped in brown paper and brought it to him. "For you."

"Did you frame our marriage license?" He smirked.

"No. Something better." She watched eagerly as he peeled the paper back to reveal a framed crayon drawing.

His gaze flicked over it, surprise lighting his expression, then he looked up at her, eyes widening slightly. "Is this . . ."

"You and me. I drew it when we were kids, apparently. My father gave it to me." Tears pricked her throat, and she smiled. "So you see, it was always you, Aiden. And whatever winding path we took to get here, I'm just glad it led me to you. I love you."

"I will cherish this for life. I love you, too, Miss Skye." He furrowed his brow playfully. "Or should I say, Mrs. Skye?"

He set the picture down and leaned to kiss her, then paused. "Dammit, I don't want to ruin your makeup again."

Isla wrapped her arms around his neck and shrugged. "You've never ruined anything for me, Aiden. You make everything better. You're my home. Where I belong."

He smiled, then his mouth dropped to hers, and he kissed her thoroughly.

Every road, every obstacle had brought them here—to each other. To love. To Paris, once again. And this time, surrounded by their family and closest friends—and a film crew—they'd remember and cherish every moment.

NEWSLETTER AND NEXT BOOK

I hope you enjoyed Isla and Aiden's story! This was one of those books that I truly LOVED writing, from start to finish—the story really came quickly and naturally (sort of like Isla and Aiden fit together).

Thank you so much for reading; my readers really are what make this possible and I am so grateful for you! If you enjoyed this book, I'd love it if you took the time to leave a rating or review at your favorite book retailer. It truly goes a long way.

And if you'd like to stick around and see more of my work and see more of Kyle, check out the next and last book in this series, *The Route to You*, which will be available in August 2026.

Want to keep up with me and hear what's going on in my world? Join my newsletter on my website or Facebook Reader's group! I have freebies and giveaways, exclusive content and, of course, you get to hear all about upcoming book news, my life, and my small army of children.

ACKNOWLEDGMENTS

I'll keep this one short and sweet, not because I'm not grateful to all the people in my life who make these books come together, but because I'm not actually convinced any of you read this. If you DO though, this is your assignment: drop me an email and tell me you saw it, haha! (Don't you love books that come with homework? Call me curious, but I like to know!)

One Time in Paris was a joy to write after one of the MOST difficult edits I've ever undertaken (from October 2024 to February 2025—different book/series). The result? I was suspicious about how easily this flowed. It really did feel like a homecoming to the fun part of writing and that was wonderful.

To my wonderful editor Marion Archer, I couldn't do it without you.

To Julie Simms, Caitlin Lengerich, and Amanda Coleman —you all are gems. Thanks for the care and attention you give all my books—and for loving Isla and Aiden so much!

Huge thanks to Patrick Knowles for the wonderful cover— this series has been a fun one to cover, and I think this is my favorite one so far.

To Ellie from LoveNotesPR—thank you, thank you. Having your help on promoting this while social has become a bit more challenging was CRUCIAL and you are amazing.

And to my kiddos and Patrick . . . you show me the meaning of home every single day—and you're it.

ALSO BY ANNABELLE MCCORMACK

The Windswept WWI Saga:

A Zephyr Rising: A Windswept Prequel Novella

Windswept: The Windswept Saga Book 1

Sands of Sirocco: The Windswept Saga Book 2

Whisper in the Tempest: The Windswept Saga Book 3

The Brandywood Small Town Romance Series:

All This Time

I'll Carry You

Once We Met

Until Forever Ends

Ever With Me

Wanderlust Contemporary Romance Series:

See You Next Fall

He Loves Me Knot

One Time in Paris

The Route to You

To find out the latest about my new releases, please sign up for my newsletter! I love hearing from readers and have some great offers lined up for my subscribers.

ABOUT THE AUTHOR

Annabelle McCormack writes historical romantic fiction and contemporary romance packed with sprawling adventures, epic love, and soulmates who just can't stay away from each other (even when the world is falling apart). If there's a sweeping love story with high stakes and deep emotions, she's probably writing it—or at least dreaming about it while chasing down her next cup of coffee.

When she's not wrangling words, she's wrangling five home-schooled kids, a couple of dogs, and an unreasonable amount of books in Maryland. If life had more hours (and less laundry), she'd be traveling, painting, or becoming a professional pastry chef. For now, she's content with baking, reading, lifting heavy things at the gym, and plotting her next great escape—er, novel.

Visit her at www.annabellemccormack.com or http://insta gram.com/annabellemccormack to follow her daily adventures.